The Portable Pierre V. Comtois

Tales of the Outré and Others

Stories and Essays

Pierre V. Comtois

"The Portable Pierre V. Comtois – Tales of the Outré and Others Stories and Essays," by Pierre V. Comtois. ISBN 978-1-60264-505-9.

Published 2009 by Virtualbookworm.com Publishing Inc., P.O. Box 9949, College Station, TX 77842, US. ©2009, Pierre V. Comtois. All rights reserved. No part of this publication may be reproduced, stored in a retrieval system, or transmitted in any form or by any means, electronic, mechanical, recording or otherwise, without the prior written permission of Pierre V. Comtois.

Manufactured in the United States of America.

Cover image by Richard Corben.

Contents

Introduction

Always a voracious reader, I was never able to warm up to what my teachers in school insisted was great literature. Authors like Nathaniel Hawthorne, Charles Dickens, or the Bronte sisters, gothic though some of their work might have been, didn't do it for me. Nor did the work of Edgar Allan Poe, J. Sheridan LeFanu, or M.R. James whose wordy styles and lackadaisical manner tended to make their work far from entertaining reads to me. On the other hand there was plenty of literature that did grab my attention right from the beginning.

Fantastic elements found in the Tom Swift series captured my imagination at an early age (the Hardy Boys were too down to earth) and it was at about the same time that my school offered selections from Scholastic Book Services from which I first latched onto such collections of weird stories as the Twilight Zone anthologies edited (so it claimed on the covers) by Rod Serling. It was from Scholastic Books that I would buy books of ghost stories and thinking it would be more of the same, *11 Great Horror Stories* which included "The Dunwich Horror," my very first exposure to H.P.Lovecraft. But my reading interests were always conducted on two separate tracks, the other being science fiction, especially of the "weird" variety written in the days before John W. Campbell changed the field forever in the 1940s. Put down by some critics for their twist endings, they were the kind of stories I ate up.

I didn't know it at the time, but eventually I realized that the stories I liked best featured those genres made popular in pulp magazines that flourished mostly in the first half of the twentieth century. Critics could hardly have suspected then that this street level literature was destined to replace the classic novels they cherished by putting them on the path to virtual irrelevance. In their place, riding on the rising tide of pop culture that seemed to swamp everything by the end of the century, would be such genre fiction as romance, western, mystery, and especially science fiction and horror. The coming of the paperback put an end to the pulp era but vastly increased the reach of popular literature until a whole new generation of readers rediscovered it in the mid to late 1960s when reprints of such pulp writers as Robert E. Howard, Earl Stanley Gardner, Clark Ashton Smith, H.P.Lovecraft, Raymond Chandler, Zane Grey, Ray Bradbury, Isaac Asimov, and a host of others flooded local book stores, pharmacies, and bus stations across the country.

Which is about the point where my own story picks up again.

The first paperback reprints of stories originally written for the pulps that came to my attention were the Captain Future novels by Edmund Hamilton. Once having read one of those thrilling space adventures, I had to read them all! Thus began a years long effort to collect all of the volumes in the series. It was around that time that I picked up some non-fiction books that would prove to be milestones in my literary awareness: Jim Steranko's *History of Comics* (the first volume was largely dedicated to pulp magazines), *The Pulps* edited by Tony Goodstone (a history of the pulps that also included reprints of selected stories), and Richard Lupoff's biography of Edgar Rice Burroughs, *Master of Adventure*. Importantly, the first two books were lavishly illustrated with pulp magazine covers in all their thrilling, colorful, garish splendor. After seeing any one of them, my dearest wish was to collect them all and read them…no matter what genre, even the romance mags!

Now armed with a growing awareness of the field, I began to find pulp material everywhere. I stumbled onto reprints of The Shadow and Doc Savage in a local department store and Conan around 1970 after being turned on to the character by the comic book series. I found reprints of the Tarzan series in a supermarket display of all places and attracted by their downright weird covers, latched onto the Ballantine reprints of H.P. Lovecraft in a downtown bookstore. An infatuation with fantasy borne of my speed reading of Lord of the Rings led to the discovery of the Ballantine Adult Fantasy Series which included reprints of Clark Ashton Smith as well as more Lovecraft. At that point, the tap had really opened full blast as my widening literary interests led me to paperback collections of the *Weird Tales* masters including more Robert E. Howard, Lovecraft, and Edgar Rice Burroughs, as well as a whole slew of science fiction writers who had first made their mark in the pulps and were being anthologized in paperback series like the Ballantine "Best Of" (take your pick!) and Isaac Asimov's "Great SF Stories." It was all I could do keep up with them all reading every spare minute I had, devouring two or three books a week. With that kind of schedule, my time had to be managed very carefully with little left to waste on such school assigned books as *To Kill a Mockingbird, Night, The Virginian, Light in August*, or *The Great Gatsby* (I made room for *1984* because it could pass as science fiction and *The Hound of the Baskervilles* because if you squinted, it was almost a horror story). But all good things must end, and slowly the tide began to go out. Luckily for me, however, I knew there were plenty more stories by my favorite fantasy authors out there to find: in rare editions, hard to find paperback reprints, small press magazines, or even in old copies of pulp magazines. Thus began the next phase in my bibliomania: tracking down work by my favorite authors or missing volumes in a series first by visiting every used bookstore I came across and then by mail order. (The internet of course, put an end to all that, but it could never replace the thrill of the hunt nor the satisfaction I felt those times when I finally found a much sought for volume on some dusty book shelf).

But the long and the short of it is that my first love and primary literary interest has always been for genre fiction and that's where my efforts at writing have always centered. Whether it was my early attempts to write science fiction, sword and sorcery, fantasy, or horror, or my latest work, I've seldom strayed from those subjects. Simply put, they offered the widest possible field for the imagination. Not bound by earthly laws, history, or even realism, I could write about anything my fancy chose, in whatever genre suited me best. A fact you'll soon discover after perusing the contents of this volume which includes a sort of "the best of the rest;" fiction and non-fiction that did not make it into my *Autumnal Tales* collection for one reason or another. Here, you'll find some examples of my horror stories in "The Broom" and "End Hunt;" science fiction with "The Soft World," "The Walking Dead of Mimas," and "Strange Pursuit;" and even some perhaps misguided attempts to ape my pulp writing heroes with such experiments in what publishers in the 1930s euphemistically branded "spicy," "saucy," or "breezy" stories. Finally, completing the broad sampling of my work that this collection offers, are a number of my essays on various literary topics that originally appeared in my self-published *Weird Tales* tribute magazine *Fungi*.

So, sit back and enjoy; there should be something here for every taste.

Pierre V. Comtois
October 2009

Dark Fantasy

The Broom

The old Ford pickup labored up the steep slope, an ominous grinding sound coming from beneath its cab. Behind it, the black ribbon of roadway stretched away for miles without the least suggestion of driveways or access roads to relieve the monotony. Hours of driving from Kansas City had offered little more variation in the scenery than what sped by the truck's windows even now. Endless fields of wheat and corn covered the plains of central Kansas like some vast, featureless rug. A farmhouse or silo stood out occasionally on the horizon as though struggling to free itself from yellow seas or shifting sands and the last dwelling Lily had seen was passed more than a half mile back. Inside the truck, she leaned anxiously forward, eager to catch the first glimpse of her new home as they slowly topped a rolling hill.

"It should be just over this rise," said Dean from behind the wheel, a slight smile playing upon his lips. "Pressing your nose into the windshield won't help you see the house before we do."

"Are we almost there, Mom?"

Lily dragged her gaze from the hilltop and looked down at her 11-year-old daughter. "Yes, Terry, we're almost there. Now stop fidgeting, your father's trying to dive." She reached over and gently pulled Terry closer to her away from Dean's elbow.

Suddenly the strain caused by the truck's ascent up the hill grew louder until Lily thought it would die before reaching the crest. But at last, it reached the top and as the old Bronco picked up momentum on the reverse slope, she had her first glimpse of the little white farmhouse far in the distance.

"If you were paying attention, you would've seen it first," said Dean playfully. Lily gave him a playful scowl then looked back to the house.

The pickup lurched suddenly as Dean changed gears and at the lower speed, the cornfields that had been passing by on either side of the truck came into better focus. A split rail fence bordered the road, half hidden in uncut grass and she noticed that parts of it would need to be mended.

Lily remembered when she and Dean had first come to the farm months before with the real estate agent. Although a little run down, it had been exactly what they were looking for. A nice sized, oldish house needing only a few minor repairs, a modest barn and windmill, and a few thousand acres of good land. Until they were married, she and Dean had grown up on neighboring farms in the western part of the state. They began their wedded life in Kansas City where Dean was sure he could earn decent money in accounting. But never far from their thoughts was that some day they would return to the rural life they loved on a farm of their own. Finally, through a combination of savings, a bank loan, some help from family, and some old fashioned luck, they managed to find and buy this small farm. They had no illusions about how difficult life was going to be in the future, but doing what they really wanted was the real compensation.

The real estate salesman said the house had been built around the turn of the century and had passed through two owners until the year before when the most recent owners had moved east. They had only lived on the farm for two years, but the original owners, an elderly couple with a niece who had moved away lived there for over sixty years.

Terry wriggled free of her mother's arm and tucked her legs up on the seat looking ahead in mild curiosity. "After we move in, can I have a dog?"

"Sure you can sugar," said Dean unhesitatingly. "A nice collie or a big, shaggy sheep dog."

Terry clapped her hands excitedly and broke into a broad smile. This time she looked to the approaching house with more eagerness.

Lily turned her attention back to the house and began inventorying the little things about it she loved. The peeling white paint on its ancient clapboards lent a certain sense of homey, old fashioned comfort to the two story structure. And now she could make out the old stone and mortar basement walls that sprouted a huge stone chimney on one side of the small house. Dean always said that he knew a house was sturdy and well built if the basement walls were made of fieldstone. A porch extended across the front of the house with thorny rose bushes crawling untended on old broken trellises. Some ragged hedges hemmed in the small front yard and an unpaved driveway wound its way through a small stretch of grass to the backyard. The barn was empty except for the faint smell of old manure. And all around for a thousand acres stretched the cornfields planted for the previous owner by a local farmer. Dean and Lily had been given whatever farming equipment that could be spared by their respective parents and planned to make do for the rest themselves. Chickens, pigs, and other livestock would follow later.

Dean slowed the truck down and drove into the driveway. Lily turned instinctively to check the flatbed to make sure none of their belongings jammed there were lost overboard. Behind it, a big U-Haul trailer was connected to a trailer hitch. The truck stopped and Dean jerked the stick shift into park. "Well, we're here, let's get the stuff out."

"Dean, where's your sense of romance? This is our first day alone at our new house, let's savor the moment."

"Savor the moment? Aren't we the sentimental ones all of a sudden. Well, you and Terry go ahead inside, you've got the key. I'm going to start taking some of this stuff out of here. Come on back when you're ready." Exiting the cab, he began to work at one of the ropes that held down their belongings in the rear of the truck.

Lily shrugged her shoulders, fingered the key, and said, "Come on Terry, dad's going to be a spoil sport as usual." Behind her, she heard Dean snort in mock derision. She took Terry's hand and led her to the door at the rear of the house.

"Are we going to see my new room, mom?" asked Terry looking up.

"We sure are, honey, but first we have to unlock the door."

Lily shifted the keys in her hand and finally slipped one into the lock. The door opened with a little difficulty and then she was in the kitchen. It was small but just right and the furnishings were not brand new, all slatted wood and linoleum, but clean and neat. The afternoon sun shone dazzlingly through the naked windows. Suddenly, the quiet was shattered by Terry's voice, calling her from somewhere deeper in the house. Lily left the kitchen and entered the short hallway that gave into the living room. No one there. Again, Terry was calling and Lily continued down the hall where it gave access to a pair of bedrooms, one on either hand. She found Terry as she ran from one of the rooms and getting ready for another shout.

"Did you find your room, dear?" asked Lily.

"Yes, mom, it's perfect! Come and look!" Taking Lily's hand, she led her inside.

The room was large and square. Fading wallpaper covered the walls with a weave of tangled flowers and the hardwood floor was marked with the feet of furniture that had obviously stood in a single position for too long. There was a small closet to their right and a window in the wall facing the door.

"Can I have this one, mom?" asked Terry as she moved to the center of the room and turned to face Lily.

"Certainly, dear. Now why don't we go and help dad get our things into the house?"

———

It had been three months since Lily and Dean moved into the small farmhouse. Three months of hard but happy work. For Dean, there had been fences to mend, the barn to paint (the house too), fields to clear, and windows to repair. Lily washed all of the floors in the house, cleared out the little root cellar in the back, fixed the curtains, straightened out the yard's shrubbery, grass, and roses, and just busied herself making the family a home. Terry had helped as best she could, but mostly just had fun exploring her new kingdom.

It was the end of October and was already cold, but Lily and Dean were contented with nights spent in their very own living room keeping warm before the fire.

The trees along the rail fence had long since been stripped of their leaves and a chill wind blew along the empty furrows of the rolling fields about the house. When Thanksgiving came around, they would have plenty to be thankful for.

"Terry," said Lily one day, "do you want to help mom clear out the old shed today?"

The old shed was a small, dilapidated structure tucked away in the furthest corner of their property. One of the first things Dean had done upon their arrival was to take a look inside to see if there was anything worth salvaging but found mostly rotting and broken tools. Putting the matter aside in favor of more pressing concerns, he'd decided to eventually clear it out before settling on what to do with it. Emptied, it might yet be worthwhile keeping up if only to store some tools and saving him longer trips from the fields to the house whenever he needed something. So while Dean busied himself reinforcing the root cellar, Lily had volunteered to tackle the tool shed.

And so, bundled up in their autumn coats and hats, Lily and Terry made their way across the fields to the shed. The furrows made walking difficult and by the time they drew within sight of the shed, Lily's feet and ankles were sore. Apparently the same was not true for Terry. She was running along a few yards ahead kicking clods of dirt into black spray as gaily as when they had started.

Lily was watching some white clouds scudding quickly along the horizon when Terry's shout drew her attention.

"Mom, hey mom! Look at that scarecrow. Ain't it neat looking?"

Lily turned in time to catch two large crows flying off, obviously frightened from their perch on one of the scarecrow's arms by the sound of Terry's voice. The scarecrow itself was well made. Dean had told her about it of course, but he didn't say anything about its condition. It was old, of that Lily was certain. The wood used for the crosspieces was like old driftwood and the overalls and flannel shirt were faded to what might be considered a colorful white. The head was a piece of burlap stretched down over what must have been a tightly packed wad of old socks and fastened around the neck with a short length of rope. A peaked hat with ragged brim crowned the head that teetered to one side like a man with his neck broken. The face looked almost real as if it had been worked in clay. Dried and blackening straw poked from its limbs and neck.

Terry stopped circling the figure and, looking up into its face said, "It kinda looks like the scarecrow on TV huh, mom?"

The realization struck Lily that yes, it did look a bit like that scarecrow. "Yes it does, Terry. Too bad dad said he was going to take it down."

"Oh, no, mom! He can't! He looks just like the scarecrow on TV. We couldn't just tear him down. Maybe it really is him, waiting to come to life, like in the movie."

"Well you'll have to talk to your father about that. He says it'll be in the way of his new tractor when he works this field next spring."

"I will. He can't do it. I won't let him," insisted Terry, eyeing the two crows that were circling overhead as if waiting to land again after they left.

"Let's get going to the tool shed now, we have a lot of work to do before going back to fix supper," said Lily as Terry ran to catch up.

Over her shoulder, Lily looked back at the scarecrow and a sudden chill worked its way up her spine. The resemblance was uncanny, she thought. It hung there, broken, in the center of what could have been some blighted field with the two black birds wheeling overhead…Lily forced herself to look away.

The lock on the shed door had disappeared somehow and the flimsy boards seemed ready to fall apart at the slightest provocation. There was a small window just to the left of the door where Terry, on tiptoes and cupping her hands against the clouded panes, was trying to peer inside. An old, gnarly tree grew from a rear corner and the rest of the structure was surrounded by rank, dry grasses and errant shoots of wheat. The roof sagged a little. Already, Lily despaired over any possible reuse of the building. With a sigh, she pushed carefully at the door. To her surprise, it swung soundlessly inward and immediately the dank, musty stench of a place long used as a hideaway for field creatures rather than the storage of tools puffed out at her. She had a feeling that she would find it a scatologist's paradise inside.

"P.U.," said Terry holding her nose. "Do we have to go in there?"

"Oh, come on, it isn't that bad is it? What are you going to do when we get some pigs and cows?"

Apparently, Terry recalled the promise her parents had made that she would help care for the animals when they got them. "What are we waiting for? Let's get to work."

Stepping over the high lip of the threshold, Lily entered the shed and found the inside sufficiently lit by the pale daylight filtering in from the single cobwebbed window. A scampering sound from the back indicated some animal, frightened at her entrance, was busy making its exit through a hole in the floor. It was just as well, Lily hated surprises, especially of the rodent variety.

Dean was right about the tools, most of them were broken hafts and chipped spades and axes that leaned against the walls. Old corn stalks had been lashed together and propped in one of the corners and in a ceiling joint where two beams met, Lily noticed an old bird's nest made of twigs and bits of newspaper. Finally, she put her hands on her hips and said, "I guess we better get started."

"Well let's hurry up, mom," said Terry. "I want to tell dad about the scarecrow."

"Okay. Let's start by taking these stalks outside."

Together, they began to grab bunches of corn stalks and laying them in a neat pile outside the door. Lily was using one to clear spider webs from the corners as Terry rummaged through the old hafts and tools.

After a while Lily noticed how quiet Terry had become and turned to see what she was up to. She was standing in the light of the window fingering one of the hafts.

"What have you got there, Terry?" asked Lily.

"Nothing."

Lily moved closer and saw that it was an old wooden broomstick. The end where the straw should have been was bare and blackened with what looked like charring as from a fire. "Oh, it's nothing for sure, Terry, go and throw it outside with the rest of the things."

"Uh, huh," mumbled Terry, stepping from the shed.

Lily shook her head and began scooping up the old tools and tossing them through the open doorway. In a little while, she finished and stepped outside herself. Slapping the dust from her hands, she saw Terry standing a little ways off, still holding the broomstick and looking at it intently. "Haven't you gotten rid of that old thing yet?"

Terry seemed to drag her eyes from the broomstick with obvious effort and said "No, I think I'll keep it."

"For heaven's sake, why?"

"I don't know, but it just seems a shame to throw it away."

Lily shrugged. "Well, if you want it, all right. But before you bring it into the house, you make darn sure you clean it off."

Terry mumbled agreement.

Turning, Lily closed the rickety shed door as best she could and started back to the house. Terry walked alongside her, stumbling now and then in the furrows due to her rapt attention on the broomstick. Taking her daughter by the arm, Lily gave one last glance at the scarecrow and headed home a little faster.

———————

"I finally got those trees cut out from the fencing on the south side this morning," Dean said from around a mouthful of mashed potatoes. "What a job and half that was."

"And Terry and I cleaned out that old shed," said Lily, pouring herself a cup of coffee. "There wasn't anything worth saving so you can load the junk we piled near it tomorrow in the pickup."

"Speaking of Terry, where is she?" wondered Dean. "She's late for supper." He looked over his shoulder to the hall door trying to get a glimpse of her. "Terry! Your supper's getting cold. Hm. That's not like her, she's usually first at the table."

"It's that broomstick she found in the shed. Ever since she got it, she's been acting absent minded, sometimes just staring at the thing."

"A broom? Like for sweeping?"

"Yes," said Lily. "We were cleaning out the shed and she found it behind some of the other tools, as if someone hid it there or something." A pause. "That's funny. Why should I have thought of it that way? Like someone hid it? Who'd want to hide an old broomstick?"

"What's so special about this broom?" asked Dean starting on his wedge of apple pie.

"Nothing, it's just an old fashioned broom. Except the end where the bristles belong, they've been burned off."

"Hm," was all Dean could muster. Swallowing, he called "Terry!"

"Oh, by the way, Dean. You know that scarecrow in the field by the shed?" Dean nodded. "Well, Terry's grown attached to it somehow. She thinks it looks like the one on television."

"And she doesn't want me to take it down."

"You figured that out, huh?"

"Well, if you were a little girl and thought the scarecrow from that movie was in your backyard, would you want to see it destroyed?"

Lily laughed. "I guess not!"

Terry finally came into the kitchen and sat down. She began to pick at her food, occasionally even placing a bite or two into her mouth. Finally, she refused a piece of apple pie. Lily could not help worrying that something was bothering her. She decided to break the uneasy silence.

"Terry, wasn't there something you wanted to ask your father?"

Terry looked up slowly and just stared at her with a vaguely puzzled look on her face. Lily leaned forward and whispered in a manner that was perfectly audible to Dean. "You know, about the scarecrow."

Terry's reaction took Lily completely by surprise.

"Take him down!" Terry said. "I don't want to see him ever again! Dad was right in wanting to do it. Take him down as soon as you can, I don't care. Destroy him!"

Lily was dumbfounded. She sat there with her mouth open and her eyes wide. Slowly, she turned to her husband who was mildly surprised himself; not with his daughter's words, but in the tone she had said them. It was cruel, merciless.

"But Terry," reasoned Lily, "this afternoon you were so certain you didn't want the scarecrow taken down."

"I changed my mind," replied Terry. "He's only a dirty old pair of pants stuffed with grass. He doesn't even scare the crows away. Maybe we should even burn him, he might have bugs."

The look in her eyes when she insisted that the scarecrow be burned was chilling but worse perhaps, was the way she kept referring to it as "him." To Lily, the combination only made Terry's reaction the more frightening. "Well, if you don't care…"

"I don't," came the blunt reply.

"Why don't you finish your supper Terry," said Dean in an attempt to change the subject.

"I'm not hungry. May I be excused?"

Lily looked at Dean and watched him say "Sure, honey."

After Terry left for her bedroom, Lily listened for the sound of her door being closed. When it came, she rose and began clearing the table. As she busied herself scraping the plates and arranging the dishes in the sink, she was not unaware of the sudden silence that had descended on the kitchen. Usually, this was the time when she and Dean talked about the little things that happened during the day.

Looking over her shoulder, Lily saw Dean as he fiddled with the broken toaster. As she began filling up the sink with water, she couldn't keep her feelings bottled up any longer. "Well?" she said at last.

She heard the tinkering sounds behind her stop.

"Well, what?"

"You know what. Terry."

"What about her?"

He was being deliberately evasive, trying to get Lily to come to the point. Dean hated guessing games having too little patience for them. He wanted her to come right out and tell him what was bothering her.

"What did you think?" Lily finally said.

"I think it'll be okay to take down the scarecrow."

"That's just it. This morning she was so adamant about saving it. She thought it was the good scarecrow from the movie. Now suddenly she wants it not just taken down, but destroyed."

"So we'll destroy it, no big deal."

"So don't you think a word like 'destroy' is a little harsh for a little girl to use?"

"Not really," Dean said. "She watches a lot of television, like any other kid."

"But the cruelty in her voice, her eyes," insisted Lily. "You must have picked it up."

"Well, maybe a little bit, but she uses the same tone of voice when speaking of cockroaches and spiders," said Dean. "Besides, cruelty is nothing to particularly worry about in children. Everyone knows kids can be quite cruel to each other. Not having yet developed the kinds of experiences and associations that adults have, they just don't know enough to realize when they're being cruel. Terry's no different."

Dean looked at Lily, expecting the answer to satisfy her but his wife wasn't having any.

"The cruelty I heard in Terry's voice and that I saw in her eyes was no childish whim," said Lily. "It was an adult hatred. The kind of hatred expressed by an adult who knows what they're talking about. That's what scares me."

"Lily, do you know what your sounding like? Only this morning you thought of Terry as your little angel. Now which is it going to be?"

Lily had to admit that it did sound like nonsense. Here she was talking about an 11-year-old girl as if she were...well...the devil or something. She would have laughed then except that she suddenly recalled what had started the whole thing in the first place. That broomstick. All because of an old broomstick. It was crazy. "Maybe you're right, it does sound kind of silly. Maybe it is all my imagination."

"Now don't get down on yourself," soothed Dean, getting up and delivering a kiss to her cheek. "I don't want you to start thinking your nuts or something. Now, let me finish with that toaster, huh?"

The cold October gust whipped around the corner of the house and caught Lily in its grasp. Shivering, she took another clothespin from between her teeth and fastened it to the sheet she was struggling to keep in place against the wind. It was times like these that she really missed her dryer; but then, she found it an easy sacrifice to make in return for the farm. She stooped to take another bed sheet from the hamper and pinned it to the clothesline. When she finished, she cupped her hands and blew into them a few times, thawing the fingertips. Overhead, silhouetted against the gray sky, a lone bird, too high to identify, wheeled and dipped on the shifting air currents. Lily watched it a moment then shifted her gaze to the distant fields for signs of Dean but saw nothing. She was bending to start on another item of bedding when a sudden movement from a corner of the yard where movement was unusual caught her eye. Peeking from under the edge of a bed sheet, she looked toward the doors of the root cellar.

She saw Terry straightening as she finished pushing one of the leaves of the bulkhead door to the farthest point of its arc and letting it go. Lily turned back to her work in order to avoid having Terry see her watching. Out of the corner of her eye, Lily saw Terry looking about as if to make sure no one was watching her. Lily averted her gaze a moment and when she looked back, Terry was gone. Obviously into the root cellar, thought Lily, for the door remained open. But why should Terry have acted so secretive? Was she up to something she knew her parents wouldn't approve of?

Lily moved away from the clothesline and drew toward the open door. Peeking over the top of a steep set of concrete steps leading downward, Lily saw a white square of daylight stretching across the cellar's earthen floor. As her eyes adjusted to the gloom, she began to make out the dull yellow glow of a bare bulb that lit the interior of the cellar. Listening, she could hear the sound of Terry's feet shuffling around out of sight. What could she be doing down there? Lily decided to sneak down to see, bothered not a little by the feeling of role reversal: she being wary of discovery instead of Terry.

The old masonry of the steps crumbled damply beneath her feet as her head came even with the doorframe. She was momentarily blinded by the glare of the light bulb until she stepped down to the cellar floor. Then she saw Terry farther back in the cramped space. She seemed to be poking at the ground with a little stick, now and then stopping to dig with her fingers. She did that a few times before she switched her attention to the stone walls and began probing those. Was she looking for something, wondered Lily

Suddenly, Terry turned and faced her mother and in the overhead light, her face showed anger.

"What are you doing here?" she demanded in her child's voice but in a tone that seemed to address not her elder, but her equal.

"I...I saw the door open, and thought I'd check to see who was here," replied Lily, stammering against will. Darn! Who was mother and who was child here? Conscious that she had lost the psychological advantage, Lily went on the offensive.

"What are *you* doing here?" she asked, throwing Terry's question back at her.

Terry made a face and her eyes moved over Lily as if she were trying to decide whether or not to answer.

"Just playing," Terry finally answered, but in such a manner that suggested she was forcing herself to go through a necessary charade.

Lily thought better of pursuing the matter saying instead "Well, that's enough fooling around. You'll get filthy in no time if you stay down here. Come on." She motioned for Terry to precede her up the steps.

For some reason, the thought occurred to her that if Terry had wanted to, she could have trapped her mother in the cellar by simply slamming the door shut and locking it before Lily reached the top of the stairs. It was an outlandish consideration but Lily was nevertheless relieved when she stepped outside without incident. Ahead of her, Terry was innocently skipping off in the direction of the house.

Lily was on her knees scrubbing hard at the planking that made up the kitchen floor. Working at the waxy buildup that had accumulated along the baseboards, she began to regret putting off the job for so long. In the background, the radio played dully, spitting out the latest muzak fabrications but Lily wasn't listening.

The day before, she had told Dean of the queer episode in the root cellar. As she had half expected, he dismissed the whole thing with a breezy "Oh, come on honey! She was exploring. Kids love to explore." The tone of his comment didn't invite any kind of qualification so she dropped the subject. Like the incident at the supper table a few days earlier, his reaction made her feel a bit silly. But now, alone with her thoughts, none of it seemed very silly. In fact, she had begun to feel a heightened sense of alarm. Abruptly, she wondered where Terry was at that moment and as if in reply she heard a sound from overhead.

Lily looked up toward the ceiling. Someone was in the attic. Terry? What was she doing up there? Searching again? Another dull sound. Slowly, Lily rose from the floor, her eyes still on the ceiling, sweeping back and forth. Wiping her hands on her apron, she moved toward the little hallway. Reluctantly, she took her eyes from the ceiling and headed for the large closet that occupied the space between the two bedrooms.

The closet door was ajar so Lily inched it open until she saw that the new collapsible ladder Dean had installed in the overhead trap had been extended to the floor. Through the square opening above, she could see a beam of light sweeping the interior. Terry was looking for something again this time with a flashlight.

Lily was about to mount the ladder when it occurred to her that in the root cellar, Terry had been without the old broomstick she had found. Lately, it seemed that she was inseparable from the darn thing. Backing away from the ladder, Lily decided to take advantage of her daughter's attic search to see if the broomstick was still in her room.

Quietly, Lily stepped out of the closet and into Terry's room. Safe from observation, she looked it over, inexplicably bothered by a fear of being discovered.

Her first look revealed nothing of interest. The dolls were all there, the bed was made, and the room was tidy. She moved to the closet and checked inside. Everything was very neat. Nothing out of the ordinary. Then Lily stooped to look more closely in the back of the closet.

Suddenly, she heard a gasp from someone behind her. She nearly jumped out of her shoes and found herself tangled in the hanging clothes overhead. For a moment she panicked but finally managed to extricate herself. She turned to face the room just in time to see Terry as she dashed the last few steps to her vanity and snatch the broomstick from behind it. Holding it tightly to bosom, she said very low and very menacing "Get out." Then yelling "Get out!" Lily almost ran from the room; the door slamming shut at her heels.

Some time later, Lily was still shaking from the incident. She was convinced now that Terry was not herself. Something had to be done; but what? She could tell Dean, but without the evidence of his own eyes, she felt certain all he would offer was more talk of child psychology. Feeling desperate, as only a mother of an endangered child could feel, she knew she had to do something. Not knowing what exactly was wrong with Terry limited her options but maybe if she found whatever it was her daughter had been searching for it would act as a calming agent. The more she thought about it, the more it made sense. Yes, that's what she would do.

Trembling, she drew on her coat and kerchief and stepped outside, feeling cold not from the weather but from her own fear and helplessness. She crossed the yard and began to make her way toward the old shed where it still stood leaning against the midwest wind. Maybe she and Terry had missed something when they cleaned it out before. A few stray leaves skittered across her path catching in the tall grass and tree stumps along the fence. In the distance, against the flat horizon, she could see the small, lonesome figure of the scarecrow where it stood amid the stubble of razed corn stalks. Dean hadn't got around to taking it down yet.

She stumbled amid the furrows, and almost twisted her ankle. The ground had begun to harden with the approach of winter. Now she walked with her head down, watching her feet. She had been doing that for some time when she noticed something out of the corner of her eye. It was the base of the pole from which hung the scarecrow. Looking up, Lily caught her breath, for some reason, horrified at what she saw.

The scarecrow hung there as always, but now its head was a sagging pouch that had been emptied of its brains. What there was of them had been strewn about in the form of old rages. The deflated sack and folds with its button eyes and stitched mouth, warped its formerly smiling features into a mask of pain and sadness. Its torso had been split open from neck to groin spilling its damp and rotted innards in all directions.

It was a disturbing sight made all the worse when Lily supposed the destruction had been done by Terry. Hadn't she insisted to Dean that he "destroy" it? But why not remove the scarecrow completely if destruction had been her purpose? Lily stood silently a moment, holding the top of her coat closed against the wind. Then it struck her: because she'd been searching for something…inside the scarecrow! But what? What? For one terrible instant, Lily feared that it was she who was losing her mind. Dean was right, Terry was normal and it was she who was imagining things. But then she recalled Terry's strange behavior, the change in her personality, the tone of her voice…as if she were no longer herself but someone else. On the other hand, maybe she was just going through something every child goes through, maybe…suddenly everything seemed to be spinning around in Lily's head, back and forth, back and forth. When she regained focus, it was to find the ruined face of the scarecrow looking down at her. She screamed then, turned, and ran wildly for the farmhouse and its distant yellow lights.

The screech of the nails pierced Lily's ears as Dean leaned on the hammer. The crosspiece that had supported the scarecrow's arms came loose and Dean positioned himself to hammer out the nails from the back of the beam. Lily looked away at the scarecrow where it lay spread eagled in the bare field a short distance away. The last rays of the setting sun shone redly over its disemboweled figure. Lily shuddered involuntarily. As Dean began to hammer at the protruding nails, she was reminded of the change that had come over her daughter in the past few days.

Almost hour by hour since yesterday's scene in her bedroom, Terry became further removed, distancing herself from her mother and the little world she and Dean had tried to build here on the farm. In contrast, as Terry seemed to move away from her parents, she became more attached to the broomstick. If she was not staring at it, she fondled it in a way that Lily felt was almost sinful. Gradually, Lily was convinced that such an unhealthy attachment to an inanimate object could only end up with Terry developing some sort of psychological damage or dependence she would be unable to break.

But *was* there really anything to worry about? How many times had Lily asked herself that question? Was it all just her imagination? Was she taking a simple childish fetish, like the sucking of a thumb or the picking of a nose and blowing it all out of proportion as Dean said? No, she was sure there was something more going on with Terry than a simple habit. The cruelty that was in Terry's voice that night at the supper table and the cold command in her room the day before; the former, a sudden turnabout from her concern over the scarecrow was evidence enough for Lily if not for Dean. But then, Dean just didn't spend the amount of time with Terry that she did. Lily knew better.

So, what then? All the latest pop-psychology books insist that the first thing to do to solve a problem is to admit there is one. Check. Next, it needed to be identified. As little sense though it made, Terry's strange behavior began only after she had found the old broomstick. So, crazy as it seemed, Lily concluded that it was there that she had to begin.

Lily remembered that she had started out to search the shed the day before but was scared off at sight of the mangled scarecrow. She recalled the inexplicable terror she had felt and found it difficult now to remember what exactly had frightened her so. Anyway, with Dean here and the scarecrow removed from its place overlooking the field, she found herself in much better frame of mind to finish what she had originally set out to do. Lily turned to the rickety structure that stood a short ways off. Dean was so absorbed in his work that he didn't notice that Lily had slipped away.

The interior of the shed still reeked of animal droppings and at sunset, even less light managed to find its way through the single window. Lily looked around the tiny room looking for anything that might give her an idea of what to do about Terry. It didn't have to be anything to do with the broomstick itself, just something that could serve to jog some gears and give her a fresh perspective on the problem.

She pushed the door closed to look behind it, but saw nothing. Then, as her eyes grew accustomed to the darkened corner, she made out the gray of the small bird's next in the groin of the roof beams above the door. Were there any eggs in it, she wondered? Reaching up slowly, she tenderly closed her fingers about its prickly shape and drew it down to where she could examine it. Inside, was a fleecy white whirlpool of webbing indicating that the nest was in disuse. She turned it upside down and knocked it against the doorjamb. A spider fell to the floor and scrambled for cover, but not before Lily placed her heel to it. It was then that she noticed the bits of paper woven into the fabric of the nest.

The birds must have raided every farmhouse in the area for their collection, thought Lily. Idly, she thought that if some of the pieces had dates on them, she might get an idea of how long the broomstick had been in the shed.

Gingerly, she began to pick at the bits of paper and twigs that composed the nest until at last she pulled at a piece of paper that refused to emerge from the tangle. It must have been a larger piece, stuck farther inside. Eventually she managed to work it free. It turned out to be a rather large piece of paper folded many times upon itself, and through years of weathering had fused together into a thick wafer. Lily faced more to the light and saw further that it had faint, blue lines on it, as if it had been a sheet torn from a child's notebook.

Carefully, she inserted a long fingernail along a seam and it opened with a dry sticking feeling. The blue lines were better preserved on the inside. In another few seconds she had it completely unfolded but not before a piece of string fell from within its folds. As if it had once been tied to something, guessed Lily.

It was then she noticed the writing on the paper. Or rather the printing. The ink was almost too pale to discern so she held it up before the setting sun low in the west. At first she could only make out a few phrases but eventually deduced that it was only one page of a longer work. As she read, it was with increasing disbelief that her mind began to make certain associations that logic dictated were impossible:

> ...It was a few days after coming back from that wonderful country that I was looking for a ball under my bed. I was reaching under there with one hand while lying flat on the floor when I felt something long and hard. When I pulled it out I gasped and saw that it was the witch's broom. The one I had won from her in that country. I still remembered the warnings of the people there about it, and decided to hide it in the old tool shack with this letter tied to it so no one else will touch it. If you are reading this, whoever you are, don't touch the broom. It's bad, and no good can come of it.

> Dorothy

————————

Lily stepped out from the shed and walked over to Dean, keeping what she was thinking at a mental distance. Dean was busy loading the debris from the shed that she and Terry had piled nearby into the back of the pick-up. Was it really only a few days ago that the two of them had worked so happily together?

"Dean," she called.

"Yeah?' he answered, turning from the tail gate.

"Look at this; I found it in the shed." She handed him the note and watched his face as he read it. She saw the line of his jaw set. Then he looked up.

"You don't believe any of this do you?"

"I don't know what to believe anymore. But if you don't think there's anything to it, okay. But I know there's been a change, a change for the worse in my daughter. Dean, I want you to take me home right now." She hoped she would not have to argue with him.

"All right, honey, if that's what you want. Let's go."

The cab light lit as she pulled open her door and played strangely with the shadows on Dean's face. She couldn't tell what he was thinking. As the light went out again, she said "Please hurry, Dean."

Dean nodded "Don't worry, Lily. Just relax." He was just humoring her; she knew it, but at least they were on their way.

The ride took too much time for Lily but it could not be helped; the frozen furrows of the field threatened to shake the truck to pieces. Even at the slow pace they were going, the thuds and jerks jarred her to the bone. Dean held the steering wheel tight, leaning forward against the falling night. In front, the headlights jogged up and down over the earthen waves as the first stars began to twinkle in the east. Lily saw the moon hanging low in the sky.

The far lights of the house drew nearer and Lily strained to see any movement from inside, but nothing seemed amiss. They had left Terry alone in the house, not expecting to be gone more than an hour. Dean had made her promise to stay in front of the television set because Lily could not yet bring herself to speak to Terry directly. Dean had said little about the situation, only quietly agreeing to do the talking. Since returning to the house the day before and trying to make him understand amid tears and frightened babbling, Lily at least convinced her husband not to press her with any further platitudes about child psychology or having her imagination run away with her. She was thankful for that.

The little truck fell from the field into the road in front of the house and swerved into the driveway. Dean played with the brakes and brought the machine to a halt at the back door. With more urgency than she cared to admit, Lily jumped out and dashed up the short flight of steps onto the porch, not bothering to slam shut the truck door. She had passed through the mudroom and was peering indoors through the window panes in the kitchen door when Dean came up behind her.

In the yellow light of an overhead bulb, Lily tried the doorknob but it didn't to turn. "It's locked," she said.

Dean tried next but with the same results. He pounded his fist on the doorjamb and shouted "Terry! This is your father! Come and open the door!"

There was no reply.

Even as he called again, Dean was inspecting one of the window panes and after calling one last time, warned Lily to stand back. Lily retreated a little as Dean's elbow drew back. With a tinkle of glass, he broke the pane and was fumbling for the inner doorknob. Finally the door swung open and he stepped inside the kitchen. When Lily had followed him, she saw he was looking around for something but as she drew up to him, noticed that his hand was bleeding.

"Use my kerchief, Dean," she volunteered, pulling it from her head and helping to wrap it around his hand.

By this time they both began to wonder why Terry had not come running at the sound of the breaking glass. With Dean leading the way, they crossed the kitchen and headed toward the living room. Terry wasn't there and the TV set was dark.

Dean laid his hand atop the television. "Still cold," he whispered to Lily before they continued down the short hallway to Terry's bedroom.

Lily's heart pounded against the wall of her chest, dreading the inevitable confrontation; wondering what would happen next. They paused a moment before the closed door to Terry's room, steeling themselves for whatever was on the other side. Looking around at the gloomy house, Lily saw the window in her own room and thought she could feel the black of the night pressing against its panes, trying to get in. She nearly jumped when Dean spoke.

"Terry! Are you in there, honey?" he asked, ear hovering near the door panels. "This is dad, answer me!"

But silence was the only reply until they heard a low, muttering laugh that seemed to seep from beneath the door and then rise to a cackling pitch before seizing abruptly. Frightened, Lily clutched at Dean's arm as they stared into each other's eyes.

Dean surrounded the doorknob with his palm and gave it a twist. It turned easily. Pushing slowly, he managed to open the door a few inches before it stopped. Something held it fast on the opposite side and no amount of force was able to budge it. Retreating a few steps, Dean waved Lily aside and charged the door shoulder first. With a protesting screech it skidded open, then suddenly shot forward, slamming into the opposite wall. A chair that had been jammed beneath the doorknob clattered across the floor as Dean came to a stop at the foot of Terry's bed, carried there by his momentum. Lily followed slowly, looking carefully in all directions.

"Terry, where are you?" said Dean, but there was no answer.

Dean was about to say something when the same maniacal laughter built again from a low murmur to a loud cackle. It was coming from outside the window and Lily spun in time to see a black figure skulking there, blacker even than the night. Later, she would confess that it had been difficult to make out any details but the thing seemed to be draped in a black cloak that billowed in the wind (even though there wasn't any wind that night) and a tall, conical projection reared itself from where the top of its head should have been. That was all Lily was able to see before the thing had vanished.

What she never dared tell anyone was that she had seen the thing's face and knew that she was directly responsible for all that happened later. Its greenish, satanic features were those of a woman; old yet young; wise yet demented. The face of a stranger and yet, shockingly, one she recognized: that of her daughter, Terry. But as it would appear decades in the future; her youthful innocence captured behind maddened eyes that looked out like the windows of a prison. And then, horribly, Terry's aged voice issued from the thing's mouth and the sound that resulted was as hard as steel and as piercing as chalk on a blackboard.

"Well, humans, for such I see you be, you have rewarded my patience."

The thing bent closer to the window, one arm hidden while the other stretched out a clutching hand.

"Long have I waited to be released into your world, and long have I schemed to find myself here, the home of that hated little girl," it snarled. "She was wise to have fled but I will catch up to her, never fear! In the meantime, I must thank you for handing over to me this new world to conquer; one free of wizards and good witches. Be assured I will make use of their absence."

Then that maniacal laughter filled the room again and the thing raised the arm that had until then been out of sight and in its grasp was the broomstick Terry had found but that now was strangely restored. The movement seemed to be a signal of some sort but before Lily could consider it any further, the thing spoke a final time.

"Farewell, my pretties," it laughed, vanishing from view.

Lily and Dean both raced to the window even as the laughter continued to echo as if with increasing distance. It was the kind of a laugh that froze the blood and threatened to release primal fears that had taken mankind millennia to confine to a part of the brain where they could never escape. Together, they found themselves clutching the window sash in white fingered desperation, their teeth on edge, their eyes wide in fright, but the laugh that had drawn unknown fears from where ancestral memories lay buried and forgotten now, mercifully, was growing fainter in distance. Overhead, the moon had swelled until it seemed impossibly large and it was then that they saw the thing again: a shadowy figure, robes flowing and crowned with its impossibly pointy headgear as it melted into the darkness between the stars. It was blacker than the surrounding night but for one moment as it passed across the face of the moon, they saw that it was riding Terry's broomstick!

After that, it seemed as if the world would return to normal with the surrounding fields all silvery in the moonlight, stretching off emptily into the distance…until the star flecked western sky began to darken, not with clouds, but with countless millions of black-winged creatures, an invading army all flying and flapping in the direction of the house, filling the world with a cacophonic tittering that sounded mankind's doom.

End Hunt

The quality of the hunt over the past one hundred years had been growing steadily worse.

It was late autumn and the ground, where its grassy covering lay exposed, undulated in frozen waves. Cracked and veined, it radiated little warmth from beneath the frost line, a warmth he sensed more than felt. The old grass and crisped leaves crackled beneath his uncertain tread as he picked his way through the short stretch of forest. The woodland of the New World was certainly a far cry from the deep and untouched wildernesses of his youth in the Old Country. He breathed deep, more a sigh than a breath, in recalling the dark forest of the Rhine, the clear-aired mountain reaches along the Bosporus, the misty mornings about Loch Eir, the open spaces of the Ruhr. But those days were gone and he had long since left those ancient shores.

The sun was still hidden below the horizon, though it would remain just as invisible after it rose behind the seamless blanket of clouds that encased the sky. A thin ground fog stood motionlessly around the gloomy forms of tree trunks, disturbed only when he moved from tree to tree. The bare branches reached in a tangle over his head, fracturing the sky. Over all, a heavy silence hung. Here, in the pre-dawn stillness of a Massachusetts autumn, nothing moved. All birds had flown, every rodent lay cuddled in its nook. The omnipresent hum of distant traffic was gone. The wind was dead. He liked it this way because it reminded him of the old days of hunting in the Black Forest where his solitary nature could merge with the silent loneliness of the wood. But here, in this hated New World, those moments were few, and lately, hardly existed at all.

Again he cursed the forces that had compelled him to leave Europe for America. The mushrooming industries of the Continent emptied the countryside of people, creating filthy urban centers instead. Need drove him to their populated, stinking environs and forced him to hunt the rubble strewn streets, the diseased ghettoes, the fume-engulfed rooftops. Finally, the corruption had sunk so deep that his prey began to taste of it as their bodies absorbed the pollutants in the air. Sick and weakened, he left the cities to retreat to the Ruhr valley, there he had always been able to rest and escape the constant tension of capture; but even there, perhaps worse than anywhere else, the new industries had taken root. Drawn by its rich coal deposits and iron ores, the first roots of the giant Krupp works had been laid. Sickened, he determined to leave Europe altogether and travel to America, of which he had heard so much. With its wetlands, vast tracts of untouched forest, and most of all, its tiny communities huddled against the coasts, it presented itself to him as an ideal retreat.

And so, he left his beloved Prussia, hiding for many weeks in the deepest hold of an old barnacled hulk. Emerging only when the ship finally berthed at Salem harbor, his first prey had of necessity been another hated city creature; but with the first pangs of hunger sated, he removed himself from Salem and sought the nearby forest.

And they were indeed pure and vast! For many years he idled among them. Hunting and resting as he pleased, there was always likely prey in the scattered settlements, especially in the crude mining and logging camps that dotted the land. But eventually, settlement changed that. Creeping industrialism found its way to this new continent also, and the countryside was depopulated in favor of the cities. The elements necessary to his survival were now only to be found in abundance in the larger towns.

Until now, he found himself once again in repetition of the strategy he had followed a hundred years before, hunting amid the pollution saturated inhabitants of the cities. Here, where his sojourn in America began: Salem.

He reached the edge of the forest that also topped a steep rise in the land. Below, at the end of a gray ribbon of highway, glittered the lights of the city.

Late afternoon sunlight poured into the living room through glass doors that led onto a small balcony. Throwing the apartment into pale orange relief, motes of dust were clearly visible as they settled on the few items of furniture that dotted the room. The sounds of the evening news broadcasts permeated the apartment as Maureen sat facing the television set. She leaned back on the sofa and breathed a sigh of anxiety. For the dozenth time she brought her wrist up, checked the time, and let it drop again. If only her heart would stop racing. She stood up, took two steps to the television set, and snapped off the announcer in mid-sentence.

Her hands shook slightly as she walked to the window that overlooked the street below. The early evening traffic crawled by in grim procession, punctuated by the occasional blast of a horn. She took another deep breath, held it, and exhaled. *Would I ever shake this nervousness? It wasn't as if this was my first date with Tony. I've seen him half a dozen times. So why am still so nervous?* And yet her hands still shook and as usual, she felt the need to go to the bathroom just before he was due to arrive. *Here I am,* she scolded herself, *27 years old and still nervous about going out on a date.*

I felt as though she were a teenager on her first date. And it never let up. She often wondered if other women felt the same but immediately cast the thought from her mind. All the other women she knew, including Susan, her best friend, seemed so casual about men. They were used to having them around. But she wasn't. Since leaving high school, she had gone out on a grand total of one date. Was it that long ago? The thought hit her hard, as it always did. Time seemed to go by so quickly, especially when it was measured in days and weeks. After living alone for so long, she had developed a routine, one that as time went by, she felt increasingly hard to free herself from. She was used to her life, used to the way things were going. With a man in her life, the routine was broken. Her sense of security was threatened and replaced by the unknown.

But it was a trade Maureen had forced herself to make. She was getting older, and time, she knew, was slipping away.

The problem wasn't that she was unattractive. As a matter of fact, she was quite pretty, at least so she'd been told. But she'd never really been popular. In high school she was bookwormish, reading all the time. So when it was time to become interested in the opposite sex, she found herself on terra incognita. Never having socialized before, she was shy. So how could she be expected to flirt with the boys like other girls? It struck her as completely outlandish to insinuate herself onto one using her sex appeal to draw his interest. On the other hand, some boys had asked her out, but they did it with a leer on their faces as they looked over her body. Others, those she was interested in, were either intimidated by her looks or already spoken for.

After high school, she found a job in the local library, in the stacks, where she'd been ever since. Not the sort of job with a high visibility factor; that, coupled with her habit of moving outside established social circles, kept her pretty much to herself. As a result, she'd been miserable. Periodic depression born of loneliness plagued her. Oh, sure, there was her family and Susan, but they weren't enough. She was sure that the sort of aching loneliness she felt was the kind that could only be assuaged by a man. A special someone who could be all hers. Someone who could hold her close, care for her, really love her. But each time she thought of someday being held in a man's arms, the utter impossibility of it all struck her like some great weight. She'd been so long without a man she found it impossible to imagine such a thing actually coming true. Such things happened to other people, or in books, but not in her own life.

Until one day, all that seemed to change. She had seen an advertisement on television for a dating service with all these respectable people saying how marvelous the service was. *What if they could match her up with someone who was actually like herself?* Maureen wondered. Impulsively, with the knowledge that time was against her, she signed up. The result was Tony.

She sighed softly and brought her knuckles to her chin, the setting sun suddenly blinding her as it was reflected from a window across the street. As she stepped away, Tony's Datsun pulled up in front. Immediately, she began to shake again, her teeth chattering slightly. She forced herself to stop just as Tony left the car and sprung up the front steps. A moment later, the call buzzer sounded from downstairs.

"Is that you, Tony?" she said into the intercom.

"You know it," came the response from the speaker.

Maureen pressed the release button and imagined Tony as he took the stairs two at a time. A knock indicated that he had arrived at her door and undoing the latch, she let him in.

"Hi, Moe, all set?"

A chill of pleasure ran along Maureen's spine as she heard the pet name he had taken to calling her. His smile lit the room and his dark eyes flashed. Beneath a tan overcoat worn against the late autumn chill, Tony sported a dark suit that went with his eyes.

"Just let me get my coat and I'll be right with you," said Maureen.

"Take your time."

She came back with her coat and he helped her into it. She lifted her chin as he fastened the topmost button for her. The look of studied concentration on his face made her laugh.

"Is that the thanks I get?" he asked, feigning hurt.

"Thank you, kind sir," she replied with a slight bow. "And now the door, if you please?"

"But of course," he replied, ushering her through the opening.

It was that twilight season that lay athwart the raw autumn and crisp winter.

The fur lay matted and damp against his flesh. The early morning cold had long since departed, but not before the difference in temperature from the cold of the night to the relative warmth of the muggy day had worked themselves through his system. It was one of those days where, though the sky was yet slate gray, the warmth of the hidden sun filtered through, drawing steam from the waters of the nearby rivers and lakes, turning the hardened ground to muddy inconsistency. As a result, he became overheated with the exertion of the hunt and as his kind did not perspire, the heavy moisture in the air condensed against his body. Now, he was annoyed whenever he stopped to rest and reconnoiter as his body suffered chills throughout its tawny length.

He was stopped now, in the shadow of two wood-framed tenements. The alley between them was strewn with the semi-decomposed trash and swill of months of uncollected refuse, now mushy and moldy from long exposure to the elements. An overflowing dumpster stood at the rear of one of the buildings surrounded by its coterie of bulging plastic bags. The stink was strong enough for his sensitive sense of smell to have located its exact position even in the dead of night. Piles of fallen leaves struggled with pools of rainwater for dominance in the warped and blistering tarmac of the alley. Gritty runoff dripped in steams from slate roofs onto his head and back. Normally, he would have walked along on all fours, but the part of him that was still human revolted at the thought of stepping along the putrid paths of the city.

Yes, Salem had changed considerably since his first arrival over one hundred years before. Then, it had bustled as any great seaport would have during the Civil War; these days however, it was but one of many slowly dying cities from which industry had moved on for the outlying towns and suburban sprawl.

He stumbled and then caught himself against the cheap tarry siding of one of the tenements before he could fall onto the cracked sidewalk. He swore inwardly at the curse that forced him to walk about on two legs like a man, when every instinct of his wild self screamed to use all four. It was not only clumsy but painful for him to walk upon two legs shaped for leaping and thrusting his body forward over harsh terrain. But circumstances dictated his current upright posture: each of his forelimbs terminated in a rough approximation of four fingers and opposing thumb. And though, at times their shape proved quite useful, his bestial nature prevented him from fully utilizing their range of functions. But then, what did he care for the dainty uses the affairs of a man would put them to? He preferred to see their most effective and useful purpose as rending and tearing tender flesh from its anchor of sinew and tendon, exposing the bone beneath. At thought of hot blood steaming in the cold winter air, his mouth began to water and his tongue to run along the edges of his snout. It was then that he caught the first sweet scent of prey.

———————

Tony closed the passenger door with a firm shove and Maureen watched him move easily around the forward end of the car. He looked so distinguished in his suit and coat, but then he looked like that no matter what he wore. Was it possible that she could have so easily found the man she'd always dreamt of?

He entered the car, inserted the key into the ignition, started the engine, and closed the door all at the same time. Craning his neck to look out for cars coming from the rear, he eased the Datsun away from the curb.

"What's on the agenda for tonight?" asked Maureen luxuriating in the warmth emanating from the car's heater.

"First a movie, then dinner at the Regal."

"Sounds good," she said. "What's the movie?"

"You'll like it. It's about this mild mannered librarian who gets into all sorts of trouble."

"Sounds familiar." She was more relaxed now as the easy talk soothed her nerves. The conversation waned as Tony negotiated traffic down Lafayette Street toward Essex. Maureen took the opportunity to close her eyes for a moment.

She remembered the day not long before, when she received an envelope from the dating service stating that her name and vital statistics had been duly logged into their computer and were immediately matched with a number of suitable men. *So quickly*, she thought. Two nights later, her phone rang and upon answering it, she found herself speaking to Tony and arranging for a first meeting on neutral ground somewhere. Maureen had been hanging up the phone before the reality of the situation struck home. Tony's voice was strong and firm and when they finally met, she found that her first impressions suited him in person as well. Anthony Strode was polite and cordial and spoke with an easy familiarity on almost any subject. He was the president of his own small electronics firm and lived modestly in a small duplex in the Castle Hill section of town.

Of course, she had been incredibly nervous on that first date making frequent trips to the ladies' room. But Tony appeared to understand, insisting on no explanations. Best of all, he was gentlemanly in accepting nothing more from her but a chaste kiss goodnight. And all of it resulting from a date arranged for her by a dating service! At times, she still couldn't bring herself to believe she could be so fortunate.

But always, lurking at the back of her mind, was the thought that soon she may be called upon to give more than just the mandatory kiss goodnight. And what then? Tony was such a gentleman, she couldn't see how he might raise the subject of asking for more tokens of her affections. But eventually it would have to be done. Was it something natural and unplanned that grew out of a moment of intimacy the way it was shown in the movies, or was it something two people plan, consciously agreeing with each other that they would do such and such a thing at such and such a time? Maureen shook her head slightly, opened her eyes, and thought she'd cross that bridge when she came to it.

His keen eyes watched from the alley's shadow as the girl entered the car across the street. Her male companion barely registering as the sweetest scent of all reached his flaring nostrils. A virgin! Untouched, unspoiled. The choicest prey of all!

It had been many years since he had sampled such a sweet morsel. But no sooner had the contemplation been considered, than it was superceded by his recollection of the curse. Because of it, he could only imagine what sinking his teeth into such unspoiled meat would be like. Unfortunately, only despoiled flesh could pass his fangs. Such was the curse of the beast.

A beast! Yes, how long had it been? Once again his feeble brain attempted to pierce the fog that filled it. His past was a subject that filled his thoughts when they were not being dominated with the desire for prey. Dimly, he knew that he had once hunted the fields and forests of Europe before the coming of industry drove his prey into the cities. His stomach more than his head reminded him of the how lean those years had been.

It was only in these later times, in America, that prey had become so plentiful that his belly always remained full. He knew the churches in this land had begun to empty of believers. He saw fewer people pass through their doors. He saw the corresponding increase in violence and perversion until they no longer drew any special attention. So pervasive had casual violence become, that he was able to hunt almost with impunity. Assuming his depredations just part of the culture of violence, humans rarely associated them with anything out of the ordinary. With the general collapse of the unstated, unwritten codes of society, all forms of aberrant behavior were now accepted. So had his prey increased in numbers and he seldom went hungry.

But the thought of prey, reminded him of this latest find. He ached to taste her flesh with all–consuming fervor but was restrained in the gut-knowledge that one drop of that precious blood would surely kill him. And centuries of learning and honing the skills that had become his very life could not be thrown away, even for such a feast.

But there was yet one thing he could do that could approximate the pleasure of drinking the blood of a virgin. If she were to lose her purity and he were to strike immediately afterward, he could savor a feast as near to the sweet taste of purity as he was able short of death. He had had his fill of soiled and unclean meat. Now, he hungered for the clean and wholesome.

But a precious gift given in lust, in some moment of animalistic passion, never failed to render the sweet meat rotten and coarse. It smelled forever of fetid decay and tasted of maggots. The kind of smell he had too often in years past traced to its source. Too often in those times he had settled for what was at hand rather than what remained in the field. But as that pure scent once more reached his whirling brain, he knew that this time he would plan, and stalk, and really hunt rather than simply, artlessly, pluck whatever quarry crossed his path. The game would serve as a tantalizing entrée for the main course.

———————

Maureen laughed lightly as Tony recounted a humorous episode from the film they had just seen. She was feeling a lot better now, her nervousness had passed. She really felt relaxed and natural with Tony tonight. It seemed like it came easy to him, acting as if he hadn't a care in the world, rubbing it off on her. But with a company of his own, of course, he must have had plenty of concerns. Maureen sipped her after dinner champagne slowly and regarded Tony from over the rim of the glass, unashamedly. Was she actually growing bolder?

"I'm glad you find that funny Moe, because I have a real surprise for you next week," he said pushing his empty plate aside.

"Oh, no," she said, in mock alarm.

"Oh, yes," he rejoined. "There's a Red Skelton film festival next weekend at the museum and we're going."

His reply was couched in mock command but Maureen kind of liked that.

"Why the sudden interest in comedy?"

"I've always loved Red Skelton; and besides, admission is free."

"I should have known," she said. "Financial trouble at work?"

She said it in a light, non-serious tone, but she really did want to know. She wanted to know all about him.

"Of course not. I'm a financial genius, remember?"

Maureen laughed again and said more seriously, "I know, but really, how are things going?"

"Wonderfully. I have more orders than I could fill. But I'm determined to take it slow, I want to put out a good, solid product, so I don't want to rush my people. Quality, not quantity is the name of the game. But if things continue as they are, I could be very comfortable in a few more years."

Was that a hopeful note in his voice, or was she looking too hard for hints?

More and more, Maureen found herself convinced that this was the kind of man she always wanted to spend the rest of her life with. Was it fate? Kismet? Or was she just being foolish, letting her desires run away with her, leaving her reason behind. But reason be damned! For too long she'd spent her life alone, seemingly without hope. Now her heart was saying even as her head reminded her to "think, think." Wasn't that how it always was? She thought of all those marriages ending in divorce, most of them seemingly because the two partners had rushed ahead on infatuation alone? Hadn't she believed that things would be different with her? That when the time came, she would be more level headed than others, she would never allow herself to fall in love in such a way as to lose all reason and make a terrible mistake.

"Did you enjoy yourself this evening, Moe?" Tony's query broke her chain of thought, dragging her mind back to the present.

"Oh, yes I did. I always enjoy myself when I'm with you Tony." She didn't mean to say it exactly that way, it sounded too fawning, too girlish, but not only was it too late to take it back, she found she didn't want to change it. Perhaps he'd take it as a hint.

Unbidden, an image of she and Tony making love entered her mind. Reluctantly, she banished it from her thoughts. She was finding herself fantasizing more and more easily these days with the imagery becoming more natural, more acceptable all the time. But if the chance ever came to make her fantasies come true, would reason compel her to reject it or would she simply follow her desires? She really didn't want to know the answer; it was one that she might not like.

"Thank you, I'll accept the compliment graciously," Tony was saying.

"And thank you for a wonderful meal. I thought I'd never see the inside of the Regal."

"Are you kidding? This place is rock bottom, wait till you see the places I have in mind for us later on!" As Tony took in the large dining room with a wave of his hand, Maureen couldn't help following its sweep across the darkened room, the sequestered tables, the chandeliers, the waiters as they drifted soundlessly from table to table.

She looked back to Tony as he leaned forward on his elbows.

"I'd do anything to make you happy, Moe," he said. "I don't know what it is, but you've got something that just makes me want to do thing for you, to care for you..." His voice trailed off as he dropped his eyes in embarrassment. It was obvious that he hadn't intended to reveal so much of his feelings.

Maureen opened her mouth to speak but halted herself, unable to finish. She had been about to say "I love you" but common sense rescued her in the knick of time. Or had it been so well timed? Maybe she missed the perfect opportunity to have said such a thing. While her reason urged her to beware, her heart compelled her to go on. But she only said "It's late, maybe we should be getting along."

———————

He had waited.

The patience of the hunter was his.

He had long learned the futility of following a motor vehicle through the streets of the city. The neighborhood around him was quiet, as it had been all day. Now it was night and the tenements were dark. He grinned, exposing yellowed canines, bits of still undissolved flesh from an earlier meal still clinging to them. His keen eyes jerked here and there along the face of the apartment building across the street; it was mostly dark as well. And now, in the stillness of the night air, after the thick blanketing of pollutants present during the day had settled, the myriad smells of the city became more apparent. The trash in the dumpsters, the rat and dog droppings, cigarette smoke, human sweat, the stink of the sewers as steam wafted from openings in the gutter. He crouched in the alley, oblivious to all of them in anticipation of the one scent that was to come. Following the pattern of the females of this society, his prey would lure her desired mate into her lair and couple with him there. Soon after, he would leave, and the hunter would creep to the building in his wake and seek ingress. Finding it, he would then attack lightning swift and eat of the female's flesh, so recently unspoiled, but just then still clean enough to allow him a feast too long untasted.

———————

The drive home was conducted in an awkward silence as Tony concentrated more than he needed to on the road ahead. Maureen, for her part, debated fiercely with her heart whether to take what was for her, a momentous step. After her fumbled attempt at the Regal to say something really meaningful about their relationship, she had stopped herself short. Almost immediately, she began to doubt whether she had done the right thing. Looking surreptitiously at Tony limned in the dashboard lights, Maureen thought she owed him something in return for his own attempt at honesty. *Lord knows it was difficult enough for men to show any of their affections,* she thought. And for her to have ignored his overture was a cruel blow. Yes, she was determined to make it up to him. Besides, she didn't want to take the chance of losing Tony because he misinterpreted her caution for disinterest. So by the time the little Datsun halted along the curb facing her apartment, she had made up her mind to ask him in for a real visit, not just to wait as she slipped on her coat.

"Home sweet home!" said Tony in forced joviality. He sprung from the car and sprinted around to open the door for her even as Maureen steeled herself for the big step.

He let her out of the car and steered her by the elbow along the short walk to the door. Between the inner and outer glass doors of the apartment entrance, she turned to face him as he made the preparatory motions to kiss her goodnight, but before he could, Maureen said "Tony, would you like to come upstairs for a while? For some coffee or something?" Her voice trembled a bit as she said it, and she was sure he knew it. She half hoped he would decline the offer, recognizing it as a sort of apology; but another side of her hoped that he would accept the offer. *Oh! She didn't know what she wanted!*

"That sounds great, thanks," Tony was saying. "There's nothing like a good, slow cup of java after a good meal."

She sensed immediately his relief and happiness; he had taken the offer for what it was and accepted it. But did he read more into it than Maureen had intended? She turned and unlocked the inner door and led Tony up the short flight of stairs to her apartment.

As she fumbled with her keys, she found she had trouble handling them. Her hands began to tremble again. She finally got the door open and ushered Tony into the kitchen, closing the door snugly to behind him.

"Here, let me have your coat."

"Thanks," he said, letting it drop into Maureen's waiting arms.

As she retreated to the vestibule she remembered just having cleaned the parlor rug, and without thinking, blurted out "Oh, do you mind taking your shoes off, Tony? I just cleaned the rug."

"No problem."

Presently, she heard the sound of his shoes as he kicked them off onto the hard linoleum. Immediately, she began to regret her rash demand. How could she have suggested such a thing? The two of them could have just as easily, less threateningly, taken their coffee at the kitchen table. But she hadn't thought the situation through far enough. What could possible be going through his mind now? Did he think she was setting him up? *I hope not!* thought Maureen. *He couldn't possibly think that could he?*

She hung his coat in the closet and now was obliged to kick off her own shoes as well. As they tumbled from her feet into the recesses of the closet, silly as it sounded, she realized that she and a man were now alone in her apartment *without their shoes on*! With the thought, she had to stifle a laugh with her hand.

Calling back to the kitchen she said, "Make yourself comfortable, Tony. I'll be right back."

"Take your time. I'll start the coffee."

Returning from the bathroom, Maureen heard the clinking of sounds cups and spoons from the pantry and found Tony by the Mr. Coffee. Mustering her courage, she said "Well, look who's getting all domestic!"

"A fine thing," said Tony, laughing. "I'm invited up to have coffee and I'm the one who ends up having to make it. If I didn't know better, I'd swear I was set up."

Maureen sobered. Was he kidding, or was it just an innocent remark? She finally decided it was just a figure of speech.

"Okay, shoo!" she said. "Get in the living room while I handle this. You men are all thumbs in the kitchen."

"A woman after my own heart!"

Presently, the rich smell of coffee wafted up to her from the counter as strains of Brahms floated into the pantry from the living room. Was Tony trying to set up a romantic mood? Was it possible he was thinking she'd meant a lot more than coffee when she invited him in? Nervously, she poured the coffee and slowly brought the two cups into the living room. There, she was momentarily startled to find that Tony had divested himself of his suit and tie.

"Let me get those," he said as she entered the room. Springing from his place on the sofa he cocked his head to where he had been sitting "Sit down there." When she had taken her place, he sat down beside her saying "I took the liberty of putting on a bit of Brahms; you don't mind do you?" She shook her head and reached for the cup he was handing her. "I wasn't sure if the neighbors would complain, but then, who in their right mind would complain about Brahms?"

"Not me," said Maureen as her eyes followed Tony down to the sofa.

"You didn't tell me you were interested in classical music, this opens whole new vistas of possibilities," Tony said.

"You never asked, to coin a phrase," replied Maureen, sipping her coffee.

Was it warm in the living room or was it just the coffee? She blinked her eyes and her head dipped slightly, but she recovered quickly.

"What's wrong?" asked Tony suddenly concerned.

"It's nothing," she insisted. "I think it's those two glasses of champagne. I don't drink too often, and when I do, my defenses crumble. I'm still a little dizzy I guess."

"Well that shouldn't last too long, just keep working on that coffee. On the other hand, it is a little warm in here. That's why I took off my coat."

"I thought the warmth was my imagination," said Maureen.

"Don't think so. And of course the tie had to come off too…to tell you the truth, I hate the darn things," he added in a stage whisper.

She laughed and said, "But you have to wear one all day long at work."

"The cost of success my dear, the cost of success," he finished his coffee and set the cup aside.

"Add that to your interest in classical music as a character trait needing further discussion," said Maureen.

She set her own cup on the lamp-stand half finished as Tony launched into a monologue regarding the merits of Schubert over Chopin. And interesting though it was, Maureen found herself struggling against the combined effects of the champagne, hot coffee, and the apartment's warmth to stay awake. Finally, against the hope that Tony hadn't noticed her drowsiness, she felt her head easing back onto the couch as his voice receded into the distance…

———————

At last the car had returned, and by the light of the new risen moon, he saw the two humans leave the vehicle and enter the little foyer at the front of the building. Instantly, he had risen to all fours, crouching for instant action. Head lowered, his eyes followed the couple's progress as they crossed into the interior of the building and disappeared upwards on the stairs. He rose onto his hind legs and continued to watch the building opposite for some minutes until he saw a dim light shine from one of the second story windows. Still waiting, he saw it grow suddenly still brighter as someone inside advanced deeper into the apartment.

It was then he began to move.

Half-walking, half-stumbling on legs never meant for upright movement, he reached a spot at the front of the building he had previously planned on using should he find the woman's abode to be on the side facing the street. Grasping the dusty branches of the ivy that grew thickly about the brickwork, he used the claw-like hands he had frequently cursed as a man would use them and began to negotiate the clinging growth. Rear paws scraping silently for holds, he finally reached the small veranda that overhung the front of the apartment and that allowed him to look into the rooms beyond without himself being observed.

As his wet nose pressed against the cold panes of a sliding door, his snout cracked in the semblance of a grin. The scene revealed to him inside proved that his knowledge of the mating habits of this new society was sound. How these humans had grown so pathetically predictable! The female lay back dreamily on the couch with wordless invitation to her chosen mate for the evening.

He backed away carefully from the doors and soundlessly retreated back across the empty street. In the alley, he watched the light tumbling from the distant windows. Soon now, his patience would be rewarded.

———————

Soft, soft as the brush of a butterfly's wings.

Maureen sat up suddenly, eyes wide, fingertips pressed to her lips. Asleep. She had fallen asleep...after fighting so hard not to. And Tony! Her eyes focused at last and she saw him sitting alongside her, his face a mixture of surprise and apprehension.

"Tony...?"

"Maureen I..." he started, then halted.

They both were sitting on the sofa, so close, their bodies touched. Maureen honestly couldn't tell which of them was the more discomfited.

"Maureen," Tony tried. "When I realized that you had nodded off, I decided to let you sleep. But looking at you lying there so natural, it occurred to me just how attractive you really were."

Maureen felt herself blushing.

"This is going to sound pretty silly, but the situation reminded of the story of Sleeping Beauty who only needed a kiss to be woken up," continued Tony. "I couldn't resist that element of fantasy and for a moment, the thing I most wanted in the whole world was to brush my lips against yours...I...I'm sorry. I'll leave now, if you want."

Tony started to get to his feet, but Maureen motioned for him to stop.

His sincerity had been real; she knew that as certainly as she knew she wanted his kisses. In her heart, she had already forgiven him but he didn't know that so she leaned forward, tilting her face upward, imagining herself looking angelic in the glow of the lamp behind her. They were close enough that she didn't have to move far to be near him.

"It's all right," she managed. "Please, kiss me again."

She had whispered it so softly, she hardly heard herself speak, but as Tony came forward, she knew he had heard her well enough.

"Thank you, Maureen," he whispered back.

As she heard him say her name, Maureen knew he was taking the moment seriously, not at all lightly. And as their faces drew together, she also knew that she couldn't stop what was happening between the two of them even if she wanted to.

The warmth of Tony's nearness washed over her as their lips brushed lightly, tentatively, together. His kiss was gentle, caressing, not forceful at all. She yielded and her lips parted involuntarily as her head bent backward to receive him. Distantly, she felt her pulse pounding and even the roots of her hair tingled with heightened sensitivity. Tony slipped an arm behind her, supporting her body as it began to fall backward. His other arm circled her waist. With rising passion, she felt the play of his tongue about her lips. Somewhere in the back of her mind, she heard herself saying no, that it was wrong, but the warning went unheeded as she slipped her arms upward around Tony's neck.

He removed his hand from her waist, bringing it up to stroke her cheek, but in passing, it brushed one of her breasts. She breathed sharply inward at the brief contact and the reaction freed his lips to roam her face. She was reacting instinctively now, without much conscious thought. She caught his rising hand and replaced it gently on her breast. Leaving it there, his lips again sought hers and as they rejoined, the sensations she had been experiencing up to that point redoubled in intensity. She held him tighter and was only able to breathe again when his lips left hers and moved downward to the hollow of her throat.

As he moved lower, Tony's hand abandoned her breast and began to fumble with her blouse; staring at the ceiling, Maureen helped by undoing the lower buttons herself. Parting the folds of her blouse, Tony's kisses found the soft swells of her breasts. Unwilling, or unable to stop, Maureen freed them from their restraints and in another moment, Tony had grasped them in his hands and cupped them upward to his eager lips.

Maureen thought she had blacked out then but realized that she had only grown faint. But the momentary seizure had brought her briefly to her senses. Her rational mind struggled to come to the surface, but its efforts were still too weak to resist the repressed desires that had been set loose. As time passed, seconds seemed like hours, and her mind grew clearer. Suddenly, it seemed as if she were outside her body looking down at herself in Tony's arms. Just the way she had pictured it in her fantasies.

As she watched, her blouse lying whitely where it had fallen on the rug, her skirt undone and lowered to mid-thigh, Tony began to maneuver her onto her back. Her legs dangling over the edge of the sofa, it suddenly occurred to her how awkward and unromantic the act of sex could really be. Her strange out of body experience over, Maureen seemed to feel the excitement of lovemaking begin to ebb. Again, her lifelong convictions regarding the proper place and time for such activity, removing the awkwardness of spontaneity and replacing it with genuine affection and tenderness, reasserted themselves. At that moment, she felt the cool touch of Tony's hand as it slid along her belly and came to rest gently between her legs. She felt the muscles of her inner thighs quiver in anticipation; but instead of invitation, it served as an alarm. Weakness on the part of both she and Tony had allowed events to progress to a point beyond which they would regret; a point that Maureen knew would mean the end of any kind of serious, long lasting relationship between the two of them. To spare them that fate, and preserve a chance at happiness in the future, she had to stop things before they went too far.

"No," she said. Too weakly to arrest Tony's attentions. "No!" she said more firmly, moving to push away his probing hand.

Reacting slowly, like a man awakened from a deep sleep, Tony raised himself on an elbow. Freed from the pressure of his body, Maureen pulled up her skirt and fastened the waist strap. Then, scooping up her blouse she shrugged into that. Finished, she stood and paced deliberately to her bedroom.

A slight, quick movement in the light. The coupling was over; the two were now moving about, making the obligatory motions for the leave-taking. His entire body tensed in anticipation. From the damp fur lining his tail to his heaving torso to the whiskers on his snout. He bunched the legs beneath his rear quarters. As soon as the male's car was gone, he would strike.

Leaning against the bedroom door, she began to cry. She shivered against the cold surface of the door as sobs wracked her body. After some minutes, she wiped her tears with the back of her hand, straightened her clothing, and passed a comb through her hair. Straightening, she exhaled loudly and prepared to go to Tony.

The short hallway leading from her room to the living room seemed endless. What was she going to say? *I hope you enjoyed your coffee, Tony. See you next week?* She was suddenly struck by the absurdity of the situation and it was all she could do to keep herself from laughing. Restraining the impulse, she forced herself to confront the fact that she had nearly done the very thing she swore never to do. And how easily she had let it happen! She'd never suspected how strong the tide of passion could be. Once begun, it was almost impossible to stop. She was surprised to have found the strength within herself to beat those odds.

That explained herself; but what about Tony? Was he after all, just as weak as anyone else? But then, the realization struck her: it was she who had invited him to kiss her that second time. It was she who had manipulated his actions to some degree during the lovemaking! She never knew that she had that potential. But knowing it now, she suddenly felt purged; recognizing weakness was the first step in protecting oneself against it. Reassured, she was ready for the moment when she finally stepped into the living room to face Tony.

Upon seeing her, Tony stood quickly, his hands, searching for support and finding none, came together behind his back. Maureen noticed that he had replaced his coat and tie. Suddenly, he stepped forward, raising his arms slightly in supplication.

"Maureen, I'm sorry, really I am," he began. "If I could take it all back, I would. I...I've never done anything like that in my life. I've always thought of myself as a gentleman."

Maureen crossed her arms and looked down. "I know, Tony. I feel the same way. It was all I could do to stop it when I did."

"I'm glad you had the presence of mind to do it because I couldn't have."

"It wasn't entirely your fault, Tony, I led you on..."

"No, you didn't. What you did was hardly a seduction."

"Just the same," she sighed. "Maybe the blame lies on both sides. In any case I've learned something tonight."

"But at what price, Maureen?" Tony wanted to know. "Weeks or months of regret and self-recrimination with myself as the villain? I don't think I'd like that very much. And imagine my own frustrations: seeing the kind of woman you truly are, I'm more certain now than ever that you're the kind of woman I want to spend the rest of my life with. The price

I'll pay for this incident is how I'll have lost you due to my own weaknesses."

With that, he began for the kitchen to fetch his shoes and take his leave.

"Tony, wait," said Maureen. "We're only human. We all make mistakes. But you're goodness asserted itself when it counted. You could have tried to force the situation further, but you didn't. You stopped when I asked you to stop. This doesn't have to be the end. Maybe...maybe we could see each other again sometime." He looked up hopefully. "Not right away, but soon."

"I said it before, and I'll say it again Maureen, you're a beautiful woman; more inside than out. That price I spoke about before...I think it's been considerably lessened. Thanks."

He finished slipping on his shoes, opened the door, and stepped out.

Maureen looked at the floor and hugged herself. Absentmindedly, she wandered to the veranda doors and looked out. There was the sound of an engine starting from somewhere below and in the same instant, she recalled Tony's overcoat that still hung in the closet. Retrieving it, she dashed out and down the stairs to the front door. As she reached the landing, she wondered if she were simply returning the coat out of necessity, or because what she really wanted was to let Tony know that they need not wait too long before seeing each other again? Whatever the reason, she burst out into the frigid night air and ran down to the sidewalk in time to see the Datsun's receding tail lights. Her shoulders sagged in disappointment as the coat sleeves trailed on the pavement. She really had wanted to give him some more hopeful signal after all. Sighing with regret, she felt for the first time the cold of the autumn night through her thin blouse. Shivering, she turned to go back inside.

———————

With the departure of the automobile, he rose onto his hind legs and, using the side of the tenement building for support, stepped out into the street. The rising of the full moon

51

filled him with renewed vigor for the hunt. Though not necessary for his livelihood, the full moon always affected him in a most primal manner; to the point where he felt like howling his excitement for the whole world to hear. But where in the solitude of the forest he would not have hesitated to do so, here amid the dwellings of man, he refrained from painful experience.

He fully expected to have to scale again the front wall of the domicile and gain entrance to the woman's abode through splintering glass doors when suddenly, to his amazement and good fortune, the woman herself emerged from the front entrance and came out into the street. He froze where he stood, in the center of the road, and drunk in her still-fresh loveliness. She stood with her back partially to him, looking after the departing vehicle. He appreciated how well her actions fit in with the coupling process. Where at first she had acted as the lure and control, she now seemed to acquire some emotional attachment where she did not formerly expect one. All to the good, as it served to draw her outside, providing him with easy prey. Without the need for a noisy attack, he could now kill with ease. He longed to grasp the shapely head, like some ripe fruit, in the crook of his mighty jaws, dragging her lifeless carcass to some secluded spot to relish at his leisure.

Suddenly, the stink of the alleyway once again permeated the air, dulling his senses. But before he could lend further thought to the bothersome phenomenon, he saw the woman turn and begin to reenter her building. With sudden decision, and with more grace and speed than his former difficulties had suggested, he charged headlong across the street.

———————

Maureen had just started up the front steps when she heard the sound of movement behind her. Not alarmed, for it hardly resembled the sound of running feet, she turned and saw charging furiously across the street, the form of a giant dog; running so fast in fact, that it seemed to her that it ran on its hind legs like a man. But she had little time to ponder such an absurdity as the creature quickly reached her and knocked her to the ground. Falling to the sidewalk, she didn't even have time to scream as her head struck the iron railing at the side of the door and for the second time that night, she lost consciousness.

———————

He had reached her in seconds and in even less time, subdued her with a mighty sweep of his arm, stifling any cry for help. Standing now over his victim, the scene lit in the glare of a nearby streetlight, his chest heaved with increasing excitement as his hungry gaze fell on the pink flesh of her face and trailed down to her bare throat. Her feet lay against his crooked legs and with the contact his own flesh tingled in what he imagined was the vanishing aura of her cleanliness. Although the polluted air of the city still prevented him from fully appreciating her sweet scent, he could not restrain himself any longer. Bending, he grasped her limp form in his hands and drew his fangs close to her neck in anticipation of the hot pulsation of her soon to be gushing blood.

Overcome by desire, unable to wait any longer, he dragged his long tongue over the woman's flesh. Not quite as satisfying as he had hoped, he allowed his teeth to break the surface of the skin. Blood welled up and lapping at it, he recoiled in distaste. Where he had expected to enjoy the sweet taste of innocence, he felt only the searing, scolding action of bitter disappointment and pain!

Letting the woman drop from his grasp, he reeled back in shock. His entire being was wracked in piercing pain. It shot with lances of fire along his arms; it coursed with rivers of acid down his legs. Eyes wide and holding his head between his hands, he crumpled to the pavement looking desperately about for the source of his suffering. But it was useless. In the same instant he knew that he had tasted the blood of a virgin! Looking back through fading vision at the form lying a few yards away, he found the strength to howl a curse of anguish at the hated pollution that fouled the air and prevented his being able to recognize the telltale scent. His legs numb, he managed to drag himself back to the alley across the street, seeking refuge amid the trash of a civilization he hated. Five hundred years of the hunt had evolved him from an inexperienced quasi-human wolf to the coldly efficient dealer of death he had finally become. And in that fading pride, he breathed his last.

On the sidewalk, Maureen slowly regained consciousness; her hand straying to the side of her neck where blood still pulsed from where the skin had been torn. Whimpering, she recalled the charging dog and realized that it must have bitten her. Looking around, she satisfied herself that it was nowhere about. Relieved, she hauled herself to her feet, bothered that now she would have to make a trip to the emergency room, probably for a tetanus shot. *A perfect way to end the night,* she thought. *Wait until Tony hears about this*...but then, she remembered she wasn't seeing him anymore...well, not for now at least. Recalling the events of the night, she wondered if she really had done the right thing in stopping things before they went too far. If she hadn't, Tony would still have been with her and she wouldn't have ended up being attacked. But then, neither of them would ever have been quite sure if the reason they were staying together was really out of love or simple lust. No it was better this way. Now a genuine relationship between Tony and herself could be possible without sex to confuse their emotions.

Upstairs again, Maureen stepped out onto the veranda and stared down at the silent street. She was sure that when the moment had come, she had done the right thing.

Conflicting Realities

Downtown was crowded this time of year. Holiday shoppers scurrying from store to store, arms laden with a growing number of packages. Women pulling reluctant children along snowy sidewalks; their eager faces being dragged across toy store windows. Well dressed men in the latest London Fog outer wear clutching at collars with one hand and holding down hats with the other. Everyone, it seemed, leaning forward at dangerous angles, thrusting their way against the cold December wind. Even the occasional dog, accompanied by the constant clink-clink of license tags, struggled in the violent gusts.

One such gale, seemingly more furious than the rest, propelled Professor Curt Walters, muttering under his breath, into the neon lit glare that spilled from the windows of a popular fast food restaurant.

Pale, darkish faces seemed to look up at him from the opposite side of the steamy pane, but the street scene reflection and neon glare made it impossible to be certain. Walters ran his fingers along the underside of his coat collar lifting it to protect his neck from the biting wind. Gripping his briefcase firmly in his hand, he staggered along the busy street.

The day at the university had been a long and tedious one filled with Kierkegaard, Hegel, Satre, and Jung. Together, they continued to swirl in his thoughts even after he had left the confines of the classroom. Which bothered him more than the intemperate weather: after he was through for the day, he regarded his time as his own filled with his own experiences and his own activities. When events properly belonging to his duties at the university spilled over to his private life, it was then that he chastised himself for being weak. The university paid him a generous salary to instruct its students in the great philosophers so there was no need to spend his own valuable time with them. Consequently, it was with increasing annoyance that Walters struggled to keep matters dealing with his employment confined to the university.

A Santa Claus with ringing bell and swaying pot passed him as Walters hurried along the sidewalk to the next corner. People were all about and someone bumped into him, hurrying on with a mumbled apology. Walters barely glanced at the man as he continued to make for the corner. But upon reaching it, on impulse, he turned to look back along the busy sidewalk to the man who had struck him. To his surprise, he saw that the man had also turned, a solitary figure standing amidst a torrent of shoppers like a dividing stone in rushing waters.

The man stood there looking back at him, unmoving, until he was lost from sight when Walters was compelled to cross the intersection at the change of the traffic lights.

Once free of the crowd however, Walters decided to turn back and find the man who had looked after him so intently. Why had he been so interested in him anyway? He was a simple teacher with no books or papers printed to his credit. His curiosity aroused, Walters determined to find the answer.

A little while later, after hurrying up the street for six minutes and four blocks, Walters recognized the stranger's gray colored raincoat. The man had his back to him and was walking purposefully ahead, looking from side to side with seeming amusement. It was as if he alone were aware of some joke, some fact or circumstance, that everyone else around him was not.

Walters was thinking about what he would say to the man once he caught up with him when a small furor broke out across the street: a elderly woman was shouting something as a youth raced up the street colliding into one person after another like a pinball falling toward the bottom of its glass enclosure.

The incident reminded Walters of a pet theory he held regarding criminal behavior.

Fascinated with the concept of "personal space," that indefinable zone that can only be comfortably breached by those with the most intimate connections with a person, Walters had always wondered why most people were instinctively aware of its existence and rarely made the error of invading it? And if such a transgression was made, the other instinctively backed away, overwhelmed by a sense of violation.

Years before, when Walters first entertained it, the concept had been popularly labeled "personal space." As good a name as any, it was understood as an inborn sense shared by everyone. Also, it was something by no means confined to one's own self, but could also be extended to personal property as well. When one's home was broken into, the feeling of violation was no less acute than if the intrusion had been one of a more personal nature.

Walters turned away from the little drama of the purse snatcher and returned his attention to the man he had been trying to follow. He was still in sight but further along the street. Suddenly, even as Walters looked after him, the man turned and, catching his eye, smiled ever so slightly. It occurred to Walters then that the man was in no hurry, taking his time and checking back now and then to make sure his pursuer was on his trail. Shaking off the feeling, Walters zig-zagged along the crowded sidewalk, closing in on the stranger but even as he did so, his thoughts turned back to his notions on criminal behavior.

After having dwelled on the question for years, he had at last identified a common link shared by most criminals and malcontents. All possessed a disregard for the sanctity of personal space. Youngsters, before any thought of a criminal career entered their minds, began with bullying or stealing from their schoolmates. That kind of anti-social behavior often evolved into intimidation and more violent forms of aggression. In some, the trend eventually ended in the most egregious form of violation, the taking of a human life.

The mystery of it all was that the answer did not lie in nurture over nature. Those of an anti-social bent were not necessarily products of domestic oppression. In fact, many came from what society would deem "good homes." So what to conclude from these facts? Walters finally decided that some people lacked that sense of mutual respect for personal space that was inborn in others. But that led inevitably, to the question: were criminals liable for their actions or not? Walters was just glad that it was not his responsibility to decide.

Trying to keep the stranger ahead of him in sight, a curious thought struck him. What if all of reality was an elaborate illusion? It was a question that had been addressed from time to time by philosophers throughout history so Walters' mind did not immediately reject the idea.

Why does the death of hundreds or thousands of strangers caused by some natural disaster on the other side of the world disturb us less than that of a single person whom we know? It happens because the other side of the world, in the limited experience of each person, might as well not exist. After all, what real proof is there that whole different cultures flourish out of sight on the other side of the globe? Are stories in the nightly news or the newspapers proof of their existence? When it really came down to it, the other side of the world might as not even exist. And if that's so, then what about the world immediately around the corner that is out of sight and whose presence cannot be personally verified as actually being in existence?

In fact, what if each human being's personal space extended only as far as one could see, coming into existence only as a man's perceptions advanced or retreated? All creation would be reduced to an immediate reality accessible only for the single person imagining it all up. And everyone else in that reality? Only temporary constructs that existed to populate the temporary landscape each nevertheless complete with a full set of memories but no inkling of their own unreal existence.

Walters looked along the busy sidewalk watching as people disappeared from sight into buildings and around corners and imagining them vanishing as soon as they left his sight, his personal space. Amused at the notion, he returned his concentration to the stranger.

Following his earlier train of thought, Walters mind tried to connect some of the dots. Supposing the idea that reality was only the invention of individual "dreamers," what if what was perceived as criminal behavior on the part of some, the willingness to violate others' personal space, was actually the manifestation of dreamers trying to make contact with others? Maybe what was perceived as a violation of a person's space was actually an attempt to "overlap" individual realities?

Maybe real individuals lay dormant somewhere, in a sort of limbo, inert except in their dreams, one such as Walters was walking through right then?

Then, as a frisson of fear ran up his spine, he wondered: what if there were no individual dreamers but only one? Walters had long since dismissed the concept of God but if there were only a single dreamer what else would he be called? Suddenly self conscious, Walters began to look upon his fellow pedestrians in a new light. Could one of them be the lone dreamer? A god who held the existence of the world in his mind from one moment to the next and who might be moving about among his creations even now? If so, what guise would he take? One of two lovers holding hands strolling along the sidewalk? The woman struggling with an armful of packages? The child being pulled impatiently along by its mother? *Himself?*

Or the stranger he had been following for the last quarter of an hour?

What was that enigmatic smile that played on the man's lips? What was the attitude he seemed to have of looking around him in amusement? *What did he know that others did not?*

Disturbed at his own train of thought, Walters tried to push it from his mind but it was useless. Each time, the doubts creeped back, stronger than before until he became convinced that the only way he could settle the issue was to catch up to the stranger and speak with him.

As he made his way closer, Walters wondered if perhaps he was the dreamer in this reality. Feeling not a little ridiculous that he was even entertaining such a silly notion, he decided to try an experiment. Focusing his concentration upon the stranger, he mentally commanded him to stop where he was.

The stranger halted in his tracks!

Walters was brought up short. Despite the success of his little experiment, he refused to believe that the man had stopped specifically on his orders. Concentrating again, he ordered the stranger to resume walking...now!

The man began to walk.

This time, there could be no doubt. Walters had purposely delayed the command to begin walking so as to eliminate the possibility of coincidence should the stranger have decided to move on his own. But no! He had begun to walk only on Walters' order. But that smile! That damnable, knowing smile!

Commanding the man to stop again, Walters quickly covered the remaining few yards that separated them and at last, the two came face to face. Their meeting seemed more momentous to Walters than it had a right to be seeing as how he had acquired the notion of pursuing the stranger only a few minutes before. Nevertheless, it was fraught with drama, something the stranger seemed to feel as well.

"So professor, we meet at last," said the stranger, smiling.

"Who are you?" For the moment, Walters was at a loss for words. It would have been completely ridiculous right then to bring up the crazy notions he had been thinking about the last few minutes.

"To you, I'm a stranger. You don't need to know any more than that. But you need not be bashful about your recent theorizing regarding personal space, individual realities, or dreamers. I'm very well acquainted with them having placed them in your thoughts myself."

"You…what?"

The stranger laughed then, even as the crowds continued to pass around them.

"No need to be surprised. Don't you think it was strange that you would follow such a train of thought, from one seemingly unrelated notion to the next? Certainly, they weren't something that should have been uppermost in your mind while you pursued a stranger through crowds of holiday shoppers?"

"Are you suggesting that my conclusions were correct? That this is all some kind of personal reality for some dreamer somewhere?"

"It made sense to you at the time didn't it?"

"But it's so outlandish!"

"Just so."

"Assuming you're right," said Walters, trying to marshal his thoughts, "then you're suggesting this is my individual reality? That here, in this limited universe, I'm a god?"

"You overrate yourself, professor," said the stranger with a smile. "It is I who am god here."

"Wha...? You...?" Walters could hardly contain his indignation. Perhaps the man did not realize that it had been he who was forced to stop by Walters' own mental command.

"You find the situation amusing? "

"I'm sorry," Walters finally managed. "Really sorry. But I have to tell you that you're wrong. It's you who are the construct here."

"Oh, really? And where was it that you acquired the notion to follow me, a total stranger in the first place?"

Walters was silent. Try as he might, he could not recall any reason why he had decided to follow the man.

"And where in the world did you reach such an outlandish conclusion that dreamers outside reality were actually the reason for all existence?"

Walters had to admit his train of logic had been pretty shaky.

"You don't suppose that if I were the dreamer in this reality, that I could not manipulate you any way I choose? That I could not place the idea in your mind to test me? That I could not know what your commands would be even before you did? I did it all for my own amusement. When I became aware of the true nature of reality, I decided to test it, just as you thought you were doing. Only I tested it on you."

Slowly, Walters became overcome with doubt. What was real and what was not? Was he in control or was it this stranger? Or was the man simply mad?

"I see you're still having trouble accepting the fact of the true state of affairs," said the Stranger. "I propose a dare. I dare you to walk the short distance to that intersection and...walk around the corner. One of two things will happen...either the world will continue as it is or you and it will blink out of existence."

Walters stood and stared at the crowds that emerged from around that corner and the people who turned the corner out of his sight. None registering in any way that the world did not go on as it should have on the side hidden from his sight.

"Well?"

Walters' forehead became damp with perspiration even in the cold temperatures. He took a step in the direction of the corner then stopped.

"Why do you hesitate, professor?" asked the stranger in altogether too casual a tone. "If your convictions are correct, you are the god of this reality. Or maybe it's all balderdash and the world goes on as it ever has, without beginning or end."

But Walters merely stood where he was; frozen, unable to move either forward or backward.

"Go on, professor!" laughed the stranger. "Go on! Ha, ha, ha! Go on!"

Science Fiction

The Soft World

From where it sat at the crest of a low hill, the heavy, concrete blockhouse should have commanded an expansive view of the land for hundreds of yards in every direction. As it was, line of sight extended from the plexi-glass viewing port in the front of the building to maybe fifty feet in any direction before a whitish mist obscured the landscape. The mist was less whitish than simply an absence of color that seemed to cast the rest of world it embraced into a kind of black and white still-life. At the moment it was early morning and the sun should have been visible over the treetops, if there were treetops, but the sun was nowhere to be seen, its presence signaled only by a brightening in the composition of the mist relative to the utter blackness of the nighttime. Nothing stirred around the blockhouse. No birds, no animals; even the mist did not appear to be drifting. But inside, two figures moved.

Saul Murcheson had just stepped into the loose folds of his self-contained environment suit where it hung against the utility rack at the back of the ready room when his partner Harry Sterner, stepped away from the viewing port.

"Anything happening out there?" asked Saul. It was a rhetorical question, asked by one to the other whenever either of them came away from the window. Invariably, the same reply was given.

"Nope," said Harry heading over to his own gear on the rack, "still dead."

Saul grunted and lifted the domed helmet onto his neck ring and twisted it, *snick*, into position. He checked his internal readouts along the chin panel and pressed a stud on his cuff controls. Instantly, a hissing filled his ears as artificial atmosphere expanded into the confines of the sealed suit and stretched its space-age fibers taut like a human-shaped balloon.

The hissing stopped and Saul checked the suit's systems; all were optimal.

By the time he had finished, Harry was reaching for his own helmet and Saul wondered for the last time what it would be like out there beyond the sight of the blockhouse where, in addition to the uselessness of human eyes, even their most sophisticated radars and laser finders could not penetrate the puzzle of the anomaly area.

No one was really sure just how or when the anomaly area had come into existence. Certainly it was not a natural phenomenon of the Ohio countryside that surrounded it! After early testing by the Army Biological Warfare Office, it was discovered that the area was made up of biological material not found on earth. With that information and word from the star gazers at Palomar of intense meteoritic activity around the time of the anomaly's discovery, it was concluded that the area's origins were not terrestrial.

In any case, the origin of the anomaly area soon became a moot point compared with its other, more startling characteristic: it was spreading out from the impact point (wherever that was exactly since nothing, absolutely nothing, could penetrate the atmosphere over the anomaly area) at a rate of thirty feet a day. Already, the concrete blockhouse built by the army outside the perimeter of the area as a forward observation post was surrounded by the non-terrene matter which stretched out nearly half a mile behind it. Now, no one could get to the blockhouse except inside the protection of an environment suit.

Although scattered farms had been evacuated of their owners, at the rate it was spreading, the anomaly area would reach the nearest town in a few weeks. That was where microbiologist Saul and xenobiologist Harry came in. As the team that broke the riddle of just where all the life on Mars had gone to, they were the obvious choice to move into the blockhouse and study the problem up close. Unfortunately, they were as stumped now as they had been the day they arrived a month before, the only difference was that time now was running out. They had to find some answers. Answers that could not be found through short excursions outside the blockhouse. The one thing they did know about the anomaly area was that it was about two miles in diameter and getting bigger. They had put off Washington as long as they could, now they had to take a stab in the dark, something both of them up to now had been too methodical to do. Maybe that was their weak spot: unwilling to take shortcuts to the solution of a problem, but with no answers they had little choice.

"Ready?"

"Yeah," said Harry. "I'm opening the air-lock now."

Saul heard nothing from inside his suit as the air-lock door slid open. The two men stepped inside and Harry hit the cycle button. The inside door closed and with a light puff of escaping condensation, the outer door opened onto the white horizon. They stepped outside onto the soft, squishy surface of the ground. It was what the earth had become under the influence of the spreading anomaly area: three to six inches of a gray, biological matter that seemed more moisture than fiber. The closest thing Saul could compare it with was earthly fungi and right then, their feet were sinking in it. Behind them, their footprints were already disappearing as the spongy material slowly closed over them.

"It's hard to believe that the edge of the area is only a couple thousand feet away," said Harry trying to look into the white distance back where the rest of the world was.

Saul shuddered at the words as he followed his partner's gaze through the slight polarization of his helmet bubble. Just what would become of the world if the anomaly area just kept on spreading? Would it stop at the seashore? With a frisson of fright, he remembered an experiment he had conducted only the week before. He had placed a portion of the alien matter into a beaker of fresh water. It continued to spread until it had covered the entire bottom of the container, then slowly, the water level began to go down. In a few hours, it had disappeared leaving only the gray matter clinging to the bottom of the beaker. They soon learned that whatever the alien matter was, it was infinitely adaptable, absorbing, remetabolizing, and finally supplanting any other material that it came into contact with. Nothing they tried seemed to inhibit its progress. Even the atmosphere in the area had been absorbed and annihilated.

Thus the need for the environment suits whose artificial fibers had, so far, retarded the actions of the alien matter.

His secret fears resulting from the series of experiments made him think of Carol. Carol, who had stayed behind on Earth with an ultimatum when he was chosen to go to Mars. He had found the secret of Martian life there all right, but he had yet to find its Earthly counterpart. Carol never saw the need for him to take part in the three year project; he would be leaving her behind with two children, was his personal ambition more important than his family?

Well, he had gone and come back acclaimed throughout the scientific world, but it had been a hollow victory. Even from the first days aboard the *Ambitious* he knew he had made the wrong decision.

"Let's get started," said Saul suddenly, chasing the painful thoughts from his mind.

"I wouldn't mind these suits so much if they weren't so itchy," said Harry.

"You know, you're right," agreed Saul. "I've got the damnedest itch on my foot." He stamped his foot a few times to relieve the irritation, but it did no good.

So they began walking with Saul taking the lead. Progress was slow with the uncertain footing. Soon, they had reached the slope that led downward from the hill upon which the bunker had been built. It was not steep, but because of the viscous matter that layered it and their cumbersome suits, they had to move slowly. As Saul descended, one hand held to the side of the slope for balance, his downward movement piled up the alien substance at his feet. At the bottom of the hill, he stopped long enough to peer into the rut left in his wake and he found to his relief that ordinary earthly stone still existed beneath the surface. Then on closer inspection, he saw that it had been worn down to a glassy smoothness; every imperfection was erased leaving a uniform sameness. But had the adapting process halted or was it continuing? Was there after all a limit to the stuff's voracious appetite?

His question was soon answered when, after taking only a few steps more, he plunged waist deep into the alien matter. Forcing down a moment of panic, he warned off his partner.

"There's a sink hole here of some kind," said Saul. "I don't seem to be sinking any deeper so try to find the edge and make your way around it. When you get to the other side, throw me the emergency tether and I'll try to haul myself out."

"Sounds good," said Harry nervously. "But I don't like the looks of this, Saul. Topographical maps show this whole area to be almost featureless, so where'd a depression like this come from?"

Saul did not answer, preferring to watch his partner's progress around the depression. It took nearly an hour to find a way around it and by then Saul was convinced that it was no natural phenomenon. Harry was right; they had spent weeks poring over surveyor's maps and geographic profiles of the area and found it perfectly regular. Gentle hills and grassland was all there was. If a sinkhole the size of the one he found himself in had not been here before the arrival of the alien matter, it meant that the matter was continuing its erosion of the earth's crust, with occasional cave-ins in places as the effect continued.

When Harry had at last thrown him the line, they soon found that a lack of footing forced Saul to wriggle out of the depression under his own power. Breathless, his suit covered in the slimy matter, he finally reached safety.

"I must be getting old," puffed Saul. "I can hardly get my breath back."

"Nothing a cold beer won't take care of, old man," laughed Harry, thumping him on the back. "If we ever finish with this job that is." He coughed.

They continued on more carefully now, soon confirming their worst fears: there were sinkholes everywhere indicating a continued metamorphasizing action by the alien matter.

More than once, either one of them slipped into these depressions and each time found it more and more difficult to climb out again. Breathing became harder. The bunker had long since retreated into the whiteness and they began to feel as though they were castaways upon some fog bound desert island. At last however, they began to notice a change in the contour of the land. A gradual slope began to form until there could be no doubt that everywhere around them the land was tending downward.

"What do you make of it?" asked Saul.

"We must be approaching ground zero," Harry said, peering vainly into the distance.

"At the rate this stuff is eating away at the earth, it stands to reason that the closer we get to the impact point, the shallower the ground is going to be."

They were both silent a moment.

"What the hell is this stuff?" Harry blurted in sudden frustration. "How long will it keep eating away at the earth? Until there's nothing left?"

"The grade of this slope suggests that it isn't an ordinary meteoritic impact crater. It's too smooth, too gentle. But if projected outward and downward, I'd guess that the center of the impact point has sunken a good thousand feet into the earth's crust since the object first hit."

"And it's still sinking," added Harry.

"Well, let's go," said Saul, adjusting the atmosphere in his suit.

"You know, I could take being covered in all this slime, but when I've got an itch I can't scratch..."

Saul laughed for the first time since leaving the bunker.

"Know what you mean," he said, still looking at his atmosphere gauge from inside his helmet. It was showing plenty of oxygen, but he was still having trouble with his breathing. "I've got one on my leg that just won't quit."

More carefully now, with a combination of measured steps and short slides, they began making their way down into the screen of whiteness that obscured the bottom of the pit. As they descended, the alien matter piled up at their feet, covering their calves; and their breathing became more labored. At last, with the upper rim of the crater invisible above their heads, Harry spoke and pointed downward from where he clung to the slope behind Saul.

"I think I can make something out down there," he said.

Saul stopped his downward motion with some effort and looked up. Sure enough, there seemed to be the suggestion of a shadow lurking in the featureless white at the bottom of the crater.

"What can it be?" he wondered aloud. "This stuff has been eating through everything it comes into contact with; how can anything still be standing at ground zero?"

"If there *is* something down there that this stuff hasn't been able to assimilate, it could hold the answer to stopping it for good," said Harry.

"Then what are we waiting for?" said Saul, once more starting downward. "But let's approach with caution, huh?"

"Sure, sure; but after wading for hours in this muck, I can't see what could be worse."

A few minutes more was all it took for the object to emerge from the concealing whiteness as the two men were forced by their own consternation to come to a halt. What stood before them was obviously a machine, but one whose origin and purpose they could only guess at. Such musings however would come later, at the moment, they were too dumbfounded at the unexpected discovery to do anything but stare at the thing's strange instrumentality and unfamiliar workings.

"What the heck is *this*?" said Harry at last, craning his neck to look up at the object as it teetered slightly to one side, the greater portion of its vast bulk obviously hidden beneath the spreading muck. Around its base, the greyish alien matter stirred gently as an occasional bubble rose and burst against the skin of the machine.

"I don't know," Saul admitted. "I'm a biologist, not an engineer, but I think I'd be on safe ground if I guessed that this thing represents no technology in the public domain."

"You think it's something those bastards in the Pentagon could be mixed up with? Or maybe it doesn't even belong to us. The Russians are still sending things up from Tyuratam...but no, it'd be in a million pieces."

"You know what I think, Harry? I think we're looking at something from another world, another planet!"

"Whoa, now wait a minute, Saul. No need to jump to conclusions..."

"Just add things up," said Saul, absently trying to scratch his arm through his environmental suit. "We've got an object here that's impacted hard enough to create a crater but not to destroy itself; the object itself is built with a kind of technology we've never seen before and most of all, we've been walking in a whole environment completely alien to anything that exists on earth: from this biological matter we've been wading through to the strange, opaque atmosphere that blocks out every known form of radio or light waves. What more evidence do you need?"

Harry was silent for a few minutes as his eyes continued to play about on the object that towered over them. It was nearly thirty feet tall and devoid of a smooth outer casing or fuselage. Instead, it seemed tightly wrapped in a confusing tangle of what looked like conduits, relays, piping, and a myriad other unrecognizable instrumentation. No lights blinked, no parts moved, but there was sound.

"Say, do you hear that?" said Harry, avoiding an admission as to the object's possible origin. "A kind of a hum."

Saul took a step closer. "Yeah, I hear it. Wonder what it means?"

They began to circle the object, trying to zero in on the source of the sound, then stopped.

"Does that look like a hatch to you?" said Saul, pointing to a dark opening in the object about three feet from the ground.

"I think hatch is too kind a word for it," said Harry.

"Give me a boost up," said Saul, lifting his foot.

Harry knitted his fingers and grunted as Saul placed his foot in them, grabbed hold of the irregular surface of the object and hauled himself up into the opening.

"Hey, Saul! Hold it!"

The fear and anxiety in his friend's voice froze Saul into place. "What's the matter?" he said, trying to look into the darkened interior of the object for signs of danger.

"Your suit," said Harry. "It's being eaten away! That stuff's turned your atmosphere recirculation pack into swiss cheese!"

His heart suddenly pounding, Saul reached back and although it was difficult to feel anything through his bulky gloves, he could still tell when his fingers fell into the holes worn into his backpack. No wonder he was having trouble breathing! Quickly, he checked his internal atmosphere gauge and saw that it was nearly down to zero. Why hadn't he noticed it earlier? Even more important, why was he still breathing?

Perched on the lip of the opening, he looked over his shoulder to Harry and was shocked again to see that his friend's environmental suit was also being worn away.

"The suits' plastic fibers must have only slowed down the metabolizing action of the bio-matter," he said. "But now that it's adjusted itself to them, the pace of its assimilation is accelerating. It's why we didn't notice anything until now."

"Except our breathing...and itching!" said Harry. "The suits must've been compromised on some level long before the major intrusions. But then, what are we breathing now?"

Saul thought desperately, his mind racing. Then the answer came to him: the unearthly bio-matter, its steady outward spread, and its properties of transmuting anything that it came into contact with, the altered atmosphere itself and finally this strange machine, undamaged and operating, thrust into an impact crater the size of which suggested that the machine should have been destroyed instantly, all indicated a single conclusion. He shivered against what it meant to the world...he looked down at his now useless environment suit...what it meant to him. To any possible life he may still have had with Carole. "Harry, I think I know what this machine is all about," he said, hating the clarity of thought that suddenly struck him. Then he tried to explain his conclusion to his friend, a conclusion that he himself found hard to accept.

"You mean this machine is terraforming the earth?" asked Harry, not at all with the tone of disbelief in his voice that Saul had expected.

"Why not? We've often discussed using such technology on the Moon or Mars."

"Sure, but taking centuries to do it; melting frozen ice, introducing bacteria, creating an atmosphere and soil...not dropping some machine from space and doing it in..." He thought a moment. "...I don't know. A few years?"

"All true," agreed Saul. "But whoever's doing this, isn't human. They're obviously operating under a completely different set of scientific principles both mechanical and biological. Just look at the rate this bio-matter is metabolizing indigenous material. Earthly natural law just doesn't apply. In fact..." Then Saul did the unexpected. Undoing the locking ring, he pulled off his helmet before Harry could protest. Both men stood silent until it became clear that not only were Saul's lungs accepting the alien atmosphere, the trouble he had been having breathing disappeared. In addition, the pallor of his skin had become an anemic blue.

"You're breathing an atmosphere that doesn't have a trace of oxygen in it," said Harry in disbelief.

"Take off your helmet, Harry," Saul said.

A moment later, both men were bare headed and breathing easily.

"There's only one explanation for this," said Saul "Since we noticed some itching and coughing problems from the time we left the blockhouse, the suits must have been compromised almost from the beginning."

"The alien matter has been working on us the same as it's been working on everything else," Harry added. "But instead of killing us, its adapted us to the new environment."

Suddenly, Harry began stripping himself of the rest of his environment suit. When he was finished, the two men could see that in addition to the blue pallor of their skin, Harry's fingernails had begun to recede into his fingers and his torso had begun to swell indicating accommodation to a greater lung capacity.

"My God," said Harry almost beneath his breath, "do you know what this means? We wouldn't be able to survive outside this damned anomaly!"

Saul was silent as the full realization of their uncanny predicament dawned on him. They were as good as dead unless a lifetime spent in the controlled environment of a containment suit or isolation chamber appealed to them. He was more completely cut off from Carole now than when he was on Mars! But he would have grieved more for his lost humanity if he really believed that he may have had a chance at reconciliation with her, but Carole had left him in no doubt the day he returned to earth that there was no going back. During their three year separation, she had learned to live without him, could he learn to live without her? He knew then, as he knew now what the answer was: no. And he had no one but himself to blame for the way things happened. Carole had been pleading for his love that day before the *Ambitious* took off and in his blindness, he hadn't seen it.

But hope and regret aside, he knew where his duty lay, but did its fulfillment necessarily mean their deaths as well?

"Harry, I think all we've got is one long shot chance to save the earth and ourselves, but it isn't going to be pretty," he said at last.

"Damn it, this isn't the time to keep it to yourself; what is it?"

"Well, if we're right and this thing is something from another world then there's a good chance its operations are being monitored..."

"I get it; we fiddle with some of its wires and someone's going to have to come and check it out."

"You got it."

Harry thought it over for a minute. "So you figure to take a ride back with the owners to wherever they're from?"

Saul nodded. What did he have to lose? Even if there was never any hope of getting back together with Carole, at least he could leave her and the kids a world to live in.

"Ever figure they might be angry with our throwing a wrench in their plans?"

"Yeah, but what choice have we got?"

"If it works, it'd be a xenobiologist's dream come true."

"How about that?"

"Give me a hand up there and let me at those wires."

If Harry was having any tortured thoughts of life as a mutated monster or the loss of family and friends, he didn't show it, thought Saul. Was that something to admire or to pity?

As Saul drew his friend up into the opening of the machine, he discovered some of the limitations of his new body: it was a bit weaker than a human's, its joints prone to ache with too much strain and its posture tended to fold up into a semi-crouch.

Inside the machine the hum they had heard from outside was slightly louder and they soon discovered that the opening

74

they had entered was less access to the machine than simply empty space left by its design. All around them wound a bewildering array of what they guessed was machinery but could not be certain.

"Where do we start?" asked Harry.

"How about right here?" replied Saul taking hold of a handful of stuff and yanking it from its moorings. Nothing happened.

"Looks like we're going to have to get rough," said Harry, doing the same.

Minutes later, they were surrounded by piles of paraphernalia that seemed to be draining liquids as well as giving off the occasional spark. The humming had stopped.

"I think that did it," said Saul.

"Wonder how long it'll take before they get here?" said Harry looking outside the machine at the alien matter spread out around it. The viscous movement they had observed immediately against the base of the machine was now absent.

"Whatever this thing was doing out here has stopped," said Harry looking up into the white of the sky and expecting any moment to see the flare of a descending vehicle. Then, turning back inward he said, "Think you'll like it, wherever it is they come from?"

Saul shrugged. "No, but I expect it to be interesting for a while at least."

"Then what?"

Saul was silent. He suddenly realized that he did not want to answer that question. Could he face life trapped in a prison more inescapable than any ever built? Worse, could he do it without any hope at all? Of escape or of reuniting with Carole? No prisoner who ever lived faced such a bleak prospect. If he told Harry what he really felt, deep down, he knew he would not have the strength to go through with their plan. But before his thoughts could go any further, they were mercifully interrupted by a tremor in the machine around them.

Harry dashed back to the opening. "They're here!" he said, as he looked about for an arriving craft.

Instead, there was a second tremor and the machine began heaving violently as if something were trying to pull it from the ground.

"Harry, the makers of this thing aren't coming to us, their bringing us to them!" shouted Saul over the growing din as a lurch sent both men tumbling.

When they got back to their feet, they could see that the opening they had entered by began to seal itself up as portions of the alien instrumentality draped themselves over it. Soon, it had been completely obliterated and the two men stood in darkness.

The concrete blockhouse sat at the crest of the hill, empty but for a short wave radio whose speaker had come to life with static after a long silence. Around it, other instruments glowed with renewed life: real-time satcom video received from space, the jabber of geiger counters, the green glow of screens come to life with a bewildering variety of oscillating waves tracking the ebb and flow of ultra-violet and infra-red. Outside, stars began to peek through the whiteness like light through the rent fabric of flimsy gauze. Gray, mucous matter that until recently had eaten greedily of the vitals of the earth, now began to recede and wither, the unseen forces that had quickened it now evaporated.

There was a slight tremble, flakes of concrete fell from the blockhouse and the sky suddenly became lit with a blinding flash while the atmosphere resonated with the boom of a vast object lifted into the air. And when it ended, the stars shown down upon an earth undimmed by strange fogs.

Swimmers in the Sea of Time

Finlay Gower fingered the key-pad in front of him and brought the *E.R.Burroughs* about, easing it into the gravity well surrounding the planet below him, whipping the spacecraft into a high orbit that would take it over most of the planet's northern hemisphere.

"Not too shabby," said his wife from her position at the navigator's console. "I barely felt it when you jinked the ship into orbit."

"Thanks, Pris," said Finlay, giving a final command to the computer, "your calculations were right on the money."

"Oh, come on, are we going to have to listen to all this mutual admiration the whole mission?"

Finlay and Pris turned together in time to see Jules Ince step fully into the pilot's cabin, with a big grin on his face.

"I see someone's glad to be here," observed Pris.

"Not just one," said Jules, "Joan's already getting our gear together." He moved up until he was standing between husband and wife, trying to see the planet's surface from the limited-area view port over the control console. "Have you tried to locate the site yet?"

"Not wasting any time, are you?" said Pris. "I haven't gotten to that yet, but if it'll make you happy..." She leaned forward and enabled the look-down sensor array that bristled on the underside of the spacecraft. Immediately, a variety of data leapt to screens spread out around her. A greenish glow suffused the cabin as computer enhanced grids, graphs and sine-waves registered their information. Under the woman's practiced eye, the confusing jumble of information came together and made sense. "We've covered most of this hemisphere on the way in; the sensors have something, but it's ill defined. As if something's distorting the readings."

"I'd say a planet whose surface is completely submerged in liquid methane would tend to be difficult to read," said Finlay.

"That shouldn't matter too much," Jules replied, not taking his eyes from the readings, "after all, the sensors aboard the *Saint John of the Cross* found the site pretty easy, and that was only a Naval cruiser."

"Don't kid yourself," said Pris. "Those military ships have sensor gear that'd put these survey vessels to shame. The Empire gives them all the best."

"Just the same, how about it?" asked Jules.

"Well, it's here anyway. Maybe we won't be able to identify it clearly, but we should be able to zero in on its general area as an anomaly against the remainder of the surface." She sighed. "But I'll need to map the whole area and have the computers study it all. It'll take a few hours."

Jules sighed. "Okay. Let us know when you've got something. I'll be with Joan in the hanger." Jules exited the cabin and began making his way to the rear of the ship. He'd been with the Interplanetary Geological Survey for over ten years spending most of his time with his wife cataloging near-Earth worlds prior to terra-forming operations. They were a team although it was Joan who was the actual xeno-geologist; when he wasn't playing engineer aboard ship, he provided mostly muscle for Joan when off of it. It wasn't the most glamorous of jobs, but it was something the Empire wanted done and it got them out of the solar system. This time however, was different, it was their first inter-stellar assignment and he intended to make the most of it.

Joan was still lugging heavy seeming equipment from the storeroom into the shuttle that sat in the center of the hangar; her efforts made easier in the lighter gravity of the ship. Jules waited until she disappeared inside the shuttle before he dashed over and slipped in behind her.

"Jules!" she giggled, dropping the diving gear she held in her arms.

"How'd you know it was me?"

"Because Finlay wouldn't dare do something like that."

"Like what? Kiss the back of your neck?"

"No, squeezing my..."

"Hey if you're going to make such a big deal of it, forget the whole thing," said Jules in mock seriousness, gathering her into his arms and pressing his lips to hers. When he was much younger, he used to resent the Empire's policy of allowing only single sex or married couples on interstellar flights. To avoid certain anarchic incidents similar to those that had plagued early forays in long distance space travel they said. But now, with Joan's warm body pressed to his, he couldn't imagine a more pleasant idea for long geological expeditions.

At last, they pulled themselves apart long enough for Joan to ask, "Has Pris found the site?"

"Not yet, but she'll let us know soon." Jules saw the look of impatience on his spouse' face and cast a hurried question. "Is all the gear set?"

"I was just getting the last of the oxygen recycling units aboard. All that's left is an itemized check."

"No, I think there'll be one more thing we have to do before casting off..."

———————

"All systems are green," said Pris' voice from the speaker.

"Initiating green sequence...now," said Jules as he rather heavy handedly entered the command in his key-pad. Immediately, the on-board computer commenced a systems check that was completed before Jules' fingers could return to his lap. "All systems are green," he said.

"Acknowledged," said Pris. "We're making our final approach now, you two. Time minus eleven minutes and counting."

"Got it." Jules ordered the computer to open the hangar doors and in seconds felt the soft vibrations through the shuttle's deck that told him deep space was opening up directly beneath him.

"Time minus two minutes and counting."

"Line of approach is perfect," said Finlay.

"Time minus ten seconds and counting," said Pris at last. Jules began counting with her. "Eight, seven, six, five, four, three, two, one. Disengaged."

Only the instruments on his control console told Jules that the shuttle had been released from the parent ship and was in an orbit of its own that would take it into the preplanned flight path to the surface of the planet.

"Have they assigned a name to this planet yet?" asked Joan from where she was strapped in behind him.

"No, it's still just a number. Hold on."

In another few seconds, the shuttle was gliding only a few hundred feet from the surface of the planet, the greenish waves of the methane ocean moving desultorily in the minuscule atmosphere. Then they were down, and being thrown forward in the terrific shock of the contact.

"Are you okay, honey?" asked Jules, with no little concern, he never got used to the rough landings.

"No problem," was the reply, as Joan busily undid her straps.

"Don't get up yet. Let me set the stabilizers first." Jules flicked a switch that activated a separate bank of computers that would continually collect data on the planet's gravitic forces and adjust the shuttle's equilibrium on the surface of the ocean to keep it steady; an absolute necessity when its occupants would be three miles below the surface of that ocean.

"Are we positioned correctly?" asked Joan again, going through a series of calisthenic exercises to limber up before the dive.

"Right on top of it. And so far, no sign of life."

"That's good." She had begun to empty out the equipment lockers leaving Jules nothing to do but stare in admiration. Since the planet had no atmosphere to speak of, the one real danger of diving through the liquid methane was eliminated: if there had been any oxygen in the atmosphere at all, one spark could have turned the entire world into a miniature sun. Otherwise, no special difficulty was expected.

They stripped and took turns in the microwave shower that eliminated any bacteriological remains on their bodies that might have reacted negatively to any of the alien atmosphere or methane that might seep through their wet suits. It was a tricky business to put on the suits in the close confines of the shower, but it could be done in minutes. While Jules showered, Joan began clipping on her utility belt that held their equipment and portable data hook-up with the shuttle's computer. When Jules had caught up to her, he pulled out the two plasma blasters they would carry with them, and checked the charges. He handed one to his wife and clipped the other to his belt.

"Are we set?" he asked.

"Let's go." Together, they moved to the airlock and sealed themselves in. Before triggering the exit code, they double checked their re-breathing apparatus and throat microphones. "Can you hear me?"

"I wonder what it's like to make love under three miles of liquid methane?" said Jules in response. "Do you think..." But he didn't finish the thought; he heard the definitive click that told him she had turned off her receiver. He winked at her through his helmet's big visor. In response, she triggered the exit code and immediately, they were sinking slowly toward the surface of the greenish liquid at the bottom of the air-lock tube.

———————

In minutes, they were surrounded by the greenish haze of the sea with the broad underside of the shuttle blocking out the weak light from the planet's sun. Together, they moved to the forward end of the shuttle and manually opened a sliding panel beneath the nose that revealed a small cage-like device. Jules tugged on the cage and felt its hidden mechanism come to life.

There was a man-sized door in its side, and when it came down even with the two of them, he opened it and waved Joan inside. After following her in, he hit a green foot switch that allowed the cage's powered descent to the ocean's floor.

An hour's uneventful ride later, the couple emerged a few hundred feet from the sea floor, the powerful set of lights mounted on the top of the cage were just enough to illuminate vague formations looming further below.

"How far off the mark are we?" asked Jules, pushing himself toward the bottom.

Joan consulted the computer. "If we aren't right on top of it, we're mighty close. All the computer can tell me is that it's having a hard time scanning the area."

Jules nodded inside his helmet. "Have any idea what we're looking for?" The question was a variation of one he'd been asking her since the *E.R.Burroughs* left Titan Station over six months before.

"No more than I did yesterday," Joan replied.

"What exactly does the Survey expect a xeno-geological team to find out here, a radioactive volcano?"

"All we know is what the data from the *'Cross* told us; and that was made in haste."

"Yeah, I know, it was limping back from action around Procyon, the Outer Arm Coalition tried to move in on some of our colonies out there."

"Right. At first, the military thought it might have been a downed ship or something, but the readings were all wrong, not regular enough. So the whole thing was bumped down the ladder until it got to us."

"Well, whatever gets us out of the Sol system is okay by me," said Jules. "But if it *is* geological, you must have some ideas about it."

"I did until a few minutes ago, but looking over these readings now, I'm being forced to go back to square one."

"What kind of readings?" Jules drifted closer to Joan to look over her shoulder at the data link on her cuff.

Joan shook her head. "Mostly the ship's sensors just can't penetrate the anomaly area. They can't even give us accurate global mapping data."

"You mean we're swimming blind?" Jules hadn't meant for the remark to sound like a joke.

"That's exactly it."

"What about life signs?"

"Right now I can't get anything out of this thing, but according to our generalized readings before coming down, the sea holds only microbial life forms."

Jules grunted and said, "Your the boss down here, what do you want to do?"

"Are you kidding?" Joan punched off the data link and dove forward.

They continued to swim for another hour or so until, in the glare of their chest beams, the ocean bottom began to appear from the murk. Presently, the outlines of strange geological formations resolved themselves in the reaching light. They were high, conical, bee-hive like structures that, as they continued to move downward, reached up all around them, most with their crowns collapsed from the incessant erosion of millions of years of being the victims of corrosive methanol.

"What do you make of these?" asked Jules, peering down into the pitchy blackness of an open cone.

"Tectonic pustules; sometimes when a planet's tectonic plates are thin enough and its molten subsurface hot enough, magma can force its way through the thin crust in serial piercings."

"Recent?"

"Hardly," said Joan as she gently paddled over the black hole of one of the cones, directing her personal light source into its inky depths. Jules watched her from his position at the hole's edge, admiring her shapely form dimly outlined against the greenish glow from the distant cage.

"Jules, I think I saw something..." was all Jules had time to hear over his helmet speakers when he was thrown back by a sudden gust of pressure in the surrounding sea. When he had recovered his balance, it was with Joan's screams in his ears. Kicking furiously, he pulled his way back up the steep slope of the cone coming back into the circle of dim light and almost tumbling down the other side into the hole. Overhead, where only seconds before, he had admired his wife's beauty, there was now the horror of ropy tentacles, thick as a bundle of straw, whipping and waving in blind groping, as if the creature that owned them had been surprised by Joan's beam of light. Frantically, he forced himself to remain calm and search the confusion of limbs for a sign of her, unconsciously taking his blaster in hand. Perspiration creeping down his forehead, he began making his way around the rim of the hole, Joan's screams still in his helmet's receivers. "Joan! Joan, listen to me! I can't spot you! You have to get hold of yourself and help me find you." He waited three agonizing seconds before he noticed that her screams had faded and her voice began to come over the communications link.

"Jules, Jules, hurry, it's all around me! I can't see where..."

There was silence then, and Jules could only wait and agonize on the fate of his wife when he heard the unmistakable click of the homing beacon being tongued on from her helmet. Suddenly, the head-up display just over his eyes gave him an exact fix on her position. Purpose giving his actions impetus, he made his way in as close as he could to where the beacon indicated Joan ought to be; she was still completely hidden from him by the forest of tentacles. Using his blaster as a surgeon might use a laser scalpel, he began to cut away at the intervening limbs, clearing a path to Joan. At last, a gasp of relief punctuated her pleas for haste.

"Jules, I can see you! And I think the creature's grip is easing away."

"Can you get your blaster free?" asked Jules, a sudden shadow covering him.

"I think so." A grunt. "I just have to squeeze past...I have it!"

"Good, start helping yourself out!" Suddenly there were pencils of light over his head and the shadow he had only just begun to notice was lifted.

"Thought I'd help you first, Jules!"

"No argument, Joan! I can see you now. We'll have you free in a minute." Finally the last ropy appendage had been severed from around Joan's ankle and the two terrans began to swim away from over the opening as quickly as they could. But it wasn't fast enough as the creature, whatever it was, dragged itself out from the gaping pustule to follow them into the open sea. "I thought you said there wasn't supposed to be any macrolife on this planet!" yelled Jules looking over his shoulder at the behemoth on their trail. An icthyic horror of gargantuan proportions.

"I don't understand, there wasn't supposed to be anything this big," Joan panted back as the creature's true size began to make itself apparent. "It seems to have made its home inside that pustule, maybe something in the formation's composition was able to mask the creature's signature to our sensors."

"Then the pustules themselves might be the source of the anomaly we came here to investigate."

"Possible. We'll have to get inside one of them to get some definitive answers."

"You're getting ahead of yourself, my dear," said Jules, chancing another look behind him. "Because if Pris and Finlay aren't tracking us topside....what the hell?"

Joan hesitated, slowed and turned cautiously. "What's the matter?"

"Depending on how you look at it, nothing. Our pursuer seems to have vanished."

"Vanished? Where? It was right behind us."

"Don't know, but wherever it went, it must have teleported there because nothing could've moved that fast."

Joan shrugged, checking her sensor pad. "It's not registering here."

"It wouldn't if those pustules really do have interference properties," said Jules, then "Hey, where are you going?"

"To check out the composition of that pustule," said Joan as she angled her body downward in the direction of the opening from which the creature had emerged. "Wherever that creature went, I doubt if it would have had the time crawl back inside before we could have spotted it."

"It sounds logical on the surface, but I wouldn't take it to the bank," Jules replied, following her down.

With his stronger legs, Jules soon caught up to his wife and took her by the arm.

"Hold off a minute while I bring in the cage."

A minute later, Jules had directed the shuttle to take up a position directly over the pustule. The two divers watched as the glaring cage was again lowered to the opening in the strange formation.

"Let me ride the cage down first, if it's safe, I'll signal you to follow," said Jules.

"No argument," Joan replied.

Jules entered the cage and shut the gate. In seconds, he was being lowered past the rim of the opening into the murky interior of the pustule. He just had time to catch a glimpse of his rocky, striated surroundings when the cage lights went out...then on again...then out again. It wasn't a regular flicker but a more intermittent off and on effect. Sometimes the light would remain on for a few seconds, then a few minutes, creating a kind of off kilter strobe effect.

He checked the cage's status board and could learn nothing from its conflicting signals. That was one thing, but how to explain the fact that his own on-board instrument packages began to act up? Status lights began to flicker, digital readouts began to run on in endless streams of nonsensical data, range-finders and sensors went haywire. Jules, alarmed, stopped the cage, relieved that for the moment it still seemed to be functioning and motioned with his hand for his wife to hang back.

"What's wrong?" asked Joan from where she hovered a few feet above the rim of the pustule.

"I don't know for sure, but it looks like I've got a complete systems crash on my hands. How's your suit behaving?"

Joan ran a fast systems check. "Okay for the most part, but my environment indicator is acting a bit wonky."

"Then hold back while I troubleshoot."

While he worked, he began to notice that he didn't feel so good. Feelings of nausea alternated with those of unaccountable weakness, pain in his joints and irregularity in his heartbeat. In the meantime, he had to admit defeat in trying to determine what was wrong with his instruments. As far as he could tell, they were fine when they weren't going haywire and when they *were* haywire, he couldn't do a thing to run a diagnostic.

"How are you doing?" asked Joan, her voice moving in and out over Jules' helmet receiver.

"Good question," Jules admitted. "There's definitely something down here that's interfering with our instruments, but without them, I can't identify it. Also, I'm starting to feel ill."

"Anything serious? Should we pull back?"

"No, not yet. But I think we shouldn't stay in the cage, there's a chance we won't be able to get out if its systems fail too."

"What about sign of that creature?"

"If it hasn't attacked the cage by now, it never will. Maybe the strong lights are keeping it at bay. Anyway, the lights are still working, however intermittently."

"I'm coming down."

"Okay, but take it slow, honey."

Joan began to paddle toward the flashing glare of the suspended cage, the figure of her husband now visible now hidden in darkness just outside its opened gate. As she neared him, not only did her own instruments begin to malfunction, but she began to experience the same physical symptoms as Jules.

"How are you feeling?" asked Jules when she reached his side.

"Weird, like my body doesn't know whether it has a cold, the flu, or malaria..." For a moment, she held a hand over her visor in an unconscious attempt to rub her head.

Jules held her by the shoulders and drew her close, tapping their helmets together. When Joan removed her hand from her visor her face was hidden in darkness from the momentary failure of her interior instrument lights. Then the lights came back on and Jules had the shock of his life. But then, in a flash, what he thought he had seen was gone.

The surprise and consternation must have been written on his face, because Joan, her eyes wide and riveted to his, asked, "Jules, what's wrong? Are you all right?"

Jules shook himself. "Yeah, yeah, I guess so...say, you'll never guess what I spotted on the bottom of this pustule!"

Relieved to see Jules back to normal, Joan was eager to play along with his enthusiasm. "The nest of that creature that attacked us?"

"No, a spacecraft!"

"You're kidding! How on earth...?"

"It must have crashed here somehow. It's hard to judge for sure in this on again, off again light, but it looks like a Coalition ship but of a design I've never seen before."

"A Coalition ship? Then it must be hiding here from their defeat at Procyon!"

"I don't think it's hiding, although it's possible that that may have been its original intention," said Jules. "But from what I can see, it looks severely damaged. Ruptured hull, crushed bow. I think it was forced to make a crash landing here and sunk like a rock. Uhh..."

"What's wrong, darling?" said Joan, gripping Jules' arm in sudden desperation.

"Don't know, just another of the weird bodily effects this place is causing. Wish I could figure out why..." He stopped suddenly, looking intently at the shipwreck hundreds of feet below him. Straightening, he took hold of Joan, and again pressed his helmet to hers, again waited for the light inside her helmet to come on and allow him a good look at her face.

"What?" asked Joan worriedly.

Jules didn't answer, but kept studying her instead. For a brief moment the same look of shock had flickered across his face to be quickly replaced with a frown; the kind of frown Joan was used to seeing on him when he was concentrating on a particularly knotty problem.

He whirled suddenly, involuntarily moving in closer to the Coalition wreck below them.

"Well, I'll be damned...!" he said at last.

"Jules, what's wrong?"

For a few more minutes, Jules remained silent then, turning slowly, said, "Joan, I think I've got the answer for what's happening to our instruments, to us, hell, to what's even been effecting the sensors of the *Burroughs* and military craft farther out in space. It's that ship down there." He took hold of Joan and directed her gaze at the spot where the Coalition craft lay. "Look closely at the area immediately surrounding it."

Joan, still holding her husband's arm, did so, but saw nothing.

"Look harder."

"There's some kind of shimmer..."

"Exactly. That distortion in the sea surrounding the ship is the only clue we have to what's causing all the trouble." He spun her around and tapped his helmet to hers. "Watch my face closely and tell me what you see."

For a few minutes, Joan's face remained blank then, eyes wide, recoiled and would have lost her equilibrium if Jules hadn't had a good hold on her. He drew her closer again until once more they could observe each other's faces. "Do you see what I'm talking about?"

"I...I don't know. I thought I saw you as an old man...I mean...they way you'd look if you were seventy or eighty years old! But it must have been a trick of the light." Just the same, she resisted looking directly at his face again.

"No darling, it's not a trick of the light," said Jules. "The feelings of nausea and weakness we've been having are because our bodies have been shifting back and forth from youth to advanced age at a rapid rate. As a matter of fact, the shifts have been keeping almost regular time with the flickering of the cage lights and our suit systems. Joan, we're being shifted in time from the present, to the past and to the future! When we're shifted to our future, aged selves we feel the symptoms of age: heart disease, arthritis, shortness of breath and when we shift to the past, our strength is renewed. The nausea comes in the moments of transition. Even our instruments, the cage, everything around us as a matter of fact, is caught up in the same phenomenon. That's why the lights keep flickering: they keep shifting from different points in their powered lives from high power reserves to low. And the gibberish our instruments keep reading isn't just nonsense, its the readings for this place in different times, but because the changes come so fast, our instruments can't keep up with them!"

"Jules, you're rambling!" complained Joan, hardly able to keep up with her husband's speculations. "How can time be shifting like you say?"

Jules let her go and turned his body enough to throw his glance back down toward the wrecked spacecraft. He nodded inside his helmet.

"It's coming from that ship. I think the Coalition have been secretly using some form of faster-than-light temporal technology to power their ships..."

"What kind of technology?"

"Temporal technology; a way to travel faster than the speed of light using time," said Jules. "The Empire experimented with it years ago, but discontinued the research when it became apparent that there was no way to guarantee containment if there was an accident with the technology. After all, if it could be used, temporal technology would have been applied first to war craft, and during battle the likelihood of a hit striking the temporal equipment was way too high to risk."

"What would they be risking?"

"A rupture in time. No one knew exactly what that would mean, but there were theories: time could be bent, twisted, mixed, the immutable laws of nature would become elastic and unpredictable. It would make civilization itself an impossibility. Even individual human life would become unrecognizable as it was shifted from the past to the future at always alternating speeds. Just the effects we're experiencing right now."

"But...what's doing it?"

"I think the Coalition is using black hole technology. They've managed to somehow create...or trap...a temporal black hole and install it in their ships or at least in the one we have here. Maybe it was damaged in the action off Procyon, the protective casing used to contain the black hole was damaged and now the temporal distortion effects have become loosed, if they're not stopped, they'll keep spreading at a geometrical pace until they've encompassed the entire galaxy!"

"And it's this temporal black hole that they've used to travel faster than light?"

"Right. It's a lot more efficient than your standard photon drive that the Empire uses. Properly controlled, the temporal black hole can be made to fold time; in effect, transporting the ship that contains it from one place to another in no time at all. You can see the advantages such a system would have for any spacefaring civilization."

"Jules, we've got to get out of here," gasped Joan. "We've got to warn the authorities..."

"There's no time," shouted Jules through his balky helmet microphone. "Already the event horizon is moving outward, at the speed it's expanding, it'll engulf this whole planet in a few hours, after that, it'll be too late for anyone to do anything about it; by the time help can arrive here from Sol the temporal effects will be so pronounced so far beyond the planet's surface, that they'll disrupt anyone trying to make an approach.

On the other hand, there is one chance to stop it, but it might be dangerous..."

"For who? You? Jules, I won't..."

"It's our only chance, the only chance for the whole galaxy," said Jules desperately.

"If I don't take this chance now, it'll be too late later."

"All right, all right, I guess I have no good argument against it if you feel it's that important." If Jules' guesses about the danger were right, then she could have no logical objection to his trying to end it except that she loved him and didn't want to see him dead. But that was illogical wasn't it? She had to keep telling herself that, otherwise she might pull her blaster and force him to come away with her. Instead, she said, "But what can you do about it now? You can't put the genie back in the bottle."

"That's a good analogy Joan," said Jules, fighting a twinge of nausea. "But in this case, the genie has peculiar qualities that might allow me to do just that."

"How?"

"Well, it's only theory of course," Jules admitted. "But if my guess about this being a temporal black hole is right, and if I can place myself at its core, I might be able to restore whatever containment mechanism its coalition designers had used to keep the time wave in check."

"Those are a lot of ifs."

"Nevertheless, the more I think about it, the more I feel it can be done," said Jules, "providing I don't get caught in a time stream where I've died already..."

Joan's eyes grew big but Jules cut her off before she could say anything more.

"Just hold my legs as I reach out for the event horizon. There'll be some physical distortion as I move closer to the black hole, but don't worry, they'll be kind of like the distortion you see in an object lowered in the water. From my perspective beyond the horizon, I'll be perfectly normal. Ready?"

"What do you want me to do?"

"That's a brave girl. Let's move in a little closer."

They swam downward a few dozen feet more until Joan could plainly see the distortion effect in the surrounding sea as it shifted from how it would be in the future to what it had been in the past.

"Anchor me here," said Jules as he stretched himself out.

Joan did as she was asked and watched in amazement as Jules' body seemed to stretch and lengthen toward the alien vessel. Soon it appeared to her that he must be hundreds of feet long, stretched taut like an elastic band ready to snap. She fought down an urge to panic, to yank him back; repeating to herself over and over again that it was only a trick of the eyes...

Farther down, near the rocky, uneven floor of the pustule, Jules was making his approach to the downed spacecraft. As he swam closer, the alternating effects of the area's temporal flux became more pronounced. At times, he could hardly concentrate on what he was doing the pain was so great. He felt certain that he was in a race not only against the rate of expansion of the event horizon, but of the rate of shift from his own past and future selves. If he didn't find a solution to the crisis fast, he'd be dead of old age. Nevertheless, he took the time for a quick glance back at Joan. His heart leapt, not with the effects of the black hole this time, and a lump rose unbidden in his throat. He could barely make her out beyond the event horizon, but his knowledge of her presence spurred him on to the task he had set himself.

Now the Coalition craft loomed above him as he swam in close. He passed the ruined bow where the ship's crew would normally have stayed and continued on to a gaping slash in its rear portion. Careful to avoid cutting his diving suit on the ragged edges of the ruptured hull, Jules slipped into the darkened interior. Inside, in the strobe-flicker of his personal light source, he could make out the tangled remains of the ship's propulsion system. Vast conduits and thick, ropy cables twisted off into the gloom in either direction. Recognizing the conventional configurations of standard sub-photon drive engines, he ignored them and moved deeper into the ship's insides.

Presently, he came upon the expected photon shifters and beyond them the glare of the singularity. He hadn't known quite what to expect when he finally came into the direct presence of a temporal black hole, but somehow the glaring white, the absolute absence of not only color, but shadow and substance, texture and even place did not surprise him. He moved forward, slow not with hesitancy but with careful appreciation for the marvel he found himself suddenly a part of. Terror then, slipped from him, replaced with awe and wonder and curiosity. Time continued to fracture, but with such a rapid pace that it ceased to be differentiated as past, present, future. Now it was all one. A smile of delight came unbidden to his lips. Then he laughed. Not with madness but with sudden knowledge and appreciation. How simple it all seemed now/then. His body had ceased to give him trouble. He felt the best he ever had, did. In a moment of severe clarity, he knew how it felt to be God...to be able to see the past, present, future all at the same time. To see every choice, every random event, and all their attendant effects on the time stream. It was like a vast pool constantly aflicker, ashimmer with change. Oh, how wonderful it all was!

But amid that transcendent feeling, he seemed to remember another life and another soul. Dimly at first, then more strongly, he recalled...Joan. And he at last remembered that he was but a man after all.

Focusing all the consciousness he could, he forced the infinity of happenings, occurrences, possibilities aside; he threaded his way past the surface of the shimmering lake to the underlying fabric. He found the human texture of its strands and thrust apart the individual events of a universe of chance until at last, he arrived in the here and the now. He remembered the reason he had come, shifted a bit this way then a bit that way and found what he was looking for.

Jules reached for Joan and hugged her fiercely to himself. She yielded for a moment then began to struggle and wriggled free.

"What...happened?" was all she could muster, before some kind of instinctual understanding returned and she threw her arms around his neck. The embrace was awkward in the diving suits and bulky helmets, but the emotions exchanged were nonetheless real. After a few moments, they came apart.

"I fixed it," said Jules simply.

"The containment unit for the black hole?"

"Right. Oh, I guess I could've fixed it so that the hull rupture had never occurred, but then that would've left me aboard a Coalition war craft with no explanation of why I was aboard, let alone while wearing a diving suit! Instead, I got the idea of restoring the containment unit only a few minutes before I dove down to fix it in the first place; this way, the ship stays here as proof of the technology's danger and allows the Empire to negotiate with the Coalition to refrain from using such technology. Hopefully the enemy will come to realize that not using it is to their advantage as well as ours."

"But how did you do it? Contain the black hole that is."

"Oh that." Jules shrugged. "I'll admit those Coalition scientists were ingenious in finding a way to contain and at the same time harness for use a temporal black hole. They built a radical cube and then grew the temporal black hole inside it. It must have been a long process so my hope is that this ship was actually only a first working model. It'll make stopping the use of such technology so much easier."

"You're getting ahead of me, Jules. What's a radical cube?"

"A concept that we've known about for a while, but never dared build. A radical cube exists in four dimensions at the same time: height, width, depth and time. It's the last quality that makes it perfect for containing a temporal black hole. The only problem is, the part of it that exists in time is the easiest part to disrupt. That was the part that gave in when the ship was struck, releasing the time distortion effects of the black hole. What I did was to go to the moment just before the ship was hit off Procyon, dismantle the cube myself, take it with me to a point in time just before I began my descent over the event horizon and rebuild it around the black hole. That way, time wasn't changed, the effects of the black hole were still released during the battle, but this time not as a result of battle, but because I had dismantled the cube. The resultant time distortions affected the crew enough to make them once again crash land here thus allowing us to do again what we had done in the previous reality. Get it?"

Joan shook her head. "No, but just so long as you're safe."

They held hands then and didn't let go until the cage had deposited them back on the shuttle.

There were some things Jules would never tell Joan about his experiences within the time flux, but unknown to him, there was nothing more she needed to hear from him that she did not learn in the many secret lovers' embraces they would share in the years to come.

The Walking Dead of Mimas

Doug Giroux leaned hard on the steering column of the Ford All-Terrain Rover, narrowly avoiding a series of micrometeorite craters that pot-holed the trail to the gravity measuring station just over the next rise. Straightening the Rover out, he glanced over to his safety partner, Jerry DeBule, who was trying to hang on to where he sat in the passenger seat. Jerry's face was invisible behind the polarizing lens of his helmet's visor, but his voice came over the suit-to-suit intercom pretty well. "Shit, Doug. What are you trying to do, dump me?"

Doug grinned in the confines of his own helmet, stretching his neck to get a better look at Saturn as it sat on the horizon of the little moon, its wide band of rings wafer-thin at this angle, but the bulk of the gas giant dominating the view. "C'mon Jerry, that's about all the excitement you're gonna get on this trip." He was unconsciously counting the multi-colored bands of gas that slowly revolved over the giant planet up ahead. Two more of its ten moons, Rhea and Titan, were just visible far off to the left. Behind him, only the velvet black of space with its scattering of stars leading the long way back to Earth.

"Following Saturn's gas currents is excitement enough for me," said the planetary geologist. "Beats me why I have to even be on this trip."

"You know as well as I do, the safety partner rule is written in stone."

"Sure, but why couldn't you get Andrew or the Doc for the job; they're always looking for excuses to get out of the Observatory."

"You know if we start that, the system is gonna get all screwed up, we gotta stick to the schedule, no trading places."

Jerry grunted and thumbed the on switch to the communications array that hung in front of him. Long distance communications was established with his own in-suit gear.

"Rover calling scouting party one; Rover calling scouting party one, come in Lenny." He waited a moment. "Come in Lenny...Bill...Tanner?" He flicked the off switch with a show of impatience. "I don't know why they're not answering."

"Oh, it's probably something wrong with their communications gear or maybe another one of those freakish gravitic storms that's always whipping up here from Saturn." Mimas was the closest of Saturn's moons to its massive parent and was at all times at the mercy of its whims. Jerry grunted again, nodded, and settled back in his seat.

A half hour Earth time later, the Rover topped a low rise between a break in the jagged spine of the cordillera and came into view of the little gravitic measuring station on the open plain below. Doug stopped the vehicle and flicked down the binocular lenses from inside his helmet. Immediately, the little station zoomed up for closer inspection. He didn't like what he saw. The measuring equipment was untouched, with the team's second Rover still parked a few dozen feet away; but what looked like three bodies lay sprawled darkly between the two pieces of hardware. Without saying a word, he set the Rover in motion again and started down the gentle slope to the station.

"I got all the sensors going," said Jerry, "but there isn't anything to register."

"Then forget them, and just do it the old fashioned way; keep your eyes peeled."

Presently, Doug brought the Rover to a stop a few hundred feet away from the station and disembarked. "Stay here with the frequency open, Jerry," he said. Slowly, trying to keep his pace under control in the moon's almost nonexistent gravity, he made his way to the nearest of the bodies. When he reached its side without incident, the sight was no better close up than it was from the rise. He could tell by the name tag on the front of the shredded space suit that it belonged to Lenard Sentos, the Scout Party's provisional leader. The body inside was too mangled to have been recognized otherwise. Holding his revulsion in check, he managed to inspect the other bodies before waving Jerry to bring the Rover in.

———————

"So what do you make of them, Doc?" Doug wanted to know.

"Only that these men have been torn apart in exactly the way a wild animal would have done it." Doctor Walt Hernandez wiped the sweat from his forehead and faced his commander from across the stainless steel table that stood between them.

"That's fine, Doc," said Doug, looking down at the mess that had been Lenny Sentos only the day before. "Except there aren't any wild beasts on Mimas."

Walt shrugged and covered the remainder of the corpse with a sheet; even he was getting sick of the antiseptic smell of the operating room turned morgue. "Nevertheless, there doesn't seem to be any other explanation. The only other possibility would be explosive decompression; but even that's crazy. To get that level of decompression out there," he nodded toward the desolate landscape outside the thick plasticene dome of the operating room, "you'd have to come down from twice or three times normal atmospheric pressure instantaneously, but even if that were likely, its results still wouldn't look like this."

"Overheating; gravitic forces..." Doug was rattling off any explanation that came to mind no matter how outlandish.

"No, no, no. Impossible. Any activity like that would've been detected by our instruments. No, there's something about Mimas that's gone completely undetected by us up until now."

"Listen, Doc, nobody's claimed that we know all about this giant ball of ice," said Doug. "But I'm positive if there was anything big, we would've found some evidence of it by now." The two men lapsed into silence then, their thoughts racing along different paths, but with the same goal: some explanation for the unexplainable. Then Doug spoke again. "Doc, do you think you can rig up a synaptic viewer?"

Walt looked up slowly, his sense of professional ethics rising to the fore. "Now look, Doug, you know that's illegal. I can't in good conscience acquiesce to any use of the synaptic viewer process to..."

"Look, we're eight months from Earth with three dead men on our hands, without the foggiest idea of what it is that's killed them. Desperate situations call for desperate measures and as Project Coordinator, I'll take full responsibility for the use of the synaptic viewer."

Walt saw the efficacy in taking advantage of the process and thought he could live with being involved in its use. "All right, I'll set it up as soon as I can."

They were in the plasticene domed operating room again three days later: Doug, Jerry, the doctor and Andrew Fitz, the team electronics man, everyone that was left in the Observatory. Though the room was fairly large by the standards of the rest of the Observatory's layout, it seemed a good deal smaller just then with the four men grouped around the shallow tub of the operating table. Odd bits of medical machinery had been pushed to the periphery of the room and a roll-away platform housing a tangle of wires and electronic components that had an air of having been hastily thrown together stood at the head of the operating table. On the table lay the body of Lenard Sentos, the top of his skull surgically removed with the gray matter of his brain exposed to the air, glistening wetly in the bright light of the room's spot lamps. From certain portions of his brain, thin wires trailed loosely, drooped slightly toward the floor, and climbed back up to the conglomeration of electronic hardware that was stacked on the wheeled platform near the table. A large viewscreen capped the platform.

"It was the best we could do on such short notice," Walt was saying.

"Yeah," added Andrew. "It's not like we expected to use the hardware I had on hand for this sort of thing." He inclined his chin toward the bluish corpse on the table.

"I know, I know," sighed Doug. "But will it work?"

"It will," said Walt again. "Andrew and I checked it out earlier, of course. But be warned, the resolution won't be good. You must understand that the process was never meant to be used so long a time after death; it's best immediately after, while the tissue is still alive."

"I still don't like it," mumbled Jerry from where he stood in the half shadow well beyond the end of the table.

"I don't like it either," said Doug. "But it's got to be done. We have to find out what happened to Len and the others before it happens to us." He looked at the corpse on the table again and then up to Walt. "Okay, Doc, let's start."

Walt nodded to Andrew who leaned forward and tapped a command into the microcomputer that would interpret the brain's stimulated synaptic impulses. As the viewscreen before them slowly built up a visible picture, Walt began to speak. "What you'll be seeing is an electronically enhanced picture of the visual impulses from the vision centers of the brain. Through a series of connections I've made to certain areas of the cerebrum and cerebellum, and other, more esoteric portions of the brain, we'll be able to see the last dying thoughts of the subject. Unfortunately, as I've just said, because of the lateness of the connections, our resolution may not be all that could be hoped for. Also, you should be aware that what pictures we *do* get will not be exactly what the subject saw, but an interpretation of the actual events by the thinking process we call the 'mind.' You see, depending on the life-experiences of the subject, the mind tends to sort out facts in a manner best suited to the means by which it interacts with the physical brain through its higher functions."

"But the visuals will be a close enough approximation of what happened," said Doug.

"Yes."

As if that affirmative reply was a signal, the picture on the view screen finally resolved itself into a recognizable pattern. It flickered frequently and was quite indistinct with blurring, but was still enough for the four men to make out what was happening with relative ease. The picture showed, in eerie black and white, fleeting images of what Lenard's mind had interpreted his activities to have been like. The intensely personalized worldview that made the whole procedure inadmissible in a court of law and illegal on Earth except in the most dire emergencies.

"Can you skip ahead to the gravitic station?" asked Doug, his eyes never leaving the screen.

"It won't be that easy," Doc warned. "Memory is holographic, not sequential. But by changing the frequency of the electrical stimulation I think we can access the more recent images."

Andrew punched more keys and the image wavered, creating an unsettling strobe effect in the quiet room. Suddenly, the screen was filled with the stark, airless surface of Mimas, sharply lit by the sphere of Saturn against the horizon. Three spacesuited figures moved languidly about, alternating with only two figures as the mind picked and chose which image would be most understandable to Lenard. Unconsciously, Doug leaned closer, his face pallid in the bluish glow from the screen. Suddenly, amid the routine work schedule and general horsing around by the figures, there was an intrusion. One of the men began to point to the near distance and as Lenard turned to look, all four of the spectators gasped in unison as they saw two more figures enter the picture.

"What the hell...?" Andrew stammered, momentarily forgetting his keyboard.

"Doug, what..." began Jerry, advancing into the light.

"Quiet," hissed Doug, all his attention on the events unfolding on the screen.

Of course the three men of the Scout Party halted what they were doing, slowly grouping together, watching the awkward approach of the two newcomers. As the figures drew closer, they could all see that there was something strange about them. Most distressing of all, was the fact that neither wore a space suit; on the contrary, all they wore were standard issue coveralls for use inside the Observatory. Also, they seemed unable to control their limbs as their arms swung wildly about and their heads jerked spasmodically from side to side.

Their gait was steady, but hardly regular. At last, Lenny, Bill, and Tanner seemed to emerge from their surprise and rushed toward the two men. It was then that the picture suddenly scrambled into a jumble of images that made no sense at all to the viewers and at last went blank.

There was a heavy silence then in the room, a silence no one seemed ready to break. "Andrew," said Doug at last, "did you get all that recorded?"

"Yup."

"Have the computer process and enhance it and let's see it again, but this time freeze on those two guys; then give me an extreme close-up of their faces." A flicker of shaky fingers, and the desired image was flashed on the screen. Again there was a gasp from Jerry and the Doctor.

"That's...that's..."

"Seiji and Dave," finished Andrew, his hands frozen in his lap.

"Doc, I need your help here," pleaded Doug, for once looking as shook up as any of the others. "Those two men died over five days ago. We buried them ourselves." No one bothered to correct the commander. They all knew that bodies couldn't actually be buried in the rock-hard ice of Mimas, only be entombed, but habits of language were hard to change.

"I..." was all Walt could muster just then as his mind wrestled with the apparently insoluble dilemma.

———————

It was a few hours later, in Doug's little office on the far side of the Observatory. "It's an even crazier idea than my suggesting that a wild beast had torn those men apart."

"You weren't that far wrong, Doc. If this idea you got makes any kind of sense, I want to hear it."

"Okay. You know how I've been keeping busy studying ice samples from around the Observatory right?" Doug nodded. "Well, I think I found something. It was so insignificant and so completely unfounded that I didn't want to say anything about it until I had the chance to make a few controlled experiments, but now, with this situation, I figure I better let you know about it, because if I'm on to something, it could just explain the whole thing."

Doug sank back in his chair, his black skin almost invisible in the shadows, "Go on."

"A few months ago, I began trying to grow Earth-type plants in hydroponic media made from melted ice taken from around the area of the Observatory. There were plenty of base compounds in the ice samples to make the effort at least worthwhile. Anyway, the plants routinely died. But in one interesting case, the dying plant dropped a number of leaves onto the surface of the media. I neglected to clean them up and a few days later, I noticed that instead of shriveling up and decomposing, the leaves were still green. And they stayed that way, even when I separated them from the media and placed them in a bell jar without a change of air or water. Well, I took a sample of the media from that tank, subjected it to a number of tests, and found evidence of life." He held up his hands, cutting off Doug's questions. "More importantly, I found evidence of waste products, the kind produced by bacteria rather than plants. As you know, a hydroponic medium is supposed to be sterile or it is after we load it up with antibacterial agents that kill any microbe that might get into it once we fill the tanks. Anyway, there shouldn't have been any bacteria in there to produce waste. On a whim, though, I plated the medium and within 24 hours there were numerous colonies. I seeded one of them in some agar and examined it under a microscope."

"And…?"

"And what I found was a microbe unlike any I've ever seen before. "Genetic testing and protein analysis proved it's not from Earth. That means it came from right here, on Mimas, dormant in the ice for who knows how long!"

"Assuming you're right, where did it come from?"

"What I think is that once life got started on Mimas, but was cut short when Saturn didn't turn out to be a sun after all. Reverting to dormancy with the lack of friendly weather, all these microbes needed was an environment to help them get started again." He clasped his hands behind his back and paced a moment. "I think melting the ice revives them, then they react to the proximity of other biological organisms, revivifying them if dead and using them as hosts. The animation of dead tissue is only a by-product of the process. At least that's the idea I was going on with my plants. Maybe when we buried Seiji and David…"

"But Doc, we've been drinking melted ice water since we landed here, seven years ago. Why haven't Seiji and David, or any of us for that matter, been infected before this?"

"We purify our drinking water, first by double-distilling it, then by passing it through filters that remove all particulate matter at least as big as a bacterium, plus any metallic, ionic, and organic material. I retested the drinking water after I discovered the microbe; it's clean. It must have infected Seiji and David when we melted the crust to entomb their bodies."

Doug stood up. "If these microbes exist at all, then your idea makes about as much sense as walking dead men, Doc. And I know that's impossible. But how can they animate a dead man? And why attack the rest of us?"

Doc spread his hands helplessly. "I don't know," was all he could say.

Doug started to say something but changed his mind. Instead, he said, "We'll have to go and get them, Doc. We can't allow them to wander around Mimas like that. It…it's the only decent thing to do."

"Not to mention for our own self-protection," said the Doctor. "But what about weapons? We don't have any guns."

That was true, no reason for them. And no knives either, not even a kitchen knife; who needed them for processed foods? "Your surgical instruments Doc, do you have anything we could use?"

"You're planning to use them on Seiji and David?"

"It's all we got…why?"

"Because they're dead already; even if you managed to cut them to pieces, the pieces would still be animate."

———————

Doug drew the Rover to a halt near the edge of a wide plateau that jutted out high over the plain below. The stark landscape of Mimas stretched out down there for miles before disappearing beyond the horizon. Jerry shifted his weight in the passenger seat, hefting the sledgehammer in his hands, turning his head this way and that, searching the surrounding country for any movement. Behind them, hidden by miles of rough hills, the Observatory sat quietly, waiting their return.

"Nothing," said Jerry disgustedly. "We've been out here looking around for almost twelve hours, and we haven't spotted so much as a footprint." It was true, most of the ice surrounding the gravity station was too hard-frozen to show any sign of passage. The two walking corpses, or whatever they were, could have been anywhere.

Doug sighed and reversed gear. "Might as well head back and let Walt and Andrew try their luck." Taking a wide turn, he brought the Rover about and began the slow way back to the Observatory.

It was creeping up on fourteen hours since they'd been out, when they pulled up in the reinforced lean-to where the Observatory's two Rovers were housed and made their way to the airlock. In addition to Jerry's sledgehammer, Doug carried a good length of pipe with a wedge sawed off at one end, forming a point. They didn't waste any time in stripping off their space suits and heading directly for the biology wing where Doug hoped to run into the doctor. As it turned out, run into him he almost did. Stepping inside the operating room, he almost tripped over Walt's body sprawled before the threshold.

"Oh, no..." Jerry began, stepping back out into the corridor.

"Shit." Doug went to one knee, but he didn't need a closer look to know that the man was dead. A great pool of blood had already begun to coagulate beneath him and his coveralls were shredded enough to reveal the horrible carnage that was done to his throat. For a minute, Doug's mind went blank. It was only Jerry's pleadings for direction that brought him out of it. He straightened and said, "We've got to find Andrew." He was past Jerry and half way down the corridor before the other man caught up to him.

"Commander," he said, just managing to keep up with Doug. "They're in here sir, those damned..."

"I know, I know," said Doug impatiently, his mind racing, his heart hoping against hope that Andrew was still alive. The thought of those two...things...inside the Observatory was driving logic from his brain. He forced himself to think straight; they weren't going to get out of this mess unless he did.

"So what are we gonna do, sir?" asked Jerry, looking around, walking backwards and generally failing to keep calm.

"The first thing we have to do, is get more information. We'll get that in the security office." He stopped at the juncture of two corridors. To the right and left, they led to the Observatory's two shuttles in their separate launch bays; straight ahead, was another intersection that gave access to the Observatory proper: the kitchen, astronomical labs, communications with the half dozen satellites around Mimas and probes around Saturn, the geology labs and the crew's private quarters. With nothing in sight, they crossed the intersection to the next hallway, took a left and slid into the first door they came to, not missing the smears of blood that trailed farther on to the living quarters.

Fortunately the security office was empty and Doug was able to access the closed-circuit television system. A quick rerun of the airlock camera revealed the chilling fact that the walking corpses were able to use them on their own from the outside, demonstrating that they were acquiring a rudimentary intelligence, or at least were able to use what memories remained in their dead brains.

"Commander, look at this," cried Jerry.

Doug went to look over his shoulder only to be given another rude shock. The two corpses were coming down the hall from the living quarters hauling a service wagon with Andrew's body lying torn and bleeding on top of it. The jerking motions of Lenard's memories were almost gone now, and the two corpses walked with more assurance. "They're getting used to their hosts," said Doug.

Jerry wasn't listening. "Where are they taking Andrew?"

Doug answered without thinking. "To the airlock. They're going to bury him outside; for future occupancy." He stared. "I think they're a kind of group mind or something," he whispered to himself. Then shaking the sudden chill out of his shoulders, he said, "Jerry, this is bigger than we can handle.

There's no way we can kill those things, even if we could chop them up. We've got to get to the shuttle."

"But Commander," said Jerry looking up, "those ships were only meant to rendezvous with an Earth ship, not make the whole trip back home by themselves."

"I know that; we'll send a distress call to Earth, wait the eight months in orbit, and then come back down with them to finish this job." Merely to voice the plan gave them both more courage, and in another few minutes, the message was relayed with all urgency to Earth. All that remained was to reach the shuttle. "Look, Jerry. Those things are at the air-lock now; you'll be able to make it to the *Mimas One* and get it primed; I'll go to *Mimas Two* and pull a few wires to keep it on the ground. I'll meet you in ten minutes so get going." He slapped him reassuringly on the back in the way of shoving him off.

It was almost ten minutes later as Doug squeezed out of the access hatch beneath *Mimas Two* and began walking along the long, empty corridors that separated him from *Mimas One*. He still had his length of pipe as he moved cautiously up the north-south corridor to the intersection, trying not to notice the smeared streaks of blackening blood on the floor. He was almost up to the shuttle bay and could hear the preparatory sounds of take-off when a door burst open directly in front of him. In another moment, he was face to face with what used to be Seiji as the dead man reached out for him.

Stifling a panicked shout, Doug fell back, almost falling, but the fleeting brush of a dead hand against his cheek galvanized him into action. With a savage thrust, he launched himself toward the creature, burying the length of pipe half way into its mid-section, its pointed tip, viscera trailing from it in a tangled mass, jutted out a good two feet from the monster's back. Still holding on to the pipe, Doug overcame his revulsion and tried to yank it free, but only managed to draw the creature closer to him. He ducked to avoid the reaching grasp and scrambled from beneath it to the far side. He looked back and saw it was hopeless to try to overcome the thing, and so, swallowing his pride, he turned and ran as fast as he could to the access hatch beneath the shuttle.

Still gasping for breath, trying to fight down his fright, Doug sealed the hatch and made his way up toward the nose of the vehicle where Jerry had everything ready for launch. "What took you so long?" he demanded, panic in his voice.

"I ran into Seiji...I..."

But Jerry could see the beginnings of shock that were slowly creeping over his commander, and wisely chose not to press the subject.

"Let's get out of here." In another moment, the fiery plumes of the atomic engines cut in and the safety harnesses dropped from the outside of the ship. With a low rumble vibrating through its body, the shuttle lifted off from its cradle in a plume of dust from the surface of the moon. It wasn't without a certain sense of relief that the two men saw the slightly curved surface of Mimas fall away from them through the view ports. Now all they had to do was husband the emergency supplies for the eight months until the rescue ship came from Earth and they'd be able to get their revenge on the monsters that had taken the lives of their friends.

With a nervous laugh, Jerry fingered the controls, ordering the computer to put the shuttle into a permanent orbit about the little moon. "Well, I guess we're safe now. Do you think the food and water will hold out?" He knew the answer was yes, but still needed some reassuring words from Doug.

"No sweat. We got it made...what's wrong, Jerry?"

Jerry's euphoric mood had suddenly vanished as his fingers flashed over the command console. "I don't know...something's wrong!"

Doug sat down next to him and took control of the keyboard. "The ship's not responding. The computer's not putting us into orbit!"

"Then...what's it doing?"

"The Observatory master computer is overriding the shuttle's command systems." The damned creatures, they were learning *too* fast! "We're heading back..."

Slowly, inexorably, the shuttle began to drift back to its berth, thrusters firing at intervals, guidance systems correcting when needed. And somewhere below, the Observatory stood empty of life...human life...

The Space Picket

"Hey Skipper!" called out Luke McMana, the navigation officer of the *Belerafon II*.

"What is it, Luke?" I asked, crossing the control deck to his post.

"Not sure," he said. "I mean, I know what I've got, but I'm not sure what it means." He handed the earphones over to me and I pushed one of them to my ear. A series of high-low frequency patterns registered against my brain, trying hard to mean something to me, but failing. I shrugged and gave Luke back his phones. "You know I can't usually make anything out of this stuff except the standard signals; you said you knew what they were but not what they meant. Tell me what I just heard and I'll fill you in on what it means."

Luke looked skeptical but gave me what I wanted anyway. "Well, Skipper, we just picked up these signals a few minutes ago, at exactly the same time we entered the asteroid belt."

The asteroid belt was a navigator's nightmare of chunks of ice and rock circling the solar system between the orbits of Mars and Jupiter creating a belt of moving rock set right in the path of the best trade routes between the two planets. The Holy Roman Empire Bureau for the Regulation of Space Commerce strictly prohibits any civilian ship from cruising anywhere near the belt, instructing them to make a detour above the plane of the ecliptic and avoiding the dangerous zone. Of course, Space Cargoes Inc. would never have become number one if I never took any chances. So I routinely took the *Belerafon II* slowly through the fields of rock, effectively cutting our travel time in half, making it possible for Ruben and I to shave twenty percent off the price of our cargoes on arrival in Mars Central.

"I zeroed in on the readings," Luke was saying. "And found that it's coming from one of the bigger chunks out there."

"Is it a distress signal?" I hoped it wasn't, the time I'd have to spend checking it out would cut deep into my profits, but the law of space superceded any monetary interests.

"Like none I've ever heard before; no, it's not a distress call Skipper, I'm sure of that." Luke leaned forward and threw the pulsar search switch, watching the screen in front of him for a few seconds. "It's not a distress call that's for sure." I breathed easy, but my curiosity had been aroused; just what was it that was sending these signals way out here? Then Luke answered my unspoken question. "It's coming from one big chunk of metal and rock, bearing two-two-zero... Now this is nuts."

"What?"

"The asteroid isn't tumbling like all the others, it's keeping absolutely still; it's been that way for the last few minutes."

"That's impossible, Luke. Check your instruments."

He did as he was ordered and came up nominal. There was an asteroid out there acting in a way no asteroid ever did before. In a way that no asteroid possibly could. In a second, I calculated the advantages of making some sort of important find against the disadvantages of lost time and came up even.

"What's all the excitement over here?" broke in the element that tipped the odds for investigation.

It was Delores Benetto, Ruben's daughter. Dede to everyone else, and Deeds to me. For the dozenth time, I cursed my partner for forcing me to take her along on the run. She had been attending advanced language studies on Ganymede Station until she graduated and Ruben wanted her back at the office as soon as possible to start handling our foreign language accounts from Earth. I held out as long as I could of course, but in the end, Ruben's senior partnership won out. That was one of the reasons why I made the interplanetary runs and he sat at the office counting the money: he had the connections for the loans we needed and all I had was the *Belerafon II* and my pilot's skill. And although Deeds and I have been more or less engaged for the past couple of years, it still didn't mean a thing to my crew who felt having any woman on board ship was unlucky. And now this happens; maybe there was something to it after all. I didn't like that course of thought, but knew if I didn't check out that asteroid, Ruben would get wind of it and I'd never hear the end of it.

I turned to face her and said, "Something funny on one of the asteroids. We're going to have to check it out."

Deeds looked at me with those doe eyes that made me putty in her presence ever since Ruben first introduced her.

"When do we go down?" She smiled, the dimples appearing on cue, and kind of tossed her long, brown hair in that careless fashion that dared me to say she wasn't going.

"Would it mean anything to you if I told you that it might be too dangerous for a woman down there?"

"Alexander King, if you don't let me go with you, I'll make life for you so miserable..."

"Okay, okay, you can come." I already knew what that threat meant, and tried to console myself that I'd never have her aboard ship again. "But you stay close to me and do exactly as your told. Got that?"

She saluted smartly. "Aye, aye Skipper," and bounced away to check the pressure suits.

I felt more than saw Luke looking at me, a grin playing at the edges of his mouth. "Alright, mister, back to work!"

———————

I tongued the viewer switch on the inside of my helmet and watched the tiny television screen as it was lowered from over my head to stop just before my right eye. I closed my left and said, "Okay, Luke, run that piece by me again." In a space of time too short for the brain to register, a picture appeared on the tiny screen before me showing the rough surface of the asteroid from which the signals had emanated. Slowly, the camera panned across its face until it bisected a great and regular trough that stretched off the screen to either side. The first time I saw the thing, I drew a blank. Then all the excitement of my boyhood returned as the thought struck me that I was looking upon a man made object. An object obviously hidden from prying eyes in the asteroid belt, an area where to come across it by accident was a one in a million chance.

I tried to control my mounting excitement with the reminder that the Empire had strict laws against any unauthorized excursions into the asteroid belt. To hide secret projects? I had to consider the thought, after all, the only other explanation was extra-human, and that was almost completely impossible. Never in the entire history of man in space had there ever been any evidence for other than human occupation of the universe. And if this was some new, spectacular find, it could be the single greatest event in the history of man since the defeat of the rising tide of Protestant rebellion in the sixteenth century.

Now I watched again, as the camera pulled back until the entire length of the trench was visible. From end to end, it measured at least five miles and at one end was situated a featureless blockhouse of enormous proportions. From the position of the asteroid and the direction in which the trench was pointing, my ship's engineering officer made the incredible conclusion that the whole setup was a weapon to be used against the Earth. A version of a rail gun, an early industrial design to mine ore on the moon and to catapult the raw diggings into Earth orbit to be collected by ships from the planet's surface. "Clint," I called over my microcom, "tell me again what you think about this thing?"

"I haven't changed my mind, Skipper," he answered. "I'm sure this is a rail gun of a design similar to those I once studied in early Earth space exploration efforts. Only in this case, from its configuration and the paucity of any sort of ore on this piece of rock, I can only conclude that it's a weapon of some sort. Until I get more information, I stand on that opinion."

"Thanks," but I still didn't like it. I tongued the off switch and the camera swung away clearing my vision for another scan of the terrain immediately in front of me.

The blockhouse and trench stood on a relatively small piece of rock that stuck out of a larger field of rock like a small island. Not knowing what was in the blockhouse, I ordered the landing party placed at the end of the track farthest from the alien structure.

The *Belerafon II* stood glistening against the glare of stars and the duller gleam of stone-encrusted asteroids that moved slowly overhead, enhancing the feeling that we stood on a piece of floating jetsam on the ocean of space. I looked back at the trench and saw Junior as he reached the summit of its opposite side, straightened, and waved to me in signal. I waved back and faced Clint and Deeds.

My throat mike was still operational as I said, "Clint, you stay up here and walk parallel with Junior and me. Don't get ahead of me and don't fall behind. Keep your eyes open for anything out of the ordinary." Then I turned to Deeds. I couldn't see her face through the polarized face shield of her helmet, but could easily picture its soft, white oval framed in the brown hair that was now pulled tightly back in a hairnet. "And you," I said as sternly as I could, more to impress the men than Deeds, "follow me and do everything I say, got that?"

Her helmet nodded yes while her voice drifted through the ether into my earphones, "Aye, Skipper!" For a moment, I thought she was going to salute me as well, but was relieved to see that she didn't. If our little exchange was too formal to fool the men, a salute from her would have been just too much.

"Wait up here," I ordered her as I turned and hunkered down at the rim of the trench. Slipping my legs over the side, I shoved myself off and slid slowly along the almost perpendicular decline of the wall to the bottom. The lack of any real gravity on so small a body of rock made the descent minutes long, but when my feet finally bumped bottom, I realized that it had not been long enough. Despite appearances, the desolation of the asteroid and the installation on it gave me an uneasy feeling that overwhelmed any desire for a momentous discovery. I physically shook the feeling off and craned my neck upward toward Deeds. "All right, come on down. And take it easy."

In a few minutes her lithe form touched down, the circle of my arms catching her in their embrace. She lingered there a little longer than she needed to and finally disengaged. In that moment, it was as if she wasn't wearing an inch of reinforced permadyne against her body or a pressure resistant space helmet over her head. I didn't need to see her without it, my mind's eye and the fondness in my heart provided me with the image of her from life. The girl I met and fell in love with a few short years ago was perfectly apparent to me even now on one of the most inhospitable shores in the solar system.

Somehow, she sensed the same thing, because she reacted the same way I was about to. "Where to now, Alex?"

I shook the image of Deeds from my mind and gestured toward the center of the trough. "We'll head out to the middle of the trench there, and walk on toward the blockhouse; real slow." I took a slow step in that direction and sauntered buoyantly over to where I had pointed, Deeds right behind me. There was no need to look out for her, she was more at home in a pressure suit than half my crew.

I wasn't too surprised to find the trough completely barren of dust or detritus, not much activity way out here, and whatever kept the asteroid aligned with the Earth kept it away from collisions with other asteroids as well. "Say Clint," I thought aloud, "do you suppose there could be some sort of gyroscopic mechanism inside this piece of rock that keeps..." I had looked up instinctively to the man I was addressing, and noticed Clint wasn't listening to a word I said. His mind was on other matters, and so was Junior's. Both of their gazes rested, I noticed, on Deeds, whose pressure suit hugged her curves in all the right places. I tongued my mike to full frequency and repeated my sentence.

The piercing resonance of the transmission went right through their ears and halted them in their tracks; they got the message.

"You're right Skipper, I thought of that. I just thought it was too elementary to mention. But I catch your drift." He looked at Deeds. "I copy."

"Me too," chimed in Junior.

It was all no secret to Deeds, who merely chuckled softly over the transmission line.

Together, in parallel formation, we all moved forward toward the blockhouse that loomed gigantically ahead, with myself slightly in the lead. Deeds surprised me by obeying orders and keeping to my right and rear; I guess she was as awed as the rest of us.

At last, we arrived at the base of the wall of the cubed structure where, to our utter confusion, we couldn't find a single means of entry. I ordered Clint and Junior to draw their hand weapons and circle round the building in a more thorough search of ingress, but in a few minutes they returned to the edges of the trench and shrugged their shoulders. No more needed to be said. I thought a moment and decided to risk damage to any possible artifacts hidden on the other side of those blank walls by forcing entry. It was worth the gamble if we found something important; if we didn't, we'd be no better off than if we hadn't tried at all.

"Clint, go back to the ship and get out the industrial blaster. Bring it along this trench, it'll be easier on the treads."

"We're going to blast our way in?" he asked, the engineer in him getting its hackles up.

"Yeah, it's the only way we can do it...Relax, Clint, we'll take it easy."

"How do you take it easy with a Continental Hammer?" he asked rhetorically as he leaped off in the direction of the ship.

We waited there at the base of the blockhouse with Junior standing lookout above, his laser pistol still drawn, none of us in the mood for conversation. Then my receiver began to pick up the slight electronic interference generated by the big blaster. As I saw Clint bringing it along the trench, I picked out a spot on the wall's surface where I wanted him to start the beam. The Continental Hammer was a proven industrial product of Ford's Heavy Interplanetary Machines Division, designed to cut down to size the toughest of ores on any planet. We used it primarily to cut our cargo to manageable size for the hold of the *Belerafon II*. In utter silence for a machine so big, Clint brought the Hammer in close to the wall and waited for my instructions.

I took a piece of colored chalk from my utility belt and marked off a segment of wall big enough for the Hammer itself to fit through if need be. I could tell Clint didn't approve of the dimensions I had indicated, but he didn't say anything as he revved up the Hammer's generators. We stood back as the nozzle began to glow, and when it reached a bright white, Clint let the high intensity laser beam have its head. It was the work of minutes for its cannon to carve out the opening I had outlined and then to slice the piece of wall to rubble. Clint cut the engines, but left the powerful searchlights on as they pushed back the darkness from inside the blockhouse.

I moved past the hulk of the Hammer and led the way inside the building, perhaps the first human being to ever come in contact with evidence of extra-solar intelligence. But it was Clint who spoke first.

"I don't think I like this Skipper."

I shook off the first moment's bewilderment at the sight of so much strange looking machinery packed into the confines of the blockhouse. Machinery seemingly of gargantuan proportions, as if made for giants. All of it still throbbing with electronic life as its vibrations traveled through my feet and into my body. Directly in front of me stood what could only have been a huge rail gun mechanism. Deceptively primitive in shape, it looked no more menacing than the old catapults of medieval times, yet it still conveyed an air of menace about it that seemed to intimidate both Junior and Deeds for the moment. "What don't you like, Clint?" I knew *I* somehow didn't like *any* of this.

"See those casements over there?"

I looked; it wasn't as if I hadn't noticed them of course, it was just that they seemed no different than all of the other paraphernalia in the building. "What about them?"

"Those are receptacles of some kind," he said, "and by their shapes, I'd say they were meant to be placed in front of that gun." He inclined his head toward the machine in the center of the room. "If you notice, they're a perfect fit for the trench we just came down on."

I looked back, not really needing any confirmation, but just to have something to do while I thought fast. "If this is some sort of weapon to be used against the Earth, how was it we got in here with so little trouble? Where are the operators? All this stuff in here is still operational; with the looks of permanence about it." Clint didn't answer. And I wasn't sure I wanted him to.

"Look, there's a doorway over there," said Deeds, pointing over to the rear of the building. It was the first time she had spoken since we entered the blockhouse and I had begun to worry about her.

But there was a doorway where she pointed, over to the side of the rail gun machine and wide enough to haul heavy equipment through it with no trouble. "Let's have a look people," I said at last, "and have your hand lasers ready for anything." I took my pistol in hand even as my words were sent along the electronic pulses of my radio. The others followed suit and cautiously, we moved ahead.

I took the lead and reached the door first. I saw right away that it was an airlock not unlike those the Empire used and once again wondered whether the builders of the complex had been human after all. That question became even more poignant after I entered the airlock and noted that my atmospheric readouts were registering at Earth type levels. It could only mean that the builders of the blockhouse breathed the same air as that of humans. But any further thoughts along those lines were abruptly terminated as the surface beneath my feet shuddered slightly and the whole airlock began to sink into the flooring. In seconds, the double doors opened up and I was bathed in the glow of a light that shone intermittently from behind a bulkhead far up ahead. The atmosphere was still Earth-type, and so I removed my helmet, not without a bit of relief. Slowly, the airlock ascended back to the ground floor and I called ahead as to its safety.

In a few minutes, my small exploring party had assembled again before the airlock and we all quietly moved forward in the direction of the pulsing light. I led the way with no small amount of reluctance; but having come this far, there was no question of seeing the affair through. I felt the nearness of Deeds's body as she tried to stay close to me without seeming to convey her fear to the men. But she needn't have worried about that, there was plenty to go around.

I had my laser pistol raised in readiness as I rounded the bulk of strange machines that crowded the floor of the sub-level, all of it throbbing with electronic power that told of mighty energies harnessed for some mysterious purpose. Then, suddenly, that purpose was made quite plain. I stepped into that vast, ultimate chamber and stood confronted by a sight, I can safely say, no space traveler from Earth had ever seen before. The bright, pulsing light that had led us into the chamber, was almost a single, constant presence there, its fluctuations hardly noticeable in its painful brightness. But it was its source that halted me in my tracks, brought a gasp of amazement from Clint and Junior and forced Deeds to cling openly to my arm.

In the sharp light that seemed to become almost audible in its throbs, like some invisible heart, a long row of perhaps twenty bodies suspended upright in glassite receptacles were ranged along the base of a pedestal over which hovered what could only have been an enormous brain. I say "brain," not because the form was shaped or colored like that of the master organ in a human body with its folds of gray matter and blood vessels, but because of the intricate network of filaments that twined about one another in a bewildering array. The source of the powerful beats of light was apparent in the giant arcs of electrical power that surged from one neuron to another; the level of mental activity was indicated in the sheer number and constant speed of the sparks, each representative of a particle of thought in the human brain. But the thought inevitably came: was this, in some way, a reconstruction of the human brain?

"It's a brain. A giant, mutated brain." Clint said it almost matter-of-factly, but the look in his eyes told a different story.

"But is it human?" I asked him, as much to snap him out of his stupor as to reassert my own confidence.

Clint stirred after a few moments and said, "No...no it's not. It's been stripped of all tissue leaving only the neuronic fibers to carry on the basic mental activity. Higher thought patterns must be completely impossible in this state, reducing the brain to an instinctive level."

"But why?"

I saw his eyes follow the fine strings of wire that trailed from the lobotomized skulls of the human shapes before the antigravity pedestal and disappeared into the glare at the base of the neuron cluster. "Somehow, its higher thought processes have been sacrificed in order for it to more easily assimilate itself to the mental activity of the bodies there."

Junior had moved in a little closer than the rest of us and finally spoke out. "Skipper, I don't think these bodies are even human."

Together, we all approached to confirm his opinion. He was both right and wrong. "These are human beings, but like none the Earth has seen for thousands of years." I stepped back involuntarily, the others unconsciously following, Deeds was a physical reassurance in the circle of my arms. "Those are Neanderthals."

But it was all I was able to say as a deep booming sound echoed all along the empty corridors between the towering machinery and hit us like a plasma piledriver. In seconds I was flat on my stomach, an invisible force pinning me to the floor with such strength that I was barely able to breath. Slowly, I forced open my eyes against the waves I felt trying to keep them shut. There was no way I could move my head from the position it held; but I didn't need to, I could see all I wanted to. Right alongside me lay Clint, his face away from me, but obviously as helpless as I was. And farther away, from his position ahead of the rest of us, lay Junior. Except now, he was dead. His pressure suit slunk along the flooring and out ahead of where the neck ring stood slightly in the air, a mess of blood and viscera sprayed out for a dozen yards into the deeper reaches of the chamber, his body squeezed from his suit like toothpaste from a tube. I would have shut my eyes if it didn't mean such a fight to get them open again. Instead, I noticed that one of Junior's feet was still whole, his leg flattened only above the knee, as if the force that held us was just enough to keep us in place and inside a proscribed area, certain death.

Suddenly, the sweat began to stream from the pores of my body. Deeds! Where was she? Frantically, I dredged back the last memories I had of her position. Was she too far back or over towards Junior? Then relief mixed with bewilderment washed over me as I saw her standing just inside my peripheral vision. It was infinitely good to see her safe, but at the same time, agonizingly puzzling to see her free. I tried to speak, but only a vague shadow of my usual voice managed to squeak out. "Deeds, are you all right?"

It was a moment before she overcame her own bewilderment to answer. "Oh Alex! Yes, yes, I'm all right! But what about you?" She rushed to my side, bent, and tried to get me up, but failed. "Oh Alex, Alex...what's happened? How can I help you and...and..."

I could see that the sight of Junior was unhinging her nerves and felt there was only one thing I could do. "Deeds. Deeds, look at me!" She did. "Now listen to me. You said you'd do everything I ordered didn't you?" She nodded slowly, tears frozen on her pale cheeks. "Look, I think whatever's keeping us pinned here has to do with that brain there. You've got to destroy it. Use your laser pistol...Deeds! Are you listening?"

She shook herself and straightened. "Yes, I know what you want me to do." She picked up her blaster and held it out in both hands at arm's length. She sighted carefully along the barrel and pulled the trigger. Nothing happened. She tried again. Nothing.

"Check the safety," I said. "Check the power source."

She did both things and still nothing. Finally, she flung the pistol from her and began to move closer to the brain.

I didn't need to watch her go all the way to guess what she had in mind. "Deeds! Wait! Don't go any closer! It's too dangerous!"

"I have to, Alex," she called from over her shoulder. "I'm not leaving here without you, and I can't get you free. It's the only way. I have to find some way to deactivate that thing, even if I have to pull it apart with my own hands.

"Deeds, no!" But she didn't listen.

She didn't rush at the thing, but moved toward it with deliberate steps, plenty of time for the thing to activate its other defenses. Defenses that must have been planned against the contingency of failure of the first trap. It seemed that with every step Deeds took, new sounds erupted from the bowels of the heaps of machinery that were ranged on either side of the big room, but nothing more happened. It was as if electronic processes were begun and just as suddenly halted or broke down. I knew somehow that they were all further traps aimed at Deeds, but that for some strange reason, none affected her. It was maddening to lie where I was, completely helpless as the girl I loved braved dangers never dreamed of by human beings. But of course, I had to.

At last, she moved abreast of the row of Neanderthals and looked at the wires streaming from their craniums. Vaguely, her hands moved to her head and her fingers gently massaged her temples as if some invisible tendrils of thought tried to insinuate themselves into her mind. It was the last, desperate attempt by the brain to stop the danger to its existence posed by the slender figure before it.

Then Deeds' hands left her head and she turned purposely toward the row of Neanderthals; a look of determination crossed her face, as if the fleeting touch of the brain had left her with the knowledge of what to do. She approached the first wired man and yanked out the bundle of wires that grew from his head. Immediately, the cave man shuddered and began to turn swiftly blue; in seconds, his body withered and crumpled out of its near vertical receptacle and fell to the floor. But by that time, Deeds had done the same to almost half the Neanderthals and in the same amount of time, finished her grisly business. With the shrunken carcasses of the twenty cave men dried and dead, the pulses in the giant brain became visibly weaker. Slowly, the electric arcs of energy faded and slowed, more and more of the filaments grew dark and cold, and the throbs of light dimmed gradually, their pace slackening in proportion. Finally, all of its remaining processes seemed to pause in their mutual deterioration.

I held my breath, still pinned to the floor, watching the delicate form of Deeds as she was limned in that ghostly light. It was a moment frozen in my mind forever.

Suddenly, there was one, single pulse of light that flashed painfully in our eyes, piercing our own brains to the core.

I think I lost consciousness then for a few minutes, because the next thing I knew, I was sitting up and trying to get my feet under me. Nearby, Clint was swaying a bit, not sure about his own legs. Then there was the scent of roses and a puff of warm breath on my cheek and I realized Deeds had come back to help me up. She came in handy as I said, "What happened?" But in the same instant, I knew.

I knew something I didn't know before. My head seemed to be filled with scrambled, alien thoughts; and just when I seemed to have them pinned down, they scattered again. I looked up and saw an expression on Deed's face that spoke of the same perplexity. Clint stumbled over to where Deeds was propping me up and tried to say something I couldn't make out. I was scared. With that last big pulse, the giant brain had done something to us. Maybe induced some sort of brain damage on the three of us as a sort of last ditch defense; a suicidal one. But then, as the three of us came close together, it dawned on us that it wasn't anything of the sort, but something a lot more miraculous.

Somehow, that last pulse had imprinted on our brains all the primitive information it possessed. But it was still too much for any one of us to hold; and so, it parceled it out. Each of us had only a part of the story. Coming within a closer proximity, we were able to pool our portions through some kind of telepathy and make sense of the asteroid's puzzle.

The asteroid had been designed by an alien race eons before in the dim recesses of history, at a time when Neanderthal man was the only evidence of intelligent life in the solar system. But that was enough for the aliens to worry about the creature's potential. They foresaw a time when those primitive beings could become a threat to their civilization. And so, against that possibility, they had built a completely automated military station far from Earth, and so well hidden it would have only one chance in a million of ever being discovered. Envisioned as a sort of "trip wire," the station would be occupied by a facsimile of one of their own brains and attached to those of a number of Neanderthals'. Thus connected, the sentinel brain could recognize the approach of those it had been created to defend against. But because of two small errors, all those millennia of planning and waiting had been wasted. The first trap outside the blockhouse had failed to activate, and the decision by the aliens to hook up the sentinel brain with those of *male* brains effectively negated any chance of the brain's being able to stop Deeds. Being female, she was of course close enough to the male for the brain to recognize and attempt to protect itself against her; but being female also meant that at the most basic levels of her being she was *different* than the male. Equal in all things save what made them two genders. In any other context, two separate and alien races inexplicably intertwined at the mystery of creation. And so, she had been able to pass through the alien gauntlet unharmed and to detach the sentinel brain from its only contact with the outside world. I even wondered over the powerlessness of the laser pistol in Deeds' hands when she tried to fire it, and the answer came to me that it was a product derived from a male mind, enabling the brain to extrapolate its function by following the almost endless chain of events that led to its invention, and thus neutralize it.

The irony was, that the brain had received information a thousand years before which indicated that the alien race that had created it and which feared danger from prehistoric man, had in the end destroyed themselves through the simultaneous destruction of all the suns of their colonized systems.

And even as the explanation manifested itself to us, it quickly faded, the last effort of the last outpost of a dead civilization to keep the memory of its origins alive.

It took us only hours to retrieve Junior's remains and to verify that all of the strange machinery contained in the blockhouse had been reduced to slag in the same burst of light that imparted to us the knowledge of the race that had built it.

Later, Deeds felt good in my arms as we both watched the video monitor holding the image of the asteroid in its cold gaze. Slowly, it receded from the camera's field of view and presently, was lost in the rubble of the asteroid belt.

Strange Pursuit

Shartfil was on the run and he didn't know why.

Someone had been on his tail for the last two weeks, or at least, that's when he'd first noticed him; from Bston to Washtn to Phil, he'd tried everything to lose him but nothing had ever worked. Oh sure, he'd lose him for a while, and every time that he thought that he'd succeeded, the man would appear again, usually on the road ahead of him, or in a dive where he'd stop for a drink, or in the lobby of a crash joint where he'd decided to catch some winks.

And to make things even weirder, in Balt, he'd scooted at random along the blasted sections of the city, picking a crash joint completely out of a hat and still, he'd find the man slinked in a rest-rack or sagged on a stool in the joint's darkest corner. There was no way in the world his choices could have been predicted; no way! But the guy was there. All the time, every time. Cool and breezy as you please.

It was easy to recognize him. He wasn't trying to make himself unseeable. He was pretty normal sized like Shartfil, and was always swathed in a long coat that wrapped his body from head to toe, hiding his features so that no one could get a good skance at him.

Anyway it was darkside now, and Shartfil was trying to haul his battered zipper along the empty stretch of pathway between Balt and Nwyrk while at the same time, keeping in sight the distant point of light that trailed him. He'd given up trying to lose his tail on the open pathways. The man was either too smart for that, or just had a better zipper. No, this time, Shartfil had a foolproof plan of escape that didn't involve anything so crude as outracing the snooper. No one knew Nwyrk better than he did, and it was there that he knew he'd lose whoever it was that was following him once and for all.

It was almost two numerals before dawn when he eased his zipper into the outer ruins of Nwyrk and began a series of evasive moves designed to confound the most experienced of snoop-trackers. Satisfied at last that he'd given him the ditch, Shartfil slammed the pumper and propelled his zipper down the aisle of cleared rubble near the center of the city and plunged recklessly into the heart of Nwyrk. It was still dark when he pulled into an alley behind a row of stacked sleep boxes and hid the zipper beneath a pile of trash. The neighborhood's mutts raised a turbulence, but a few kicks silenced them.

He squeezed himself through a narrow slit in some of the sleep boxes and stepped out onto the avenue on the other side where the sleepless kept up a lively series of interests. Not twenty steps from where he was pancaked against the wall, stood a match. Watching out for the zipper that had been on his tail, Shartfil walked up to the match and said, "Having a full day?" The male reached out and they shook hands; the female turned her back to him and he warmed his other hand at her buttocks. "I have a pocketful of pleasure pennies for the both of you if you'd help me with something."

The male eyed him then glanced at his match.

The female looked at him from over her shoulder and then at Shartfil, but allowed the stranger's hand to remain where it was.

Shartfil breathed a silent sigh of relief.

"There's a snoop-tracker on my tail that I need to get rid of," he told the male. I want you to take my zipper for a turn around the city while I take your place with your match. While you're away, I want her to take me to any crash-joint she wants, I don't want to know the place before I get there."

"Where are the pleasure pennies?" the male asked.

Shartfil produced them, poured them into the other's hands and gave him directions to the hidden zipper.

"Keep the zipper if you want," Shartfil told him. "I know where I can get another." The male only raised his eyebrows. "Don't worry, I don't want to keep your match, I just want to get rid of those snoop-trackers."

Reassured, the male nodded to his match and moved off into the narrow alley leading to the zipper.

Shartfil turned to the female and said, "What's your label?"

"Ellaia," she said. "Where do you want to go?"

"To any crash-joint you care to take me to."

Ellaia shrugged and said, "You'll have to act like my match."

Shartfil held her left buttock with his hand as Ellaia led him down the pathway edge in the coming dawn.

It was full light when they reached a particularly nasty crash-joint near the edge of the ruins where the old forest crept around the huge heaps of rubble. As they stepped into the dim interior of the joint, he could see a few matches slinking about and felt Ellaia loosening his belt and snaking her hands deep into the backside of his trousers. He bellied up to the swill counter and demanded a joint for the two of them. Two pleasure pennies yielded him a key and with his hand warm on Ellaia's buttock, they made their way to the second tier. He was just beginning to think that maybe he'd ask Ellaia to stay with him a little while longer, when upon opening the panel to his joint, he was astounded to find the snoop-tracker there waiting for him.

"Having a full day, Shartfil?" the man asked.

Shartfil reeled back into the corridor, all thought of Ellaia gone, his mind mixed in confusion. How did the guy find him? There was no way he could've been followed; he had made absolutely sure. Even he didn't know where he'd wind up!

The man remained where he was as Shartfil edged along the corridor toward the stairway and finally stumbled down their dark length to the lobby.

Back in the room, the man folded back the collar of his coat, revealing his face and watched Ellaia's eyes widen in recognition. Then she placed her hands before her face as fear and uncertainty filled her dull mind.

"Won't you sit down, Ellaia?" the man said, motioning toward the rest-rack. "You'll have to excuse me, I have an appointment with your match to keep." He stepped toward the door, allowing Ellaia to slink aside and fall to the floor.

Outside, Shartfil had plunged recklessly into the forest, shoving himself through the scratching, clinging branches of the denuded trees and underbrush; falling and stumbling along the steep slopes of ancient rubble and half buried chunks of concrete. Dimly he was aware of pursuit close behind him and despite himself, couldn't help wondering why he was the object of the snoop-tracker's attention. All these weeks, all this trouble; he could have caught him any time he wanted and yet he didn't. Why? His thoughts came back to the present as the sounds behind him grew louder with the approach of his nemesis. Crazily, he clawed his way to the top of a mountain of rubble, lost his footing, and fell painfully down the opposite side and through a thin sheeting of rusted metal that had lain buried beneath a covering of dirt and grass. With a scraping crash, he broke through the surface and tumbled into a black cavern below. The fall from the surface was fortunately short but when he rose, he still ached with pain. He felt his head and a smear of blood came away on his hand.

Suddenly, he knew he wasn't alone.

A light flashed from above and a voice he thought vaguely familiar echoed softly in the hidden chamber. "Stay where you are and you won't be hurt." A rope was lowered into the hole and in another second he was confronted by the coat-wrapped man who had been chasing him for so long. He had a kill-grip in his hand leveled at Shartfil's chest. Confidently, as if familiar with the cavern, he edged back and fumbled in the darkness until a dim light came on, illuminating the room and demonstrating that it was some sort of ancient laboratory filled with strange machinery. Then the man shrugged out of his coat and Shartfil saw that he was staring into a mirror!

He stared open-mouthed as the man before him, his exact double in every feature, except for a faint scar on his forehead, smiled. "Yes, Shartfil," he said, "I'm you. Funny, isn't it? You see, I'm from your future, or rather, another time stream. In my own stream, I was chased through these same woods and fell into this same room. Only in my stream, I fooled around with the machinery you see around you and discovered too late that it was a time machine built by the Pre-Ignition People long ago; maybe to escape the Burn Times into another, safer time period. Who knows? Anyway, because of my ignorance, I wound up cast backward three years in time without any way of getting back to my own period. Since I'd fallen accidentally into this room while being chased through an unfamiliar wood, and had suffered temporary amnesia in the transition from my time to yours, I'd found that I'd wandered away from the laboratory and hadn't the foggiest idea of how to find it again. Until I realized just when and where I was. It was then that I decided that I had to find you, my double, and in three years' time, recreate the event that allowed me to discover the laboratory in the first place. I spent the years of waiting studying the old manuals and found what I needed to know in order to operate the machine and get myself back."

"But why bother, if your world is the same as this one?" said Shartfil, finding his tongue.

His double snorted. "This sinkhole? The Earth of my time stream may have been blasted too, but life there is a good deal more tolerable than it is here."

Shartfil wasn't sure whether to believe any of it but he was given no more time to think it over.

"Step over against the wall, Shartfil," ordered his doppleganger, pointing the kill-grip at him. Shartfil did as he was told and watched as the other man moved before a sheer white panel and began to shimmer. In another moment he was gone. That was it. So simple. Then there was a slight sound and he saw a thin wisp of smoke rise from the contraption and knew his double had fixed it so that no one else could fool with it.

Somehow, he found his way out of the forest and made his way back to the city, but one thought stuck in his mind long after the whole strange episode had receded into the years: If he had been chased by his double from the future and forced into the hidden chamber, who was it that had chased the other Shartfil into it?

Splendid Isolation

Father Alexander Xickler, abbot of the Cistercian monastery on Rigel IV, stood in an empty pastureland of gently rolling hills and studied the readouts of his environmental data link to the little satellite that followed him in geo-synchronous orbit high overhead. Satisfied with its conclusions, he hitched the unit back onto his utility belt and looked around. Everywhere, waist high grasses swayed slowly in wavelike motion as far as he could see; everywhere except for a small patch of darker green on the horizon to the east. Overhead, the sky was a perfect blue, undisturbed by flying creatures. He breathed deeply of the clean, fresh air, untainted by the stinks of worlds occupied by men.

It was a virgin world, far outside the accustomed pathways of the Holy Roman Empire; a world that had once belonged to his own race, the star spanning Krone. He grunted at that. He was, after all, only half Krone, his mother being of the Empire. It had been a good three centuries since the Krone culture had been absorbed by the more vigorous and expanding Earth Empire. Not without a struggle of course. There had been elements of the Krone that had held out militarily for almost fifty years after the first uprising, but even that was a dim memory now. His family had been one of the first to convert and he himself came from a long line of Xicklers that had taken Holy Orders. But he had preferred the contemplative life of a Cistercian to the more active priesthood and despite that, he had found himself as abbot of the monastery on Rigel IV. The true irony was that here he was, playing the part of explorer, searching for a newer, more secluded site for a new abbey for his order. Looking around him now, he felt this world was ideal. But earlier scans of the planet had told him that a more advantageous site for the abbey buildings would be best situated atop a nearby plateau. Accordingly, the Navy cruiser that had brought him here had dropped him as close to it as possible. He checked his chronometer and found he had almost a week, Earth time, to thoroughly reconnoiter the site.

He took note of his surroundings and double-checked his coordinates with his personal satellite and began walking east. The satellite would follow the signals given off by the power source of his data link and remain directly overhead. It was one of a number of advanced models manufactured by the brothers as part of their program for self employment; much as earlier houses used to raise crops for market or work at handicrafts. As the day wore on to noon, the dark green smudge in the distance resolved itself into the face of the plateau and in short order, he found himself on its lower slopes. After a simple meal, he began to negotiate the incline as it grew steeper and steeper. At first, the climb was relatively easy, but as he neared the crest, it became more difficult to keep his footing.

Slowly, the landscape began to change as well. The tall grass of the fields below gave way to scrub, then to a form of stunted trees. By the time he was half way up, a regular forest came to dominate the slopes. At last, as he neared the crest, and noticing that the temperature too had risen with the altitude, the vegetation had altered into that of thick jungle. His footing was aided by lengths of creeping vines and lianas, great drooping branches of trees that leaned and swayed crazily against the face of the escarpment and that increasingly blocked out the warm sun.

It took a lot less time than it seemed to reach the level top of the plateau and it wasn't with a sense of relief that Xickler fell to the ground to catch his breath. In front of him was a sight not made to discourage him. The thick canopy of trees continued with their towering trunks reaching branchless to the hidden sky hundreds of feet overhead allowing only the stray shaft of sunlight to pierce greenly from their leafage to the ground below. And amid the pools of greenish light, thousands of varieties of shrub, grass, and fungus grew in generous profusion here and there dotted with the wildly colorful flowers that made Xickler think of Eden. For in truth, the sight before him was not displeasing. It was rather beautiful and it would be a shame to spoil it with buildings. He was coming to the conclusion that the better site for the monastery would be on the plain below, leaving the plateau as a natural location perfectly suitable for meditation. He was entranced by the relative openness of the land beneath the trees and began walking aimlessly, enjoying the natural beauty all around him. Perhaps it was this preoccupation that almost got him killed.

If asked, he probably wouldn't have been able to explain what it was that made him jump, leap, and roll the twenty yards to a shallow hole in the ground. He probably couldn't even say how he instinctively found his way to a hole he certainly could not have known was there.

Perhaps it was some residual memory of the time he spent with the Imperial Troopers years before entering the Order. Whatever it was…instinct, training, or divine intervention…it saved his life. An instant after he had tumbled into the hole, the air was alive with the crackling hiss of immense power and the green gloom of the forest shimmering in the glow of a great energy-web that crisscrossed the entire area for what looked to the abbot like two or three hundred yards in every direction. He was able to judge that distance by peeking over the edge of his hole and seeing that the web lay only a foot above the surface of the forest floor and had slashed the entire forest at that height like a giant scythe. Everywhere, the giant lengths of the trees that had stood only minutes before, high over his head, were now lying about in haphazard chunks, covered with the shredded detritus of the lower lying vegetation.

Consternation dominating his thoughts, Xickler was hardly able to concentrate on even that as a new threat presented itself. Disturbed by the sudden tumult overhead, a score of ground worms began wriggling their way to the surface of the earth, making the ground beneath the priest come alive with their frantic efforts to come to light. One by one, they began to show themselves from hidden openings at the base of the hole, their blindly searching heads weaving disgustingly in the air. Faster than their great bulk would seem to indicate, they emerged wetly in a tangle and, sensing the presence of life nearby, and perhaps determining it as the cause of their discomfort, they began to drag themselves in Xickler's direction.

Appalled at the prospect of being done in by such a horrid form of life, and seeing the multiple rows of sharp teeth displayed by the leaders, Xickler edged himself as far back up the side of the hole as the energy web permitted then drew his gamma pistol. Firing at the lead monstrosity, he reduced it to gelid slag and then did the same for its fellows. Anxious minutes later, he determined that he had destroyed all of the worms in that particular cluster and holstered his weapon. Finding that the episode had enabled his mind to clear itself of its previous consternation, he was better able to study the situation that confronted him.

Once again, he looked out under the web and the mass of destruction that lay there. He recognized the web as an old Krone death trap, meant to catch anyone venturing too near one of their hidden bases. In this case, knowing this world to have been in one of the rebel sectors that had risen up and held out against the Empire when the Krone civilization had been almost completely absorbed by the Earth culture, Xickler guessed that this particular world had been missed by Naval mop-up operations when the rebellion was stamped out. Somehow, his emergence onto the plateau had triggered the area's defensive systems. But he wasn't ignorant of the way the Krone thought, being one himself. They had a weakness for using overwhelming power when only a little would suffice; just a look at the elaborate energy web confirmed the notion. Consequently, he concluded that the power needed to energize the web would need to come from a source too large to hide completely. All he had to do was to find it.

As it turned out, that wasn't too hard to do. Directly before him, about two hundred yards away, stood a white-walled blockhouse visible now where before it had been well hidden by the surrounding forest. But there was no way he could even crawl to it with the web so low to the ground. He thought a moment before settling on a course of action.

Taking his communications link to his overhead satellite, he punched the necessary commands that would allow the satellite to refocus all of its power to his gamma pistol and through it, unleash a tightly focused beam of radio waves at the blockhouse. He realized that the operation would leave the satellite virtually useless to him, but he was willing to trade that for his life.

The commands completed, he aimed his pistol at the blockhouse and waited for the ready-light to come on. It did, and he fired. Immediately, the blockhouse was pierced by the invisible beam and the energy web disappeared. Xickler stood up, the faint scent of ozone in his nostrils, and looked at his pistol. A thin wisp of smoke dissipated from its nozzle and the slagged circuits within. He threw it aside and walked over to the blockhouse. It was easy because the heaped vegetation that had been piled up in front of him had been pulverized by the residual radio waves that radiated from his unidirectional beam. He entered the blockhouse through the gaping hole that had been blasted into its side and could easily see daylight from the hole in the opposite wall. In front of it lay a mound of heaped and unrecognizable machinery that had lain in the path of the radio beam. He was still congratulating himself on a job well done when he noticed something else.

A section of the flooring had melted away revealing a hidden niche below the main floor. A complex mechanism was revealed that had every indication of continued life. Hurriedly, knowing the Krone penchant for double and even triple-layered booby traps, he probed the device with his environmental data link, now on limited mode. What it revealed didn't make him feel any better. The air was charged with residual radiation, the by-product of crashing atoms. Instantly, he knew the device before him was a primitive sort of atomic bomb, meant as a last ditch denial weapon. If the Krone forces could not hold their base world, they meant to deny its use to the Empire, much as the ancients used to poison the wells outside the walls of fortresses to deny besieging armies their use.

There were only two things he could do: disarm the thing or destroy it. Unfortunately, he had too little time to attempt the former and so he was forced to try the latter. He had no idea how long he had, but he was sure it couldn't be too long. Quickly, he gave his satellite one last command, hoping there was enough energy left in it to shove it into a radically deteriorating orbit that would allow it to plunge to the planet's surface. Throwing himself into the hole he had so recently vacated, he prayed the satellite's shields would protect it long enough for it reach the ground.

In quick, economical motions, he had assembled his portable shelter and had it stretched across the top of the hole, reinforcing it with small stones and soil. The last sight he had of the outside, was of a rapidly approaching streak of light from the west before he huddled deep inside the shelter. Reciting a last prayer to God for protection, he waited a seeming eternity for the coming impact, and when it came, he could hardly have prepared himself completely for the shock of the spacecraft's landing. A great, deafening crash filled the air and popped his eardrums, setting them to ringing, and immediately behind that came the shock wave that set the earth to shaking so violently that it almost threw him clear of his shelter. Luckily it didn't, as a hail of debris came crashing down about him, resulting in a broken wrist.

At last, all was calm, and he emerged from his shelter to see the small crater that sprawled where the blockhouse once stood. He checked his environmental data link and allowed himself a sigh of relief; no evidence of radiation. He smiled. It looked as though the Order would have its new location after all. Then the smile froze on his face as he thought of the fate of his expensive satellite. What would the Superior General say?

Essays

Romantic Elements in Frank M. Robinson's "The Power"

Once, before the age of the internet, Frank M. Robinson's novel *The Power* (1956) used to be a difficult book to find but for those who took the trouble to search it out, proved to be well worth the search. It was first published in 1956 and later brought to the silver screen by director George Pal in a relatively faithful adaptation that underlined the monstrous nature of a man possessing the limitless power of the mind.

Although the subject of the novel was not a new one for science fiction, not even for the mid-50s, it did succeed in examining the subject from a different perspective, one having more to do with the dark side of man's nature and the horrors that can arise from it than with the usually mechanistic trappings of science fiction. Science is necessarily an exact field, filled with finite conceptions, beginnings and endings. The realm of the mind and of the soul, is conversely infinite; its ideas and concepts eternal with their different facets broken and staggered into mirrors reflecting endlessly into each other.

In the novel, one man has discovered that he possesses the infinite power of the mind, a power that makes him "as different from his fellows as they are from the apes." Realizing that his power set him apart from others and could make him the object of their fears, he sets out to destroy the members of a committee who were present when his existence was discovered. Through the course of the story, the committee members are disposed of until only one remains. The survivor finally comes face to face with his nemesis and it is at that point that the novel truly transcends mere science fiction and becomes the masterpiece of gripping fear, loathing, and distrust it truly is.

But before going into more detail, one more thing need be said about the nature of the novel. In order for a story of the supernatural to truly pass from the mundane bluntness of the popular terror novels, it must have certain literary attributes. Not only good grammar, plot, climax, and resolution, but also elements that certainly other novels may possess, but without which a story of the supernatural falls flat. Beginning with Edgar Allen Poe, the terror tale has since attained a style and shape that has made it one of the most popular forms of literature. Before Poe, horror stories concerned themselves mainly with ghosts, castles, and creepy dungeons; certainly elements calculated to send shivers down the spines of less sophisticated audiences. But since the days of Victorian horror, the industrial age has come full upon us with its requirement that every horror must be explained; so why do tales of horror still strike deep chords in modern readers? With the coming of the Romantic writers in the eighteenth century, literature became more introspective, turning from the classical period's adherence to art, order, and mortal perfection to lust, chaos, and the labyrinth of the human mind.

The Classical writers regarded their work as an imitation of life, "a mirror held up to nature" in a way that would both teach and give pleasure to the reader. In a reversal of this idea, the Romantics theorized that the inspiration of literature originated in the mind of the author; not in men and their actions, but the imaginative vision of the writer. Elements of Romantic fiction include spontaneity and freedom, the glorification of the commonplace, individualism, nonconformity, and apocalyptic vision. But for our purposes here, its emphasis on the supernatural is of the most importance.

Romantic writers were the first to actively use their dreams and nightmares, and particularly in Coleridge's case, their drug induced experiences. Though Coleridge's "Kubla Kahn" is the recognized masterpiece it is, other works in the gothic genre of the time by such authors as Baudelaire and Swinburne, carried the movement of blatant perversity to its extremes thus establishing what was called "European decadence."_Other writers of the period, such as Lord Byron, flaunted their immorality by their deliberate exploration of the Satanic hero. Matthew Lewis effectively predated the current trend in the similar areas by delving into the forbidden areas of diabolism, sensuality, and sadism. Indeed, the reliance of the Romantics on the combination of man's aspirations for the infinite and his belief in the power of the individual mind sets Robinson's *The Power* firmly in the Romantic tradition.

As noted earlier, it was Poe, with his moody, depressed outlook on life and his frequent bouts with alcoholism who, as a latter day Romantic, combined the spirit of Romanticism with the supernatural horror story. His tales were more often than not studies of the dark side of man's mind. In stories such as "The Telltale Heart," "The Mask of the Red Death," and "The Fall of the House of Usher," he explores the fears, guilts, and doubts that plague the hearts of men. Since then, the best horror stories have been those that dwelt on these inner conflicts, the enlightened and dark sides of man's nature. These emotions can and often do eclipse the physical terrors the author may introduce to his plot.

Perhaps the most basic difference between Classical and Romantic horror to the modern reader is the former's reliance on logic and science and the, latter's preoccupation with disorder and chaos. The ideological basis being the idealized as opposed to the deformed. The past and the future.

Robinson's *The Power* is a literary curiosity. On the one hand, it is clearly based on a pseudo-scientific idea: that a new race of superior men will evolve from the old but on the other, it still owes something to the Romantic preoccupation with the mind and individual man's dependence on the vagaries of his own or other's thoughts. Here, aside from the novel's basic pseudo-scientific premise, Robinson concentrates his attention on the struggle between two minds: one that seeks to manipulate the emotions of its victim and the other that uses logic to resist. The denouement being what the Romantic would consider to be the ultimate horror: the surrender of logic to emotion. Victory is achieved through increased mental turmoil and in the end, instead of good being triumphant over evil, the victor simply replaces his opponent as a new menace to mankind. Between logic and emotion, the mind has become morally neutral: neither good nor evil.

In *The Power*, Robinson's hero, Tanner, is helplessly buffeted about at the whim of a hidden telepath named Adam Hart who leads both the protagonist and the reader from the familiar world of science, logic, and realism through many twists and turns of a plot that plunges them into increasingly surreal situations. At the same time, the author manages to intertwine his genres, as the story alternately switches from a detective yarn to horror.

In the course of his novel, Robinson manages to touch upon many elements common to the Romantic era. For example, through the course of the story, Tanner struggles to free himself from the danger posed by Adam Hart. But true to the Romantic spirit, when freedom is at last attained, he loses it. As the full horror of the novel reveals, freedom, as it turns out, is only an illusion.

The one element that allows Tanner to survive the pitfalls set for him by Adam Hart is his reliance on spontaneity and instinct, unrefined thoughts that become superior to the Newtonian idea of an ordered universe. Only thus can he hope to keep Hart psychologically off balance and at the same time, reverse reader expectations: in being forced to react to Tanner's thrusts, Hart becomes the champion of order while Tanner that of chaos.

Quite apart from the plot and main action, certain scenes are accentuated by Robinson in the breathless persona of Tanner as he stumbles through the nighted streets:

People...on the fire escapes, stretching in the early morning sunlight and hawking and spitting and scratching themselves. The women in dirty bathrobes, their hair in curlers and their tired faces sagging at the edges. Fat men in pajamas too small for them and skinny men in shorts and T shirts looking at the world as if it were a suit they had bought at a second floor walk up and they were just getting a good look at it in the daylight.

The homely little people who made up ninety percent of the world, who made all the mistakes and committed all the crimes and regretted everything they had ever done which had given them a little pleasure in life. The decent little people who were kind to strangers, and had kids who got their heads shot off in the once-every-generation-war. The poor slobs who lived in ratty little apartments that smelled of cooking and human sweat...There were the few who would plant grass and flowers in their backyards year after year even though they knew flowers would never grow on a diet of broken glass and city soot...They were the few who stood to lose the most if Adam Hart were running things.

A vivid example of the novel's Romantic allusions glorifying the common man, this passage is made all the more chilling as, later in the story, Tanner's earlier sympathies give way to total unconcern.

By contrast, throughout the course of the story, Tanner perceives Hart's own lack of empathy for his fellow human beings as an expression of his extreme individualism, the total nonconformist who exists outside of society. Indeed, Tanner thinks that Hart's superiority over ordinary human beings must have finally purged him of such baser emotions as hate, fear, and disgust. In reality, Hart lacks higher emotions as well achieving the status of ideal Romantic hero, a situation that ironically, is to be reversed by the conclusion of the novel.

Thus, as will be shown below, Robinson's final apocalyptic vision becomes self-evident as well as self-fulfilling.

As previously stated, the horror of The Power lies mainly in its exploration of the human soul, but in some instances physical horror can be equally as powerful. Witness this scene as Tanner, fleeing wildly from Hart, finds refuge beneath a porch that has been used as a storage place for the detritus of suburban life, dirt, rats, and cobwebs. Tanner, panting in exhaustion and fear like some hunted animal, watches as Hart's attention is drawn to a dog scratching on the opposite side of a nearby fence.

"...The boxer growled and the hackles on its neck rose. It trotted stiffly forward, then suddenly froze in a patch of moonlight. It began to whimper.

"...A muscle on the dog's left hind leg hunched and jerked and there was a brittle, snapping sound. He could see the muscles of the throat work as the boxer tried to howl, but not a sound came out.

"...The end was quick. The dog's skin rippled and it went into convulsions, circling around with its useless leg and frothing at the jaws. Suddenly there was a louder snap and it sagged, broken, to the ground. It jerked once, as if somebody had kicked it, and a growing depression showed faintly in its side. Blood gushed abruptly from the mouth and then the yard was still and empty.

"Footsteps sounded faintly down the sidewalk..."

"(Tanner) glanced at the boxer, lying crushed in the middle of the yard and imagined himself lying there."

The scene of Hart, framed in the opening beneath the porch and standing in the shadows watching calmly as the helpless canine is killed in such a gruesome and callous manner, is made all the more powerful due to being depicted in such an understated way. Adding to the chilling effect, is the peaceful suburban setting with its whisper of trees and twinkling of stars overhead.

Imagery also plays an important part in a key scene running up to the novel's climax. Here, Tanner and fellow committee member Arthur Nordlund, watch as a trap they had set for Hart springs shut at an amusement park. Reasoning that Edward DeFalco, the last surviving member of the committee besides himself, must be Adam Hart, Tanner watches as DeFalco is chased through the empty park by police until cornered in the funhouse. Escaping, DeFalco then runs toward the roller coaster.

"The lights and the cars and the hunters moved after him, flowing down the street like a giant amoeba. In the shadows of the wooden framework, a figure worked its way rapidly towards the top, leaping from beam to beam with an agility that far surpassed that of any human being.

...A scattering of shots from the figure high in the framework. Then the lights were on him, first one picking him out, then clinging tenaciously and then the others until the whole roller-coaster framework was bathed in light. DeFalco was caught in the center, like a fly in a web. Somehow Tanner thought he heard the man scream, "Oh my God!"

Then the riot guns caught him and he fell and the guns still clung, their invisible fingers plucking at him while he was still in the air. He hit the ground and bounced and it was all over. All over."

But the novel's more traditional Romantic horror is reserved for Adam Hart himself. Throughout the novel, Hart has been portrayed as evil personified: the chaotic elements of man's psyche freed of the moral shackles of twentieth century civilization. A true Romantic hero, Hart possessed many of the elements that defined the movement including spontaneity, nonconformity, supernaturalism, personal freedom, and apocalyptic vision. Hart's ultimate goal, though ill defined, was to possess the world and to use it however he chose with humans reduced to mere cattle or puppets as indeed, many of his hapless victims had been. In the course of the novel, Adam Hart encapsulates the Romantic conception of man at once at the mercy of, and in control over, his own emotions. As a consequence, the real horror of the story issues forth.

The reader's first true insight into the soul of Adam Hart comes when Tanner follows a lead to Hart's hometown. There, he discovers that as a boy, Hart had been the darling of the town. Through his use of the Power, he was able to present to everyone the appearance best fitting each person's notion of what the perfect teenager should be. To the coach he was the perfect athlete, to the teachers the perfect student, to the girls the perfect lover. Consequently, Tanner is unable to find any single description of the real Hart. For years Hart had treated his best friend as a puppet and made of the man's sister a slavish concubine willing to condone anything Hart felt like doing. So completely under Hart's influence is the woman, that she even condones his murder of her brother after he became a member of Tanner's committee. It was an unwholesome influence that Hart readily practiced on every woman in the town whether married or single; behavior happily accepted by his neighbors as the doings of a fun loving teenager. Finally, Tanner learns of the mysterious death of the entire Hart family soon after Hart's departure from the town. It seemed that the family was found burned alive in its own home with all of the bodies huddled against an unlocked front door. To keep his existence a secret, Hart had killed every member of his family and left psychic commands in other townspeople to kill anyone who ever came around asking about him. Tanner, after a narrow escape from one of the human booby-traps, manages to speak to a doctor recently moved to town before the fellow dies a convenient death.

Hart repeated his performance of the house burning when he killed committee member Prof. Van Zandt together with his wife and children after the man's usefulness to him had ended. Hart served DeFalco in the same way when he forced him to run like a mouse in a maze through the carnival until he was shot to death.

But the ultimate horror comes as part of the novel's ironic climax when Nordlund, who is revealed as Adam Hart himself, attempts to destroy Tanner with his psychic powers. The killer has his comeuppance when his assault inadvertently releases Tanner's own pent-up powers with which he kills Hart.

From the story's beginning, clues have been set pointing to Tanner's own psychic abilities. In the opening chapters, the reader is told that the purpose of the committee is look into the reasons why some men are able to endure the stress of combat while others cannot. As the story unfolds, it becomes apparent that those who are the most successful soldiers are those whose psychic powers give them an edge, the same kind of edge that Tanner himself possessed when he became the only member of the committee able to survive against Adam Hart. It was against that possibility that Hart positioned himself as a member of the committee: to be on hand if others with similar powers were discovered and to be able to destroy them before they had a chance to challenge him.

The final irony however, is that though Hart is portrayed throughout the novel as evil and Tanner good, when Tanner becomes aware of his power he also comes to understand what his adversary had known for years: that he was in fact superior to other human beings. The point is driven home to the reader with Tanner's final thought:

"It was going to be fun playing God."

Clark Ashton Smith and the French Romantics

Of course it would be obvious, in fact more than obvious, to say that Clark Ashton Smith was heavily influenced by the French symbolist and surrealist, poetic movements of the nineteenth century. The subject has been mined more than once in the past to prove that point, if Smith's own unequivocal remarks on the matter were not enough. What the following paragraphs seek to accomplish has less to do with seeking out those influences on Smith's work, than to explore, albeit superficially, the origins of those influences. Who were the symbolists? What were the surrealists trying to say? What brought some decadents inevitably to existentialism and even dadaism? Clark Ashton Smith was a complex human being whose inner life, no matter how much we know of it from acquaintances who knew him and even from his own writings, can only be imperfectly guessed at; still, enough can be learned from these sources to say, with some measure of certainty, that he felt a close affinity to the thoughts, aims, and feelings of those exponents of the French romantic era. The one thing they certainly had in common, was a taste for Edgar Allan Poe, his greatest French admirer being Baudelaire. Is it coincidence that just as Baudelarie translated Poe into French, Smith translated Baudelaire into English? But where exactly did the trail begin that would eventually lead from the early centuries of western poetic development to these romantics and thence to a young man living on the farthest shore of the New World?

The long climb of French poetic expression began in the early fifteenth century with the widespread use of the Alexandrine stanzaic formula. Before the time of Charles D'Orleans (1394-1465), French verse had struggled slowly upward from the essentially didactic form of *The Song of*

Roland to the great Alexandrine flowering of the fourteenth century. The Alexandrine became the most common meter of the Middle Ages after the dearth of popular narrative poems based on the adventures of Alexander the Great. This poetic form was to last over three hundred years as French poetry sank into the doldrums until revivified by the emergence of the symbolists in the 1800s. The symbolists, led by the brilliant and erratic Charles Baudelaire, attempted to depict the revelation or suggestion of abstract conditions and truths through the medium of their art. The written word transcended its limited nature as essentially the communication of mutually recognized sound patterns to that of connotation that would strike each reader differently according to his unique life experience. And the life experiences of the major contributors of the symbolist movement were unique indeed.

The symbolists as a group, led generally Bohemian lives and died young. Some even wrote their entire life's output of verse before they reached twenty. All seemed disturbed in some way whether drunkards, drug addicts, or homosexuals, and that these debilitating qualities, far from being detrimental to their art, gave it the wild revolutionary quality that enabled them to leap from the printed page into abstract realms of thought and emotion. Among these ideologically restless men of the mid-nineteenth century was Charles Baudelaire.

Baudelaire was born in Paris in 1821, but by the time he became a teenager, his family had become so scandalized with his lewd lifestyle that he was sent on a long voyage to India. He never got there. Instead, he returned to Paris and immediately continued his profligate ways. He had his first work published in 1845 and in 1853 he published his translation of the works of Edgar Allan Poe, an author whose personal life and somber prose that rejected an increasingly mechanistic world, captured Baudelaire's imagination. Perhaps influenced by Poe's rejection of the modern world, Baudelaire published in 1857 his masterpiece of symbolist thought, *Les Fleurs du Mal* (The Flowers of Evil). Soon after, he was brought to court on charges of indecency and blasphemy that resulted in a fine for the author and the excision of six poems from the collection. If the following poem is any indication of the content of *Les Fleur du Mal* it is no wonder that the French state felt obliged to work for its censorship.

Melancholy

I am like the king of a rainy country,
Rich, but powerless, young and yet very old,
Who, scorning the bows and scrapes of his tutors,
Is bored with his dogs as with other animals.
Nothing can cheer him, neither game nor falcon,
Nor his people dying opposite his balcony.
The grotesque ballad of his favorite jester
No longer smoothes the brow of this cruel invalid;
His bed adorned with fleurs-de-lis becomes a tomb,
And the tirewomen, who find all princes handsome,
Can no longer contrive a shameless costume.
That will draw a smile from this young skeleton.
The alchemist who makes gold for him has never been able
To eliminate the corrupted element 'from his nature,
And in those blood baths bequeathed to us by the Romans,
And which the mighty recall when they grow old,
He has not been able to restore warmth to this dulled corpse
In which, in place of blood, the green water of Lethe flows.

The poem is clearly depicting the French state; the "I" of the poem being France and the condition of its politics in post-revolutionary times is described as "a rainy country," that is, dull and gray. The I's identity is confirmed in the line "His bed adorned with fleurs-de-lis becomes a tomb;" the fleurs-de-lis, symbol of France covers its people as though a nation dead. The condition of the country is further characterized and delineated with words and phrases of such negative connotations as "dogs," "animals," "people dying opposite his balcony," (reminiscent of Marie Antoinette's inflammatory rhetoric prior to the revolution), "cruel invalid," "shameless costume," "young skeleton," "corrupted element," "blood baths," "dulled corpse," "place of blood" and finally the deadening sleep of the "Lethe" in the underworld. Baudelaire's emphasis on the seamier side of life and its use in his poetry was explained by him in a single phrase from the introduction to *Les Fleurs du Mal*, "...to extract beauty from evil." Just as Poe, Baudelaire's inspiration, was able to conjure beautiful prose imagery from sordid subjects, so too did Baudelaire; as shown above when he uses carefully chosen phraseology to create at first reading, a beautiful piece of verse, but on second reading to present the reader with the base sight of a rotting corpse.

This theme of Beauty from Evil is again utilized in conjunction with another Baudelairian and symbolist motif; that of nature as infinitely unknowable.

And now the depth of the sky consternates me; its lim- pidity exasperates me. The insensitivity of the sea, the immutability of the whole scene revolts me...Ah! is it necessary to suffer eternally, or to flee the beautiful eternally? Nature, pitiless enchantress, rival always victorious, let me go! Refrain from tempting my desires and my pride! The study of the beautiful is a duel where the artist screams in terror before being vanquished.

In this excerpt from *Le Confiteor De L'Artiste,* Baudelaire at once juxtaposes the infinite and unknowable universe of Nature (the sky, the sea) with his concept of Beauty from Evil. Though the sky is "limpid," the sea "immutable," and Nature an "enchantress" yet the whole thing "revolts me" and forces the speaker to "flee the beautiful eternally." Baudelaire had stood the poetic ideal on its head and soon other young artists would follow his example and, decades later, Smith as well.

Having stated his position in much of his correspondence his attitude to the human race and his pessimism toward any of its more altruistic motives, Clark Ashton Smith clearly sympathized with Baudelaire's depressing and contradictory world view as well as his poetic method of expressing it. The contrast of beauty and the grotesque became a constant motif in almost the entire body of his work, with the following excerpt from "Soliloquy in an Ebon tower," fittingly addressed to Baudelaire, a perfect example:

In my room

The quick, malign, relentless clock ticks on,
Firm as a demon's undecaying pulse,
Or creak of Charon's oar-locks as he plies
Between the shadow-crowded shores. Evoked
Within the vaults of my funereal brain,
Voices awaken, sibilant and restless—
Tongues of the viper's charnel-fostered brood,
Half-grown, amid the shreds of winding sheets
And crumbling wicker of old bones. They sing,
Those little voices, all the poisonous,
Importunate melodies you too have heard,
O Baudelaire, in midnights when the moon
Sank, followed by some cloudy hearse of dreams,
Into the skyless nadir of despond.
Black-flickering, cloven tongues! Though we
Distill
Quintessences of hemlock or nepenthe,
We cannot slay the small, the subtle serpents
Whose mother is the lamia Melancholy
That feeds upon our breath and sucks our veins,
Stifling us with her velvet volumes.

Stephan Mallarme was born in Paris in 1842 becoming a teacher of English as an adult. Like Baudelaire, he fell under the sway of Edgar Allen Poe and quickly developed his own poetic style that yet owed much to Baudelaire. In his *Confiteor*, Baudelaire explains his idea of Infinite Nature as horrifying and beautiful, that he is revolted at its insensitive immensity. Mallarme grasps this concept also, and extends it still further; from the example of Baudelaire's Nature as a recognizable bridge into the infinite, to his own totally abstract thoughts on language and Truth.

In a letter to Francois Copee, Mallarme writes: "And now having arrived at the horrible vision of the pure work, I have about lost my mind and all contact with the meaning of the most common ways of speaking." Language as we understand it has lost its meaning in its total inadequacy in explaining the unknown of the poet's "nothingness." "An undeniable urge of my time is to separate, in view of divergent attributes, the two-fold status of language; on the one hand, the crude or immediate, and, on the other hand, the essential." Thus Mallarme developed his theory of language. That certain words could have at once their literal meaning, and their intrinsic, connotative meaning. The poet will from now on strive for the ideal work of language and, in doing so, move away from ordinary forms of everyday speech. This direction of movement, from the literal to the ideal, from the limited to the Infinite, from the mask of reality as we see it to the Truth is implied by Mallarme as somehow horrible to behold; echoing the sentiments of Baudelaire who is revolted at the sight of naked Truth. Not many men can behold the face of the Medusa and live.

Apparition

The moon grew sad, Seraphim in tears,
Dreaming, the bow in their fingers, in the calm of the vaporous
Flowers, drew from dying viols
White sighs gliding on the azure of the corollas.
—It was the blessed day of your first kiss.
My daydream, taking pleasure in torturing me,
Became knowingly drunk on that perfume of sadness
Which even without regret and without disappointment is left
By the culling of a Dream in the heart that has culled it.
Thus I wandered, my eyes fixed on the pavement grown old,
When with sunlight in your hair, in the street
And in the evening, you appeared to me laughing

And I thought I saw the fairy with the hat of brightness
Who once would pass through my beautiful spoiled-
child's
Slumbers, always letting her not-quite-closed hands
Snow down white bouquets of perfumed stars.

"I am in Truth on a voyage, but in unknown lands, and if I
like to evoke cold images in order to escape from torrid reality
I should tell you that for a month now I have been in the purest
of glaciers of Aesthetics....that after having found nothingness,
I have found the beautiful...and that you cannot imagine the
lucid altitudes in which I venture." "Apparition" seems to touch
on that absolute nothingness as Mallarme takes the most
common subject matter of poetry, the first young love, and in a
symphony of words, uses language to paint in the mind's eye
the sweep of the cosmos and the infinity of "white bouquets of
perfumed stars."

In a letter to Samuel J. Sackett, Smith explains his
thoughts on language and his sources for proper names by
saying: "I hope I have made it plain that my use of rare and
exotic words has been solely in accord with an aesthetic theory,
or, one might say, a technical theory." One derived from his
readings of Mallarme, perhaps? Furthermore, in the same letter
Smith echoes both Baudelaire's and Mallarme's contention of
the horrifying nature of cosmic truth when he says, "...if the
infinite worlds of the cosmos were opened to human vision, the
visionary would be overwhelmed by horror in the end, like the
hero of ('The Hashish Eater')."

Arthur Rimbaud became the link between the symbolists
and the surrealists; cherishing the new-found freedom
bequeathed by Baudelaire and Mallarme and anticipating its
exploration by the coming of Verlaine and Eluard. This
intoxication with symbolism and the open armed acceptance of
Surrealism is best illustrated in Rimbaud's "Departure."

Departure

Enough seen. The vision was met with in every clime.
Enough had. Sounds of cities, in the evening, and in
the sun, and always.
Enough known. The decrees of life.—0 Sounds and
Visions!
Departure in new affection and new noise!

In his "Enough seen...Enough had...Enough known..." the
poet expresses his exuberant satisfaction with life and work and
announces his readiness to accept new experiences: "Departure
in new affection and new noise!" But where Baudelaire's
experience of art was based on Nature and Mallarme on
language, Rimbaud's was grounded in work, labor, the
everyday toil of the proletariat in the new mechanistic society.

Born in 1854, Rimbaud was tyrannized as a child by his
mother, forcing him to leave home twice in adolescence.
Beginning to write early (he would complete his entire output
of poetry before the age of 20), he soon met up with the
celebrated decadent and salon patron, Paul Verlaine in a life of
bohemian, homosexual, hashish ridden travel and developed
his ideas on the poet-seer as the true arbiter of the modern (read
industrial) world. In 1870 he completed his collection of short
prose poems "Illuminations" and in 1873 (after a stormy
farewell to Verlaine that ended with Verlaine's being shot in
the wrist), wrote his masterpiece and final contribution to verse
Un Saison en Enfer (A Season in Hell).

Ostensibly a collection of poetic prose work with veiled
allusions of his relationship with Verlaine and their drugged
travels, it is actually Rimbaud's paean to the working class, as
A Season in Hell could very easily be seen as a good
description of nineteenth century steel works and other
difficult, labor intensive work. (Europe at the time was just
entering the full vigor of the industrial age with expanding steel

and munitions works across the land, especially in Germany where the giant Krupp works armed the Prussian *Wermacht*, a country quite possibly visited by the young poet).

But *Un Saison en Enfer* was ultimately the work of a disillusioned man. Unable to "change life" or "reinvent love" Rimbaud at age 20 gave up writing to "embrace rugged reality." Living what he wrote, that in physical labor does man find the purest expression (reading Rimbaud, one is often reminded of another artist who found physical labor as somehow mystical, Millet; both men felt the elemental spirit of being close to Nature in simple toil). And so, Rimbaud spent the rest of his life traveling the world seeking work. In England, Germany, Italy, Denmark, Sweden, and Egypt. In 1878 he worked in a quarry in Cypress; from 1880 to 1891 he was a trader; an explorer in eastern Ethiopia; in 1891 he returned to France with a tumor in the leg, dying from it despite the limb's amputation. In "My Bohemia," written in 1870, Rimbaud describes the uncontrollable urge to wander that prophetically illustrated his world travels after 1873.

Mv Bohemia (Fantasy)

I went off, my fists in my torn pockets;
My overcoat, too, became ideal;
I walked beneath the sky, Muse! and I was your liege;
Oh ho! What splendid love affairs I dreamed of!

My only pair of trousers had a wide hole.
—A daydreaming Hop o' My Thumb, I strung out rhymes
As I went along. My inn was on the Big Dipper.
—My stars in the sky had a sweet rustling

And I listened to them, as I sat by the roadsides,
Those good September evenings when I felt drops
Of dew on my forehead like a heady wine;

When, rhyming amid the fantastic shadows,
Like lyres I pulled the elastic bands

Of my wounded shoes, a foot close to my heart!

On the road to the surrealists however, the symbolists had to cross the barren landscape of the Decadents and Existentialists. Of the former, its leading exponent was the psychologically erratic Paul Verlaine. Writing verse since the age of 14, (his most uninspired work coming at the end of his life but paradoxically, his glory grew as his poetic powers waned), fits of violence, alcoholism, and homosexuality all contributed to his *Romances Sans Paroles* ("Songs Without Words") his most admired work and the most personally hellish. It was this volume and later works of outspoken pornography that established him as the leader of the poetic school of decadence.

In "Geometries," Smith skirted the borders of Verlainian decadence with a deft mix of eroticism and intellectualism:

Your body and mine, upon the bed opposed,
Presented changing forms and lines Euclidean.

Our heads' irregular and hairy spheres
Pillowed in close conjunction, or describing
Tangents, diagonals, parabolas,
In the unresting play of love.

And lastly,
The lingham's rigid rectilinear line
Bisecting the yoni's cloven, soft triangle.

All these were figures formed in time,
Figures that changed and vanished,
And passed, perhaps, into eternity,
Rejoining their Platonic absolutes.

And afterward
You went away, and I was left to ponder
On love's geometries of straight and curved.

Guillaume Appolinaire was born in 1880, the illegitimate son of an Italian nobleman and Polish girl. Never seeing his father again after 1885, he became a tutor and finally a journalist, writing erratic verses on the side. In 1914, Appolinaire enlisted in the French army and was wounded in the head and discharged. He died of influenza two days before the armistice. But in his short years, Appolinaire was able to help bridge the gap between the Symbolists and the Surrealists with many fine works. Among them *Les Calchiques* (The Meadow-Saffrons) a work that juxtaposes the innocence of youth alongside the spectre of death.

The Meadow-Saffrons

The meadow is poisonous but pretty in autumn
The cows grazing there
Are slowly poisoned
The meadow-saffron like bruised flesh and lilacs in
color
Blooms there your eyes are like that flower
Purplish like their dark ring and like this autumn
And my life for your eyes is slowly poisoned
The schoolchildren come with a clatter
Dressed in smocks and playing the harmonica
They pick the saffrons which are like mothers
Daughters of their daughters and are the color of your
eyelids
Which beat as the flowers beat in the crazy wind
The keeper of the herd sings very softly
While slowly and lowing the cows abandon
For ever this great meadow with its evil autumn
flowers

From the ranks of the decadents came the first two surrealists, Paul Eluard and Aragon. Surrealism attempted to express the workings of the subconscious with the use of fantastic imagery and incongruous contrast of its subject matter. The latter has already been touched upon in Appolinaire's *Les Calchiques* with its poisonous flowers and young girls. Though Elouard has been acclaimed the greatest of the surrealists (his range of free floating images created patterns of meaningful and emotional boldness; a form of stream of consciousness adapted to verse) he early on abandoned the form in his love of Communism. But in *Le Phenix,* ("The Pheonix"), those free-floating images are immediately recognizable and lend a very personal and individualistic interpretation to the poem.

The Phoenix

The Phoenix is the couple—Adam and Eve—which is
and is not the first.

I am the last on your path
The last springtime the last snow
The last struggle not to die

And here we are lower and higher than ever.

There is a little of everything in our pyre
Pine cones vine shoots
But also flowers stronger than water

Mud and dew.

The flame is beneath our feet the flame crowns us
At our feet insects birds men
Will fly away

Those who fly will alight.

The sky is bright the earth is dark
But the smoke goes up to the sky
The sky has lost all its fires

The flame has remained on earth.

The flame is the heart's cloud

And all the blood's branches
It sings our melody

It dispels the vapor of our winter.

In night and horror anguish blazed
The ashes have bloomed in joy and beauty
We still turn our back to the sunset

Everything has the color of dawn.

Aragon was an army surgeon during the First World War
and later as he began to write, became the most brilliant of the
Dadaist and Surrealist writers. Like Elouard, Aragon joined the
Communist Party and during the Second World War, achieved
the zenith of his Surrealistic powers. In "Les Lilas et les
Roses," ("The Lilacs and the Roses") first printed in the
collection *Le Creve-Coeur* in 1941, Aragon successfully and
spectacularly uses the Surrealist device of juxtaposition in
almost every line of the piece, creating one of the most
exquisitely balanced works of poetry in all of literature. One
can almost see the plane on the fulcrum. Its fantastic imagery
almost hides the fact that the poem was written to commemo-
rate the retreat from the Battle of the North and the fall of
Paris. In fact, only the word "tank" in line six, "turrets" in line
ten, and "cannons" in line eighteen serve to remind us that this
story takes place at a particular moment in time, and in a sort of
every-time. Finally, the use of simple language (not
immediately apparent in the translation), in the Alexandrine
meter brings the poetic innovations of the past one hundred
years (Baudelaire's first published work was in 1845, *Les Lilac
et les Roses* in 1941) full circle to the roots of French verse.

The Lilacs and the Roses

O months of flowerings months of metamorphoses
May that was cloudless and June that was stabbed
I shall never forget the lilacs or the roses

Or those whom the spring kept within its folds

I shall never forget the tragic illusion
The cortege of cries the crowd and the sun
The tanks burdened with love the gifts of Belgium
The trembling air and the road with that humming of
bees
The thoughtless triumph that anticipates the conflict
The blood prefigured in carmine by the kiss
And those who are to die standing in the turrets
Encircled with lilacs by an intoxicated multitude

I shall never forget the gardens of France
Like the missals of vanished centuries
Or the agitation on the evenings the enigma of the
silence
The roses all along the road that was traveled
The flowers that gave the lie to the wind of panic
To the soldiers passing by on the wing of fear
To the frenzied bicycles to the ironic cannons
To the pitiful get-up of the mock campers

But I do not know why this whirlwind of images
Always leads me back to the same stopping place
To Sainte-Marthe a general black patterns of foliage
A Norman villa at the edge of the forest
Everything is still the enemy is resting in the shade
We were told this evening that Paris has surrendered
I shall never forget the lilacs or the roses
Or the two loves that we have lost

Bouquets of the first day lilacs of Flanders
Sweetness of the shade whose cheeks death rouges
And you bouquets of the retreat tender roses
Color of far-off fires roses of Anjou

As was said at the beginning of this piece, there is little
doubt that Clark Ashton Smith drew more than a passing
inspiration from the French romantics; it is also true that after

the passing of his friend, George Sterling and the San Francisco literary circle of which he was a member, Smith became almost the sole disciple and practicioner of romantic poetry in the United States. The country had less and less time to spare on the ephemeral fantasies of its poets after the twin tragedies of two world wars; in a new world that was to be dominated by the spectre of the atom bomb, a hard-edged realism would be the criterion. But Smith, perhaps rightly, saw in the delicate word-tapestries of the romantic tradition an esoteric language rich in connotative power that would serve him well during his most creative years. After all, he said more than once that the modern world could claim none of his affection; the poisonously exotic worlds of his imagination at least had their hauntingly beautiful sides as well, while the real world held only the cold, careless touch of an increasingly mechanistic society. But if the French romantic tradition had to have its last echo, what better legacy for its admirers than to have had Clark Ashton Smith as its final arbiter!

Beyond the Clouds Lie the Pastures of the Sun: Robert Ervin Howard

Somewhere outside, a cock crowed. In the narrow bed against the rear wall, Robert Howard held his eyes tightly shut and stretched his arms in pleasurable exaggeration. The cock crowed again and the boy yawned contentedly as he threw back the bedclothes and swung his feet to the cold linoleum floor. Pausing a minute there on the edge of his bed, he looked out over the backyard through the row of windows on the opposite wall. The long field of dried and bedraggled grass stretched along the road to the right. A thin, early morning mist covered the ground as the sky in the east lightened, presaging the coming of the Texan sun. Slowly, the boy rose and began preparing for school; for a moment as he dressed, he felt the absence of his cousin, Earl Lee Comer, who had shared his previous bedroom for years when he lived with the Howard family. Robert did not particularly miss him since his cousin graduated from the Cross Plains school system and found a job in Dallas. After a quick trip to the bathroom, he collected his books and crossing his parents' bedroom, entered the little kitchen, already smelling of eggs and bacon. His mother placed a dish on the table before him and after gulping down the food and with a cheerful goodbye, Robert ran from the house into the crisp morning air, screen door slamming noisily on the front porch. Outside, under the branches of the big cedar tree and leaning against the peeling picket fence, were his friends, Lindsey Tyson and Tom Ray Wilson. At Robert's spirited hello, the two boys straightened and, tossing their books over their shoulders, broke into smiles echoing their friend's greeting. Together, the three friends walked to the nearby school along the newly graded road, merging with fellow students as they neared the schoolhouse.

So began another long day at school. Long for young Robert whose natural hardheadedness and creativity found the constraints of conventional education a heavy cross to bear indeed. And though he tried his best, he could not bring himself to excel in any subject save one. To Robert, the one exception, the one subject that fired his imagination and fueled his desire to put on paper and make come alive in words and prose (an ability he had developed a knack for) was history. To him, Alexander and Ceasar, Washington and Houston, were alive and vibrant. The Peloponesian War and Punic Wars, the Revolution and Indian Wars happened just yesterday. He excelled in history. Other classes were places not to be attentive, but to dream and plot of heroes bold and brave striding across the globe, making and changing history; heroes of his own creation whom he had committed to paper such as El Borak and Bran Mak Morn. Stories and adventures already having been sent and returned from the big magazines in the faraway cities of the east, New York and Chicago. But the dry, hot days of summer would soon arrive, and with them, at last, graduation and he would be free from the dreary classroom for good and able to devote all his spare time to writing.

Finally, after a seeming eternity, the school day ended and the students poured into the dusty schoolyard, some to linger, others to drift home. Robert found himself walking along Main Street, swirls of dust pirouetting from its unpaved surface in the light breeze. The afternoon sun grew increasingly hot as spring wore on to summer. Finally, Robert bid adieu to his companions with a promise of meeting them later at Tom's house.

Walking leisurely south on Main Street, Robert passed the two town banks, the First State Bank and the Farmers National. Across the street, the Higginbotham Department Store stood with its tan brick building baking in the sun. Expensive looking clothing, popular with city-slickers thought Robert, draped the sexless mannequins in its big windows. A few horse drawn wagons and a couple of automobiles stood outside with equal patience. The spires of the little town churches peeked over some rooftops; not a special achievement since all of the buildings lining Main Street were of a single story. Switching his books from his right to his left hand, Robert stepped up out of the street onto the steps of City Drug Store and entered the cool interior. Dusty hardwood flooring received the clump-clump of his workbooted feet as he moved unerringly to the magazine rack, pausing only long enough to wave to the proprietor. The initial dark of the drugstore brightened as his eyes accustomed themselves to the dim light; the myriad smells and aromas of medicinal supplies, unwrapped foods, fresh fruit, ice-cream, tobacco, and paper nearly overwhelmed his sense of smell. But he did not mind because the smells reminded him of the pleasurable anticipation he always felt for the latest issue of *Adventure Magazine;* a feeling that forced his mind back to the first time he had discovered the gaudily covered pulp magazine. He had found himself in the drugstore one afternoon when he had run out of books to read. A voracious reader, he read almost everything he could lay hands on; as a conse-quence, in a town with a population no larger than 1,500 he had soon exhausted its meager supply of books and had resorted to rereading many of them. Then one day, he suddenly realized magazines could be read also, and after reading half of that issue of *Adventure* in the store, he bought it, or rather, charged it. Paying for it on the arrival of the subsequent number, he then charged the newer issue. After that, it had not been long before the idea struck him to submit his own stories of El Borak and Bran Mak Morn to the magazine, but with his first rejection slips, he discovered how difficult it would be to see his yarns published.

Now, dragging his eyes across the scores of gaudily colored magazines that crammed the display rack to bursting, he saw many titles that promised action and excitement unparalleled for only a thin dime. Which to choose? *Blue Book, Black Mask, Detective Story, Saucy Stories, Weird Tales, Strange Tales, Argosy.*

Finally he found the one he wanted, almost completely camouflaged amidst the colorful spread: *Adventure Magazine.* Heart thumping in anticipation, he took the copy furthest to the rear of the batch, where they were less thumbed, and threaded his way back through the maze of wire wrapped bundles of newspapers and magazines to the end of the soda counter, where a group of little girls giggled excitedly while picking a nickel's worth of penny candy from the huge assortment behind a glass case. Paying his dime for the previous month's *Adventure* and charging for the new one, he left the drug store and stepped out into the street. The walk home seemed short that afternoon as he thumbed eagerly through the magazine looking for his favorite authors (there was a new Howard Lamb story!) and let his feet guide him to his house through back lots and familiar streets.

At home, he said hello to his mother as she swung contentedly on the porch swing and made a beeline to the kitchen; the precious magazine having been deposited in his room. A quick glass of milk and he was out again to meet Tom and Lindsey in the woods just down the road but was delayed by the approach of the ice wagon. After a few moments of mock argument with the delivery man, his efforts were rewarded with a large lump of crystal clear ice and, juggling it from hand to hand, he dashed back to the house for a napkin to hold it with. Later, sitting on the front stoop and sucking appreciatively on his chunk of ice, Robert waved thanks to the ice man and watched as he walked to the neighbor's house, the horse pulling his wagon faithfully following, long since having memorized the route.

At last, finished with the ice, mouth aching with cold, Robert waved to his mother and trotted down the road to meet his friends. The final hours of the late spring afternoon were filled with imaginary adventures he had cooked up and turns at riding a neighbor's horse. At last, as the sun hung low in the west and lights twinkled in homes all across the little town, the calls of mothers at kitchen doors drifted forlornly over field and scrub and the three friends separated for the evening, exhausted from the rigors of play.

Entering through the kitchen door at the rear of the house, Robert saw his father already sitting at the table, napkin tucked in the collar of his shirt. His mother was just setting down a steaming bowl of mashed potatoes and the radio muttered in the corner. Supper was conducted amid recitals of the day's activities and concluded by a warning from his father to finish his homework before reading any dime novels. Later, rushing through homework of math and grammar and history, Robert left the company of the kitchen for the privacy of his room. There, he settled before his "worktable," shoving a sheet of paper into his rickety Underwood typewriter and paused a minute or so contemplating the black sky outside his bedroom windows where dim stars gleamed high overhead. Somewhere beyond the horizon, hundreds of miles away, big towns and bustling metropolises still throbbed with vibrant life even as Cross Plains wrapped itself in gloom to sleep. But Robert did not need to see those cities or to know first hand their inhabitants. He already knew of fabled Carthage and Rome, Pompeii and Athens, the Danube and the Nile, the Matterhorn and Everest. He knew of Picts and Roman Legions, of Spartans and knights errant. Even of men and gods.

And gradually, from those dreamy heights, Robert's thoughts returned to Earth and his old Underwood and as his fingers began to poke at its keys, he acquainted himself with one of those figures out of history as Solomon Kane whispered to him his story...

Robert E. Howard and the Southern Folk Tradition

"Black Canaan" and "Pigeons From Hell" are Robert E. Howard's two most powerfully compelling tales. Though Howard is justly renowned for his other stories of Americana, most notably his tall tales of the American west featuring Breckinridge Elkins, these two stories are perhaps closer to his roots than any other. Despite frequent avowals of his association to the Gaelic tradition by blood, and his identification with John Wesley Hardin of the American west, his association with the old South both through actual blood ties and the early recitation to him of ghost stories by his relatives proved the strongest. And though only two real stories of the South came from his pen, the sheer power and force of their narration easily mark them as Howard's greatest tales and those actually closest to his personal sensibilities. It is no coincidence that both stories involve elements of the supernatural and that both dwell on the contrasts of White and Black culture (and their inevitable inter-relations), the dark, oppressive quality of Nature and the once aristocratically genteel lifestyle of the great plantations. All formed strong currents of creativity and influence in young Howard as he grew up in the small west Texas town where he lived, a lone poetic spirit among a citizenry apathetic and sometimes hostile to him.

Howard's emphasis on folk tradition in his many tales certainly is not unique to storytelling. Thousands of years before the rise of civilization, when primitive man huddled fearfully about his campfire, information was passed verbally from person to person. Mostly information of the utilitarian sort: Where were the best hunting grounds? Who had killed the largest bison? Who had died on the hunt that day? Quite possibly the earliest known non-verbal communication between men was in the art of cave painting. Though cave paintings are fairly common throughout the world, those in southern France seem to be the most numerous. Though the subject matter was mostly man hunting beasts, these cave paintings accurately portray the urgency of early man's efforts to communicate. This urgency was quickly transferred mainly to verbal communication as the spoken word became a more versatile instrument for the passing on of information. Soon, early religious rites were secretly being passed on from master to student, each jealously guarding the information. Great feats of heroism were told by father to son, and finally, fanciful tales of strange forces and stranger beasts growing out of a lack of understanding of the natural world were used to explain the unexplainable. Systems of belief, stories of great heroes, were told to succeeding generations, each adding and refining the tradition until whole epics, taking many hours for a person to recite were created. All races and countries seem to have developed such epic tales. The Welsh with the Mabinogean, the English with Beowulf, the Germans with the Ring Saga, the French with the Song of Roland, the Italians with Orlando Furioso, the Spanish with El Cid, the Sumerians with Gilgamesh.

But aside from these great national epics, whole systems of minor and disjointed legends have grown. Where the epics told of fierce fighting, gloomy lands and tragic events, these other legends were mostly humorous or imparted useful information to the uneducated peasants of pre-industrial Europe. Little people abounded. Elves, dwarves, trolls, leprechauns. All with their attendant do's and don'ts. Popular formulas for curing the pox or for finding a lover abounded. But there seemed to be a division between those who embraced the folk tradition and those who disregarded them for the more important historical epics. As civilization spread, the gap between the two grew wider until the intellectual class turned their collective backs on popular folklore and accepted the epics as the sole source of ancient, pre-civilized art to be respected. Folklore was left largely to the ignorant peasant.

Under the constant pressure of collective disdain, folklore lost much of its cultural force. Peasants became farmers and land holders, merchants and artisans, and the traditions of folklore were transformed into fantastic tales told to children at bedtime. In contrast, the part of folklore dealing with more practical matters of cures and signs, were still held by most people to be true even if the admission was never spoken aloud. As the migration of Europeans spread all over the world and in particular to North America, people brought many of these still extent folk traditions with them.

The evolution of American folkloric tradition thus had its origin in two important developments resulting from the great influx of immigration. One was the early settlement of America by a variety of peoples, mainly European but later Asian with each group importing their own special folk traditions: the Spanish in the far west, the British in the northeast, the French in the midwest, and everywhere, that of the American Indian. The second development, uniquely American, involved the sheer size of the American continent. At first unsuspected by early European colonists, the eventual realization of the size of the American continent staggered the European mind. Used to centuries of civilization, one built upon the ruins of the other, Europeans had long lost their sense of the isolation and the anarchism of the wilderness. There were no more lands that lay hidden in the Old World, no roads not yet traveled. But in America, all was new, primeval, and what was more, vast beyond comprehension. The single state of Texas for instance, could encompass the entire land area of Europe and it was possible that a single rancher there could own land greater in size than some European countries. In this new land everything was big; plains, rivers, mountains. Consequently, American folklore grew to match the size of the land. Davy Crockett and Daniel Boone assumed the proportions of Roland and Beowulf with their heroic deeds, Pecos Bill rides a tornado, Paul Bunyan carves out the great plains and raises the Rocky Mountains, famous gunslingers rack up an unbelievable tally of corpses. Thus the folk tradition came to America, changed, and adapted itself to the needs of a new breed of men. But different parts of America and different regions of the country saw the formation of their own peculiar variations of folk myths.

The American South had existed for over two hundred years as a dual society. The dominant portion of this society was made up of the White, aristocratic land owning gentry and their less prosperous cousins who were predominantly small landholders. While the plantation owner held the choice bottom lands and many of the port facilities, the backwoodsman worked the undeveloped land farther inland. The other, powerless, half of the society were the Black slaves held in bondage mostly by the large landowners. The slaves had no rights of their own, but lived as the property of their White masters. Largely uneducated, slaves were obliged to teach themselves what they could and as a result, much of their knowledge was derived from the folk tales of their native Africa fused to what they could pick up from White society.

In time, a dual folk culture arose as well. The folklore of the Whites assumed that of an aristocratic European tradition. Perhaps the most widely known folk tradition of the Old South is told in the anecdote of the Mississippi planter who was once asked by a visitor if he knew where a night's lodging could be found, to which the planter replied, "Why at any house in the state sir." Aside from its legendary hospitality, the Old South held the values of European aristocracy as its highest aspirations; of these, the one that became a legend among the gentlemen planters was that of dueling. Duels were fought over trifling insults, a rude word, a wrong glance, or a mere brush against another. At first, duels were fought with rapiers, later with rifles, shotguns, pistols, and eventually the very American tradition of hand to hand combat with the Bowie knife.

Black folklore on the other hand, was richer and more varied. Composed of their relatively recent memories of Africa coupled with their lives as slaves, Blacks took what they saw of the White lifestyle they could only view from a distance and the little education they received in Christianity to invent a system of stories and anecdotes intended to define their status in Southern society or to make sense of the inexplicable. Humorous stories such as that of B'rer Rabbit, Jack O'Lantern, and stories about the smart slave who gets the best of his master were enduring favorites. But there were also the dark tales of ghost mansions, voodoo men, cotton magic, Plateye who attacked wayfarers, evil spells, and curses. It was these latter stories that were told first-hand to the young Robert Howard by his family's Black cook, Mary Bohannen, herself born into slavery.

Howard was a natural storyteller, turning out stories and tales of exotic adventure, sports, and horror at a prolific rate. It came easy to him; indeed, he once said it was the only thing he could do. For hours, and sometimes days, he would work at his typewriter turning out page after page of prose and poetry; almost never revising a piece once completed. Instead, if unsatisfied, he would put it aside and create a whole new yarn. He manipulated words like other men did wood, fashioning them, polishing and fitting them together in seamless wholes until he had a finished product. And after the impulse to create had been torn from his heart, ripped from his experience, drawn from a longing only someone stranded in a small Texas oil town in the Depression ridden 1930s could have, his best work was inevitably dazzling in its simple virtuosity. In "Robert Ervin Howard: A Memoriam," H.P. Lovecraft defined Howard's qualities this way:

It is hard to describe precisely what made Mr. Howard's stories stand out so sharply; but the real secret is that he himself is in every one of them, whether they were ostensibly commercial or not. He was greater than any profit-making policy he could adopt...for even when he outwardly made concessions to Mammon-guided editors and commercial critics, he had an internal force and sincerity which broke through the surface and put the imprint of his personality on everything he wrote. Seldom, if ever, did he set down a lifeless stock character or situation and leave it as such. Before he concluded with it, it always took on some tinge of vitality and reality in spite of popular editorial policy...always drew something from his own experience and knowledge of life instead of from the sterile herbarium of desiccated pulpish standbys. Not only did he excel in pictures of slaughter, but he was almost alone in his ability to create real emotions of spectral fear and dread suspense.

Robert E. Howard was born in West Texas and grew up in the small oil town of Cross Plains. Having few friends and even fewer distractions, he took to reading avidly at an early age; reenacting many of the tales he read later on excursions into the neighboring wilderness. With little time spent in college, Howard filled in the blank areas of his education by reading voraciously in his favorite subject areas: Irish lore and Southwestern history. His interest in the American southwest began when he was a small boy listening to hair raising tales of ghosts and horror told by his grandmother, Eliza Howard:

"No Negro ghost story ever gave me the horrors as did the tales told by my grandmother. All the gloominess and dark mysticism of the Gaelic nature was hers, and there was no...light and mirth in her. Her tales showed what a strange legion of folklore grew up in the Scotch-Irish settlements of the Southwest, where transplanted Celtic myths and fairy tales met and mingled with a substratum of slave legends.

The Last Celt

Indeed, "Pigeons from Hell" is based on a number of these very recollections. In L. Sprague DeCamp's *Dark Valley Destiny*, the author cites another influential source of folk tales for Howard, the family's Black cook, Mary Bohannon.

(Mary Bohannon) had ghost stories enough to produce a neverending tingle down the spine. A plantation house haunted by a headless giant; footseps heard when no one else was present; rattling chains, chill winds, hot blasts; dismembered bodies; groans, moans, and other eerie sounds…all were part of (Bohannon's) repertoire.

These stories made a strong impression on the young Howard, and though he wrote few stories using elements from

Bohannon's repertoire, the raw power in those that he did is such that there can be little doubt about how close to the author's heart those eerie legends were.

As to the historical feel of his stories, though others have pointed out their blatant and sometimes offensive characterizations, they are undeniably real. Howard himself regarded historical writing as his ultimate element of literary expression.

There is no literary work, to me, half as zestful as rewriting history in the guise of fiction. I wish I was able to devote the rest of my life to that kind of work. I could write a hundred years and still there would be stories clamoring to be written, by the scores... I try to write as true to the actual facts as possible; at least I try to commit as few errors as possible. I like to have my background and setting as accurate and realistic as I can, with my limited knowledge; if I twist too much, alter dates as some writers do, or present a character out of keeping with my impressions of the time and place, I lose my sense of reality, and my characters cease to be living and vital things; and my stories center entirely on my conception of my characters. Once I lose the "feel" of my characters, I might as wall tear up what I have written. And once I have a definite conception of a character in my mind, it destroys the feeling of reality to have that individual act in any manner inconsistent with the character in which I have visualized him. My characters do and say illogical and inconsistent things...inconsistent as far as general things go...but they are consistent to my conception of them.

In "Pigeons from Hell," Howard takes a number of the different folk elements told to him by his grandmother and puts them together to create a seamless whole: the dead man descending the staircase of an old plantation house at midnight, the wicked woman who sadistically mistreats her slaves, strange sounds and whistlings from behind closed doors, and the ghostly pigeons flying in the night.

The story itself tells of two northern travelers stopping to rest for the night at an abandoned mansion. As they approach the entrance, there is a foreshadowing of events to come as the two friends see "...pigeons (rise) from the balustrades in a fluttering, feathery crowd and (sweep) away with a low thunder of beating wings." Later in the story, the sheriff explains:

"I've seen men who'd swore they'd seen a flock of pigeons perched along the balustrades just at sundown, "...The niggers say they can see the pigeons, but no nigger would pass along this road between sun-down and sun-up. They say the pigeons are the souls of the Blassenvilles, let out of Hell at sunset. The niggers say the red glare in the west is the light from hell, because then the gates of hell are open and the Blassenvilles fly out."

As the story unfolds, one of the two friends is mysteriously killed. Later, after seeing his dead friend walking as a reanimated corpse, the second man flees the house into the arms of Sheriff Buckner. The sheriff investigates the wild story and concludes by the evidence and his knowledge of local folklore that there may be something in the man's story of a walking corpse. After a visit to the local "conjure man," the two return to the house and this time, it is the turn of the surviving friend to be effected by the curse. But before he can meet the same fate as his friend, he is saved by a timely shot from the sheriff into the body of the creature that has been inhabiting the house for fifty years.

In this story, Howard concentrates on the White, aristocratic folklore of the Old South as he weaves details told to him by his grandmother into a tale of allegory and mutual master-slave destruction. According to Howard's legend of the aristocratic Blassenville family, four sisters lived in the house after the Civil War with their former slaves still working the land. Pride, the bane of the pre-war southern aristocracy, prevented them from leaving the property or asking help to maintain it. Soon, a relative named Miss Celia arrives from the West Indies where the custom has been to treat slaves with great severity. Continuing the practice, Miss Celia takes sadistic pleasure in whipping her naked maid until one day, both mysteriously disappear. Soon afterward, Elizabeth, the youngest Blassenville sister, arrives in town and confesses her belief that Miss Celia is not gone but still in the house somewhere. Later, the three older sisters vanish one by one until Elizabeth, frightened, flees from the house. A thorough search of the premises by a posse yields nothing, but for the next fifty years, folklore has it that Miss Celia still remains in the house, waiting for a hapless victim to fall into her insane clutches. In the course of the story, the conjure man visited by Buckner tells about a mysterious visit by Joan, Miss Celia's maid, who had asked for a special brew by which the drinker would be turned into a deathless zombie. The conjure man assumes wrongly that the brew was meant for the maid, but instead, the maid gives it to her mistress and leaves the mansion. And as Sheriff Buckner says at the conclusion of the story:

"Griswell, I understand now; the mulatto woman had her revenge, but not as we'd supposed. She didn't drink the Black Brew old Jacob fixed for her. It was for somebody else, to be given secretly in her food, or coffee, no doubt. Then Joan ran away, leavin' the seeds of the hell she'd sowed to grow."

The allegorical threads of the story wind together to describe the slow fall of the Old South of folklore. The ruined plantation is antebellum south in microcosm. Just as the pre-war south lived in genteel ignorance of the coming holocaust, so too did the Blassenville family, and when disaster struck, neither were prepared for it. Aristocratic families such as the Blassenvilles fell with family members vanishing one by one until both the family and the land which had supported it lay fallow and empty for long years afterward. When Miss Celia arrived on the scene, she brought a renewal of the old ways as the South in general endured the rise of vigilantism and the Klan. Finally, the victim of Miss Celia's sadism turns on her and destroys her forever, as the homogenizing effects of American society softened the hard edges of the South. The past, although golden in memory, lay quite dead, as dead as the old Blassenville house.

The system that left one man master and another slave, eventually debased the Black man as well as his White master. As Miss Celia mistreated her mulatto maid, so did the maid mistreat her in turn. The former with torture, the latter with arcane magics. The system that in real life was the root of master-slave self-destruction, became an anachronism that ended in a paroxysm of violence and was personified by Howard in his portrayal of the two women.

Howard frames his tale of abuse, murder and revenge in a flight of pigeons:

From the balustrades of the gallery rose a whirling cloud of pigeons that swept away into the sunset, black against the lurid glare.

Both men sat rigid for a few moments after the pigeons had flown.

"Well, I've seen them at last," muttered Buckner.

"Only the doomed see them, perhaps..."

Of "Black Canaan," Lovecraft asked who, after reading it, could forget,

"...its genuine, regional background and its clutchingly compelling picture of the horror that stalks through the moss hung shadow-cursed, serpent-ridden swamps of the American far south.

But for all that, "Black Canaan" still must remain Howard's most powerful tale. With its opposing forces of White settlers and townspeople and Black backwoods folk carrying on their symbiotic relationship in a setting of dark, depressing swamp country, Howard's jack-hammer prose style pounds relentlessly forward, urging the two sides into inevitable conflict. The Whites, motivated by the fear of an uprising much as had occurred in the antebellum South and the Blacks terrified by a mysterious conjure man who threatens to bring back the primordial horror of ancient African folkways, are drawn together over a land as dark and oppressive as their own guilt ridden souls.

"Black Canaan" follows the story of a threatened Black uprising led by a mysterious conjure man named Saul Stark who uses voodoo magic to terrorize his followers into leaving their homes and joining him in the nearby swamps. The White population, led by prominent citizen Kirby Buckner, organizes for its defense. But Buckner (no relation to Sheriff Buckner in "Pigeons!") is hypnotized by a beautiful Black woman and in a particularly suspenseful sequence, is compelled to pass through the swamps into Stark's presence. There, Buckner witnesses the Dance of the Skull and the death of the woman who had captured him. Her death releases him from his hypnotic state however, and thus freed, he kills Stark and aborts the uprising.

Once again, the story's racism is often criticized but as Howard himself had once said, his overriding concern in writing period pieces was historical accuracy and in recreating the world of 1870 Arkansas, how could he draw an accurate picture without showing it with all of its prejudices? At the time, the post-Civil War South was still raw with open wounds and ancient hates still seethed close to the surface.

And so, due to his accurate depiction of life in the 1870's, Howard is able to set up a conflict of cultures between White settlers who live on neatly tilled farms or in town and Black backwoods people who either live deep in the jungle-like forest or beyond the farthest White farmstead. Ironically, Blacks live side by side with Whites in town, as their maids and servants. The old aristocracy has gone and only the smaller landowners remain in the region with Kirby Buckner's family assuming the leadership role in the community once reserved for the local plantation owner. As the story unfolds, the White community is motivated by old fears born of earlier slave uprisings while the Blacks, freed but in possession of only the most unwanted land, have retreated into the Ouachita River and Tulip Creek swamplands. Isolated from the civilizing effects of White society, Blacks living in the fringe areas have reverted to a quasi-primitive lifestyle reminiscent of the lives led by their forbears in Africa.

In the story, Howard sets the stage with a vivid description of the black and gloomy, piny woods; the stagnant, snake infested swamps and the ominous, rhythmic drumming that comes from deep in the forest. As the reader follows the White settlers into this ominous landscape, he feels more like he is entering the Dark Continent than the American bayous. Meanwhile, from his solitary hut deep in the swamps, Saul Stark, the conjure man, works his old magic, enthralling the local people. Howard had modeled Stark on folk tales of a huge, enigmatic Black shaman who had lived in Arkansas in the 1870's. The folklore of voodoo conjure men and aspects of Christianity had long been a powerful source of imagination and fear in the Old South, not only to the Black population, but to the Whites as well. Around 1830, Marie Laveau became the most successful of voodoo practitioners with a following of rich and well-born Whites parading to her door in a constant stream until her death in 1881. Thus, from the beginning of Howard's tale, the lines are drawn between the White community which still observes the frontier credo of eternal vigilance and self-dependency and the Black community which continues to live only a step removed from one form of slavery and another as they come together in a collision of cultures.

The story opens with Kirby Buckner on the road to the town of Goshen when he is met by a beautiful mulatto woman whose presence has a disquieting effect upon him:

...a strange turmoil of conflicting emotions stirred in me. I had never before paid any attention to a black or brown woman. But this quadroon girl was different from any I had ever seen. Her features were regular as a white woman's, and her speech was not that of a common wench. Yet she was barbaric, in the open lure of her smile, in the gleam of her eyes, in the shameless posturing of her voluptuous body. Every gesture, every motion she made set her apart from the ordinary run of women; her beauty was untamed and lawless, meant to madden rather than to soothe, to make a man blind and dizzy, to rouse in him all the un-reined passions that are his heritage from his ape ancestors.

The woman assumes the proportions of a Dark Eve, at once attractive and dangerous, offering undreamed of pleasure in return for betrayal. But Howard's description of this garden is hardly that of Eden. Dark and gloomy, it appears as the road to Hell should look, and the woman takes on the added significance of a satanic temptress, drawing Buckner from his duty, the promise of his family to the people of Goshen.

One of the most powerful and gripping scenes in the story is that of Buckner's mesmeric trek through that dark Eden of swamps and forest. Accompanying him is Jim Braxton, unaware that Buckner's single minded drive is the result of the witch woman's spell that compels him into the wilderness. As the two men stumble ever deeper into the swamps, through the morass of the lower Ouachita River, Howard paints an oppressive picture of inky blacks and shadowy grays:

With an oath he sprang toward the houses on the bank of the creek. I was after him just in time to glimpse a dark clumsy object scrambling or tumbling down the sloping bank into the water. Braxton threw up his long pistol, then lowered it, with a baffled curse. A faint splash marked the disappearance of the creature. The shiny black surface crinkled with spreading ripples.

....The pulse of the drum was fitful, growing more distinct as we advanced. We struggled through jungle-thick growth; tangled vines tripped us; our boots sank in scummy mire. We were entering the fringe of the swamp which grew deeper and denser until it culminated in the uninhabitable morass where the Tularoosa flowed into Black River, miles farther to the west.

...The moon had not yet set, but the shadows were black under the interlacing branches with their mossy beards. We plunged into the first creek we must cross, one of the many muddy streams flowing into the Tularoosa. The water was only thigh deep, the moss-clogged bottom fairly firm. My foot felt the edge of a sheer drop, and I warned Braxton: "Look out for a deep hole; keep right behind me."

His answer was unintelligible. He was breathing heavily, crowding close behind me. Just as I reached the sloping bank and pulled myself up by the slimy, projecting roots, the water was violently agitated behind me. Braxton cried out incoherently, and hurled himself up the bank, almost upsetting me. I wheeled, gun in hand, but saw only the black water seething and whirling, after his thrashing rush through it.

"What the devil, Jim?"

"Somethin' grabbed me!" he panted. "Somethin' out of the deep hole. I tore loose and busted up the bank. I tell you, Kirby, something's follerin' us! Somethin' that swims under the water."

At this point, Howard stacks the deck; after describing the realistic setting of the swamp, he next includes an element of the supernatural as the two men become aware of something following them beneath the black waters and with it, the oppressive reality of the landscape is suddenly transformed from one of a simple metaphor for evil to the real thing.

He splashed after me without comment. Scummy puddles rose about our ankles, and we stumbled over moss-grown cypress knees. Ahead of us there loomed another, wider creek, and Braxton caught my arm.

"Don't do it, Kirby!" he gasped. "If we go into that water it'll git us sure!"

...I climbed down the sloping bank and splashed into the water that rose to my hips. The cypress branches bent a gloomy moss-trailing arch over the creek. The water was black as midnight. Braxton was a blur, toiling behind me. I gained the first shelf of the opposite bank and paused, in water knee deep to turn and look back at him.

Everything happened at once, then. I saw Braxton halt short staring at something on the bank behind me. He cried out, whipped out a gun and fired, just as I turned. In the flash of the gun I glimpsed a supple form reeling backward, a brown face fiendishly contorted. Then in the momentary blindness that followed the flash, I heard Jim Braxton scream.

Sight and brain cleared in time to show me a sudden swirl of the murky water, a round, black object breaking the surface behind Jim...and then Braxton gave a strangled cry and went under with a frantic thrashing and splashing.

...As I struggled up I saw Braxton's head, now streaming blood, break the surface for an instant, and I lunged toward it.

It went under and another head appeared in its place, a shadowy black head. I stabbed at it ferociously, and my knife cut only the blank water as the thing dipped out of sight.

...Jim Braxton...was dead. It was not the wound in his head which had killed him... But the marks of strangling fingers showed black on his throat. At the sight a nameless horror oozed out of that black swamp water and coiled itself clammily about my soul; for no human fingers ever left such marks as those.

Once again, as in "Pigeons from Hell," Howard explores the theme of southern decadence as his White protagonist trudges through the swamp, his surroundings becoming more primitive as he goes. Finally, he arrives at the scene of the Dance of the Skull, symbolic end of the slide into decadence made by his Black foes. Thus, both sides meet on common ground, arriving there by different paths. The tangled swamp becomes a metaphor for the wrong path taken by Whites in the pre-emancipation South, with its moral compromises and deadly choices that seek to drag them down. Under this interpretation, the beautiful African woman who at once revolts and attracts Buckner now becomes the personification of the corrupting allure of the slave system; the Dance of the Skull stands in for the agonies of the Civil War; Buckner's soul laid bare, becomes the land ravaged and pillaged by Northern forces; Saul Stark is the haunting shadow of slavery that seeks to return the Black population to its former servile status, an evil the rest of the world has long condemned.

For the real essence of folk tradition in the American South, one must look past the more accessible and popular stories to the deeper motivations that inspired them. The cultural experience of the two peoples they involve is what forms genuine folk tradition and those currents run deep enough so that their influence, if only unconscious, will continue to influence writers such as Robert E. Howard for quite some time to come.

Nature As Evil In Hawthorne's "Young Goodman Brown"

Though the Puritan influences in Nathaniel Hawthorne's "Young Goodman Brown" are deeply rooted in the sect's European experience, through their voyage to America and subsequent experiences on those shores, they had become uniquely American.

In Europe, a long tradition of belief in the supernatural had developed from ancient times long before the coming of Christianity. Up until the arrival of that religion, the continent of Europe was occupied by various barbaric peoples each with their beliefs of how the world ran and what forces governed its existence. Aside from the usual pantheons of gods and demons, a legion of spirits existed in nature, quite apart from the gods. Nature spirits who existed inside various natural objects and places: trees, rocks, lakes, crossroads. The belief in these spirits was widespread and actually much stronger than that of the pantheistic gods. Upon the arrival of Christianity, it was relatively easy for the early missionaries to supplant the belief in the gods with the belief in Christ. But in the subconscious of the recently converted was the hidden belief that the gods were really expendable; that in reality it was the nature spirits with their attendant power over the people's crops and fertility that were most important. It took much longer for Christianity to subdue these beliefs, but over time it succeeded, albeit by supplanting a new superstition over the old in the form of the devil. But the original beliefs in the nature spirits lived on subconsciously with the people, the understanding that nature being somehow against man, that man has a right to subdue it, bending it to his will. Nature became an adversary and somehow darkly alluring. Like Satan and in league with him, it sought to seduce man with its hidden evils. Algernon

Blackwood described this feeling nicely in his story "The Wendigo" when he recounted the Indian aphorism that a man whose mind had been lost to those temptations was said to have "seen the Wendigo."

Hawthorne was uncannily close to his Puritan roots and built a literary career around such themes as nature and evil. In "Young Goodman Brown," the author comes closest to synthesizing all of the above themes in a single story of allegory and personification made all the more remarkable for its brevity.

But the transition from belief in nature spirits to that of Satan acting through nature to subvert man did not come overnight; hundreds of years were needed to complete the change. In the end with the coming of the Renaissance, even these fears receded into the past, but with the rise of Protestantism and its more literal view of the Bible and the abrupt confrontation of the Massachusetts Bay Puritans with the singularly hostile environment of America, the old suspicions rose again to prominence. Although this was by no means a solely American phenomenon (at the same time the witch trials in Salem were taking place, a similar wave of hysteria swept Europe) it is all that necessarily concerns us here.

To better understand the Puritan ethos one must go back to 1536 and the publication of John Calvin's *Institutes of the Christian Religion*, in which the author expresses his belief in the more literal interpretation of the Bible. Calvinism first took hold in the Netherlands and eastern Europe before gradually spreading west to France. In Britain, the movement greatly influenced the Church of England which was then seeking a more clearly defined identity to that of its parent in Rome. Expecting to encourage great change in the Church, Calvinists were disappointed when Queen Elizabeth decided on a more parochial approach. Those Calvinists unreconciled with events were labeled "Puritans" and many of them found refuge from persecution in Holland and later, led by John Winthrop, to America.

Upon the arrival in America of those first Puritan settlers, the wildness of the land and the savagery of its natives immediately began to work their spell. Author H. P. Lovecraft, in *Supernatural Horror in Literature,* has illustrated the facts succinctly:

"The vast and gloomy virgin forests in whose perpetual twilight all terrors might well lurk; the hordes of coppery Indians whose strange, saturnine visages and violent customs hinted strongly at traces of Infernal origin; the free reign given under the influence of Puritan theocracy to all manner of notions respecting man's relation to the stern and vengeful God of the Calvinists, and to the Sulpherous Adversary of that God, about whom so much was thundered in the pulpits each Sunday; and the morbid introspection developed by an isolated backwoods life devoid of normal amusements and of the recreational mood, harassed by commands of theological self-examination, keyed to unnatural emotional repression, and forming above all a mere grim struggle for survival. ..all these things comprised to produce an environment in which the black whisperings of sinister grandams were heard far beyond the chimney corner, and in which tales of witchcraft and unbelievable secret monstrosities lingered long after the dread days of the Salem nightmares."

Although Lovecraft described the influences on the Puritans' American experiences, his idea of the oppressive, brooding woods contrasted sharply with the Calvinist view of nature in God's scheme. Calvin thought that God had from the beginning committed to man the responsibility to act as the great prophet and king of creation. That man is to interpret creation, as God's possession, to lead it in the worship of God and to govern it for God. That God gave man the right to rule over, subdue, and to replenish the earth, involving both the development of its resources and the organization of man to this purpose. Thus it is easy to understand the early antagonisms of the Puritans toward their wilderness.

In addition to this, Calvinism's "five points" of the total depravity of man, unconditional election, limited atonement, inevitable grace, and perseverance of the saints all forced the Puritan settler to view almost everything with suspicion. As a result, the Puritan leaders were always on watch for devious or Satan inspired behavior. One case that involved a group called the Merry Mounters was chronicled in *The New English Canaan* by its leader, Thomas Morton. Although Morton's version described the Merry Mounters as merely participating in harmless revelry, governor of Massachusetts William Bradford reached the opposite conclusion in his *Of Plymouth Plantation*. According to Bradford, the Merry Mounters had erected a Maypole around which the participants danced in a lascivious manner. In addition, rhymes were created and recited and various liquors consumed in a style that was all too devilish and disgusting. In a subsequent police action, Bradford sent Captain Miles Standish out to put a stop to the accursed worshippers of Dagon.

With this understanding, the later witch trials of 1692 can be seen as the culmination of the combative nature developed by the Massachusetts Puritans in defense of their beliefs. Their suspicions of nature might even be considered the culmination of a struggle begun in the Garden of Eden with its forbidden fruit, representative of the dark allure of untrammeled nature of which man had once been the master.

In "Young Goodman Brown," Hawthorne taps into all of the themes derived from Puritan thought and feelings; the brooding presence of nature; the devil assuming the shapes of trusted individuals; native Indians as devils; distrust; and suspicion. These themes form the backbone of many of Hawthorne's tales and in "Young Goodman Brown," they all come together with a virtuosity and economy of word as take a reader's breath away. Here Hawthorne presents material enough for a novel and yet nothing is rushed.

Chief among the elements of the story is the forest itself which acts as a physical representation of the mental turmoil suffered by Goodman Brown as his mind see-saws between good and evil. Here, Hawthorne draws an imperfect parallel between Brown and Christ and just as the latter was tempted by Satan three times, so does Brown.

The story opens as Brown bids his wife "Faith" goodbye to keep a prearranged meeting in the forest with an unnamed stranger.

"He had taken a dreary road, darkened by all the gloomiest trees of the forest, which barely stood aside to let the narrow path creep through, and closed immediately behind. It was all as lonely as could be; and there is this peculiarity in such a solitude that the traveler knows not who may be concealed by the innumerable trunks and the thick boughs overhead; so that with lonely footsteps he may yet be passing through an unseen multitude."

Later Brown asks rhetorically: "What if the devil himself should be at my very elbow?" Thus, from the beginning, the forest is characterized as a malignant entity, the abode of devils, Hell.

To Hawthorne, Lovecraft says,

"Evil...appears on every hand as a lurking and conquering adversary; and the visible world becomes in his fancy a theatre of infinite tragedy and woe, with unseen half existent influences hovering over it and through it, battling for supremacy and moulding the destinies of the hapless mortals who form its vain and self deluded population...he saw a dismal throng of vague specters behind the common phenomena of life..."

The association of the oppressive nature of the forest with the man whom Brown is scheduled to meet is strengthened when the stranger tempts the young man three times, just as Satan once did for Christ. The stranger challenges Brown to walk further into the forest with him to a meeting deep in the woods but at the same time advising him to use his reason in deciding to go forward or not:

"We are but a little way in the forest yet."
"Too far! Too far!...My father never went into the woods on such an errand, nor his father before him. We have been a race of honest men and good Christians since the days of the martyres; and shall I be the first of the name Brown that ever took this path..."

Failing with the first appeal to logic, the stranger tells Brown of his acquaintance with his grandfathers and father. But Brown refutes him in disbelief. Immediate authority figures having failed, the stranger tries a third time with reference to supreme authority in the colony, that of his companionship with the "deacons of many a church," "selectmen of divers towns" and "a majority of the Great and General Court." But Brown once more refuses the stranger's suggestions. Thus nature becomes for Hawthorne a substitute for evil. Just as Christ went to Hell before ascending to Heaven, so must Brown venture through the "forest" before finding freedom outside it.

Another important element of the story is the stranger's ability to make himself resemble Young Brown:

"As nearly as could be discerned," the stranger "was about fifty years old, apparently in the same rank of life as Goodman Brown and bearing a considerable resemblance to" Young Brown "though perhaps more in expression than features. Still they might have been taken for father and son."

The ability of the devil to assume the shape of familiar persons loomed large in Puritan belief. During the witch trials, the possibility was brought up over and over and in *Wonders of the Invisible World*, Cotton Mather explained the phenomenon:

"Some Popish Authors argue, That the Devil cannot personate an innocent Man as doing an act of Witchcraft, because then he might as well represent them as committing theft, Murder etc. And if so, there would be no living in the World. But I turn the Argument against them, he may ...personate honest men as doing other Evils; and no valid Reason can be given why he may not as well personate them under the Notion of Thieves, Murderers, and Idolaters."

To the Puritans then, as in the works of Hawthorne, the devil was a very strong and real force in the world; not just random, but deliberate! A deliberation for which the Godly man must always be on guard. In "Young Goodman Brown," Hawthorne pursues this interpretation as Brown, with increasing vigor, continues to refute the stranger's entreaties even as he introduces people the young man has respected all of his life. But now, they're not the kindly, God fearing people Brown has always known them to be; instead they appear as grotesque opposites of their normal selves.

And so, as Brown accompanies the stranger along the woodland path, they run into old Goody Cloyse who had taught Brown his catechism. Not wishing for his old teacher to see him in the company of the stranger, Brown ducks into the woods

From the concealment of the trees, he listens to the conversation between his companion and Goody Cloyse and any doubt about the stranger's true identity is removed:

"The Devil!" screamed the pious old lady.
"Then Goody Cloyse knows her old friend?" observed the traveler.

After a short conversation, the stranger and Goody Cloyse vanish, leaving Brown hiding in the undergrowth where he suddenly overhears more familiar voices, that of the town minister and the Deacon Gookin as they talk of the meeting in the forest.

As the climax of the story unfolds, Brown, after a delirious run through a particularly evil tinged forest, succumbs at last to its brooding malignancy when he suddenly emerges at the meeting site and beholds all those he has admired as good people apparently celebrating the arrival of Satan himself. But as astonishing as all of it is, most incredible of all is sight of his "Faith" as the girl willingly gives herself up to the devil. Recovering from his shock, Brown implores his "Faith" to "Look up to Heaven, and resist the wicked one." At that outburst of resurgent faith, the hellish ceremony and its celebrants vanish, defeated, just as the wilderness was finally subdued by the faith and determination of Hawthorne's ancestors.

Hawthorne ends his tale on an ambiguous note as Brown returns to his wife and neighbors a changed man. Never again could he look upon them with the same eyes. The suspicion and distrust that plagued the early Puritans and that resulted in the notorious witch trials stayed with him till his death many years later. Just as with the Puritans themselves, he could never be sure what was real and what was false.

Until the time came when the Indian menace had been eradicated and the forests of New England tamed, the old Puritans were never off their guard. Whether the dangers were real or imagined, the Puritans' faith in their God pulled them through those difficult times, just as William Bradford claimed at the very beginning of the Puritan Odyssey, "through the help of God, by fortitude and patience, might (this) be borne, or overcome."

Although Nathaniel Hawthorne has become the most well known example of the Puritan influence in American literature, he was not alone. When the Puritans arrived in America, they were not the only settlers who had to face the wilderness and overcome it, so did those in Virginia and the Quakers in Pennsylvania and a dozen other groups. The American experience did not limit itself only to the Puritans, and did not limit itself in time. For the next three hundred years their descendents would face the same hazards as the nation expanded westward until today, they push a different kind of frontier, the frontier of science. And as these new vistas open, other writers of the supernatural have emerged with a clear debt to the colonizers of Massachusetts. Washington Irving, perhaps the most American of American authors of the nineteenth century, was able to synthesize the inborn American understanding of nature most effectively in his humorous "The Legend of Sleepy Hollow." Edgar Allen Poe delved deeper into the human psyche seeking the exposed nerve of American unease over nature with his tale "The Masque of the Red Death" which has men literally walling themselves up in panicky fear of an unknown force of nature that seeks to destroy them. H.P. Lovecraft carried the theme over into the twentieth century when he combined the old fear and distrust of nature with the newer scientifically based fear of an unknown universe in such tales as "The Whisperer in Darkness" and "The Colour Out of Space."

Thus, the process continues with newer examples of purely American supernaturalist writing appearing all the time albeit with less force and vigor in these latter days than before. But that is not to say that readers (and writers) have overcome their latent fears. The ancient pre-Christian beliefs still lie imbedded in the subconscious and it will take time to work them out, beliefs that are more basic than mere superstition. They are born in man's uncertainty and doubt, his feelings of inadequacy, and those are feelings that will never die, insuring a steady stream of weird fiction for the foreseeable future.

The Christian Dialectic: C.S. Lewis

Clive Staples Lewis, though recognized as the author of the Narnian Chronicles and the Perelandrian space trilogy, was more than just a literary fantasiste. Lewis' schooling and later professorial and Fellowship positions at Cambridge and Oxford respectively in the first half of the twentieth century, all combined to instill in him as in many of his contemporaries in British letters, a strong interest in theology and philosophy. For up until that time, philosophy and the medium of the written word (particularly in the form of a fantastic tale) were very closely associated, an approach to fiction writing almost completely lost today. In Britain at least, it may have been J.R.R. Tolkien's *Lord of the Rings* that set the precedent (rightly or wrongly) of a fantastic story written merely for entertainment and without a philosophical sub-text. The trend, to readers' and the literary world's loss, has sadly continued to the point where few imaginary stories written since convey anything but plot. But in the years before the twentieth century, the philosophical fantasy tale was the preferred literary form for communicating new ideas. Francis Bacon used it for a number of his ideas in *The New Atlantis* (1627); Jonathan Swift laid bare human foibles in his *Gulliver's Travels* (1726) and Mary Shelley explored the danger of science to the soul in her *Frankenstein, or The New Prometheus* (1817). In the same tradition, C.S. Lewis used the fantasy genre, not because it was a popular form but because it was the traditional one.

In the Perelandrian trilogy, Lewis was moved by his particular philosophical viewpoint, to challenge the conclusions reached by his English contemporaries, Olaf Stapledon (*Star Maker*, 1937) and H.G. Wells (*When the Sleeper Wakes* etc., 1899), that the universe was governed by a sort of blind, all-powerful force or spirit that was neither good nor evil, but both. It was their essentially hopeless and unsatisfying vision of man's ultimate place in the universal scheme of things that prompted Lewis to respond in kind: writing up his opposing position as an allegorical fantasy. For the human condition and its eventual elevation from its currently base nature was what concerned Lewis. That man had the innate ability not only to rise above himself, but to come to full joyous union with and beside the godhead not as some nebulous part of him. Wells and Stapledon insisted that the answer to man's eternal search for meaning and peace lay in science and logic. But in his efforts to refute science as a possible salvation for mankind, Lewis inadvertently painted a pessimistic view of the world. A world in which man is trapped on Earth unable and unwilling to leave its embrace. On the other hand, his depiction of an era of brotherly love and peace through the teachings of Christianity create a comforting feeling of well being. Is he optimistic or pessimistic? That would depend on one's viewpoint. From the purely physical, scientific point of view, the view of numbers and logic, the latter; from the spiritual point of view, where man's inner qualities transcend mere finite concepts of time and space, the former. Lewis substituted limitless spiritual development for a limitless yet paradoxically, finite one.

In the first novel of the Perelandrian trilogy, *Out of the Silent Planet*, Lewis uses his protagonist Dr. Elwin Ransom, as the spokesman for his own Christian-based philosophy. His antagonist, Dr. Weston, becomes the representative of Stapledonian and Wellsian science and, by extension, the devil, in *Perelandra* the second novel of the series. It is through these two characters that Lewis expresses his view on the human condition and the mutual antagonism of science and religion, raising the level of the trilogy to a degree of didacticism that could be compared in some respects to the Greek *Dialogues*.

Born in Belfast, Northern Ireland in 1898 and surrounded by the books of well read parents, Lewis began an early fascination with the written word. His interest in fantasy may have surfaced as a boy when he and his brother made up imaginary lands of wonder. His early years were spent in private schools such as the Wyngard School in Hertfordshire and Cherbourg House in Malvern where he encountered many works of the fantastic by authors such as William Morris (whom many consider the founder of modern fantasy) and George Mac-Donald. As an adult, he became Professor of Medieval and Renaissance English at Cambridge and a Fellow of Magdalen College, Oxford. At the time, it had been the fashion in intellectual circles to spurn religion (and later, to embrace socialism). It was because his later convictions ran counter to these prevailing attitudes that Lewis felt compelled to leave Oxford or forever be frustrated in his desire for promotion or award. Accepting Christianity after years of agnosticism, and with the heat of the newly converted, he wrote at least a score of philosophical books including a collection of radio talks called *Mere Christianity; The Screwtape Letters* written in the form of letters sent from an old devil to a younger nephew; and *The Great Divorce,* about a journey through heaven. *Out of the Silent Planet* appeared in 1943, followed in the next year by *Perelandra,* and in 1946 by *That Hideous Strength.*

Together, the Perelandrian series expresses Lewis' position regarding the relationship between Christianity and the human condition. Told in the form of an allegory, the books' two protagonists (one good, one evil), travel from world to world confronting each other at crucial moments along the trilogy's theological plotline. In the first, *Out of the Silent Planet,* Dr. Elwin Ransom finds himself kidnapped by Dr. Weston and his partner Devine. Placed aboard the former's spaceship, Ransom is taken off to Mars, (or Malacandra as it is called by the natives). Devine it seems, is going for gold while Weston for science and the advancement of the human race. Ransom is to be held as a sacrifice for the Malacandrians if such an emergency should arise. But through various adventures upon that strange world, Ransom becomes separated from his captors and, after having learned the Malacandrian tongue, is taken before the planet's leader, the Oyarsa. He is soon able to prove his worth to the Oyarsa when Weston reappears in need of a translator. From there, as events in the story unfold, the reader is left in little doubt that in Malacandra, Lewis has created a world bereft of the taint of original sin.

In the following book, *Perelandra*, Ransom is sent from Earth to Venus (the world of the book's title) to prevent the seduction of a new Eve by the devil. For in this world, Lewis has created a new Garden of Eden before its own Adam and Eve had fallen to original sin. In the story, Ransom encounters an innocent Eve who is searching for her Adam. Just as in our world, the two beings have been forbidden a single thing: overnight residence on solid land. On Perelandra it seems, the whole world is covered with water with only grand, floating islands to break the monotony. But there is one exception: a lone island of fixed earth.

In the story, Ransom is at a loss to explain the reason why the Oyarsa has sent him to this watery world. But with the arrival of his old adversary Dr. Weston, he is soon left in no doubt. Because it quickly becomes apparent that Weston is now not only familiar with the Malacandrian language, but that he has been made a tool of the devil. Weston approaches the naive Eve figure and assails her with cold relentless logic, slowly working her mind to accept the notion that staying the night on the fixed land could do no harm. In the meantime, Ransom tries to present an equally logical argument not to stay on the fixed land but fails to convince the woman of his position. Finally, desperately, Ransom is forced to resort to physical violence to destroy Weston then wages a fierce inner struggle to keep himself from giving in to despair at the deed. In the end, the new Adam and Eve decide to obey God and are rewarded with becoming almost godlike themselves. What the children of the first Adam back on Earth could have been if not for the first man's own weakness.

That Hideous Strength, the third book in the series, falls short of its predecessors in allegorical meaning by trying to cover too much ground. It has some science-fiction in the form of the N.I.C.E., a secret society trying to take over the world; some fantasy with the presence of Merlin and magic; a dash of contemporary events by having the NICE resemble certain European powers and finally, some religion as Ransom continues his efforts on behalf of good versus evil.

On the surface, the trilogy presents itself as an imaginative exercise in fantasy and science-fiction, but below this outward appearance, rages a fierce philosophical counterpoint that Lewis deftly (and sometimes blatantly) juggles in order to address questions raised by non-believers and scientific absolutists such as H.G. Wells and in particular, Olaf Stapledon.

Although the plot of the first two books in the series is more well defined than in the third, it is the conflict between Ransom and Weston (as they stand in for the arguments between religion and science or even good versus evil), that is at the heart of the story being told. In addressing the human condition, Lewis, through Ransom, argues for the Christian point of view. However, in *Out of the Silent Planet*, Lewis cheats a little by filtering the scientific arguments made by Weston for the Oyarsa through the translations of Ransom. What emerges, comes at the expense of Stapledon, whose ideas of scientific determinism prove to be untranslatable in their cold blooded, purposeless logic.

In *Perelandra*, the sides are more evenly matched as both Ransom and Weston share an easy facility with the language, bringing more subtlety and complexity to their long arguments. But where Ransom's character is a more or less nebulous agent for the Oyarsa (who is not necessarily intended to represent God, but maybe a high ranking angel of some sort), there is no uncertainty regarding Weston's motivations:

"Idiot," he repeated. "Can you understand nothing? Will you always try to press everything back into the miserable framework of your old jargon about self and self-sacrifice? That is the old accursed dualism in another form. There is no possible distinction in concrete thought between me and the universe. In so far as I am the conductor of the central forward pressure of the universe, I am it. Do you see, you timid, scruple-mongering fool? I am the Universe. I, Weston, am your God and your Devil. I call that Force into me completely..."

With those lines, Lewis establishes Weston's intended identity, leaving no room for conjecture: he is the devil come to corrupt another world. Stripped of guile, his nature and purposes obvious, he is easily bested by Ransom.

Weston's role in *Out of the Silent Planet* however, is not so simple. There, he assumes the role of a typical scientist, blithely expounding upon his ignorant attachment to scientific determinism. This makes him all the more dangerous and seductive while his calm reasonableness compares well against Ransom's increasing desperation.

In *Perelandra* Weston is essentially harmless as his conclusions about the universe, though erroneous, are arrived at seemingly without malicious intent. But in *Out of the Silent Planet*, he is armed not only with newer, more complex arguments that cunningly blend Christian theological principles with those of science, but also with an earnestness that lends conviction to his positions. But as the novel wears on, Weston's body begins to reflect physically the ugliness of his twisted nature. Echoing Dante's presentation of hell as the opposite of everything in heaven, Lewis paints a particularly grotesque portrait of his villain.

Then horrible things began happening. A spasm like that preceding a deadly vomit twisted Weston's face out of recognition. As it passed, for one second something like the old Weston reappeared--the old Weston, staring with eyes of horror and howling, "Ransom, Ransom! For Christ's sake don't let them---" and instantly his whole body spun round as if he had been hit by a revolver-bullet and he fell to the earth, and was there rolling at Ransom's feet, slavering and chattering and tearing up the moss in handfuls.

Then Lewis reveals to the reader the true target of his novel as Weston, now speaking in the name of the devil, recites Stapledonian philosophy to Ransom:

"...I plunged into Biology, and particularly into what may be called biological philosophy. Hitherto, as a physicist, I had been content to regard Life as a subject outside my scope. The conflicting views of those who drew a sharp line between the organic and the inorganic and those who held that what we call Life was inherent in matter from the very beginning had not interested me. Now it did. I saw almost at once that I could admit no break, no discontinuity, in the unfolding of the cosmic process. I became a convinced believer in emergent evolution. All is one. The stuff of mind, the unconsciously purposive dynamism, is present from the very beginning."

"The majestic spectacle of this blind, inarticulate purposiveness thrusting its way upward and ever upward in an endless unity of differentiated achievements towards an ever increasing complexity of organization, towards spontaneity and spirituality, swept away all my old conceptions of a duty to Man as such. Man in himself is nothing. The forward movement of Life--the growing spirituality—is everything."

The "stuff of the mind" and the "unconsciously purposive dynamism" of which Weston speaks, describes exactly Stapledon's idea of the great single, inarticulate "spirit" to whom all conscious beings belong and to whom one day they all will return. According to Stapledon, this "consciousness" created the universe and an infinite number of others before it, in an effort to perfect its invention. In its mindless quest of this perfection, it will continue to create new universes ad infinitum until such time as it gets the process right. Thus man is merely another ingredient making up the stuff of the universe which is fated to merge and reform into other universes, endlessly recombining with no purpose other than to seek some unknown idea of perfection. A similar concept was explored by E.R. Eddison in his Zimiamvian trilogy (1935-1958), where a god, unaware of its own godhead, creates new worlds (including the Earth, which is created and destroyed during the course of *A Fish Dinner in Memison*!) in its quest for Beauty and Perfection. The whole idea of such a deity was repugnant to Lewis, who believed in a Christian God who was not only conscious of His own nature, but cared enough for his creatures to interfere on their behalf. A God that cared so much in fact, that He created an entire universe for His creatures and gave them the chance to share, however minutely, in His Godhood.

In *Perelandra*, Lewis allows the reader to see that care in action as he recounts in allegory, the Biblical story of Adam and Eve. Ransom, determined to follow God's will, is sent to Perelandra to prevent that world's own dawn parents from a seduction that those of our own had long ago embraced.

Upon arriving on the surface of the planet, he meets a beautiful, green woman. Wasting little time, she tells the uncomprehending Ransom of her true nature:

"Look here," said Ransom. "You must have had a mother. Is she alive? Where is she? When did you see her last?"

"I have a mother?" said the Green Lady, looking full at him with eyes of untroubled wonder. "What do you mean? I am the Mother..."

"But the King--had he no father?"

"He is the father."

"You mean," said Ransom slowly, "that you and he are the only two of your kind in the whole world?"

"Of course."

Further emphasizing the innocence of the Perelandrian Adam and Eve, the woman then expresses surprise at Ransom's way of dividing time into past, present, and future. She, it turns out, views it in a quite different manner. A manner described by the fifth century philosopher Boethius, in his *Consolation of Philosophy*. It was Boethius' contention that God existed outside of time and thus was able to view the past, present, and future all at once. God lived in a kind of eternal present, a perspective the human condition lost the day Adam and Eve fell from grace. Trapped now by the inexorability of time, man's outlook on life is necessarily limited, trapping him in a mindset of now and then, unable to imagine being totally free.

"This looking backward and forward along the line and seeing how a day has one appearance as it comes to you, and another when you are in it, and a third when it has gone past...I have never done it before...stepping out of life into the alongside and looking at oneself living as if one were not alive."

So saying, the green lady not only dissociates herself from the circumscribed lives of men, but indicates how much closer she is to the Godhead in their shared vision of reality.

The full range of her innocence is revealed when Weston tries to induce her into spending a night on the fixed land. To do it, Weston starts small. Using logic and common sense, he begins to familiarize the naive girl with smaller mortal vices such as vanity, greed, disobedience, and sloth. Meanwhile, Ransom attempts to challenge him on every point but it is a losing battle. As the devil, Weston needs no rest, no sleep. Slowly, his influence over the green lady grows even as Ransom's wanes. To be sure, Ransom wins his small victories, but he has to sleep sometime, and in those moments, Weston increases his efforts, hammering away at the girl's resistance with illustrative stories and logic. Eventually, Weston turns his attention to Ransom, keeping him awake and denying him rest by constantly repeating his name: "Ransom...Ransom... Ransom!" underscoring the fact of Weston's supernatural identity.

Here, Lewis (as Ransom) spells out his position on the attractive and seductive nature of pure logic; a method energetically propounded by contemporaries such as Stapledon and Wells (as Weston). Ransom's use of logic in the story to counter Weston's arguments, shows the illusive nature, the objective heart of logic that owes loyalty to no argument; it can be twisted and reshaped to support both sides of any issue (moral relativism). So of what use could it be in the search for ultimate truth? Can a purely logical approach to the human condition and the purpose of life even offer the possibility of an ultimate answer? Lewis' position is that without the dead reckoning of instinct, the unswerving faith in God and the God of Christianity in particular, man must be doomed never to know the truth. Without that faith, every logical position must be qualified with an "if," "and," or "but." Stapledon then, with his reliance on logic to make his arguments, cannot offer a final answer. A series of facts that lead to a certain conclusion, which Weston has called an "unconsciously purposive dynamism," must be anything but conclusive. At any point along the delicate links of the factual chain, a case can always be made for an alternate interpretation, leading the search for an answer in an entirely different direction. To Lewis, a universe as indefinite and "illogical" as this, was not only intellectually and spiritually unsatisfying, but purposeless. His faith in Christianity and its own "logic" (embodied in its theology and based on unshakeable philosophical and Biblical principles), imagined an order to the universe that left little room for doubt and much more for hope.

Lewis expresses this hopeful interpretation of man's role in the universe at the conclusion of *Perelandra*, as the green lady and her mate, now the Queen and King, are raised up and transformed. Unfallen, they come face to face with God; still individual, still man and woman, but more than man and woman. Masculine and Feminine yet sexless. Where Stapledon pictured an end for man's quest for the meaning of life in a mindless, whorling, semi-sentient chaos, Lewis found man's destiny not as an ending but a glorious beginning...

It was hard even for Ransom to tell me of the King's face. But we dare not withhold the truth. It was that face which no man can say he does not know. You might ask how it was possible to look upon it and not to commit idolatry, not to mistake it for that of which it was the likeness. For the resemblance was, in its own fashion, infinite, so that almost you could wonder at finding no sorrows in his brow and no wounds in his hands and feet. Yet there was no danger of mistaking, not one moment of confusion, no least sally of the will towards forbidden reverence. Where likeness was greatest, mistake was least possible. Perhaps this is always so. A clever waxwork can be made so like a man that for a moment it deceives us: the great portrait which is far more deeply like him does not. Plaster images of the Holy One may before now have drawn to themselves the adoration they were meant to arouse for the reality. But here, where His live image, like Him within and without, made by His own bare hands out of the depth of divine artistry, His masterpiece of self-portraiture coming forth from His workshop to delight all worlds, walked and spoke before Ransom's eyes, it could never be taken for more than an image. Nay, the very beauty of it lay in the certainty that it was a copy, like and not the same, an echo, a rhyme, an exquisite reverberation of the uncreated music prolonged in a created medium.

Why Didn't Robert E. Howard Write Any Science Fiction?

In his creative output, Robert E. Howard was one of the most diversified authors of the pulp era. Writing everything from horror to westerns, he was able to make himself a living in the hard pressed times of the Depression. Yet despite the fact that the science fiction genre comprised one of the largest categories of pulps, Howard, with very few exceptions, virtually ignored it.

Saying that he just did not care for the subject matter seems too facile an explanation in the face of his wide ranging output. After all, he himself had said that he hated the mystery genre; hated to read it, hated to write it, but he did. In another place, he even suggested to H.P. Lovecraft the possibility of writing sex stories for profit using one's own fantasies for fodder. So clearly, his preference regarding the subjects he chose to write about were dictated not by taste, but by monetary considerations. And yet the evidence is there that this practical attitude toward writing for profit found its limit with science fiction.

So did Howard hate science fiction? Was his aversion (if any) for the genre so strong, so reactionary, that writing it must have been more than even he could stomach? In letters on the subject compiled by Glenn Lord for *The Last Celt* (Berkley, 1974), Howard writes:

> *Though I seem to be fairly versatile in a small way, having written and sold weirds, historicals, sports, detectives, and adventures there is so little of the scientist about my nature that I feel no confidence in my ability to write scientific fiction convincingly. Frankly, it seems to me that the average pseudo-scientific tale--is pretty poor stuff below the average level of*

the weird, detective, or adventure yarn. I attribute this partly to the necessity of bending plot action, and atmosphere to fit some scientific or mock scientific theory or formula, and partly to the fact that readers of this type of fiction seem to demand the same plots over and over again, and to resent the slightest variation. I may be wrong, but this is the conclusion I have reached from reading the published letters of pseudo-scientific fans.

On the surface, this statement seems to put Howard's aversion to science fiction in black and white terms, but he had deeper reasons than these to ignore the genre. In the same letter, he says:

There is no literary work, to me, half as zestful as rewriting history in the guise of fiction--I try to write as true to the actual facts as possible; at least I try to commit as few errors as possible. I like to have my background and setting as accurate and realistic as I can...if I twist too much, alter dates as some writers do, or present a character out of keeping with my impressions of the time and place, I lose my sense of reality and my characters cease to be living and vital things--My characters do and say illogical and inconsistent things-- inconsistent as far as general things go--but they are consistent to my conception of them.

Thus, in Howard's own words, we discover that his aversion to science fiction went deeper than we were led to expect in the previous quote. And judging from the bulk of his literary output, Howard's attitude toward history and facts were no idle words. History was as alive for him as the present, not dead as it seemed for most others. So how could he ignore a past that was alive and vital for a future that did not even exist? But even as the course of this subject has taken us from Howard's simple dislike of science fiction to his more complex attitude toward history in general, so must the researcher look even deeper, to the most basic strata of Howard's psychological make-up:

--Always I am the barbarian, the skin-clad tousle-haired, light-eyed wild man, armed with a rude axe or sword, fighting the elements and wild beasts, or grappling with armored hosts marching with the tread of civilized discipline, from fallow fruitful lands and walled cities. This is reflected in my writings, too, for when I begin a tale of old times, I always find myself instinctively arrayed on the side of the barbarian, against the powers of organized civilization.

This is the real reason why Howard could never relate to science fiction; his attitudes were those of the instinctive barbarian. His disinterest in science fiction was not necessarily with the technology it represented, but with the increased organization that successful science demanded. The massive public works projects (such as the Panama Canal) or a space program (such as NASA) resulting from the application of science necessitated a greatly increased cooperation among individuals and even whole communities. Progress was impossible without civilization and civilization impossible without science. Thus science enforced conformity; a civilization increasingly reliant on science cannot afford uncontrolled elements in its midst. Thus, it creates more laws, more rules, more expectations that must in turn, be regulated by an establishment of legislatures, educational, judicial, and religious institutions and enforced by police. Such suffocating layers of bureaucracy was anathema to Howard which he felt constantly threatened to hem in the wild nature of free spirits such as himself.

In the area of Texas where Howard was born and raised, the days of the early pioneers, their struggles with the Indians, with Mexican authority, with anti-slavery forces of the East, the more recent oil boom and even the internecine warfare they conducted among themselves, were still of recent memory and even of experience. When Howard was only ten years old, the United States Cavalry was still regularly riding into Mexico on the trail of raiding Villistas. Consequently, Howard developed an attitude, perhaps stronger than those of his contemporaries, of intense individualism and instinctive resistance to anything that might restrain him from doing what he wanted. Born of experience, (comments he made in letters about working in the oil industry and clerking in a general store indicate that he had trouble accepting authority) and fueled by selective reading, Howard soon developed the intense feelings that culminated in his identification with the uninhibited barbarian who once lived on the fringes of civilization.

Howard's reading habits seemed to reinforce this attitude as a cursory glance at the contents of his personal library prove. (From a list recorded in Appendix A, of Don Herron's *Dark Barbarian.*, Greenwood Press, 1984). The bulk of the books cover historical subjects, particularly of the southwest, poetry, classic novels of western literature, a scattering of popular novels, and the occult. The only evidence of science fiction are a few volumes of Edgar Rice Burroughs' Mars novels and the Professor Challenger novels of Arthur Conan Doyle.

Perhaps another part of Howard's problem with science fiction was that in the 1920s and '30s, the genre still rested in the firm grip of Hugo Gernsback.

Gernsback took the lead in popularizing science fiction in the post-Wells-Verne world and brought it to the masses; but in doing so, inadvertently cemented its form and content for twenty years in a format that emphasized the gadget over the impact of the gadget on people and society. So when Howard complained of science fiction's slavish adherence to gadgets, theories, or formula, he was expressing an attitude toward the form that would not be addressed in any systematic way until the advent of John W. Campbell's tenure as editor on *Astounding Science Fiction* in 1938.

On the other hand, Howard did seem to have a soft spot for Burroughs' brand of science fantasy (which relied more on action and adventure than gadgets); perhaps seeing in John Carter's battles with green and yellow Martians a struggle to retain his individualism against the forces of a decaying civilization.

Perhaps then, it was no coincidence that Howard's only true foray into the realms of science fiction followed the precepts laid down by Burroughs' rather than those by Gernsback..

Aside from minor excursions into pseudo-science fiction with his Cthulhu Mythos-like tales (particularly his chapter in the round-robin written "Challenge From Beyond," [1935]), Howard's third novel, the 50,000 word *Almuric* (1939), was the author's only attempt in the genre. The novel follows the adventures of Esau Cairn, a typical Howardian character of the instinctive barbarian school who is on the run because of his killing of a political enemy. Howard describes his protagonist in terms that could easily fit the author himself:

Many men are born outside their century; Esau Cairn was born outside his epoch--a man of intelligence so little fitted for adjustment in a machine-age civilization.

He was of a restless mold, impatient of restraint and resentful of authority. Not by any means a bully, he at the same time refused to countenance what he considered to be the slightest infringement on his rights. He was primitive in his passions, with a gusty temper and a courage inferior to none on this planet. Esau Cairn was, in short, a freak--a man whose physical body and mental bent leaned back to the primordial.

Except for this personal touch, the story of Cairn's adventures on the planet of Almuric is one of rather pedestrian Burroughsian plot contrivances: his falling in among a stone-age tribe whose men are brutish while strangely, its women are all well within twentieth century standards of beauty; the capture of Cairn and of his newly won girlfriend by the devilish Queen Yasmeena and her evil Yagas.

Only in the foreword does Howard acknowledge the fact that *Almuric* is supposed to be a science fiction story. So fleeting is the reference that one can only conclude that it was considered by the author as merely pro forma, brought up only to satisfy the demands of a science fiction fan or magazine editor. From there, Howard never looks back as the reader is plunged into a world no less exotic than Conan's Hyborian Age or King Kull's Atlantis.

--I told him of the Great Secret, and gave him proof of its possibilities.

In short, I urged him to take the chance of a flight through space, rather than meet the certain death that awaited him.

--There was no place in the universe which would support human life. But I had looked beyond the knowledge of men, in universes beyond universes. And I chose the only planet I knew on which a human being could exist--the wild, primitive, and strange planet I named Almuric.

--*Esau Cairn left the planet of his birth, for a world swimming afar in space, alien, aloof, strange.*

The "Great Secret," (presumably the method of transportation for Cairn's arrival on Almuric), is never explained, comprising the totality of Howard's nod to "mock scientific theory and formula."

Could Howard have written true science fiction? His contemporaries from *Weird Tales*, H.P. Lovecraft and Clark Ashton Smith, though less equipped in the *sang froid* school of professional writing than he did it quite successfully in their own styles. But Howard was a paradox, though he could induce himself to write in many genres, his own internal contradictions prevented him from violating certain elements that made up his tragic soul. Science Fiction it seems, presented too much of a threat to Howard's outlook on life and if any of its worlds ever came to pass, he would most likely have chosen to be dead.

Beyond the Fields We Know: An Appreciation of Gervasio Gallardo

No literary genre identifies itself with particular artists or illustrators as do those of science fiction and fantasy. And even in science fiction there are not that many, with only Frank R. Paul in the pulp era and perhaps Vincent di Fate and Kelly Freas in the paperback years. Fantasy, on the other hand, has had many, from J. Arthur St. John and Roy Krenkel (associated with Edgar Rice Burroughs) to Frank Frazzeta (Robert E. Howard's Conan) toVirgil Finlay (illustrator for *Weird Tales*) to Murray Tinkelman (with Matheson and Lovecraft). But of all these great talents, one artist stands out from the crowd, not simply by virtue of his unique talent, but by the very nature of his approach to fantasy.

Gervasio Gallardo never intended to become a straight fantasy artist. As a matter of fact, he began his career with an eye to fine art and only later found himself in the commercial art field. Born in Barcelona in 1934, Gallardo learned the rudiments of his craft and received his first assignments in the advertising field in his native Spain before going to Munich in 1959. Later, moving on to Paris, he found work there with the Delpire Advertising Agency for four years. Finally, in 1963, he made it across the Atlantic and arrived in the United States. Returning off and on over the next few years, Gallardo displayed his work in an occasional exhibition.

But this brief outline of Gallardo's career barely suggests the wonder and sheer imaginative power that would justly earn him a place among the great illustrators forever associated with the literary heritage of Western fantasy.

Even early in his career as an advertising artist, Gallardo refused to rein in his sometimes outré tastes and bizarre visions. Looking at some of his work in that period, one can only wonder and admire the courage of agencies (never mind their clients!) who accepted and used Gallardo's work which often included such recurring motifs as oversized eyes, human figures with the heads of birds or animals and weird, juxtaposed imagery such as a moonscape with dead butterflies, an insect eyed woman with butterfly net, a still life with body parts or creatures assembled with parts from different animals. But if his "public" work was strange, his "private" work, the pieces of art executed for his own pleasure, were even more far out. But no matter how surrealist his work became, it almost always remained grounded in some measure of reality with the artist's almost constant use of such common elements as flowers, fish, birds and other wildlife (even if their species and phylums remained unfamiliar to earthly botanists and zoologists!)

And so, Gallardo's distinctive style was firmly established by the time Betty Ballantine commissioned him to execute covers for her new line of paperbacks reprinting the classics of western fantasy. The Ballantine Adult Fantasy Series, which was to be edited by writer Lin Carter, was intended to take advantage of the growing boom for fantasy fiction generated by the unprecedented sales success of J. R. R. Tolkien's *Lord of the Rings* trilogy. In providing his share of covers for the line (which he executed from sketches prepared by Ballantine art director Robert Blanchard), Gallardo joined a handful of other imaginative artists that included Robert LoGrippo and Bob Pepper. But very soon, it was left in no question as to which artist's style was emerging as the line's definitive look.

"Very rapidly a Gallardo painting on a cover became a signature which fantasy fans recognized immediately," Betty Ballantine herself confirmed.

Among Gallardo's contributions to the Adult Fantasy Series were his extraordinary group of paintings illustrating the work of nineteenth century fantasiste William Morris. Wonderfully capturing Morris' medieval settings that never were, Gallardo brought just the right feeling of idle solitude to the hills of waving grass and distant trees dim in summer haze of *The Wood Beyond the World*; the meticulous detail of the fairy-land city on the cover of *The Sundering Flood*; the fatalistic otherworldliness of *The Well Beyond the World* and the strange, yearning beauty of *The Water of the Wondrous Isles*.

For three collections of the short stories and poetry of Lord Dunsany, Gallardo seemed to have created a triptych of views from what might have been the same town as he takes the long view with *Over the Hills and Far Away*, the middle view in *Beyond the Fields We Know*, and the close up of the very odd *Charwoman's Shadow*.

Another set of covers seem to show Gallardo still up to his old tricks of juxtaposing contrasting images as he does with the cover of G. K. Chesterton's *The Man Who Was Thursday* by having two gentlemen face each other as an oncoming train descends from the air between them. For *Great Short Novels of Adult Fantasy Vol. II*, a naked man rides on the back of a sea serpent and on the cover of George McDonald's *Evenor*, a winged fish takes flight. And what is the reader to make of the cover for *Great Short Novels of Adult Fantasy Vol. I* with its group of dwarves in the process of tucking a beautiful princess into their tree-trunk hideout?

The Ballantines must have been impressed with Gallardo's work on the Adult Fantasy Series, because they also managed to press him into service illustrating a set of paperback reprints of the work of H.P. Lovecraft. For these, Gallardo seemed to abandon all connection with reality and allowed his fertile imagination to run free. And so, unburdened by the constraints of reality (and apparently, of editorial control!) Gallardo proceeded to fill an elliptical cover layout with the most ghastly and grotesque inventions of his career. *The Spawn of Cthulhu* in particular presents a menagerie of creatures as hideous and disturbing as anything found in Lovecraft's prose including a thorned plant adorned with human mouths; strange, filamented crabs, men with heads (adorned with medusa-like hair) too large for their undersized bodies and ghostly, mournful visages of the dead. For the cover of *The Survivor and Others*, a giant bird creature soars over a town with a naked body in its beak as vague, furtive figures flee in panic far below. And for Lin Carter's *Lovecraft: A Look Behind the Cthulhu Mythos*, reptilic creatures with avian style heads gnaw hungrily at bones in a graveyard even as bat-winged reptiles flitter past the moon and amorphic, rugose trees bend menacingly toward a nearby village.

Over the course of a few short years, Gallardo had launched himself from the anonymous world of advertising and the relatively rarified community of art dealers and buyers to the much wider circle of fantasy enthusiasts who lived wherever mass marketed paperbacks reached. But although Gallardo had success in the wake of his stint on the Adult Fantasy Series, creating paintings for such other markets as magazine publishing and record album covers, he soon retired to his native Spain to devote himself to more personal work.

There he remains today, continuing to unleash the weird fantasies of his ever-active mind, translating visions of the bizarre and the wonderful into mundane oil and acrylic for himself and the occasional connoisseur of the fantastic. But for all his accomplishments away from the literary field, it will be the evocative, visual doorways into the minds of writers such as Morris, Dunsany, MacDonald, Smith, and Lovecraft for which he will always be remembered with fondness and affection by fellow travelers along the byways of imagination and that will stand as the greatest monument to his unique vision.

Dualistic Nature: E.R. Eddison

Like Olaf Stapledon and C.S.Lewis, E.R. Eddison wrote his greatest novels for other reasons than mere entertainment (although they are that too!). In his first widely read novel, *The Worm Ouroboros*, Eddison creates a vast tapestry of action and conflict as the forces of Demonland and Witchland clash for control of the world (in this case, Venus, but for the purposes of the story, it might as well be anywhere in fairyland). Across this tapestry move figures who would only be numbered among the greatest of the great on our world. For Eddison, at his aristocratic best, does not concern himself with the petty lives of the lowborn, it is only the world shaking events placed into motion by great and influential men that concern him. Indeed, there is not a single character that appears in the book that one would call "minor." For instance, a particular character may play what we regard as a small role, but because Eddison imbues it with such a distinct personality, that character becomes an idealized version of real people possessing some of those same attributes. A goal Eddison would later explore with more verve in his Zimiamvian Trilogy. In regards to these idealized personalities, Eddison himself said "In that world, well fitted to their faculties and dispositions, men and women of all estates enjoy beatitude in the Aristotelian sense of ...(activity according to their highest virtue). Gabriel Flores, for instance, (the Vicars' secretary), has no ambition to be Vicar of Rerek: it suffices his lust for power that he serves a master who commands his dog-like devotion."

The larger than life characters and events in the novel are accompanied and enhanced by Eddison's own version of Elizabethan prose; a prose that, although trying for the contemporary reader, offers a sense of greatness and otherworldly wonder that more than amply rewards anyone with the patience to master its idiosyncrasies. It is with this prose and the development of his larger than life characters in

The Worm Ouroboros, that Eddison prepares the ground for the following two books of his masterpiece, the Zimiamvian Trilogy. A colossally cosmic series that moves from the strictly earthbound action that takes place in the first book and proceeds to explore the nature of God and the universe in the following two volumes using the heaven of the world of *The Worm Ouroboros* as the setting. A heavenly plane only hinted at in that first book in a scene where two of its characters climb one of that world's most inaccessible mountains and from its peak manage to glimpse in the indistinct distance, Zimiamvia:

"Juss looked southward where the blue land stretched in fold on fold of rolling country, soft and misty, till it melted in the sky. "Thou and I," said he, "first of the children of men, now behold with living eyes the fabled land of Zimiamvia. Is that true, thinkest thou, which philosophers tell us of that fortunate land: that no mortal foot may tread it, but the blessed souls do inhabit it of the dead that be departed, even they that were great upon earth and did great deeds when they were living, that scorned not earth and the delights and the glories thereof, and yet did justly and were not dastards not yet oppressors?"

"Who knoweth?" said Brandoch Daha, resting his chin in his hand and gazing south as in a dream. "Who shall say he knoweth?"

They were silent awhile. Then Juss spake, saying, "If thou and I come thither at last, 0 my friend, shall we remember Demonland?" And when he answered him not, Juss said, "I had rather row on Moonmere under the stars of a summer[1]'s night, than be a King of all the land of Zimiamvia."

In *The Worm Ouroboros*, Eddison stressed more the color and action of a world rather than philosophical ideas made in allegorical form; although more than once the author insisted his work was not allegorical, it nevertheless became so over the course of its creation despite his best efforts. Thus in the land of Zimiamvia, Eddison does not merely extend the surface qualities of characterization and description used in *Ouroboros*, but adds a subtext of deeper meaning as well.

And so, Zimiamvia, like the story in *Ouroboros*, is populated only by the mortal world's greatest heroes. And as they themselves are larger than life, so are their concerns of state, war, intrigue, love and politics. Eddison never depicts anyone preparing a meal, tending to horses or tilling the fields; instead, all these things simply are, with no explanation or, as Diana Waggoner says in *The Hills of Far Away*, "Eddison's heroes are all public men, concerned with great matters of State, power, policy and war, men whose private lives mold and are affected by public affairs. He portrayed Renaissance princes, not knights-errant." And as such, "Eddison has had no imitators; his philosophy is too repugnant for modern sensibilities." The common man's sensibilities perhaps, but even among the diplomatic dealings of today's nations, Machiavelli still is the master.

Eric Rucker Eddison was born at Add in Yorkshire, England, in 1882, and after the required number of years in public schools, entered the civil service on the Board of Trade. For eight years, he was the deputy comptroller-general for the department of overseas trade from which he retired at age fifty-five, spending the rest of his life in literary endeavors. In 1922 he published *The Worm Ouroboros*, in 1926 a work of Norse Legendry called *Styrbiorn the Strong*. In 1935 appeared *Mistress of Mistresses*, in 1941, *A Fish Dinner in Memison* and finally, thirteen years after his death in 1945, *The Mezentian Gate*.

The story of how the books came to be written is almost as strange as they are themselves. Though Eddison wrote them in the order of the above listing, the story they tell begins with the third book and moves backward (forward?) to the first. The author describes the process himself in a letter to his brother:

"Not by design, but because it so developed, my Zimiamvian trilogy has been written backwards. *Mistress of Mistresses*, the first of these books, deals with the two years beginning 'ten months after the death, in the fifty-fourth year of his age, in his island fortress of Sestola in Meszria, of the great King Mezentius, tyrant of Fingiswold, Meszria, and Rerek.' *A Fish Dinner in Memison*, the second book, belongs in its

Zimiamvian parts to a period of five weeks ending nearly a year before the King's death. This third book, *The Mezentian Gate*, begins twenty years before the King was born, and ends with his death.

In *Mistress of Mistresses,* the reader is introduced to a set of characters who will be encountered again in the later books with the insinuation that they are more than what they appear to be. King Mezentius, the man who had united all of the land of Rerek is poisoned, ostensibly at the hand of the Vicar. In his bid for power over all of Rerek, the Vicar is aided by his noble cousin, Lessingham who, by diplomatic arts, corners the Vicar and creates an uneasy peace between he and Duke Barganax, illegitimate son of the king. But the truce is broken by the Vicar and war is declared, a war that ends when the Vicar is treasonously killed by his secretary, Gabriel Flores, who, ironically, had been commissioned by his master to murder Barganax. The book is framed by segments depicting the life and death of Lord Lessingham on our own earth, and his desire for his long dead wife, the Lady Mary. The significance of this framing sequence becomes apparent only in the next book, with the only hint in *Mistress of Mistresses* being a dreamlike episode in which the Lessingham of Zimiamvia sees in a mirror, not his own reflection, but that of Duke Barganax who loves the Lady Fiorinda.

A *Fish Dinner in Memison* alternates chapters between Lord Lessingham and Lady Mary on earth and the couples King Mezentius and his mistress the Duchess Amalie, and Barganax and his lady, Fiorinda. The events in Zimiamvia lead up to a fish dinner out of doors held by the king in which the Lady Fiorinda proposes the creation of a new world. A world that the king builds for her, an ability that surprises even himself. That world is revealed as our own earth, the earth in which the Lord and Lady Lessingham reside. But upon its completion, the king and Fiorinda enter it and reside there for a lifetime that, from their perspective, only lasts a few minutes. Here the reader discovers that the alternating chapters that took place on earth had actually been telling of the lives of the king and Fiorinda while they resided there. Upon their return to

Zimiamvia, the king is suddenly filled with the knowledge that he is God and that he has created Zimiamvia and all other worlds himself; all for Fiorinda who likewise, has now realized her true nature as the personification of Perfection or Beauty. The supper ends as the guests leave the table and Fiorinda casually destroys the earth with a pin-prick.

In *The Mezentian Gate*, Eddison tells of the life of King Mezentius from his birth to his death, overlapping and weaving through the plot of the *The Fish Dinner...* Though Eddison died before completing this volume, he had finished a number of chapters at the beginning and more importantly, at the end of the book.

After the events of the fish dinner, the king's legal wife, Rosma, poisons her husband's drink; but even though he knows it is tainted, still does Mezentius drink from the cup. As the novel closes, the king and Fiorinda "mentally" communicate with each another, fully realizing their natures as God and Perfection, with Fiorinda wondering whether the universe will continue to exist after the death of its creator. Finally, Barganax dimly realizes his own nature as the god unaware of his own identity, living in a world of his own creation and seeing Fiorinda as she truly is. For the king has not died, but merely exchanged one "dress" for another, in the form of Barganax, just as Fiorinda has exchanged the "dress" of the Duchess Amalie for her own; for as the Duchess herself says;

"I have thought it, I think," she said, very low, "from the beginning: that there have been four of us. Perhaps, more than four. And yet always a twoness in that many. And that twoness so near unite to oneness as sense to spirit, yet so as not to confound to unity the very heart and being of God; who is Two in One and One in Two."

As stated above, Eddison did not write a fantasy tale simply to entertain. The author himself said "The book then is a serious book: not a fairy story, and not a book for babes and sucklings." Eddison sought to illustrate his own philosophical idea of the nature of God and His role in the universe. A philosophy crystalized by an encounter with the poet George Santayana,

"The divine beauty is evident, fugitive, impalpable, and homeless in a world of material fact; yet it is unmistakably individual and sufficient unto itself, and although perhaps soon eclipsed is never really extinguished: for it visits time and belongs to eternity." Those words I chanced upon while I was writing the *Fish Dinner*, and liked more because they came as a catalyst to crystallize thoughts that had long been in suspension in my mind."

Using Descartes' famous maxim as the ultimate proof of reality, "I think therefore I am," Eddison concentrated on its essential meaning: that to have identity, a creature must be self-aware; that consciousness was the fundamental reality of human existence and the driving force behind it was the desire for perfection.

"...it can be said that no religion, no philosophy, no considered view of the world and human life and destiny has ever been formulated without some affirmation, expressed or implied, of what is or is not to be desired: and it is this star, forever unattained yet for ever sought, that shines through all great poetry, through all great music, painting, building, and works of men, through all noble deeds, loves, speculations, endurings and endeavours, and all the splendours of 'earth and the deep sky's ornament' since history began, and that gives (at moments, shining through) divine perfection to some little living thing..."

With the desire for perfection the most fundamental of human strivings, that desire becomes the one, true Value and as such, desire defines the nature of God Himself. Seeing as the desire to create is viewed as a positive force, then the desire God felt when he created the universe can only be understood as an act of omnipotent love; and since the object of desire is to seek perfection, even for a god, it stands to reason that God created the universe in His search for perfection. In this regard, Eddison echoes Stapledon's views of the dual nature of God, that He is not perfect Himself, and consequently, must create and destroy an infinite number of universes, seeking perfection.

"In that conception, ultimate reality rests in a Masculine-Feminine dualism, in which the old trinity of Truth, Beauty, Goodness, is extended to embrace the whole of Being and Becoming; Truth consisting in this...That Infinite and Omnipotent Love creates, preserves, and delights in, Infinite and Perfect Beauty: (*Infinitus Amor potestate infinita Pulchritudinem infinitam in infinita perfectione creatur et conservatur*). Love and Beauty are, in this duality, coequal and coeternal; and, by a violent antinomy, Love, owing his mere being to this strengthless perfection which he holds at his mercy, adores and is enslaved by her, while Beauty (by a like antinomy) queens it over the very omnipotence which both created her and is her only safeguard."

But where Stapledon depicted the dual nature of God as consisting of both "good" and "evil," Eddison posited a dual-natured God who can tolerate no evil; not because it exists, but because it is all relevant.

"Ultimate reality, as was said above, must be concrete; and an infinite power, creating and enjoying an infinite value, cannot be cribbed or frozen in a single manifestation. It must, on the contrary, be capable of presenting itself in an infinite number of aspects to different minds and at different moments; and every one of these aspects must be true and (paradoxically) complete, whereas no abstract statement, however profound in its analysis, can ever be either complete or true. This protean character of truth is the philosophical justification for religious toleration; for it is almost inconceivable that truth, realized in the richness of its concrete actuality, should ever present itself to two minds alike. Churches, creeds, schools of thought, or systems of philosophy, are expedient, useful or harmful, as the case may fall out. But the ultimate Vision...the flesh and blood actuality behind these symbols and formulas...is to them as the living body is to apparel which conceals, disguises, suggests, or adorns, that body's perfections."

Thus Eddison at once repudiates both Stapledon and C.S. Lewis' ideas of the nature of God for a synthesis of the two.

In the Zimiamvian books, King Mezentius, driven by the eternal desire for Perfection (in the form of Lady Fiorinda), becomes God, creating world after world and divesting himself of one body or "dress" after another in his never ending pursuit. And so, at the conclusion of *The Mezentian Gate*, the king becomes Barganax and in *Mistress of Mistresses*, it is hinted that Barganax will become Lessingham. Fiorinda, as Perfection, exists both as the king's creation and his ultimate goal, eternally changing "dresses" following the king's suit. Thus at the conclusion of *The Mezentian Gate*, the Duchess Amalie becomes Fiorinda. And the cycle, the "new universe" is recreated, constantly evolving toward an unatainable perfection.

Man's Guts

The Spirit Hearse

"How far do you want to go?" she asked.

"All the way," I replied.

"Too bad," she laughed, "but this is as far as I go."

I pulled up alongside her and we both moved out onto the tiny spit of land created by an inlet of the rushing river. Over the years the small dike of silt had managed to reach out and embrace a goodly portion of the stream in a pool whose deep waters held the best trout fishing in the whole county. Or so Donna told me.

"I thought you said the best spot was further up the river?" I asked.

"It is," she said "but I haven't the time to take you all the way upstream this morning. I have a boarding house to run remember?"

"Sure, but your mom can handle things for a few hours can't she?"

"Not the account books she can't," said Donna with an air of finality.

Sure, I was disappointed. Donna was an attractive woman. When Bill Finley told me about the fishing in this area and recommended the Roadsider Inn to me, he never said anything about its attractive owner. But then, from what I knew of her, she wasn't here when Bill was vacationing last summer.

I edged past her and moved out onto the spit, reaching a pile of rocks that formed a natural point at its end. Facing back toward the shore and the pool, I dropped my hardware and stripped off my jacket. It took only a minute to bait the hooks, but in that time, Donna had followed me out and had settled on a large, flat rock that sloped down into the cool water. I watched her stretch out her long, white legs as she poked her bare feet into the water. As I slipped into my hip boots, she leaned back and wriggled her toes under the surface.

"I guess you're not that anxious to get back," I said.

She smiled a smile that would've knocked most men dead and said, "I've got a couple of minutes. And I do so love it out here. Especially this time of the morning."

"Um-hm," I agreed and eased myself into the water, grabbing my fishing rod as I did. I tested its tension and asked rhetorically, "So what else is there to do in Beechum's Hollow, I mean, anything exciting happen around here?"

As soon as I said it, I bit my tongue. I had forgotten what she told me earlier in the week, that her husband had been murdered not six months before. In fact, that was the reason I hadn't put any of my moves on her yet; her recent bereavement kept me at arm's length. At least, to me it did. I hadn't really gotten any signals one way or the other from her. In any case, judging by her reply, she didn't seem to be bothered by my question.

"Actually, Tim, nothing of interest ever happens in Beechum's Hollow." Despite myself, I couldn't help feeling a thrill whenever she called me by name. No woman ever had that sort of effect on me before. "That's why we get the sort of tourists we do. It's quiet and relaxing."

"So there's nothing to give the town any atmosphere, any identity?"

"Well…" She seemed to think it over for a minute, then in newfound animation, she curled those legs from out of the water and tucked them wetly beneath her. "There's the Spirit Hearse."

"The what?"

She laughed and shrugged her shoulders. "The Spirit Hearse. Stories have gone around the town for years about this hearse that rides around at night during full moons looking for the souls of the dead. It's crazy, I know, but it's the closest thing to a legend Beechum's Hollow has."

I laughed with her then and made my first cast. "Maybe I'll get a look at it before I leave."

"Maybe," she said, rising to her feet and brushing off her shorts. "Anyway, good luck with the fish and don't forget, dinner is served at the Roadside at seven."

With that, she disappeared into the forest in the direction of town. With her receding figure, I found myself thinking of other things than my fishing. I had just come off a really tough case in Boston the week before when my partner, Bill Finley, coaxed me into coming here, to Beechum's Hollow, to unwind. It was in taking a room at the Roadside Inn that I ran into Donna. She and her mother owned the place and I wasted no time in ingratiating myself onto her. Except that when I found out her husband had been mysteriously murdered only six months before, I decided to lay off. Call me old fashioned, but I felt it would've been too soon for her to think about another man in her life. At least we had grown familiar enough for her to volunteer to show me the best fishing spot on the river.

It was about three o'clock in the afternoon when I exited the trail leading from the forest and stepped into the shady interior of the bait and tackle shop where I had rented my equipment. The gloomy, two room shack stank of rotten fish and damp earth as I threw down my gear and slapped my day's catch onto the greasy counter. I figured I made enough noise for the proprietor to hear and in another second he emerged from a back room giving me a wary eye. He weighed about three hundred pounds and, dressed in filthy chinos and soiled T-shirt, sported a three day old growth of scraggly beard. Still wielding the knife he was using to hack and cut up his own catch he sold to nearby towns, he looked down at the full line of fish I had on the counter. He didn't say anything.

"Can you cut and clean these fish and have them sent to the Roadside Inn?" I asked. He grunted and thunked his knife into the counter's surface. I figured it for a yes, and walked out into the dirt road that led to a paved section further on.

When I reached Beechum's Hollow proper, I passed along the short length of the town center to the small variety store at the opposite end of the street and escaped the mosquitoes that had just begun to bite. I passed the old pot bellied stove and rockers that in winter, still hosted the town's oldsters, and slid between the narrow shelves of dusty canned goods toward the rear of the store. Johnson Peters milled about behind the high refrigerator counter whose glass face was so fogged that I couldn't see what the day's sale was. I moved over to the stand of garden tools and cleared my throat. Peters turned and smiled.

"Hello, Mr. Mons, what can I get you?"

"A can of Hellspont tobacco," I said.

"Sorry, I only stock a single brand."

He picked up a can whose label was completely unfamiliar to me and held it out questioningly. I shrugged and dug out my wallet. While he fooled with the antique cash register, I took the opportunity to eyeball the pictures he had hanging on the rear wall. They were all of a single man in various phases of his life but none older than middle age. They all seemed to be well taken care of and as a matter of fact, Peters had been busy polishing one of them when I interrupted him.

I paid for the tobacco and weaved my way out to the narrow porch again and paused there to light my pipe. After a few experimental puffs, I guessed the tobacco to be tolerable and surveyed the nearly empty street. Looking at my watch, I saw it was almost five o'clock and thought it a good idea to head back to my room and lie down for an hour or so before dinner.

The Roadside Inn wasn't too far away, and it was only a few minutes before I entered the little foyer and climbed the stairs to my back room and crashed.

A couple of hours later, I sat down at the long dinner table where all of the inn's guests shared their board. Unfortunately, because the sitting arrangements went according to seniority, those guests who'd so far stayed the longest, I was stuck a good five or six seats from where Donna sat. Conversation over dinner was consequently limited to a few bon mots with the pale cadaver that sat alongside me. His skin was whiter than the milk he habitually drank and the more I saw him drink it, the more I knew I had to have a real drink as soon as possible. It was even more unfortunate that Donna's mother didn't allow liquor on the premises. But for once, I managed to make a bit of bad luck pay off, and used it as an excuse to ask Donna if she'd like to keep me company down to the local bar and grill a few streets away.

We crossed the narrow porch and left the picket fence behind us as we moved up the street. It was completely dark by this time, and the hot summer day had turned into a warm summer night. We walked slowly, neither of us felt like breaking the mood, and so reached the bar in a relaxed frame of mind. I ordered two beers, a bottle for me and a glass for her, while she scouted for a table.

I slid in the booth she had picked and pushed her glass over to her side of the table. We sipped a bit while I took in the décor. Except for the porno pictures the proprietor had plastered behind the bar, it was a pretty quiet place.

"Thank you for the fish, Tim," she said at last. "You sure made mother happy. She'll have it fixed up for dinner tomorrow night."

"No sweat," I said. "What was I going to do with twenty pounds of rotten fish when I got back home in two weeks? Besides, the fun is in the catching not the eating. I'll look forward to more of your mom's home cooking tomorrow."

Sensing a lack of forward motion, I felt I had to keep the conversation going at all costs.

"When did you take over the Inn anyway? Bill Finley never mentioned you or your mother to me when he recommended it to me."

"Oh, it was just after John, my husband, had been killed," she said. "I just couldn't stay in the old house, so I sold it and bought the Inn a few months ago."

"I think it was a good idea," I said soberly. "You look good...but did they ever find the man who murdered your husband?"

I couldn't help it. The question slipped out before I could stop myself. On the other hand, I really wanted to get that bogey out of the way as soon as possible. Better to hammer it out now than at the last minute before I left for Boston. Still, I was surprised when she went ahead and explained.

"No, they never did catch him. They just found John's body at the bottom of Kile's Gorge with no way to find the killer. No clues, no nothing."

"If you want, I can poke around some. I am a detective after all..."

She looked up with those doe eyes I couldn't resist and said, "No, Tim. It's all over now. Let it rest. I have a new life and I'm happier now than I thought I could be. I'm satisfied."

Feeling that to be the end of the conversation, I rose and Donna followed me. The walk home was way too short and I felt that somehow we had developed a certain rapport that I couldn't explain. Just as I couldn't explain the impulsive kiss she gave me at the foot of the front steps before dashing into the house. I would've run after her then if I hadn't been paralyzed with an indefinable prickling ecstasy that washed all the way through me in the wake of that kiss. And I mentally kicked myself ever afterward, because if I had followed her, then maybe she wouldn't have disappeared the way she did the next morning.

I found out about it early on the afternoon of the following day when I got up from a long sleep filled with dreams of me and Donna to find the parlor filled with my fellow guests and a weeping Mrs. Thomson, Donna's mother, hunched in the overstuffed chair near the fireplace. Zeke Briggs, the town's sheriff, was there too trying to get some information out of her but finding it hopeless. Just as I walked in, one of the guests said, "There he is sheriff."

Sheriff Briggs turned and walked up to me saying, "You're Mr. Mons, from Boston?"

"That's right."

He cleared his throat and straightened. "When was the last time you saw Mrs. Hampton?"

"Mrs. Hampton…you mean Donna? About ten last night. Why?"

"She's disappeared. I got a call from Mrs. Thomson here about an hour ago saying her daughter never got in last night. And you were the last person to see her. I understand you're a detective, have you any idea where she might be?"

"None," I said.

"Don't believe him sheriff. I saw him leave with Mrs. Hampton last night. And I didn't see them come back," said the cadaverous albino.

The sheriff looked at me suspiciously and said, "What have you to say to that?"

I thought a minute and took a long shot.

"I was with her last night, but I had no reason for any wrongdoing," I said. "You see, we're going to be married."

Needless to say, there was a collective gasp from the assembled group, not least of all from the surprised Mrs. Thomson. I'd worry about Donna's reaction later. Right then, I was more interested in finding her. I was just about to turn the tables on the sheriff and quiz him on what he knew, when a new arrival started babbling from the window.

"It was the Spirit Hearse! I saw it! I saw it!" Everyone turned to the newcomer and saw that it was just old Jonas Bencroft, the town drunk. "The Spirit Hearse came for her soul and now she'll be trapped in limbo forever!"

"Jonas, shut your yap before I shut it for you!" barked the sheriff. "Now get on back to your cell at the jail, get on now!"

Jonas did as he was ordered, but not before one more "Spirit Hearse!"

Sheriff Briggs turned back to me and said, "All right, Mr. Mons, I don't know about you, but you'd better stick around here till either I get to the bottom of this, or Mrs. Hampton reappears." And after an obligatory word of sympathy to Donna's mother, he headed back to his office.

As for me, I was inwardly frantic. My words of marriage toward Donna were all true, at least in my heart. I knew that when I saw her next, I'd ask her to marry me, and she'd say yes. Unless her disappearance had something to do with the kiss she gave me the night before. Was she afraid of what she was feeling and decided to run away? I preferred not to think about that possibility but to concentrate instead on finding her. And like it or not, I had only one clue to go by: The Spirit Hearse.

The first thing I discovered while going through the stacks at the Amesburg public library was that there was no mention of it before 1957. Looking further, I found the biggest story ever to hit the county. It was about Armstrong McGovern Peters, the most important man in the county. Besides owning most of the business, real estate, and county commissioners, he also owned a funeral home. It seems his main occupation was as an undertaker. But in 1955, it all came crashing down. Scandal found him and hounded him from the county; leaving everything he owned and taking only what cash he had in his bank account, Peters disappeared never to be seen again. His mistake?

Peters had a sweet racket going with his funeral parlor business. Besides gouging his customers for expenses, he also managed to seduce unwary widows during the preparations, taking the fruit of his desires right in the back seat of the hearse as he drove it from the cemetery. The funny thing was, none of the widows ever said a word about it. Until Mary Mathews. He tried his routine with her the same as the others, but she withstood his advances. Peters, though, wasn't a man to take no for an answer. So he just took her there in the back seat. Later, she brought him to court but he never showed up. He took his money and skipped the county never to be heard from again. Mary Mathews was left with her shame and an illegitimate son.

Of course, it struck me right away that that son could be none other than Johnson Peters, the proprietor of the Beechum's Hollow grocery store. Peters with those pictures of his long lost father hanging all over his shop.

I left Amesburg and made my way back to Beechum's Hollow as fast as I could, I had to get to the sheriff and tell him of my suspicions. The whole drive over, I couldn't get the thought of Donna being in Peters' clutches out of my mind. But just as I was coming into Beechum's Hollow, it hit me. I knew why Peter's had done it, and worse, what he intended. I remembered the circumstances of Armstrong Peters' rape of Mary Mathews, the place, the time, the date. Desperately, I looked at my watch and saw that in only an hour, all three would coincide to the minute, thirty-two years later. There was no time to find the sheriff, so I pulled hard on the steering wheel and brought the car around and headed back out of town.

In a few minutes, I pulled up to a dirt road that led off the main highway and into a cathedral of over-arching trees. Forced to slow down, I passed the town cemetery on my right, the site of the elder Peters' unspeakable acts. Deserted of visitors this late in the afternoon, I passed the burying ground and continued on into the depths of the surrounding forest.

At last, I halted a good two miles further on where I almost despaired that the road I was following would disappear. But it had held on long enough for me to draw up to the entrance of another, even more ill used road. Leaving the car, I pushed through the initial shrubbery and managed to make my way along the faint traces of what was left of the old road. Quickly, taking occasional glances at my watch, I headed deeper into the forest toward the spot I knew from the newspaper accounts was the place the elder Peters had raped Mary Mathews thirty-two years before. The place and time his illegitimate son insanely hoped to emulate the father by raping a widow. A widow I knew had been created by Johnson solely in an effort to have her available on the fateful day when he prepared to consummate not his love of the woman, but his love of the father he never knew.

But as I finally reached the little clearing containing the old Peters' house, I found that I wasn't at all ready to face the reality of my conjectures. He was there all right, just as I thought, but as if to punctuate his madness, what I saw beside the house was enough to give me pause. There, alongside the old, faded clapboards of the house, was a perfectly restored hearse. The fresh tire markings in the soft soil of the unpaved road that wound around the house to the other side indicated that old Jonas Bencroft was a least partially right. It could well have been a hearse he saw the night Donna was abducted.

Suddenly, there was movement from the house and I forgot all about the whys and wherefores of the case as Peters pushed Donna from the front door with the encouragement of a small hand pistol. Anxiously, I scanned for some sign of injury upon Donna's person and breathed a sigh of relief when I couldn't spot any.

Peters was forcing Donna down the rickety front steps as my mind spun with thoughts of rescue. But nothing came. As long as Peters held that gun, I was helpless. I cursed myself inwardly for not having the foresight of bringing my own piece from Boston. But who would've thought I'd need it in Beechum's Hollow? All I could do now, was wait and watch for an opportunity to surprise the kidnapper.

With my heart pounding in fear and frustration, I watched as Peters led Donna to the hearse and opened the rear door. He motioned curtly with the pistol for her to get inside. I knew what would come next and so, careless of the danger, I dashed across the intervening space to the far corner of the house. Luckily, Peters had been too busy watching his captive to notice me so that I found myself in the perfect position to observe what came next. It wasn't pretty.

With Donna lying back on the rear seat of the hearse, Peters ordered her to remove her clothing. At first she hesitated, protested, pleaded; but it did no good. Peters fired the gun at the ground and the sudden report made me jump. Donna cried out at the sound and began to squirm pathetically on the seat backing farther inside in an effort to get away from Peters. Again, he ordered her to remove her clothes and slowly the frightened girl complied. She began by slipping off her skirt. Seeing Peters yank it from around her ankles and raking it out of the car reminded me that Donna was still wearing the same outfit she had on the night before when she gave me that surprise kiss. I hardly noticed my fingernails digging into the old clapboards as she had begun to unbutton her blouse next. Again, impatience clear in his every movement, Peters began to drag the stockings from her legs, his pistol still pointed menacingly toward her breast. Petrified, Donna was past resisting and I could tell even from where I hung back that she had given up hope of being rescued before the final indignity. Grabbing one of Donna's ankles, Peters pulled her closer to him. Releasing her leg, he reached out and snatched at her bra; pulling, he snapped its fastenings and tore it free of her bosom.

It was then that I saw my chance. As he climbed onto the seat, into the space between Donna's legs, his back was fully toward me. I leaped from the corner of the house, dashed around the porch, and lunged for the car. As I did so, I grabbed up the only object at hand that I could use as a weapon and in the very instant Peters was groping for the panties that were Donna's final protection, I knocked the gun from his hand and wrapped the length of the discarded bra around his scrawny neck.

A blind rage must have took hold of my brain, because I nearly killed the man then and there. It was only the pleadings of the girl that brought me to my senses in time for me to merely strangle him into unconsciousness. And as he slunk to the ground outside the hearse, Donna flew into my arms and we held each other long and hard before at last separating.

It took time to explain to Sheriff Briggs the motivations that compelled Peters to do the awful things he did, chief among them his need to belong following the early death of his mother and a blind love for a father long dead. A desperate need for affection that drove him to the point of murder and rape simply to emulate the idol he cherished. His mother probably tried to hide the truth of his father from him and it was only after she died when he discovered the truth that he became unhinged. Eventually, he had the idea of emulating his father using the Spirit Hearse legend. I was sure that with a little thought, Briggs would recall other disappearances of local widows, serial violations by Peters that finally culminated in his murder of Donna's husband and her own abduction. What made that outrage even more significant was that her planned rape would have taken place on Peters' birthday; he'd planned for it to be a twisted recreation of his own blighted conception!

Briggs took some convincing to believe my explanations but the biggest thing in my favor was Donna's corroboration of the facts and her exoneration of my hasty declaration of marriage. The only thing we both wanted after that was to find a preacher and get out of Beechum's Hollow as fast we could.

The Devil's Choreography

The whole strange story began about six months ago, in the early part of spring. Linda, my wife, had begun to take dancing classes downtown just after New Year's in an attempt to recapture the talent she'd shown before we were married. Of course, I had no objections; after all, she had to quit her budding career in dance when we were first married in order to go with me overseas where I was transferred for a couple of years. But as soon as we got back to Pacific City she wasted no time in making noises about getting back to the studio. We already decided to wait a few more years for children, giving her plenty of time to see if dancing was really what she wanted. Besides, if she were going to give it her best shot, it had to be soon, while she was still young and limber. But at twenty-three, she still had plenty of fire left. That, and her girlish good looks would make her a shoo-in once she was ready. At least that's what I kept telling myself. Deep down, I didn't want her to get caught up in any big performing kick because I knew once that happened, she may not want to settle down. It was selfish, and I felt guilty about it, but it was something that I couldn't help.

That said, there was no way that I could want it bad enough for any harm to come to her.

Anyway, as I began to say, the whole strange story began about six months ago when Linda left one morning as usual to get to her studio in the city. She gave me one of those flying good-bye kisses as she hurried out the door and the next thing I heard was the sound of her car revving up and pulling out of the driveway. I finished my coffee and left for my job at the offices of Jay & Killowan. It was a perfectly normal day until I got home that night and found the house empty. It was unusual for Linda not to be home first and have something brewing on the stove, but not unusual enough for me to get worked up over it. Sometimes that rush hour traffic along Route 93 was murder on Fridays. So I pulled out some hamburger and began something simple for supper.

It was about seven thirty when I really started to worry. She'd never been that late. I'll confess to having felt a little nervous as I dialed the number she left by the phone stand and waited for the answering voice.

"Martineau Studios in the Art of Dance, may I help you?"

"Yes, this is Vincent Parry," I asked as calmly as I could. "Is Linda Parry still at the studio?"

"Can you wait a moment, Mr. Parry?"

I said yes just after she left me hanging and waited with butterflies in my stomach. I kept telling myself to calm down, that nothing was wrong. But the answer I finally got did nothing to help me relax.

"Mr. Parry? Mrs. Parry is not in the studio. She must have left with her class at three o'clock."

"No, she couldn't have; you see, she hasn't gotten home yet, and she always…"

"Well, I'm sorry, but she's not here. Maybe she stopped for some shopping on the way home."

I didn't see the need to press my argument and said, "Yes, well, that could be. Thank you."

But I wasn't convinced of that at all. Linda always called if there was a change in her plans. These days, a woman couldn't take any chances. We didn't have any relatives in the area and we hadn't lived there long enough to make any friends so there was no one else to call. So I moped around the house for a while before deciding to lie down. I thought that maybe if I dozed for an hour or so, I'd wake up to find her home, safe and sound.

The house was pitch dark when I woke up. Out of habit, I reached across to the other side of the bed to stroke Linda's hair, but all I felt was the cold sheets that had never been slept in. Abruptly, I remembered her being late that afternoon and shot bolt upright. Quickly, I grabbed for the alarm clock by the bed and saw with horror that it was nearly two in the morning! I dashed from the bedroom and ran through the house calling Linda's name, but there was no reply. Sweat began to run along the sides of my body as I grabbed up the phone and dialed the emergency number.

"Police headquarters, Manolis speaking, can I help you?"

"Officer, I'd like to report a missing person, my wife…"

"When did she disappear?"

"This afternoon…"

"Well sir, I can't move on a missing person report this soon. We have to wait three days…"

"But I know there's something wrong," I cried, cutting him off. "She always calls…"

"Calm down, sir. What I can do is check our accident report and keep an eye out for anything that might have to do with her. Now what's your wife's name?"

I had to stop and think for a minute before replying. "Linda Parry."

I heard the soft clacking of fingers over a keypad before the officer answered. "No, there's no Parry here. All I can do is keep checking sir. Call back in three days and we can make an official report. Now what's your name and address?"

I guess I gave him the information, I don't really remember. What I do remember is running out to my car and driving down to the dance studio myself. But when I got there, the place was closed. It was only then I remembered the time: about three in the morning. So I forced my anxieties down and settled for the remainder of the night in the back seat of my car. The hours crawled by in sleepless agony until the studio doors were unlocked at nine a.m. the next day.

I was the first through them; unshaved and disheveled, I must have made quite a sight, but I ignored the looks I got from the receptionist as I told her who I was. In minutes, she had her boss out front and I have to admit, he was patient enough to hear me out. Finally, he allowed me to see where my wife had spent her time the day before.

"…and here we have the studio proper where the students can have all the room they need for the advanced movements," Martineau said as his voice echoed hollowly against the room's hardwood floors and mirrored walls. "These other rooms of course, are all designed for various styles of…"

"Yes, yes," I said impatiently. "But what I would really like is to see someone from my wife's class who may have spoken to her or seen her yesterday before she left the studio."

"Well, it is still early…" I was about to say something I would've regretted, when suddenly, he perked up and said, "Why, there's Miss Williams. She's in your wife's class. Miss Williams. Miss Williams! Yes, would you come here a moment, please?"

Miss Williams was a striking blond who was still wrapped in the long, tweed coat she wore against the early spring cold outside. As she drew up to us, she asked, "Yes, Mr. Martineau?"

"Miss Williams," said Martineau, "Mr. Parry here is the husband of Mrs. Linda Parry, who I believe is in your form?"

Miss Williams looked at me and smiled. "Hello, Mr. Parry, Linda's told me a lot about you."

I smiled back at her, and was surprised that it wasn't at all forced. I didn't wait for Martineau to explain my reasons for being at the studio but instead addressed Miss Williams myself. "Miss Williams, I'm here because I'm worried bout my wife. She never came home last night and I was hoping that one of her fellow students here may have heard her say where she was going after class or maybe even have seen her leave."

The girl frowned and thought a moment before replying. "Gee, I can see why you might be worried. But as far as I can remember, Linda didn't say anything about going anywhere to us girls. And as a matter of fact, she didn't leave with the rest of us either. I think she stayed behind in the dressing room to fix a tear in her outfit. Yeah, I think she might have been the last to leave."

My heart sank at the lack of information but was immediately buoyed at the next suggestion the girl made. "But maybe you can ask Claud about her, he's always here till eight or nine at night."

"Claud?"

"Our maintenance man," said Mr. Martineau. "At least until this morning. He hasn't shown up for work yet, and he's never this late."

All at once, a horrible thought struck me. Could this Claud have had anything to do with Linda's disappearance? But my thoughts along those lines were interrupted with Martineau's next words.

"I wouldn't suspect Claud Dalton of anything nefarious, Mr. Parry. He's quite harmless I assure you."

"I'll vouch for that," added Miss Williams.

I didn't let myself be persuaded by their assurances because they really didn't sound too sincere. Instead, I asked, "Could I see the room where my wife was last seen?"

"The dressing room?" asked Martineau, looking at the girl.

The girl nodded and said, "It'll be all right, there's no one there right now."

I thought it was kind of funny that the owner of the studio would defer to a student, but paid it no further attention as the girl escorted me to the dressing room at the rear of the building. It was a mess of clothes-trees and make-up tables; a mix of scents wafted from deeper in its interior: sweat, make-up, perfume, and the unmistakable odor of showers. Not unlike those of the men's showers I used in college and high school. I walked through the room looking around, for what, I wasn't quite sure, feeling terribly self conscious as I did so. At last, I gave up and thanked Miss Williams, exiting the building with Claud the janitor in mind.

It was mid-afternoon and I was sitting in front of the TV set in the living room. I was in a kind of mental numbness brought on by complete helplessness in the pursuit of my wife. Lethargic and listless, I just slumped in my chair, going over for the umpteenth time the events of the day.

As soon as I left the studio, I raced over to the address given to me by the receptionist to find Claud Dalton. But again, I was stymied in my efforts by an empty apartment and a landlady who hadn't seen Claud since the evening before. At least she could say that there hadn't been a woman with him. Next, I went to the Pacific City Police Station to try my luck with missing persons again but got nowhere. Again, I was told that officially, they had to wait the requisite three days before they could move on anything, and it had only been one and half. At my wits' end, I left the city for home, and if you asked me, I wouldn't be able to tell you a thing about that trip home, because my mind was numb like I said. I just couldn't believe it was all happening. And then it all turned around.

I was just sitting there staring at the TV screen when a new story came on the 24-hour local access news network. There had been some sort of police raid on a warehouse in Pacific City an hour before and the film showed a series of shots of scruffy looking men being led from the warehouse where they had been in the process of buying illicit pornographic materials. Of course, they all tried to hide their features beneath their jackets but it didn't do any good, as the film crew managed to catch the faces of a few of them and enlarge their pictures with accompanying narration. Then the electrifying news hit me. One of the shots showed a short, disheveled man as the newscaster said something about him; but the only thing that stayed in my mind was the name of Claud Dalton!

It was a miracle I wasn't stopped on the highway for speeding as I made my way back to the Pacific City Police Department. There, I cajoled the officer in charge to let me talk to Claud for a few minutes. The sergeant knew me from that afternoon and sympathized so it was an easy matter for him to let me in to see the man. Of course, Claud didn't know me from Adam, but when I told him who I was and what I wanted from him, he grew fidgety and looked about nervously.

"Look," I said, "is there anything you can tell me? I'm not asking you to incriminate yourself."

He looked directly at me for the first time, shook himself, and began to talk.

"Okay, I'll tell you what I know," he said. "It don't matter none anymore anyway. I'm as good as fired. Yeah, I saw your wife last night. Linda, the cute one." He smirked and I tried not to punch him in the face. "Yeah, she had good legs, nice tits too…"

"Shut up already, and get on with it." I already began to suspect how he came onto the information he was about to give me and it was galling to have to hold back the urge to break every bone in his body.

"Yeah, well, last night after practice, the girls all went to their dressing room as usual," he began. "And as usual, I managed to look like I had business at the back of the building. See, I got a great little spy hole back there that let's me have a good view of the room, right across it and inta the showers. Anyway, last night I took in the free show and watched until everybody left. Everybody except your wife, Linda. She stayed behind to do some sewing or something; did you know she liked to sew in the nude?"

He must have seen how my face paled at the purposeful taunt but simply snickered and continued with his story.

"Anyway, she was the last one in the room when I saw somebody else come in the window from the alley," said Claud. "I don't know who it was 'cause he had a weird sort of mask on his head, one of those rubber jobs they sell in the joke stores. It looked to me like a devil's mask with a whole outfit to match. I was so surprised to see the guy that I completely forgot about your wife. And I only remembered her when the devil guy sneaked over behind her back and whipped a rag over her face. I don't know what it was, but in no time your wife was knocked out and on the floor. The devil guy took a stretch of curtain from the window, laid her on top of it, and then rolled her up inside. Next, he heaves her in his arms and goes out by the window again. It was only then that I thought to move. I ran into the room and over to the window to try and get a better look at the devil guy but all I saw was a black limo pull out of the alley with all of its windows blacked out. That's it mister."

I was stunned. Linda *had* been kidnapped! And there was still nothing the police could do about it. But at least I had something to go on. All I had to do was find out who in the city owned a black limousine with blacked out windows and check them out for signs of Linda and pray they had nothing like murder in mind. Unfortunately, my fears weren't assuaged when the police sergeant who had allowed me to see Claud called me over to his desk.

"Mr. Parry, if you'll keep it under your hat, I'll let you in on another bit of news," said the sergeant. "Your wife is only the latest dancer to disappear in the city. Over the past few weeks, there've been at least four others. And we haven't a clue to go on. The D.A.'s office is trying to keep a lid on it until they can crack the case. So you see, technically, we are working on your wife's case."

The sergeant's information didn't make me feel any better, especially since the D.A.'s office had no clues. I would have told him what I learned from Claud but not only would it sound crazy but it was only hearsay to boot. Hurrying from the station, I determined not to wait on the slow machinery of the police but to run down Claud's story myself.

I couldn't just sit on my hands waiting for the police to find Linda; she needed me to find her right then, and the only lead I had was the sighting of a black limousine in the alley of the dance studio. So it was the first place I went after leaving the police station. It was then I got my second shock of the night. Parked right in front of the studio was a black limousine with opaque windows! Of course, my first thought was that it would be too much of a coincidence to have the kidnapping vehicle at the scene of the crime just as I got there to ask about it, but I didn't question it. If I had to look up every black limo in the city anyway, I might as well have started with that one.

And I didn't have long to wait before I had the opportunity to check out its owner. Before I even had time to step out of my car from where I had parked it along the street, Andre Martineau came down the front steps of the building and stooped into the rear of the limo. In seconds, it pulled away from the curb and accelerated up the street. I brought my engine to life and started out after them. It was crazy and illogical, but for some reason, it made sense. Who else but the owner of the studio would have the perfect opportunity to kidnap Linda? I began to wonder too if he had any connection with the other places where dancers had disappeared, but left that train of thought as it became more important for me keep the limo in sight.

While following the limo, I had time to think about the character in the devil's outfit who had taken Linda. If it was Martineau, why dress up in the crazy costume? To hide his identity, sure, but wouldn't a simple hood have sufficed? And why was he kidnapping dancing girls? I didn't really want to think too much on those possibilities. There were too many stories in the papers already about strange Satan worshippers and heavy metal freaks who got their jollies by terrorizing innocent people. Why, there was even a cult magazine called *Harem Scarem* that exploited their perverse interests by depicting the most vile acts in lavish explicitness. Then it suddenly occurred to me that it had been the offices of that very magazine which were the object of the porno raid involving Claud Dalton. But that coincidence was too much for me. If Claud was lying to me to protect himself, then by following the limo, I was no nearer finding Linda than I would have been sitting at home.

By now, it was getting dark and the limousine had led me clear out of the city and into the sparsely populated area north of town where the ground was too marshy to build anything on. I really didn't expect Martineau to stop anywhere around there, but he did. Far up ahead, his tail lights flared as his driver applied the brakes. I did the same and quickly dimmed my headlights. I tried to catch up with the limousine as fast as I could while its lights were still visible but it wasn't easy to do, as I had to be careful to stay on the raised surface of the road without the benefit of illumination.

At last, I was in close enough to slow down, and I saw the car veer sharply to the right and disappear in the darkness. I slowed to five miles an hour and crept up to the spot where I had last seen the limo and in another minute saw the dim whiteness of a road sign. "A. Martineau, 15 Drearcreek Road" it read. Nice. I rolled the car as far up against the side of the road as I could. Under the cover of some overhanging shrubbery, I got out. Two steps away from the car and I couldn't make it out at all; no one was going to see it by accident.

Satisfied, I passed beneath the sign and on up the gravel and dirt driveway that curved gently to the left and so up a slight incline to a big house that bulked heavily against the moonless sky. I was kind of surprised to find such an old house this far out in the marshes, but then figured any one of the railroad tycoons of the last century could have had the money to build such a pile out there regardless of the soil conditions.

In a few minutes I found myself alongside the parked limousine but I couldn't see inside it as the windows were tinted black and the doors locked. Just ahead, I saw the house standing quiet and dark. Not a single light burned in the entire place; it was as if no one had driven up to it in years. But I knew differently. Martineau and, I hoped, Linda were in there and I was going to find out for sure one way or another. I moved over to the first window I saw and tried the sash but it wouldn't budge, so I tried the next one and the next. All were locked and I was beginning to worry that I wouldn't be able to sneak inside without making some noise. I had worked my way around to the rear of the house when I noticed the smaller, higher pantry and bathroom windows. I figured that if any windows in the house were unlocked, it would be those. Often, owners didn't lock windows like that assuming that they'd be out of reach of any prowler.

I looked around in the dark until I found an old sawhorse in the brush and dragged it over to the window. In no time, I had the sash open and was trying to heave myself through the window as silently as I could. The sink slid by my stomach as I groped for the floor. In another second, I was on my feet and at the entrance to the dining room. I peeked in and found everything as I saw it from outdoors: dark and quiet. I crossed the room grabbing a brass candlestick as I passed and emerged cautiously out into the front hallway. I had to make a choice then: upstairs or downstairs? A squeak decided it for me and I began climbing the stairs. At the top, I paused, my heart pounding, and listened. In a few minutes, I heard another noise, this time a little scraping sound from one of the rooms. It was then I noticed the dull thread of light coming from beneath one of the doors. I hefted the candlestick and gripped the doorknob. Not unaware that I was about to save my wife or be proved the biggest fool in town, I shoved the door open.

I wasn't at all ready for the sight that met my eyes when I fell into that room. It was completely empty with all the windows caulked and sealed against the light escaping to the outside. Completely empty that is, except for the lone figure tied to a simple straight backed chair in the center of the room. He was naked and I could see that he was more than just tied;

his body was twisted into obviously painful contortions that slowly bent his bones and throttled him with any move he made. Rows of red welts, old and new, stitched his arms and torso and his face was hidden beneath a greasy hood. Somehow he sensed my presence in the room and began to speak.

"Maryanne, is that you? Please don't keep me waiting any longer. You know I'd do anything for you. You know how I look forward to your attentions...How *you* enjoy it...oh, it's cruel to keep me waiting like this..."

I thought I was going to throw up then, because I felt my gorge begin to rise, but I fought the sensation down and reached for the man's hood.

"I'm not your damned Maryanne, asshole," I said in disgust and yanked the hood from the man's head. That's when I received my second shock of the night.

"Martineau!" I gasped.

He looked up at me dazedly for a minute until his eyes cleared. "You're not Maryanne...you're...Mr. Parry?"

"Yes, yes, damn you! What have you done to my wife?"

I was sure now that Linda had been abducted by the man. It was too much for coincidence that Martineau could be involved in such perverted activity and not be connected with disappearances of the dancers including my wife who was taken from his own studio.

Suddenly Martineau seemed to break down. He began to weep and between his tears came the whole amazing story.

"It wasn't my fault, Mr. Parry, it was Maryanne's idea," he pleaded. "She was the editor of that magazine, *Harem Scarem*, when she found me. She said her readers were getting bored with the magazine's usual brutalities and that she had a new idea. She would use actual dancing girls and stage a scene from hell. Satan's Dancing Corpses she called it. She sought me out, seduced me, showed me terrible things, and before I realized it, found that I couldn't do without them. That's when she began to make her demands. If I wanted to keep her attentions, I had to help in her kidnap scheme. But it didn't include murder! You have believe that, not murder!"

"Was it you who did the kidnapping in the devil outfit?" I asked coldly, the candlestick heavy in my hand.

"Yes, and she took pictures as I did it. For the magazine she said. But I didn't murder anyone!"

I must have been in some kind of daze, because it was only then that I remembered Linda. "Where is she? Where's my wife, Linda?"

"Maryanne brought them downstairs…"

I hardly remember the exit I took from the room, the dash down the stairs, or the stumbling fall I took into the basement stairwell. I only remember things clearly from the moment I picked myself up from the dusty steps and headed for the sounds I heard of bubbling water. As I got nearer, the sound was punctuated by snapping sounds and then low moans and whimpers. I recognized them as the voices of women, and immediately, I came to the end of the corridor and a heavy wooden door. I tried it, and found it unlocked. Slowly, fighting every desire to fling it open, I inched it outward until I could see inside the room beyond. The sight that lay there will be etched in my mind forever.

The room was tinged with the reds and oranges of partially hidden fires and the floor was glowing with the reflected light as if in some madman's idea of hell. Located in the center of the room, a big, sunken pit filled with water that boiled and steamed at incredibly high temperatures created the sound that I had heard from the corridor. Over the pit, bridging it from end to end, was a narrow catwalk without railings upon which stood a half dozen naked women; all writhing and wriggling in a pathetic attempt at dance. It was then I recognized Linda. My heart leapt and every fear for her safety clouded my mind evincing from me a lone, thoughtless scream.

"Linda!"

She could hardly hear me over the sizzling water beneath her, and as she turned her shivering body toward the sound of my voice, I noticed that there was no other means of balance for the dancers on the catwalk save for the walkway itself. I halted in my tracks and began to gesticulate wildly for her to stay where she was, but her joy at seeing me there in that hellish place, was too much. She lost her balance and began to totter. I screamed her name again, but before I could see whether she had regained her balance, a sharp familiar sound cracked in my ear.

Suddenly, I felt the hot sting of a whip as it bit the back of my neck, sending me to my knees. I looked up in the opposite direction from the pit, and saw the devil as he looked down at me, laughing. I say it was the devil, but I immediately realized it was someone dressed in the costume worn by Martineau the night he grabbed Linda. The devil figure laughed again and cracked the whip toward the girls.

"Dance, you wretches! Dance for my cameras!" Slowly, agonizingly, the half dozen women began to dance again. All except Linda who had managed to grab hold of the catwalk and was struggling to lift herself back onto its surface. I could see the nicks and cuts across her breasts and buttocks from where she'd been bit by the lash and the sight had fueled my exhausted nervous system with a new surge of adrenalin. I leapt to my feet and fell toward the devil figure.

But he must have been expecting me to try something like that, because that whip wrapped itself around my neck and a good yank left a red circle on my throat and my body gasping on the floor. In another second, it cracked again and a long scream dragged my eyes to the pit just in time to see one of the girls fall from the catwalk and into the boiling water. She never came up.

"Die for the cameras, slaves!" yelled the devil.

Again, I threw myself at the creature and this time caught the whip around my forearm and locked it there. Before the devil figure could react, my other hand reached out and slapped him hard against the side of the head knocking his mask off. But any advantage I thought I had gained was lost as I saw the face beneath the mask.

"Miss Williams!" I cried in surprise.

She smiled wickedly. "Your very own Maryanne, come to take you to hell!" She jerked on the whip and almost had me loose. But instead, I fell to my knees, pulling her off balance.

Grabbing hold of the whip and yanking her in the direction of her fall, I got to my feet and kept pulling. Suddenly, she tumbled from her perch on the dais she had been standing on and fell forward. I gave the whip one more yank and she lost her grip on it, but it was too late, her careening body couldn't stop itself as it fell, then skidded, then teetered on the edge of the pit. She screamed much like her victims and fell in to the bubbling water.

It was a few moments before I caught my breath enough to worry about Linda. But then it was only a few seconds before I had her precious body in my arms again. She trembled nakedly in their embrace, the sweat drenching her skin soaking into my clothing. Quickly, desperately, her mouth found mine and we kissed violently like two thirsty travelers kept too long from water.

I scooped her into my arms and left that madhouse forever.

Anything, Anywhere, Anytime

Horst Schacter brought the PC-6 Pilotus Porter down for the perfect three-point landing, and began the short taxi up the concrete runway to the Air America terminal. From the control tower, there could have been no evidence in the landing that its pilot had just returned from an eighteen-hour run into the rugged Laotian back country with only a half-hour stop for refueling and reloading at Pnomh Penh.

As the AA terminal loomed up before his windshield, Horst nosed the craft into its slot and watched as the ground crew disappeared beneath the plane's fuselage. He cut the craft's big turbo-prop engine and pulled off his headset, shaking the cobwebs out of his head and squeezing the sleep out of his eyes. The thunk and clank coming from the rear compartment told him without his looking that his co-pilot and cabin crew were even then unloading the return trip cargo. As anxious as he was to get home and sack out for a couple of days there were still things that needed to be done. He dragged himself at last from his seat in the forward cabin and stooped out across the deck and hopped out of the cargo door. The concrete outside was hot even through the soles of his boots and the Laotian sun beat down unmercifully onto his unprotected head. But as much as he would have liked to jump onto an outgoing jeep and head home, he still had to take a look at his ship. After all, if he had to depend on it for his life every day, it better damn well be in flying shape.

He turned and almost bumped into Chris Tebert, his ground mechanic who had just given the plane a quick run through.

"What's the eyeball check show, Chris?"

Chris smiled and said, "Had it a little rough today, didn't you?"

"Uh, oh."

"Yeah, the wings are so loaded with lead, it's a wonder you brought the bird down at all. And that tail section...where is it?"

Horst groaned. If the Pilatus Porter was as beat up as Chris indicated, he wouldn't be able to fly it for his next jaunt. That meant reassignment to another of the Company's planes. Probably a Dornier or one of the older Caribous. He hated those big planes. The reason he insisted on getting a Pilatus Porter for his missions was its remarkable ability to negotiate the extremely short dirt strips that AA pilots were frequently required to use in the highlands. Thousands of feet above sea level, the tiny fields were situated on the sides of lonely mountains and plagued with high winds that more than once sent the best of pilots plunging over the side of cliffs. But the Pilatus Porter, by dint of its sturdy Swiss design and high wings, was able to take full advantage of the fierce winds and bring the plane down almost vertically onto the shortest of fields, The only drawback was that it was too damn slow, only managing a speed of 40 to 174 miles an hour. Way too slow for the trigger-happy Pathet Lao rebels that the CIA's army was fighting.

Horst knew the odds for employment with the CIA's secret airline, the Air America organization, was about fifty-fifty for coming back alive, but still, he preferred to have something in his own favor. The big automatic pistol strapped to his hip was against Company regulations, but none of the pilots took it seriously, and the Thompson sub-machine gun he kept under his seat in the pilot's cabin was extra insurance. Except that, this time, none of that mattered. He had spent most of his time in the air, a sitting duck for ground fire the whole trip. As he ducked beneath the ship's belly, he winced at the ragged holes left in its skin as they stitched their way out toward the wings and the near-miss at the engine. It was true, the tail section was nearly gone. He marveled at the remains, evidence of a almost impossible rocket-propelled grenade shot.

"I guess you'd better get right to work, Chris," he said, shuddering at the realization that he would have to settle for one of the bigger planes for a few days after all.

He found an unoccupied jeep out in front of the terminal and talked its bored driver into taking him out to the Tropic Hotel where his nice, comfortable bed and gently waving punkah were waiting A little bracer wouldn't be at all out of line before lying down as well.

The jeep drove up along the perimeter of the airport for a while, passing almost right beneath the noses of the big Russian Ilyushin cargo planes where they were parked side by side with American Starlifters. It was one of the ironies of the war that both Russian and American planes used the same airport, sometimes the same handlers to load weapons and ammunition aboard their liners, took off to supply their respective clients, and then the returned as crews swapped pernod and war stories with each other at the same clubs along the "strip."

The strip was the heart of Vientiane, the capital of Laos. Before the war had grown to its present size, the city was the best place for spending leave in the Far East. It had all the best exotic bars and specialist brothels in Southeast Asia where a man could have the prettiest girls for less than a dime. The whole atmosphere in fact, was so laid back that it reminded most of the American pilots of small-town life back home.

But the jeep lurched to a stop and broke any further reverie Horst might have had. Instead of those good years long gone, he was struck with the congested city of the present. He invited the driver in for a drink in the hotel's bar, the Purple Porpoise, and the two men left the hot street for the air-conditioned interior.

The first thing that attracted Horst's attention outside of the usual raucous gaiety of the bar was the unaccountable giggling of the nude hat check girl just inside the door. The mystery was solved when he peeked beyond the edge of the counter and saw that the girl's slim buttocks rested snugly over the bald head of Nick Sorello, a helio pilot for AA. He was trying to drink liquor from an upturned bottle but the bottle kept poking up between the girl's legs.

He sighed and looked around for his driver...he was gone from his position at the door, but Horst soon found him with a small gaggle of green American GIs as they put their money down to watch Suzie do her stuff. Suzie was famed throughout Southeast Asia for her ability to smoke cigarettes with her vagina. Well, at least he didn't have to spend any of his money on the driver.

He weaved his way over to the bar where the hotel's owner, Percy Loringham, passed out drinks and kept an eye on things. Percy claimed to be a member of the British aristocracy and affected an accent to prove it, but its authenticity was dubious. It didn't matter anyhow; he hated reporters and if he caught any in his place he had the bouncer rough them up good. The pilots loved him for it because they were apt to talk freely of Company business when they drank too much. So, if the cost of being able to talk without worrying about being overheard by the wrong people was to patronize Loringham's conceit, everyone was willing to go along with the man's genealogical claims.

As Horst bellied up to the bar, Percy spotted him and moved in his direction. "Give me a stiff one, Percy. Something that'll put me to sleep for a week."

"A rough one, my friend?" said the owner, mixing the drink.

"I don't want to talk about it, Percy."

Percy slid the finished drink over to the pilot and watched him take the first tentative sip. Then he ventured, "Are you that tired, Horst, or are you exaggerating?"

Horst eyed the man with a warning glance. "Why? What do you have in mind?"

"Well, I was going to ask you a favor. After all, I kept your room for you for two weeks last April while you were gone to Saigon. I could have easily given it to someone else during that time. We have no contract between us, after all…"

"All right, all right! Just what is it you want? Can it wait until I get some sack time at least?"

"That's the beauty of this favor, Horst. You can complete it for me and rest at the same time."

Horst put the drink down and eyed the man as he signaled to a girl who had been hovering on a bar stool a few places down. At the snap of his fingers, the girl hopped down from her perch and moved over to the American's side. Horst looked into her Oriental face and saw the beauty that seemed to reside in most of her race. She was a doll all right, he decided. And the rest of her wasn't bad, either. She couldn't have been more than fifteen.

"I got her from over at the Buddhist girl's school across the street," Percy was explaining. "As you know, I only hire quality girls to work in my place, so I recruit from unsullied flowers. No street women for me." Horst already suspected what was going to be asked of him. "She will do just fine, Horst. Except that she is...inexperienced. And as you know, most of my clientele prefer the more confident hands of professionals. I was wondering if you'd do me the favor of deflowering this little rosebud. Surely she isn't so bad to look upon."

The girl sensed the conclusion of the question and said, "You want see show?" And promptly began to take off her clothes. But her inexperience kept her from making it a smooth operation. She fumbled too long with her bra and nearly fell amongst the folds of the dress pooled at her feet.

Horst reached out and stopped her. "*Arrete la, ma petite,*" he said in his execrable French. "*Prenez votre robe et venez avec moi.*"

"Thank you, Horst," beamed the Englishman, happy at the prospect of a new acquisition.

Horst led the girl up the back stairs to his room, not at all happy with the situation. Not because he had any moral scruples about having sex with such a young girl...morality was something he had to leave behind in the real world. It didn't work here where life was cheap and swift. He lived in a different world than the one he left behind in the states, and the fact that he did that living at the very edge of endurance for long periods lent him a sort of ecstatic energy that cried out to be released. No, morality had little if any meaning in this sort of twilight existence. It was, rather, the delay in much-needed rest he resented. He really didn't feel like breaking in another of Percy's girls. Although it wasn't something he did all that often.

He unlocked the door to his room and ushered in the girl, who walked in warily, hugging her still undone dress to her bosom. He closed the door and relocked it. The girl turned and dropped her dress again in amateurish eagerness. Horst sighed, turned her around and hooked an index finger into her bra strap. Giving it a good yank, he snapped it loose and let it fall onto the floor. The girl's first instinct was to hide her tiny breasts in sudden fear. He knew the most important thing for him to do now was to put her at her ease. He smiled and laid his arm about her shoulders, squeezing her to him in reassurance. He felt her tiny body shiver against his big frame and undid her arms from about her chest. She dropped her eyes shyly as he examined her in detail. She was a beauty, or at least she would be in a few more years. Maybe it wouldn't be so bad to have a little fumbling sex before bed after all.

He went over to the bed and sat down on the edge. And, pulling off his sweat-soaked shirt, he held out his leg, nodding to his boot. The girl understood and went to her knees before him. Trembling fingers undid the laces and shapely arms wrapped themselves about the worn leather and tugged, at first feebly, then with more strength. Suddenly the resistant boot gave way and the girl flew backward onto her haunches and Horst gave out a good-natured laugh. The girl grimaced and went for the second boot with more determination. She got that one off with more ease, then began to work off his trousers. He was surprised at her initiative but didn't say anything. At last he stood above her and in a sudden move gathered her into his arms, a writhing, giggling mass, and tossed her onto the bed, all arms and legs. He leaned over to wipe a smear of dirt from about her small breasts and eased her panties off. She quieted down then and waited for him.

The next thing he knew it was morning and he was being shaken awake by none too caring hands.

"C'mon, Horst, let's go, I haven't got all day."

Horst sat up, winking the sleep from his eyes, and made out the features of Sam Fitz, Major Sam Fitz when he was on base at Tak Le. But right now, out of uniform, only Sam Fitz. The man only showed up for one reason, and right now Horst didn't want to hear it.

"What time is it, Sam?"

"Eleven o'clock."

"A.m. or p.m.?"

"It's in the morning, Horst," answered Sam impatiently. "Are you gonna get up or what?"

"Eleven in the morning? That's only seventeen hours of sleep! I thought I told Percy I wanted to sleep for a week."

"Percy was the one who let me in. He said it'd be okay. C'mon, I've got a job for you. We have to leave now."

Despite the banter, Horst knew there was no arguing with Sam Fitz. He was with the CIA's black operations unit at Tak Le air base from where the Company launched its most secret and illegal missions. Horst was one of the few pilots on their top security clearance list, and as such, was supposed to be always on call. He sighed and swung himself out of the bed, exposing his bedmate as he did so. She was still sleeping soundly, completely exhausted from her first rounds of love making. "I'll be right with you. Just let me get a quick shower and change."

Sam grunted and sat down.

A few minutes later, Horst emerged from the bathroom as Sam looked up from the month-old *Newsweek* he was reading. It was as if the nude girl on the bed was invisible. At least until Horst gave her a good smack on the behind. At the contact, the girl shot up with a shriek, tumbling off the bed onto her rump. Horst kicked her discarded clothing in her direction as she rubbed her sore backside with one hand and gathered the proffered garments with the other. In another moment she was being herded before the two men and out the door into the hall. Confused at first, she began feeble protests as she realized she was going to be pushed from the room without being able to cover herself up. Horst locked his door and left her in the corridor to the stares and laughs of passersby. Her final lesson in the life she chose to lead.

Vientiane was considerably subdued as it neared the noon hour, compared with the early evening of Horst's arrival the day before; and so, Fitz's jeep was able to cross the city to the airport with little trouble. As he passed into the air base proper, he filled in his passenger. "I've already made arrangements for your absence during the mission. You're taking some leave time in Bangkok."

Horst nodded. "What's the mission this time? Another hard rice drop?"

Horst didn't answer. It was to be expected. Black Ops were the super-secret missions of the U.S. government. Usually illegal. And very dangerous. If a pilot were shot down, his people didn't know anything about it. But AA pilots took it in stride. They were used to chances. What they couldn't tolerate was frugality. And so, the CIA paid them a lot more than the usual rate for the work.

Suddenly, the jeep pulled up at another gate. This was the entrance to Tak Le, the CIA's private air base completely sealed off from the outside world. Security was tighter than a rat's ass. Nobody got in or out if the Company didn't want them to. The mean-looking sentries checked the two men's identifications and let them pass. John Stelant's office was in a low, nondescript building alongside a big hangar that was always guarded by a small army of Marines with orders to shoot on sight anyone who came within three hundred feet of the building. Although Horst had never seen the big hangar doors open, he knew that they hid the presence of an SR-71 Blackbird, the CIA's number one spy plane. Horst felt the familiar stirring in the pit of his stomach as he contemplated the opportunity to fly that baby. Someday…

The jeep stopped and Major Fitz led him the short distance to Stelant's office. "Horst," greeted the CIA man as the two men entered his office, "glad you could get here so quickly."

He knew as well as Horst did that if he hadn't, Fitz would have brought him along under arrest, but he didn't mention that. Instead, he said, "No problem, John. Now what's the emergency this time?" He sat down in one of the two chairs facing the desk without bothering to wait for an invitation.

Stelant circled his desk and got right to it. "It's simple, Horst, all you have to do is make a night drop tonight at the coordinates we'll supply you with."

"Will I have ground signals to mark the target?"

Stelant cleared his throat and said, "Well, this time you'll have to land and unload, Horst…Now, now, I know how difficult it'll be without lights or radio contact, but there'll be a force of Mayo tribesmen and a Green Beret Alpha Team to signal you in with flashlights."

Horst still didn't like it. Why couldn't he just drop his load?

Settling on the edge of his desk, Stelant gave him the full story. "You see, there's an important general in the North Vietnamese Army that lost a wife and daughter in the war before full-scale troop commitment by the U.S. in the South occurred. He was told by the communists in the North that they were raped and killed by U.S. Advisors seven years ago, supported by manufactured evidence. In any case, the general learned to hate the South and has fought for the North ever since. But a few weeks ago we managed to track down the supposedly dead daughter. That's right, she's alive. That Green Beret team you're to meet has kidnapped the general from off the Ho Chi Minh trail and brought him to these coordinates." He handed Horst the notes. "Your mission is to get his daughter to him as soon as possible. Hopefully he'll see the light and come over to our side."

Horst stood up to face Stelant. "Okay, I can see the importance of the mission. But that still doesn't make the night landing any safer…"

"Of course it doesn't," said Stelant coolly, "but will $10,000 help?"

Horst's eyes widened. "It'll help. How about my plane?"

"Your favorite, a PC-6. Fresh from the Factory."

The Factory was the CIA's maintenance/depot base on Taiwan, the largest such facility in the world outside the U.S. There, thousands of technicians "sanitized" aircraft for the Company's Black Ops. Hundreds of the Company's people lost sleep at night worrying about downed planes being traced back to the U.S., and so they routinely erased all serial numbers and brand names on every part of the planes they purchased or "borrowed" from the USAF. But the process was so slow and exacting that they sometimes found it easier to build their own planes from scratch. The result: completely unidentifiable aircraft. That, and false commercial markings, markings taken from destroyed aircraft, and triplicated markings on several different aircraft, insured total confusion by anyone attempting to trace the Company's planes.

"Let's go," said Horst at last.

Horst took a long, careful look at the Pilotus Porter before giving his okay to it. He knew it would fit his personal criteria, but force of habit had saved his life more than once. Just as he was finishing up on the outside of the plane, a small party of three approached from around the aircraft; Stelant, Fitz, and a woman he did not recognize. He assumed the woman to be his passenger, and as she walked up to him with the others he allowed his eyes to wander over her features.

He was immediately struck by her beauty. To him, most Oriental women were in general attractive, but this woman, who could not have been more than twenty-five, the prime of an Eastern woman's allure, was irresistible. Almost as tall as he was, she was clothed in ordinary cammies with her jet-black hair held at her back in a ponytail. She stood mutely as Stelant introduced her.

"Horst, your passenger, Miss Ouan Dinh. Miss Dinh, your pilot, Mr. Horst Schacter."

Ouan looked up at him and nodded her head slightly. "How do you do, Mr. Schacter," she said in perfect English.

"Good, Miss Dinh. Shall we take off?"

"Don't waste any time, do you, Horst?" said Stelant.

Horst shrugged and helped Ouan into the plane through the cargo door. Just as he followed her in, he noticed for the first time a group of a dozen metal drums strapped against the opposite bulkhead. "Hey," he called out agitatedly, "are these drums filled with homemade napalm?" Homemade napalm was the bright idea of an overeager CIA agent. It had the same effects as the real thing, but was a lot more dangerous to handle.

"Yeah," said Fitz from outside the plane. "We didn't' have time to unload the stuff from the last mission. You don't mind, do you? I mean, for the money we're paying you..."

Horst didn't answer, but simply herded Ouan toward the co-pilot's seat. Once settled in, he fastened her seat belt , slid the cargo door shut, and assumed his own place. It was in no time at all that the PC-6 was in the air and on its way.

Some hours later, as twilight began to fall, Horst relaxed and said to his passenger, "So, what's the story of your life?"

Ouan looked over at him and smiled. "A very uneventful one, Mr. Schacter. My mother was killed by the Viet Cong for refusing to attend one of their political meetings and I would have been next but for an old woman who risked her life to whisk me away. Later she deposited me into the care of a Buddhist orphanage until I left as an adult to work for the government. It was there your fellow countrymen found and identified me. Now all I want to do is see my father once more, whether or not he wishes to change sides. And you, what is the story of your life?"

Horst laughed. "Even less exciting than yours, Ouan. I grew up in a small town in West Germany, learning English watching old American movies. When I turned seventeen, I joined the United States Army and became a citizen. While there, I trained as an assault helicopter pilot and in my spare time got my commercial flyer's license. After that, I quit the army and worked as a bush pilot in Argentina for a couple of years until a friend of mine in the employ of the U.S. government pulled some strings and got me reupped into the service. And here I am."

"Well, you…" began Ouan but was cut off then by her host.

"Sorry, Ouan, but no more talking…it's night now, and with no radio or radar, I've got to find my way to the drop zone by going from mountain peak to mountain peak." He slipped on a pair of night goggles. They helped but were no substitutes for radar.

It was a harrowing way to fly, but despite himself, Horst was actually getting used to it. In another couple of minutes he sensed the approach to his target and began a wide curve, waiting only for the final minutes to elapse before the prearranged arrival time. He was pleasantly surprised to find that he hadn't guessed too far wrong. Off to his right he could see the first lights wink on, then spread down in a ragged double line, marking off the invisible dirt runway. Now began the most dangerous part of the mission.

"Brace yourself, Ouan," he cautioned the girl. "If I'm off it could be any kind of landing!"

He began the long, slow turn that would place him at the head of the runway and, using the dim, starry horizon for perspective, brought the craft downward toward the blackness below. The landing gear clunked down and he felt the air resistance as it sought to keep the plane aloft. He softly blessed the Swiss designers of the craft who had built it with high winds in mind. Bringing the ailerons all the way down, he managed to bring the plane to an almost complete halt, until he was hovering over the land below. The stretch of lights had foreshortened into the distance and he knew the surface of the ground to be no more than a few dozen feet beneath him. At last, the moment came when he had to relinquish any real control he had over the plane as he let it find its own way the rest of the way down. A soft bump and the aircraft rolled bumpily along the dusty strip until it came to a slow halt. Horst cut the engines and breathed a sigh of genuine relief.

He turned to the girl and saw that she was staring at him. "I cannot believe it!" she gasped. "You landed the plane absolutely blind!"

Horst shrugged. "It's what they pay me for."

The girl merely shook her head as he undid her eat belt and helped her into the rear. He pushed open the cargo door and jumped down onto the reddish soil of Laos. He instinctively felt for the gun at his hip and turned to grasp the girl by the waist to lift her to the ground.

"Well, I wonder where the welcoming committee is?" he asked.

And as if in reply, a voice called out from the darkness surrounding the plane. "You will remain right where you are! If you make any sort of untoward move, you will be shot immediately."

Horst tensed involuntarily, recognizing the hostility in the voice and not liking it at all. But there was nothing he could do, as a half dozen flashlights were quickly focused on him. He raised his arm against the glare in the only form of defiance he could muster but it didn't do any good.

"You like to take chances, do you, American?" said the voice as its owner lumbered into view at last. He was a big, beefy man in the uniform of a North Vietnamese colonel. And his followers were similarly dressed. Now Horst really had a bad feeling about this set-up.

Rough hands searched them and stripped Horst of his gun. Then a surprised yelp from one of the searchers around Ouan shattered any hope that in the darkness the girl might have escaped identification. A rapid conversation in Vietnamese followed between the colonel and his subordinate until the former strode forward and grasped the girl by the scruff of her neck and drew her face into the beam of his flashlight. He guffawed in amused delight at his discovery.

"A woman!" he exclaimed. "This is a surprise. Leave it to you Americans to bring along your whores into combat! Spoiled bourgeoisie! But she will not go to waste. I will free her from the oppression of capitalism and instruct her in the delights of Marxism; and in the true spirit of communism, when I am finished with her, she may be shared among the men." Then he laughed a good-natured laugh and barked orders to his grinning soldiers.

What had happened to the Mayo tribesmen and Green Berets he was to meet? And how did the Vietnamese know of the mission? Thank God the colonel did not seem to know the true significance of Ouan's presence with him. But as it stood, her fate was not going to be any easier! He had to think fast, before Ouan could be violated by these fiends. But any plans he might have formed died aborning as the sharp rip of tearing fabric wrenched his tightly wound nerves.

As a few of the soldiers kept the two covered, another had torn the trousers from Ouan's legs, exposing the lily whiteness of her featureless limbs. Amid general hilarity at the girl's discomfiture, the soldier tore the two legs of the pants apart and with one, tied the girl's hands behind her back and with the other, tied Horst's own arms along a length of bamboo stretched across his shoulders. As the men finished, the colonel returned with a loop of leather and a long cord. Chuckling, he fastened the loop around Ouan's neck, and holding the opposite end of the leash, gave it a tug, urging the girl on.

"A leash for our little pet!" he laughed.

Another tug sent the girl to the stony ground with a whimper. Still tugging, the loop digging into her flesh, the colonel forced the girl to fight to her feet or be choked to death.

It was all Horst could do to keep himself from lunging at her oppressor. The fire kindled in his heart toward this beautiful creature in the short time they had been together in the plane surprised even him. He had known sores of women in his life, and never had any of them affected him in this way. It was a new sensation for him. But one that was destined to be frustrated because of the predicament they now found themselves in.

It was almost dawn of the following day as the band of soldiers and their exhausted captives continued to claw their way through the highlands undergrowth. It was all Horst could do to keep placing one foot in front of the other. After several hours of stumbling and falling along the uneven ground in the darkness, and in the unnatural manner he had been bound, the American was more than ready to drop. How his companion had kept up the pace, he didn't know. Of course, that damned noose around her pretty neck was good encouragement. Ouan had been brought to the fore of the column by the colonel where Horst hadn't been able to see her. But the girl's heart-rending groans of pain as she fell and her constant stream of pathetic pleadings for mercy filled the night, letting him know that she was still there. He shuddered at what condition he would at last find her in the morning.

And as the rosy dawn at last tinged the eastern sky, the column of men filed into what Horst could see was a Mayo village, with all the signs of a recent battle. So this was what happened to the Berets. They were probably followed from the Trail and ambushed here in the village. So there would be no rescue for Horst and Ouan. He would have to manufacture his own succor. And he would…he had been in tough escapes before and gotten out of all them. This would be no different. Yeah, right. But at least he didn't see any sign of bodies about the camp. Maybe there was reason to hope for rescue from the escaped Mayos?

He had little time to think on the prospect as he was led to one of only three huts left standing in the village and shoved into its musky interior. His harness hit the flooring on its tip, jarring him to the bone, and forcing a cry of pain to escape his lips. As he settled down onto his back, he sensed the presence of someone else in the room with him and looked over to see Ouan as she struggled to rise to a sitting position without the use of her bound arms.

Horst squeezed his eyes shut at the sight of her. All scratches and bruises, her once immaculate features begrimed with mud and dust, her long legs bloody at the raw knees. What was left of her cammie shirt was hanging on by a single button and her cotton panties clung wetly to her skin.

"Did they…" Horst managed to croak. "Did they…?"

"Not yet," she replied in a voice so strong that it embarrassed the American, making him ashamed he had not borne up as well as she.

"But I have decided during the night to deny them at least some of the vile pleasure they would take from my position," Ouan said. "Each time I fell to my knees, each time I was dragged naked along the trail, each time I endured the laughs of the men, I vowed to keep the one thing I could deny them."

She paused to catch her breath.

"Mr. Schacter, I would like you to make love to me," said the girl, rushing on before he could make any reply to the extraordinary request. "I want my first time with a man to be with someone I can at least respect if not love. Oh, please, Mr. Schacter, will you do it?"

Great, thought Horst, was he doomed to break in fillies all the time? Still, he could understand the desperate desire in the girl to claim some sort of control over her fate, even one as degrading as this. "I'd like to comply, but in my condition it won't be easy," he said at last. "The way we're tied won't help any, either."

But the girl had an answer for that as well. "Stay on your back and let me move up to your hand. Take hold of the edge of my undergarment and wait as I try to squirm free." Then Horst watched as the girl got to her knees and placed her hips within reach of his bound hand. When he had a grip on the waistline of the soiled panties, she worked them down until they were around her knees.

Finally, she stopped and moved to sit with her back to his crotch and, with not too much difficulty, managed to undo his trousers and pull them down far enough for her intentions. Turning, she lowered her body onto his and whispered almost in his face, "Thank you." She slid down, settling across his loins.

Night was falling again. As the shadows lengthened and the interior of the hut darkened, Horst glanced over to where Ouan was lying on her side. She had slept for most of the day; when she was awake, light sobs seeped from her lungs, tearing at the American's heart. Since their coupling the night before, they had not spoken a single word to one another. Their captors had reassured them of their continued presence with the arrival of a single rancid meal near noontime. The rest of the time, Horst had spent straining against the ropes they had replaced at his wrists, but with little gain.

For the thousandth time, he was pondering what had happened to the Green Berets and what their captors had in mind for the ultimate disposition of he and the girl, when movement from outside the hut arrested his attention.

In another moment, two soldiers had entered the building, spied Ouan lying on the floor, and moved toward her. Again rough hands seized her and fastened the noose about her neck. She made an effort to resist, of course, but to little advantage. Untying her hands, they stripped the shirt from her back, exposing her breasts. At once she began to resist more furiously, but her tormentors merely laughed and dragged her outside.

Struggling with the desperation of the hopeless, Horst fought his way to his feet and went to the doorway himself. He arrived there in time to spy the colonel as he stood on the little stoop before his command hut directing his men to fetch buckets of stagnant rain water from a barrel in the village. The girl was left standing in the village square, her tiny-seeming figure bent and filthy, her arms ineffectually protecting her bosom. Around her, a score of soldiers gawked and pointed as others arrived with the buckets. Moving right up to the girl, they each doused her roughly with their contents, turning the caked dirt and blood on her body to mud. With an order from the colonel, the girl began absently to pass her hands over her limbs in an effort to clean up. But the communist's ardor was too poignant to be long stymied. Being handed the leash, he jerked the girl in the direction of his hut. Stumbling up the wooden steps, she disappeared inside.

With that, Horst began at once furiously pulling and tugging at the bamboo pole that was still tied across his shoulders. But all his efforts were wasted. At last he stopped long enough to notice several short poles standing across the middle of the one-room hut. At one time they had been intended to support blankets dividing the room into chambers. Moving quickly to the central pole, Horst turned his back to it and slipped its tip up between his shoulders and the bamboo pole. Bracing his feet far back and leaning forward with all his might, he concentrated on bringing his hands together before his face.

For many minutes he strained there in the hot silence, fearing all the while the sudden entrance of a guard. But more than that, the horrid visions imagination insisted on showing him of the girl's plight. Sweat sheened his skin and dripped in rivulets from his face before he sensed the first kink in the joints of the bamboo. Suddenly, he was on his face on the floor of the hut and paralyzed as he waited for the investigating guard. But no guard came, and so he busied himself with ridding his wrists of their bonds.

Quietly, he searched the hut for the trap door he knew was always present for the handy disposal of rubbish and human waste. He found it handily and fell through to the ground below. Immediately, he saw the calves of a guard as he walked up to the rear of the hut. Positioning himself near the edge of the building, Horst swung out savagely with a stiffened arm at the backs of the guard's knees. The man fell at once, hitting his head against a rock. In moments, Horst had acquired an old-fashioned assault rifle with bayonet from the fallen guard and had moved to within twenty yards of the entrance of the colonel's own hut.

A single guard stood outside just below the doorway; from inside, Horst could hear the weak protestations of the girl as she fended off the advancements of the North Vietnamese. Revenge and murder filled the American's brain as he suddenly launched himself from the shadows and vaulted across the open space toward the guard. But his charge was too swift for the Vietnamese to counter in any way. Before he could call out, the butt end of Horst's weapon had broken his jaw and the pilot had dashed into the hut itself.

The glare from an oil fired lantern revealed the girl as she was being forced onto a flea-ridden cot, her soiled panties in the process of being lowered by the colonel who had positioned himself between her legs. But any thoughts of proceeding with his intentions were dissipated as he saw the American's face twist in a rictus of hate. In another moment, the colonel's belly was filled with a foot of steel and the whimpering girl had been gathered into the pilot's arms.

But there was no time to waste...the camp would soon discover the evidence's of Horst's actions. Scooping up the belt containing his own automatic from a table, Horst grabbed the girl by the wrist and hauled her through the hut's waste trap and so into the jungle just outside and to the building's rear.

Pausing only to allow Ouan to adjust her underwear, the two escapees plowed their way through the thick jungle in the direction Horst's infallible sense of place had determined lay the Pilotus Porter. For he had long since decided that the plane could supply the only hope they had for escape. They couldn't have any chance of surviving for long in the jungle, hundreds of miles from anywhere. The only trouble was that the Vietnamese would probably conclude the same thing. Horst figured their only real chance lay in that the other soldiers wouldn't discover their absence for another few minutes; enough time to allow him and the girl to reach the far side of the village and a deal beyond along the already forged path to the airstrip. He would handle any guards left by the plane when he got there.

He was beginning to congratulate himself near dawn as the trees up ahead of them cleared, indicating the presence of the field, when Ouan began to show definite signs of heat exhaustion. He knew it had to come...the woman had withstood hardships in the past few days that would have knocked out many men; it was a miracle she had held on as long as she did. But now, he could just hear the sounds of pursuit, and with the plane so near, he knew they had to make it now or never.

Since he had been half carrying the girl for hours now, it was only natural to go all the way at this point. Smoothly he lifted her to his shoulder in a fireman's carry and loped off toward the clearing.

Finally, he broke into the open and saw the CP-6 sitting there pretty as you please, without a guard in sight. Maybe there was one around, but he could not take the time to investigate. He pulled the automatic from its holster with his free hand just in case and dashed to the aircraft.

The cargo door was still open just as he had left it, and he didn't waste a second as he approached the plane and dumped Ouan inside like a sack of potatoes. He was just about to follow himself when suddenly stars appeared before his face. It was a moment before he realized that he had been struck from behind. Instinctively, he wheeled and, fists flailing wildly, he fought desperately for a time until his head could clear. He felt his blows landing solidly against unprotected flesh, and when his full senses returned, he saw the bloody remains of his attacker lying supine on the ground.

He didn't waste time congratulating himself though, but climbed into the plane. He was helping Ouan to her feet when he spotted the drums of napalm where they were the strapped against the bulkhead opposite the cargo door. An idea formed in his head then and he turned to the girl.

"Ouan, can you hear me?" he asked. The girl nodded feebly. "I'm going to strap you against the side of the plane right next to these barrels." He pushed her against the wall and secured her in a standing position with another heavy-duty strap as he spoke. "Listen carefully, Ouan. I'm going to get the plane in the air. When I'm ready, I'll yell out; when you hear me, give this strap..." he gave her the end of the strap that held the drums fast..."a good yank. Then hold fast to the wall. Got me?" Suddenly, her eyes were alert and she nodded purposefully, once more in command of herself.

Wasting no time, Horst dashed to the pilot's seat and revved up the engines. A glance at the nearby trees told him the strong mountain winds were with him. Thank God for that! Slowly, agonizingly, the plane wheeled into position and began to lumber down the runway. Tick, tick, tick! and a spider-webbed hole materialized in the left windshield. Cursing, Horst saw tiny flashes from just within the tree line as the approaching enemy tried to stop the plane before it left the ground. But they were too late as the aircraft skipped upward and caught the wind. Horst jerked the nose almost completely vertical and the plane shot straight up into the air. Pushing against the left floor pedal, he forced the plane into an extremely tight turn that brought it directly over the hidden troops. With its wingspan at a perpendicular angle to the ground, Horst shouted to the rear: "Now, Ouan, now!"

He didn't see the girl obey his command, but he heard the clunk and clatter of the exiting metal drums as they skidded down the vertical cargo deck and fell out of the open doorway. In moments, the jungle hundreds of feet below erupted in a gigantic inferno as the homemade napalm roasted it for miles around. Horst could imagine its effects on the Vietnamese; even if they didn't burn, they'd smother to death as the oxygen in the air was consumed by the flames.

Slowly, he straightened the plane and pointed it toward Vientiane. Satisfied, he turned and shouted over the noise of air rushing in from the open cargo door, "Ouan, undo the strap and come in here. But be sure to hold on tight to the handholds just in case. I don't want you falling out now!"

In another moment he sensed her presence as she squeezed into the cabin and sat down in the co-pilot's seat. Horst looked at her and shook his head. She was naked except for her panties, whose elastic waistband had snapped, allowing them to settle too far down below her hips. But it didn't matter much, as she was so covered in dirt, blood, and sweat that he could barely make out the color of her skin. Seeing her breasts jutting out boldly from the rush of cold air whipping in from the open hatchway, Horst remembered the flight jacket he had tucked down between his seat and the side of the plane. He dug it out and handed it to her. "Better get this on."

She took it silently and shrugged herself into its sheep's wool, saying, "Do you think my father…"

"I think he's alive and that he'll be out of the bush with the Green Berets two days after we get back. I never saw any evidence of deaths while in the village. And if those guys are alive, they'll get out in one piece and everyone else with them. Believe me."

"I do believe you…Horst."

"Say, that's the first time you've used my first name!"

"How else am I to address the man I've come to know so…intimately?"

"That was a sloppy job back there," admitted Horst. "I don't want you to think, being a first timer, that it's always like that…"

"I didn't think it was," she replied. "So perhaps you can show me how it is properly done while we wait those two days for my father?"

Horst just smiled. At least this time it wasn't going to be with a beginner.

Lawless Island

The whole story started when the *USS Higgins* weighed anchor at the Sonyus in the Midway group. I remember that day like it was yesterday, a sky so blue and featureless you'd never think pollution was wearing holes through the atmosphere like all those scientists keep telling us; the sea smooth and calm like opaque glass; the Higgins absolutely still on its surface; not a bird in the sky and the only sounds breaking the peaceful scene was the clank of the winches as they let down the amtraks from off the side of the ship.

I took my cover off of my head and blinked into the sun, then leaned on the rail and watched the first Amtrak hit the water with a dull splash, the rings it made in the water drifted outward thickly and disappeared. It hadn't taken as long as I thought to get out here and now that we were, I found that I couldn't wait to get ashore. I took my eyes from the sailors scurrying over the Amtrak and looked up at the little island that could just be made out from where the *Higgins* was positioned.

Just about a mile square, Sonyus Island was uninhabited as was the chain of even smaller islands that ringed it. But it was because of those islands that the *Higgins* couldn't get any closer to Sonyus than it was now. The smaller, outlying islands were actually the parts of a long coral reef that just happened to break the surface of the surrounding ocean; it was that reef, completely encircling the island, that kept the *Higgins* from just going right up to Sonyus and knocking at the door, and why me and my men, Marine Amphibious Unit 347, had to go in with the amtraks. With the amphibious vehicles, it'd be a cinch to make our way to the reef, cross over it with the belly treads of the amtraks, and then just wade in to the beach.

Yeah simple; but then came the tricky part. The brass wanted the island cleared of civilians; okay, no problem. The Sonyus Atoll was desolate as far as anyone knew. But then about three months ago, some islanders from another chain,

266

fishing in the area, were fired on from the direction of the island. Not being the shy type, they made their way ashore to do unto others, but they were beaten back by superior firepower. They weren't cowards, but they weren't stupid either; they hightailed it straight to the nearest U.S. Navy vessel and reported what happened. When they were finished, Command knew they had another "last son of Nippon" on their hands. It was common knowledge that for years since the end of the war with the Japanese, some of their soldiers refused to believe it had all come to an end. Year after year, some native or other would stumble across one of these oldsters in some forgotten portion of a jungled island and they'd have to be convinced to give themselves up. So it wasn't too difficult for Command to believe the story. Unfortunately they had plans for the Sonyus Atoll that didn't include inhabitants of any kind.

So there I was, a DI fresh out of Lejeune, with the first real active duty I've had in years and I have to go and lead a bunch of greenies against a man my father probably faced a generation ago. It wasn't the sort of action I was thinking of when I re-upped, but it'd do. I took a last drag on my Lucky and flicked the butt out over the water. For a second I thought it a shame to ruin that perfect sheen, but I forgot all about that when I heard my name being called from below decks.

"Sarge, hey Sarge!" It was Cpl. Stanley, coming up like gangbusters from the ladder. "Oh, there you are. The Navy guys say we're all set to go."

I grunted and followed him below decks, relieved to get out of the hot sun. In another few minutes, I was having the men double check their equipment before going over the side and getting a last earful from the young lieutenant in Navy khakis who insisted on following the book.

"So be sure you bring along enough emergency signal flares, ammunition, and survival rations, and…"

"Look son, I know my job, now why don't you just run along and me and my men'll take care of ourselves."

His face purpled at that but before he could say anything more, I heard the captain's voice call from his position on the deck overhead. "That'll be all lieutenant, you're wanted in the radar shack."

"Aye, sir," said the lieutenant and retreated into the hot belly of the ship. I looked up at the captain. He saluted loosely and nodded.

"Okay you lunkheads, saddle up and over. And make damn sure you get on the 'trak in one piece or I'll throw you to the sharks. I'll be damned if I have to write a letter to your mamas telling 'em how their baby boy got himself squished between the 'trak and the bulkhead."

I was darn pleased to see the practiced ease those twenty guys went over the side and clambered aboard the Amtrak. Not bad, just like any professional. I hated to admit it, especially to them, but I was pretty proud of those greenies.

After I found my spot in the rear of the Amtrak next to the sailor sitting in the steering position, I had the men settle down and hold their stomachs. It didn't take long for the amtrak to circle out away from the *Higgins* and then to make its way toward a break between two of the outlying islands. In another few minutes we all felt the sudden thump of the vehicle's belly as it came up against the sunken reef and slide back down on the inside of the atoll. There was some cursing from up front where one of the men vomited amid the laughs of those more fortunate to be in the back. I only let it go on for a minute before I ordered them to shut up and get into their assault crouches. The end of the ride came a lot sooner than even I thought as the amtrak rubbed up onto the beach and the sailor let down the debarking ramp. "Go, go, go!" I yelled. But I needn't have bothered. The men's adrenaline was pumping like mad and they burst out of the cramped space of the amtrak and onto the beach like prisoners with commuted sentences.

I moved straight ahead toward the line of trees while the men spread out in a vague crescent shape on my flanks. I grinned at their performance; just like boot camp. But I hardly had time to congratulate myself on the way I had whipped them into shape before everything fell apart.

Almost as soon as the men entered the treeline, I felt there was something wrong somewhere. It was nothing I could put my finger on, but it was something I felt in my bones nevertheless. But there was no way I was going to turn back because of some "feeling" I had, so I just signaled the others to slow down and advance with caution. The signal was relayed along the lines as we continued to move farther into the jungle.

Suddenly, there was a shot off to the right, then the left of the line. I shouted commands to take cover, but it was too late; before I knew it, half of the men were taken out and the others were scattered as they tried to find cover and return fire at the same time. At first I couldn't see a damn thing, but in a few minutes, I began to make out movement in the dense foliage farther ahead. I sent a few rounds of M-16 fire towards the disturbance and had the satisfaction of hearing the shells ripping through foliage and meat accompanied by the cries of dying men. A few more bursts from my gun allowed me to get up and dash to better cover and a quick look around showed two of my men not three feet away. They were dead all right but not in any way that I would have thought. Sure I believed the story about the old Jap holed up somewhere out here, but the evidence of my own eyes told me he wasn't alone. I definitely saw more than one figure in the foliage up ahead and heard more than a single man yell out when I hit them before. But the one thing I didn't expect, was for the Japs to have anything near the firepower we had. After all, they were supposed to be holdovers from the Second World War, the most they could have were some rusty carbines. Looking at the mangled corpses of my men, I knew I was up against hardware with a lot more firepower than that.

The two men lying there were completely unrecognizable to me because their bodies were nothing but blackened husks, like the charcoal brickettes you use in your hibachi. But the thing that hit me the most was the fact that their uniforms were completely untouched by whatever it was that zapped them. As clean and dry as they were when they put them on that morning. It was almost as if they'd been struck with a massive jolt of electricity. But those were the only speculations I had time for before I had to look out for my own neck.

I hadn't noticed it before, but I heard the distinct sound of crackling energy, like the sound lightning makes in a thunderstorm. There were more screams off to my right and I knew it came from the last of my men. Suddenly the collected anger and frustration of the last few minutes came up in me in a rush, and in a blind, unthinking rage, I stood up behind the tree I had been using for cover and sprayed the jungle in front of me with hot lead. In another minute, I was breaking through the tangle of vines and branches, shredding the rest with bursts from my rifle. I knew I was doing some damage as I heard the grunts and moans of the wounded all around me; but that was all I had time for as suddenly, a branch snapped back and whacked me in the face, slapping my eyeballs. I gasped and fell back, rubbing at my stinging eyes.

I was still practically blind when I felt rough hands take ahold of me and drag me to my feet. More hands passed over me as they relieved me of my equipment and pistol, another hand lingered and pressed against my crotch to the general amusement of my captors. I could understand that at least, after all these guys had probably been out here for years, but that didn't make me feel any better. Then they began to speak to one another, probably about what to do with me. That's when I got my second big surprise of the day: they were the unmistakable high-pitched voices of women!

Finally, my vision cleared, and slowly, from a blur to clarity, my captors came into focus. At first, all I saw was the brownish khaki of the old Imperial Japanese Army uniform, then the duller color of deeply tanned flesh. At last my vision almost normal, I blinked away the tears and tried to shrug away from the grasp of two of my captors as they held me under the arms. Their grip tightened as I looked up angrily at the others standing around me. They were almost all women! Beautiful, Japanese broads! Don't believe me if you want, but I know what I saw. Out of about ten of the Japs there, eight of them were these luscious chicks all decked out like they were right out of the Imperial Japanese Army officer corps; decked out in perfect period uniforms except for helmets. Instead, they were bareheaded, with their long straight hair tied in pony tails down their backs. And honest, they must have been the most perfectly shaped broads I'd ever seen. Not an ounce of extra weight on them! Everything they had was perfect for their height, size, and shape. If I didn't know better, I'd have sworn they weren't human! But I didn't have the time to check them out as thoroughly as I would have liked to as the two men with them grunted something, and one of the chicks whipped off her belt and moved over behind me. It's a good thing she didn't lose her britches, or I would've been in danger of selling out to them! As it was, the two dames holding me loosened their grip and the third chick tied my hands behind my back. I gave a fast thought of making a break for it, but decided to wait. They obviously wanted me alive or they wouldn't have tied me up. After all, how did they know how many more of us would be following my group onto the island?

So I was shoved toward a deeper portion of the jungle, the men at the head of the file, and the chicks trailing out behind them, me in the center. In a few minutes, we hit a narrow trail and veered off to what I guessed to have been the island's highest elevation, a small knoll at its eastern end.

It wasn't a long walk, but it was enough for the insects to begin trying to eat me alive; and with my hands tied, all I could do was grin and bear it. I tried to keep my mind off of them by studying my surroundings, but there wasn't much to see; if I got the opportunity, I could've found my way back to the beach with my eyes closed. So it was the easiest thing in the world to let my eyes take in the chicks when they came into sight. I cursed silently at the uniforms that hid most of their charms, but there was enough tension in them to let the girls' most interesting features have full play: there wasn't a bra wearer in the bunch. Unfortunately though, it wasn't long before my more professional instincts took over and I began to take notice of the weapons that hung across their backs. At first, I just took them to be simple automatic weapons, but on closer inspection, I saw that they were nothing of the kind. Small and compact, and light enough for any woman to handle with ease, those guns weren't ordinary at all. For the first time, I associated the blackened bodies of my greenies with the weapons that burnt them, and I nursed a healthy hate for their sleek barrels and funny looking energy cells forming their body. They were small and lightweight, and I had no reason not to doubt heir deadly potential.

But I didn't have too much time to think about them before my little hike ended and a couple of the girls moved ahead and parted some brush from the base of the knoll, revealing a low, black hole in its side. At first, I thought we'd have to go in on all fours, but the first man in just walked straight on and sunk into the earth. When my turn came, I saw that there was a hidden stairway that led steeply downward and I almost fell in from the encouraging shove I got from one of the girls behind me. When I finally caught my balance, I was at the bottom and blinking my eyes against the glare of phosphorescent lighting. There was a sound back the way we had come in as they closed a heavy metal hatch over the entrance and the rest of the party joined us at the bottom.

There were some grunts from one of the men as he pointed to a set of lockers by the stairs then at the girls. I was wondering what was going on, when to my shock and delight, the girls began to remove their uniforms! I couldn't believe my eyes and didn't give a damn as first one then another and another of those chicks stripped down to their skivvies and placed their discarded uniforms in the lockers and quick marched away into one of the few other tunnels that branched off from the one we were in. Of course, I was disappointed; those chicks were the most perfectly shaped morsels I'd ever seen! And I've been to all the best places; Hanoi, Manila, Tokyo, you name it! But I hardly had the time to look after all those firm legs when out of a different tunnel, comes an even weirder sight: two more chicks, no less perfectly formed but a good six inches taller than the others and decked out in some kind of samurai armor like you see in those cheap Kung Fu movies. Breast plates and mail skirts that barely came down far enough to do any good, metal shod greaves like gladiators used to wear, and a big, curving sword that they kept in their fists. When they drew up to me, their almond shaped eyes drilled right into mine so that I couldn't take my gaze off of them. Only the sudden slap of their swords on their breast plates brought me back and I heard more grunts in that Jap lingo from the men. In another second, the two broads had me under the arms and were half dragging me down the corridor they'd entered from.

Between stumbling and trying to keep up with the girls' long strides, I tried to take in more details of the place I was being held in. It turned out to be a huge underground complex with dozens…hell…maybe hundreds of rooms as far as could tell! I couldn't help comparing the place to the tunnel networks I heard the Japs built on Tarawa and Okinawa during World War II, but bigger, lots bigger. And crammed with all sorts of electronic gear too; workshops with rows of long tables filled with miniaturized tools and parts and warehouse sized places piled up with heavy, industrial equipment and other, more specialized rooms loaded up with fancy stuff I couldn't recognize at all except to think that it looked like ordinance right out of Buck Rogers or something. And remembering what those weird guns did to my men, I didn't think I was far off the mark. And everywhere, I saw chicks, beautiful dolls, all in their skivvies; thin camisoles that hung from their shoulders and ended just over their navels and cotton panties that hugged their waists. They were all working at the shops and moving around the hallways. I saw men too, but they had to be out numbered twenty to one by the girls! Whatever this outfit was, they had it over the old Corps hands down!

Anyway, I figured I was taken to one of the lowest levels of the complex before the armored chicks stopped in front of a pair of sliding glass doors and one of the men still with us slipped inside. I couldn't see past the doors as their panes were thick with steam, but I caught a whiff from inside and caught the familiar smell of a shower or locker room. I was really beginning to wonder just what the hell was going on there when the doors slid open and I was dragged inside.

My first impression turned out to be right when the first thing that caught my attention was the big pool that filled most of the room. I could hear the dull splashes of people somewhere in it, but couldn't see them yet because of the thick swirls of steam clouds that hovered over the water. As I moved farther into the room and along the side of the pool, rifts opened in the steam and I began to see Jap men here and there in the water, moving around for a better look at me. I guess it shouldn't have surprised me by this time, but it still did: each man in that pool had a couple of girls hovering around him, casually rubbing his back and legs, wiping the sweat from his face, and some even being carried through the water by girls with their arms interlocked beneath the man's buttocks. *That's the life*! I thought. From what I could tell, the men were naked and the girls wore only their cotton panties. Slowly, they all congregated near one side of the pool where another man, young, not over thirty-five years old, sat swathed in a big towel with a girl massaging his neck and shoulders and another holding a glass of wine or something to his lips. A dozen other men stood and sat around him watching me being prodded in their direction.

I didn't need a picture to be drawn for me: this guy was the big kahuna and he wanted information out of me, like what interest did the US Navy have in his island? The thought of all of that dangerous hardware I spotted on the way down didn't make me feel much like chatting, so I knew I was in for a tough time until I could think of way out of this nutty Jap tea house.

A vicious smile curled the edges of the Jap's mouth.

"So, we have an American visitor," he said. "I'm flattered." For some reason, I was surprised he spoke English and my face must have showed it, because he continued. "Of course I speak English, dog. You Americans will never change! You're so convinced of your own superiority that you're continually surprised to find that others can match you. And we Japanese have done so at every turn! We have out done you as a matter fact! But all our efforts are wasted in simple economic competition."

At that point, one of the men whispered in his ear and he smiled again. I didn't know anything about the guy, but already I hated that smile. He flicked a finger and the man disappeared, then he turned his gaze back at me and watched. Suddenly, there was movement at the edge of the crowd and it parted to let in the most beautiful woman I'd ever seen. And not just in that place, I mean anywhere! Black hair that fell absolutely straight past her waist, smooth, featureless skin of that hue that wasn't quite white and wasn't quite brown, long firm legs that tapered to strong but dainty feet. She was wearing the camisole and panties I saw the women in the upper floors wearing, but that didn't keep me from appreciating the lift of her breasts as they managed to hold out the light fabric of the shift away from her chest and belly. My heart skipped a beat when she glanced shyly my way and immediately cast her eyes to the floor.

The Jap sitting down reached over, grabbed her hair in his hand and yanked her viciously to the ground. She let out a short cry of pain before she hit the floor and I took an involuntary step forward. The Jap of course, saw me, as he had not once taken his eyes from mine. Knowing the girl was somewhere at his feet, he leaned forward and placed a bare foot on her throat. Presently, I heard soft sounds coming from the girl's mouth, she was having difficulty breathing, but that didn't stop the Jap from keeping his foot in place.

"You Americans have taught my people well, yes you have," the Jap leader said. "You've taught them to meet you on your own terms, and they have. They have beaten you on your own terms. But the cost was high! We have lost our cultural pride, our cultural identity. Traded it for the cheap baubles of western materialism. Our people grow softer by the year; our own fathers would hardly recognize their own children for the descendents of the glorious Samurai and Shogun!" He relaxed and leaned back by thrusting against the inert form of the girl at his feet. "And I am not the least to blame. I have created a multi-billion dollar empire in the east-west trade. As have others like me. But we soon came to see what a hollow victory it was to claim all those riches and to have no honor. We saw how soft and flabby our people were becoming as the years continued to go by; how even the slightest mention of increased military spending would throw the country into a paroxysm of pacific wrath. I and my fellow industrialists," he held out his arms to include the other men standing by, "have banded together in the name of Nippon resurgent! We will pool our resources to create an invincible army that will reclaim first our homeland, then the Pacific basin that is our rightful heritage, and then strike down hated American in holy revenge!" He waved an arm again. "Look around you! You've no doubt slavered over our women since entering our domain, just as you've taken them on the home islands. They are the result of limited post-pubescent genetic alteration. We have created the perfect female species. Subservient, strong, fertile; the mothers of the future rulers of Nippon. Of course, others," he rolled the girl's face toward me with his foot, "are not so perfect."

He barked something in Japanese and the girl dragged herself to her knees to face him. He said something else, and she picked up his foot and raised it to her lips. At first I thought, she was going to kiss it, but instead, she put one toe at a time in her mouth, her jaws and teeth working carefully around them. The Jap kept his eyes on me the whole time saying, "Make sure you clean them thoroughly, Kyuki, otherwise I will have your teeth for a necklace." If I didn't hate the man before, I absolutely reviled him then. To humiliate any human being like that! I wanted nothing more than to kill the bastard right there, but my hands were still tied and I was surrounded by armed guards. The Jap said something else in his own language and my guards began to take me away.

"I will be having a more in depth interview with you later American," the Jap said in English. "And you had better have the answers I seek."

The last thing I saw before being forced from the room, was the sight of that girl still bending over that monster's feet and the laughing, joking crowd closing around them in a tight circle.

The only thing that let me get through the next few hours of imprisonment, was the thought that somehow, I'd get revenge for what that Jap scum did to that girl, and revenge too for what he did to my boys on the beach the day before. And I had plenty of time to think about it too, because no sooner was I taken out of the steam room than I was tossed into a little room, it couldn't have been more than ten feet square in all, and left to think about what I'd tell the Jap leader when he asked for me. Which would be nothing as far as I was concerned. But that didn't mean I was going to hang around and find out how I'd stand up to torture either. Unfortunately, that cell was well built. The walls were of seamless concrete and the door solid steel with only a slot-panel at the foot for slipping my food through. It was well lit with a light source that was never out; I figured that was part of an effort to soften me up, but it was off-set a little by the presence of a cot with a springy mattress on it. I didn't know how long I was in there, and after a short nap, I lost whatever sense of time I had left. It helped a little knowing that the crew aboard the *Higgins* was still waiting for me and could send a search party ashore at any time.

Anyway, I had woken up and eaten the meal I found on the floor near the door and was giving the room the once over when a scraping sound behind me grabbed my attention. I spun around just in time to see a figure in a white kimono slip into the room closing the door behind it. I took one step toward the guy when he turned and threw back the hood that hid his face. Then I saw that it wasn't a guy after all! In fact, it was the last person I could have expected: it was the chick from the steam room, the one the Jap had kicked around.

I was speechless for a minute, but when she saw that I was about to open my mouth, she raised her hand and spoke. "I have come to help you escape, but first I have to know, can you get us off the island?"

Boy, talk about your guardian angels! This chick looked every inch an angel, and now she was rescuing me! It didn't take me long to give her my answer. "I'll swim us off if that's what it takes. There's a US Navy cruiser anchored just beyond the reef, even we do have to swim for it, we ought to make it easy."

She thought about that a minute, then said, "It is good. I will help you, but first you must prove yourself worthy. Tell me, are you a real man? A man of honor and strength?"

I didn't know what the hell she was talking about then. What the hell did all that have to do with us getting out of there? Then I told her so. "Listen, I don't know what kind of screwy dame you are but if you want out off this rat hole, then I'm with you. Just say it, yes or no." I was getting set to jump her if she changed her mind, but her next words caught me by surprise.

"I do want to escape, but it cannot be so simple. I have my own code of honor, my own concept of Bushido to live by. My father taught me that at least. I will allow no man into my confidence who cannot best me first in combat."

"You mean you want me to wrestle you? What, two throws out of three?"

"Your flippancy is wasted with me American. My father was an honorable man of the house Ikito, an old and ancient lineage. He taught his children the value of honor and the value of dying for it."

"Now you're sounding like that Jap nut in the steam room."

She lowered her eyes. "He is my brother…"

"Your brother!" I cried. "And he did…*that*…to you? Humiliated you the way he did? You call that honor?"

"In a way, I understand him. He was taught by my father as well. It was what drove him into his present enterprise, and myself as well. In the beginning it was to be his genius and wealth, and my body."

"Your body? What do you mean?" I didn't like the way the conversation was going.

"I am the living incarnation of the Nippon Mother. It was from me, that the genetic material was removed, mutated and transplanted in pre-pubescent girls. By the time they had passed their pubescent period, the genetic matter had become part of their physiological make-up and reformed them into the perfect vessels for the future rulers of Nippon resurgent."

It was fantastic, unbelievable, but if it was true, those lunatics couldn't have picked a better model for their army of girls. "But why did your brother treat you the way he did?"

She straightened then and looked directly into my eyes. "Because I would not stand by while he treated the mothers of Nippon in the demeaning manner he did. My protests became more and more insistent until one day I broached the society's protocol and upbraided him before his fellow industrialists. He has returned the humiliation a thousandfold since then."

I was quiet there for a minute until, "So do you still think we ought to fight?" I half hoped the little heart to heart would have gotten that idea out of her system but it was no go.

"We must. I can not sully the honor of my father's memory." With that, she threw back her kimono revealing the strange armor I'd seen on the other dames. She pulled free her sword and said, "Remove your clothing."

"What?" I stammered. "Why?"

"It is the way. You must be completely unarmed, no hidden weapons are allowed."

I thought it was stupid, and felt kind of silly doing it, but I complied. "What about you? It's not very honorable to go into combat against an unarmed man with a sword."

"Remove your clothing."

I shut up, realizing that if I was ever going to get out of there, it was going to be through her, and it'd be a whole lot better if I had her to show me the way out those tunnels. But time was running out. We'd been standing there talking for ten or fifteen minutes. Sooner or later, and probably sooner, someone was bound to decide to come by and check up on the prisoner.

I got out of my uniform, peeled my skivvies off, and straightened, not without noticing her eyes move slowly over my body. She was impressed. Then she shook herself and tossed her sword on the cot and assumed a fighting stance. "Defend yourself, soldier. Defeat me, and we go. Lose and I leave you here."

"I got news for you sister, I'm out of here no matter what you think." Before the last word was out of my mouth, I was under her guard and had an arm between her legs. The leverage was there, and I intended to lift her up and down onto the cot, but it never came out that way. She scissored her legs together, catching my arm, and reached for the other. Easy as pie, she bent me back, exposing my throat and let fly with a karate chop to the adam's apple. I twisted enough for the blow to glance off of my skull, sending sparks through my head, but it was enough for me to drag her onto me as I fell to the floor.

The breast plates and metal links of her skirt ground painfully into my flesh, but my arm was still between her legs, so all I had to do was flip her over onto her back. I had her almost completely up-side-down, and ready to slam her down for the count, when she made a grab for my crotch. I have to admit, I didn't expect such a low blow from someone who claimed to be honorable, but I didn't wait until she had me in her grip either. Guilty until proven innocent in a fight, I always say. So I let her go and slapped the hand away while she collapsed in a heap and rolled away.

We were both on our feet in seconds and she wasted no time in coming at me again. It was all I could do to side step her rush, but just the same, this time, she swung her arm and caught me good. I doubled over with a grunt and got a good swift kick in the ass for it from the metal sandals she wore. I fell forward, hitting my head on the corner of the cot, and the next thing I knew, she had me around the neck with one arm pinned behind me and a knee twisting into my back. I think I felt a couple vertebra grinding before I got my brains together and grabbed her sword from the cot. It may not have been strictly within the rules, but neither was her armor. I didn't even bother to look where her head was, but just swung the hilt over my shoulder, I knew she was right behind me, and whack! I got her.

She reeled back and I managed to get to my feet and turn. She was standing there, holding her head when I charged. A knee to the abdomen took the wind out of her and a flying kick, knocked her legs aside, throwing her onto the cot. I dove and pinned her there, not really knowing how the fight was supposed to end.

She was still groggy, and as my face wasn't two inches from her's, I could see that she'd have some nice bruises come morning. But right then, she was still the most beautiful woman I'd ever seen; in fact, the sweat that sheened her legs and arms and rivered along her face and body, made her a whole lot more enticing to me. I smelled her body odor, the thick muskiness that comes with exertion or sex and I think that that's what made me do what I did next.

I planted a good one on her mouth. Not the dainty kind of kiss you give your best girl, but a raw, hungry one that seemed to suck up her whole insides. In another second, I plucked away her breast plates and tore apart her metal skirt, then I took another drink from her mouth. Of course she resisted, it was like trying to hold down a hurricane. But I wrapped an arm around her head, pinning her mouth to mine, and gave her a rough massage across her back and thighs with the other. I felt the excess perspiration run over my hand when it slid along her buttocks and breasts. In a few minutes we both calmed down, and the visit to the oasis became more congenial. In fact, once her initial panic was over, it was hard to get her mouth away from mine. But we managed when I turned to get those hobnailed sandals off her feet, they were beating up my legs something fierce. She didn't seem to mind the hiatus, keeping herself busy with other things. At last her breathing got more regular and I was able to take more time with her.

Finally, it was time to pull away and get down to business. At first, she didn't know what I was up to, probably thought I was changing position or something, but when she saw me reaching for my clothes, she sprang up and grabbed hold of my arm. I shrugged her off and she tried again, this time offering me one of her breasts, bringing it close to my lips. I bit it and she squealed, falling back onto the cot.

"That's enough baby," I said. "Time to get out of here."

She pouted, examining her breast where red teeth marks were already spreading.

I scooped up her kimono and tossed it to her. There was no way she was going to get those plates and the skirt back on.

She wriggled into the kimono and said, "We should not have dawdled so long, it must be nearly dawn now."

"Sorry, baby," I said. "But you're not exactly made to ignore."

She smiled despite herself and stood up. "At first, I did not want your...attentions." She looked me in the eyes. "But now, I'm glad you had your way with me."

"So am I. Now how do we get out of this madhouse?"

She moved to the door and opened it. When we stepped into the hall outside, I saw the figure of a girl slouched in a chair, her camisole was gathered up around her armpits revealing her breasts, spread out like huge, perfect saucers. I almost forgot the dish I had in hand when Kyuki spoke. "She will remain unconscious for hours longer, but we should still leave this area as quickly as possible."

As we moved down the corridor, I decided to ask her a couple of questions that were on my mind. "How did you manage to get away yourself?"

She stopped at the juncture of two halls and said, "Without a boat, there is no way to escape the island. My brother knew that, and so I was not closely guarded. He knew he could summon me for another humiliation any time he chose. In fact, the only chance I took tonight was that he might have send for me for just such a reason."

"So for all you know, you might be wanted right now."

"I doubt it, these corridors are too quiet. If my absence was known, they would be in an uproar." She turned down one of the corridors and we reached a flight of stairs. She didn't waste any time in flying down them, and when we reached the bottom, I grabbed hold of her arm and stopped her.

"Wait a minute, I haven't been in this place longer than a few hours, but even I know we're not headed for the surface, we're going deeper."

"Quiet! Now listen. The corridors above are too well lit, I am all right, but you would be spotted in an instant. Our only chance is to reach the power room and dim the lights along our route."

"Why not all of them?"

"Because that would surely alert the guards to there being something wrong. A partial power outage happens here every now and then when some experiments are going on. With luck, that is what will be the assumption while we make our way to the exit. Also, in the dimness, it will be easier to mask our identities."

I had to hand it to her, she'd thought of everything. So I let her have her head, and in no time, we reached the power room. There was only one chick there, and Kyuki decoyed her in her kimono and took her out easy; then she pulled the plug on certain connections in the power panel and sure enough, if the corridor outside didn't get darker, but not dark enough so's you couldn't see where you were going.

It took less time than I thought to get to the main corridor near the surface and there still wasn't much commotion going on, not even any sirens. I guess Kyuki was right again, no one was too concerned. Anyway, we got to the head of the hallway that led into the antechamber with the lockers when Kyuki stopped me with an upraised arm. She held her finger to her lips and motioned me to look around the corner to the stairway that led to the surface. I looked and saw two armored chicks standing there with those funny electric guns. Although they didn't seem too concerned about the lights, they still blocked our escape up the stairs to the exit.

"Go on up to them like you did in the power room," I whispered to Kyuki, "get them to turn their heads away from here so I can sneak up and surprise them. You can handle the one on the right, I'll take the left." She nodded without a word and walked slowly out toward the guards.

The guards saw her right away, but didn't act too surprised. They let her get right up to them and when she started to talk, she kind of sidled over to the right, drawing their looks away from the mouth of the hallway where I stood waiting. When they were facing away from me, I didn't waste any time; I ran up to them on tip toe the short distance and rammed my shoulder in the back of the nearest of the two. I hit her so hard, she slammed into the wall a few inches away with a smack that knocked any sense out of her. I didn't wait to watch her body slide to the floor, but turned to the other broad. I didn't need to worry too much as Kyuki had her kimono over the guard's head, blinding her. She drew the woman's sword and although I didn't like it, watched as Kyuki put two feet of cold steel between the girl's ribs and yanked. Blood was everywhere and so were her dying screams. Immediately, there were yells and warnings from the different halls leading into the complex.

I didn't waste any time in grabbing Kyuki and hauling her up the stairs. She tried to make a grab for her kimono, but I didn't give her any time. In a few seconds, we were at the top of the stairs and I was pushing against the steel hatch, swearing and cursing. All the time those shouts were getting closer and the sweat began to pour from my body. I felt Kyuki's buttocks pressing against me as she backed away from the lower part of the tunnel. At last, I got the hatch open and we tumbled outside.

Sunshine and overpowering heat hit me like a physical thing and all I wanted to do was to flop over and rest, but there wasn't any time, I could hear those high piercing shouts and the bump and scrape of metal armor almost at my heels.

I had Kyuki by the arm and together, we dashed crazily through the surrounding underbrush, the branches and thorns tearing and scratching at my skin and uniform. If I had had the time, I'd have spared some pity for Kyuki's exposed flesh, but couldn't. The breath was suddenly coming in short gasps from my mouth and I felt unaccountably weak in the legs, probably the first signs of malaria. But the sudden burst of crackling fire and sizzling bolts of electricity that came from behind us and exploded to our right and left, was all I needed to keep going.

Finally, the jungle thinned and we fell onto the beach. I almost yelped for joy and felt new strength come along, like a second wind. I didn't waste any time thinking about what to do, I just pushed Kyuki ahead of me into the surf and waded out after her. "Start swimming for those islands out there; the *Higgins* ought to be just over the horizon."

"I...will...try," she managed to gasp. Poor kid, she was completely worn out by that run; and the tussle we had back in the cell hadn't helped her stamina any either. But she kept going and in a little while we were far enough out to be over our heads with those Jap chicks and their male masters howling up a storm on the beach. But I didn't start congratulating myself yet; with all that hardware I saw, they were bound to have some water transportation somewhere, and it was only a matter of time before they thought to use it. With a little luck though, this crew were the only ones to have seen us make our getaway and just chased us without thinking to warn anyone else. Anyway, they kept trying to zap us with those guns but the salt water acted as pretty good insulation and after a while, I was able to grab Kyuki under the arms and haul both of us the rest of the way to the reef. We weren't there two minutes before I spotted an amtrak making its way to the gap between the islands where me and my men had passed the day before.

I stood up as best I could on the submerged reef and waved my arms. They spotted me easy and veered off their course and into my direction. It was Sgt. McGivney's Maulers, the B-team, and were they surprised to see me with Kyuki who was naked as a jaybird!

They were all shouting and yelling and ogling at the same time, so it took a few minutes for me to figure out what they were saying, but it didn't matter because the pilot turned the boat around and headed right back to the *Higgins*. I found out later that the test had been due three hours before, but that Command had delayed the firing until the fate of my squad could be discovered. But with my report, McGiveney radioed ahead, and advised an earlier firing, like as soon as his boat was out of range, and in another hour, the new low-yield, neutron personnel bomb was on its way to the target island. I didn't waste any tears on those Jap rats, mostly because Kyuki was keeping my mind off of such things with some tricks she learned in geisha school...